WIND RIVER INCIDENT

WIND RIVER INCIDENT

DB JACKSON

Irongate Books

Irongate Books
PO Box 1860
Oakdale, California 95361
irongatebooks@irongatebooks.com

Wind River Incident

ISBN: 978-0-578-48562-1

Printed in the United States of America

ACKNOWLEDGMENTS

With special thanks to the love of my life, my wife and best friend, Mary, without whose support and tireless help Brady and Franklin would never have embarked on this epic journey.

And to those whose love inspires me: Josh, Amy, Mateo, and Lucas.

WIND RIVER INCIDENT

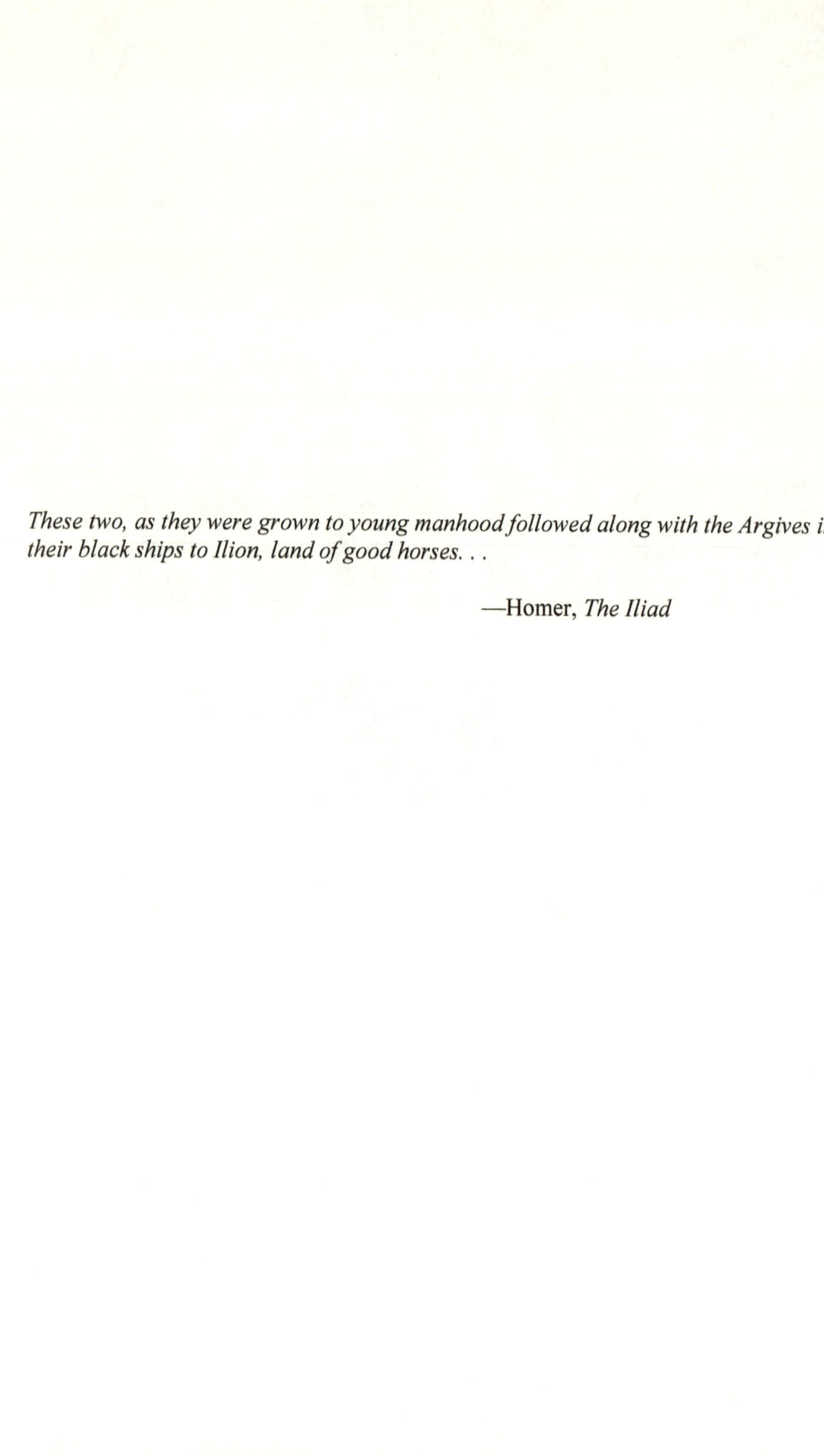

These two, as they were grown to young manhood followed along with the Argives in their black ships to Ilion, land of good horses. . .

—Homer, *The Iliad*

ONE

Madison River, Montana — 1891

Brady McCall grew up believing cowboys were the chosen ones—the privileged few—consecrated by an ancient calling over which they had no control and, if they had, they would have chosen it anyway. McCall cowboys because that's all he ever wanted to do. By nature he is a horseman. Afoot he appears somehow incomplete. And in his presence the horse appears incomplete without him—as though the hand that created him created the horse with him in mind.

Age beset McCall before he knew he was old. First a few grey hairs. Then a few more, and a few more until that's all there were. The creases at the corners of his eyes set in gradually and soon enough he grew accustomed to seeing them there. Now his muscles ache and he no longer remembers when they didn't. He does not accept old age and he allows himself no concessions because of it. Each morning he rises and his fingers fumble, stiff and gnarled, with shirt buttons that seem to grow more difficult each year.

On cold mornings he is drawn to the heat of the stove. He washes up in a porcelain basin above which hangs a looking glass. An old man stares back at him. He is drawn to the irony that his image in the looking glass is older than the image of his father in the tintype that sits on the bureau top. It often occurs to him he never saw his father get old.

But the old man who is Brady McCall walks erect. His back is strong and straight. In his eyes resides a trace of the recklessness of his youth.

Spring approaches and he grows restless. The days are short and night comes early. The night air has yet to lose its chill, but winter was loosening its grip. The old man's thoughts turn to spring, and to cows and long days in the saddle. Each year it's the same and each spring the restlessness within him returns. This year it is no different.

At night, he sits alone and works by the light of a kerosene lamp, oiling his saddle and repairing bridles and bits and broken spurs. Every scuff on the stirrup leathers and every scar on the saddle skirts hold a memory. He smiles at some and shudders at others. Memories are now his life and he regards them all with respect.

A cowdog lies at his feet as he does each evening, a ritual they both take for granted. The smell of leather and mink oil and horse stir within the man an impatient spirit and the dog senses it. McCall puts up the saddle, hangs the bridle on a wall peg by the door. He leans over the table and blows out the lamp.

Neither he nor the dog sleep much that night.

Before dawn the old cowboy had set off alone on horseback. By the time the sun came up, he had his branding fire built. Midday, the shadow of McCall and that of his horse crept over the rocks where once a creek ran.

At a bend in the creek the horse turned and its shadow turned to catch up. A set of wary eyes watched the man and the horse from the concealment of the brush as McCall stopped to study the tracks. The horse, its ears erect and its head held high, alerted on the brush and the eyes of the young bull that looked out at them.

McCall leaned forward in the saddle, his eyes following the hoof prints leading out of the rocks and up onto the dirt bank. The tracks appeared to have been made fresh. He glanced back across the dry wash where his camp lie a distance above a bluff in the clearing. He kept his bearings by the smoke that spiraled skyward from the branding fire he built earlier.

Above the camp circled a pair of Redtail hawks looking down with no interest in the man as they rode the thermals higher and higher into the clouds.

Ahead in a willow break, the young bullock stared out at the horse and rider and remained dead-still until McCall began to closed in it, then it bolted. McCall nudged the horse into a trot and followed the yearling up a shallow bank, and then over the crest of a hill and down through the buckbrush where it circled back onto the creekbed.

The bull trotted ahead. The horse followed without being asked to do so. McCall tied his catchrope on hard and fast and shook out a loop. He carried the extra coils and the bridle reins between the fingers of his left hand. In his right, the loop hung at the ready. He knew would only get one shot. It had to be a good one. There would be no second chance.

A flurry of upland game birds exploded up from the brush in front of the bull. The bull stopped. McCall let loose a quick loop that sand as it sizzled through the air. The bull turned its head. The loop settled over it and closed down around the thick neck. When he felt the rope tighten, the bull spun away tossing its head, lunging forward in a desperate attempt to shake off the loop.

McCall jerked the reins and sat deep in the saddle. The gelding set back on its haunches to brace for the coming jolt. Sweat ran down McCall's face and he tensed as the slack tightened and the rope stretched. He stood his weight in the left stirrup and turned the horse to face the bull. When he did, the bull swung around and faced off with the horse. It hesitated. Then it charged.

The bull crossed the horse's path at a full run, passed him on the offside, circled behind and, as it did so, the rope caught and jerked the horse's legs out from under it and laid it to the ground.

When the horse went down, McCall was thrown violently from the saddle to the rocks. He took the full weight of the impact on his brittle ribcage and lay splayed out in a pitiful heap, his body bent grotesquely over the boulder upon which he came to rest. His arm shook involuntarily. He gasped for air. He fought to clear his head and he fought to breathe.

McCall held onto to the rope stretched from the saddlehorn to the bull. The horse trembled, lying helplessly on its side. The downed bull struggled to its feet. It pulled back on the rope. Choking itself down further. Its eyes bulged. Its tongue lolled. It began to totter. The bull took a step forward. The rope went slack, and it could breathe again. It took another step forward, and then stopped to take in the fresh flow of air. The bull recovered quickly, pawed the ground, and sent rocks and dirt flying up behind him.

McCall lifted himself up onto one elbow. The bull watched him get to his knees, holding the loose rope like a lifeline. He eased himself up next to the horse and clucked it to its feet. The horse stood, its nostrils flared and its eyes on the bull.

There they stood, the horse watching the bull, the bull watching the old cowboy, and McCall holding onto the loosely coiled rope, hoping for a chance to get back into the saddle. It was that moment of indecision where the man, the horse, and the bull all waited for the other to determine what happened next. The bull reacted first—it turned one way, the horse bolted the other. McCall just hung onto the rope, hoping for the best as he waited for the scene that played out like a slow-motion nightmare in which all he could do was watch it unfold.

The horse and the bull, as though summoned by a higher force, panicked and took off in opposite directions. McCall could see what was coming next and he tried to drop the rope, but he was too late. The rope stretched tight and the loose coil wrapped itself around his thumb.

He watched the coil tighten and the thumb swell. He felt a quick burning sensation and heard a sucking sound as the thumb popped from the socket in a spray of blood and loose tendons. He watched the thumb rocket skyward in an arcing circle of red and felt warm spray hit his face the same time the pain shot through him and took him to his knees.

He fell to his back and blacked out. When his head began to clear some, he sat up. He stared at the deformed hand, and then down at the sand-encrusted thumb in the dirt at his feet. His stomach wretched. When he saw the exposed tendons and blood surging from the empty socket, he tried to vomit but couldn't. And then he tried not to and couldn't stop himself.

He closed his eyes hoping to dream it all away. He tucked the bleeding claw beneath his arm and sat like that a long time. The blood that ran from the wound soaked his shirt and trousers and pooled on the ground around him.

McCall's anger kicked in—he opened his eyes, slipped a battered old Indian knife from its scabbard with his good hand, and then hacked off the tail of his shirt. He wrapped the bloody mess as best he could with one hand and knotted it off with his teeth. The dressing hid the wound but did nothing to slow the blood dripping from his elbow into the widening pool where he sat.

McCall was shocked at how small the deformed hand appeared, and he wished it wasn't his. His chest heaved as he closed his eyes and tried to relax his breathing. He knew he had to get back to the fire to cauterize the wound and stop the bleeding.

He turned and looked up the steep embankment. He could see the smoke not a hundred yards away. He looked back down at the thumb lying in the dirt and kicked it away with his boot. He had second thoughts, and then leaned forward and stretched to reach the thumb with his good hand. It felt cold to the touch and he gagged.

He wiped the dirt from the thumb against the leg of his trousers and looked away from it as he tucked it into the pocket of his vest.

He looked back at the intimidating height of the embankment. His mind wandered and he felt detached from the pain and his circumstances that now, somehow, felt remote and unimportant. Some primitive voice deep within him urged him to close his eyes.

He lay back with his eyes shut and listened to the sounds the chittering birds and the rustling wind. He had no sense of time as he floated untethered in cerebral darkness.

After a few moments, he panicked and his eyes snapped open. He rose to his feet and stood there wobbling. His breathing was labored and shallow. He turned and leaned his body against the wall of the creek bank. He dug in with the toe of one boot, clawed a finger hold with his good hand, and then raised himself high enough to see his branding fire. He secured a hand hold on the grassy ledge and began to pull himself up. He grunted and dug his fingers in. The fingers slipped and he tried again. Then the gravel fell away in a large mass and he plunged back to the bottom.

He tried again, but the loose gravel continued to give. The third time he lacked the strength to rise to his feet and he lay there, back against the dirt bank, barely able to summons a clear thought.

McCall's brain swirled about like a rowboat caught in the vortex of a whirlpool that carried him into a euphoric state much like a dream—a place where no pain existed and where there was no sense of urgency. He felt warm and comfortable and light, as though he were dreaming a dream from which he could awaken at any time had he chosen to do so. Brady McCall took a deep breath, let his arms drop to his side, and closed his eyes. He began to feel cold as the darkness comforted him. He lay back imagining himself a young boy becoming drowsy before a warm fire. At that moment, he knew he had resigned himself to his fate with the fight bled out of him.

TWO

Fifty-one years earlier—St. Joseph, Missouri:
September 1840

Brady McCall, ten years old on his last birthday, balanced himself behind the rough wooden seat of the overland wagon while his father, William, clucked the mule team out of a grove of hardwood trees and up onto the roadway at the eastern edge of St. Joseph. William McCall reined the mules in at the crest of a hill overlooking distant rows of plank-board buildings situated with casual imprecision along rutted dirt streets that stopped at the edge of the Missouri River. The entire town stopped there, abruptly and rudely, as though the river itself was the final boundary between the civilized world and the forbidden wasteland beyond.

Brady's mother, Elizabeth, sat on the seat beside her husband. She looked down at the small settlement, and then turned and smiled at her husband. This was his dream and she embraced it. While his was a vision of opportunity and adventure, Elizabeth was less certain. Her reservations remained unspoken behind a veil of grace that William interpreted as her support of the move.

Elizabeth gazed down upon the citizenry of St. Joseph with a mixture of interest and relief. It was good to see people with homes conducting day-to-day business.

Something she missed dearly since leaving Virginia. She smiled and took her husband's arm.

Her eyes danced with excitement. She wore her dark hair back, complimenting her strong, refined features. She looked up at her husband and squeezed his arm. The smile and her reassuring touch were all the confirmation William needed, and it pleased him.

Elizabeth turned back and called the children forward. Eight-year old Rachael climbed up on the seat between her mother and her father. Brady lifted three-year old Matthew from the soft bundle of blankets in the center of the wagon and brought him forward. They stared and no one spoke. When they did speak, they all spoke at once.

For Brady, Virginia was fast becoming just a memory. Vague and now far removed—a place he thought about less and less but already a place he was sure he would never see again. Now, overlooking the demarcation line between The United States and The Frontier, the thought of starting over in a territory called Montana loomed more and more real.

Beyond the outer reach of civilization, beyond the familiar, lay the vision only his father seemed to see with clarity. But, as the father saw it, so did the child. Brady McCall would listen to his father speak quietly over the evening fire. The Montana Territory of which he spoke gripped the boy in the same intoxicating way it did the father until it was unclear to the boy when the dream of his father became that of his own making.

He would recall this point in his life many times, for it was the crossroad beyond which everything changed. He would spend the rest of his life with one unanswered question — *Would he have changed any of it if he could?*

Brady McCall was unsure what to expect when his father urged the mules between the long rows of cabins and brought the wagon to a creaking halt near the door of the small utilitarian structure that would be their home until spring. The boy stood, looked up and down the narrow street, and then climbed down the wheel to the ground.

"What do you think?" his father asked.

Brady smiled up at him, "I don't know. It looks kinda crowded to me."

"It does to me too," his father said. "But, it'll get us through."

Rachael climbed down and waited while Elizabeth helped young Matthew to the ground.

Elizabeth smiled and she set the toddler on the ground and handed him over to his sister.

"Take him by the hand, Rachael."

"I've got him," Rachael said in a motherly way.

After they surveyed the cabin inside and out, Elizabeth and the two younger children stayed inside to manage the cleaning and unpacking while Brady and his father began unloading the wagon.

Brady stood at the rear of the wagon and noticed a long-legged boy strutting across the street in their direction. The lanky kid walked with an ambling, cocky gait and wore a man's hat tilted to one side. Brady diverted his eyes but watched the boy as he approached. Brady stepped to one side to give the boy room. He wasn't sure why he did so, but there was an air about the long-legged kid that seemed to warrant the extra respect.

William regarded the boy with a quick glance as he handed an armload of quilts and bedding to Brady.

"Mornin," McCall said.

The new boy looked up at Mr. McCall nodding and touching the brim of his hat.

"Morning. How y'all doin?"

The older boy spoke with such confidence that Brady couldn't stop staring at him.

"I live over yonder," he said, nodding toward the cabin across the street near the corner. "Can I give you a hand gettin unloaded?"

McCall looked the boy over. He was solidly built with dark eyes and a polite manner. The wide-brimmed hat set back on his head gave him the cocky appearance of a rounder much older than he was.

The boy stood firm, still looking directly at McCall but trying very hard to make sure Brady was adequately impressed.

"Well, sure" McCall said. "We could use some help if you're not too busy. What's your name, son?"

"Franklin T. Stilwell, sir."

McCall smiled. "They call you Frank?"

"No sir. They call me Franklin."

McCall nodded and shook Franklin's hand.

"Franklin, this here's my son, Brady."

McCall turned and gestured toward the younger boy, then backed through the door with his load and left Brady standing there unsure of his next move. Brady hesitated then stepped forward and offered Franklin his hand.

"I'm Brady McCall. Brady C. McCall," he said as he stood up straight and tipped his head back to make up for some of the height difference.

Brady extended his hand. Franklin reached forth and grasped him about the wrist, leaving Brady's fingers nowhere to go but to grasp his wrist in return.

"This is how the Blackfeet do it, B.C." Franklin said. He didn't smile, and the look in his eyes was one of great seriousness. "This will be our secret handshake."

"My name ain't B.C.," Brady said, not sure whether to be offended or flattered.

Franklin adjusted his hat and pulled it low over his eyes. He dropped Brady's arm and looked at him. His voice lowered and he put his face close to Brady's.

"B.C. sounds more growed up then Brady. It makes you sound interesting—a kid your age ain't all that interesting."

Brady bristled. "I never said I was interesting."

"Did you ever think about it?"

"No, not really."

Franklin looked down at Brady. "There ya go," he said.

"Okay, then how about if I call you F.T.?"

"No, my name's Franklin and I'm already interesting."

Brady gawked at the older boy. He thought about it a moment.

"What do I gotta do to get interesting?" Brady asked.

"I ain't sure you're cut out to be interesting," Franklin said as he pushed Brady and laughed then picked up an armload of supplies and headed into the cabin.

Brady laughed and followed Franklin's lead. He pushed Franklin back.

"You ain't really all that interesting yourself," he lied.

Two days later, Brady stood at the back of the small church with his father at the conclusion of the first meeting of the *Oregon Provisional Emigrating Society*. He watched his father shake hands with Captain James Garrett, the wagonmaster. He watched his father sign his name in Garrett's ledger book, and then he followed him to a group of men gathered near the door for an informal discussion.

The men stood about the room in small clutches. All reluctant to leave—talking amongst themselves as though they may somehow resolve collectively the growing doubt that individually each felt after hearing of Garrett's assessment of the challenges of the trail.

Those with the gravest doubts seemed to be those who earlier professed the greatest confidence. William McCall mostly listened and Brady listened with him. The boy's head was filled with the names of rivers and mountains and what lay before them. The dangers, the opportunities, the overblown accounts of abundance presented in the promotional flyers and testimonial letters from those few who had gone on before them.

When Ansel Belshaw, the representative from the Massachusetts based Oregon Provisional Emigrating Society, presented the details of the journey and the land at the end of it, the grandeur of it all diluted the impact of the seriousness of crossing the largely uncharted frontier. When he explained this would only be their third organized expedition west, Belshaw neglected to mention the absence of reliable maps and the inexperience of the guides. He also failed to mention this was Garrett's first trip as a wagonmaster. Garrett's previous experience was that of a fur trapper, not a guide—a critical point that did not escape William McCall or Franklin's father, Thomas Stilwell, both who knew the full story on Garrett's background.

The grandness of it all overwhelmed Brady. But, when he looked into the faces of those smiling men gesturing and pontificating in loud voices, he was struck with a great revelation, for in those faces he saw something lacking that was far beyond his ability to comprehend. He had no way of knowing how inalterably their flawed assessment of their own cleverness would affect the course of his own life.

Thomas and Emily Stilwell and their fifteen-year-old son, Franklin, had arrived in St. Joseph from Georgia three weeks ahead of the McCall's. Divested of everything they owned save the contents of their wagon, the Stilwell's settled in St. Joseph for the winter. Along with fifty-three families, they all would cross the river in the spring with no expectations of ever returning. Theirs was an unlikely combination of courage and naiveté like nothing the world had ever before witnessed.

Thomas Stilwell—tall, thick-wristed, raw-boned, and direct, was a quiet man. With his penetrating eyes and no-nonsense demeanor, men tended to regard him with caution. But those who knew him found him to be friendly and disarming. His easy manner led men to underestimate him. He had a noticeable lack of regard for convention and authority that, combined with his good nature, only added to his charm.

These same traits ran clear in Franklin's make up. But those traits in the boy had somehow sidetracked toward reckless irresponsibility. Franklin's handsome features came from his mother's side of the family, but there remained little doubt which side of the family should be held accountable for the personality that many foresaw as the downfall of a potentially good man. Whatever conclusions those that met him reached, none would regard Franklin Stilwell with ambivalence.

Stilwell, a hunter and a woodsman, passed his outdoor skills onto Franklin. Stilwell could overlook his son's shortcomings in terms of social graces, but he could never abide a lack of self-sufficiency. Franklin, as independent and capable as any man, never disappointed his father in that regard.

As Brady McCall would learn over the years, there was no clear line between Franklin's caring nature and his reckless disregard for his own well-being. For as often as Franklin proved to be the consummate statesman, he just as often chose to fight instead. But, Franklin was adaptable. From the backwoods of Georgia to the back streets of St. Joseph, Franklin was always on the hunt for adventure. By the time the McCall's arrived, Franklin had scouted every inch of the new town and staked out every spot a young boy could find the excitement it took to get through a long winter coming.

Fall lost its color—the weather turned grey, the days grew short, and in the mornings the ground lay white with frost. Franklin and Brady were like a boy and his shadow. Where you found one, you found the other. By mid-November there had been little snow, but a cold front from the north held temperatures below freezing day and night.

Wearing heavy gloves, a wool scarf, and a thick jacket, Franklin was barely recognizable when he climbed up on the corral fence and waited for Brady to finish feeding the family mules. Franklin spoke and his words floated out into the freezing air in billows of white smoke.

"Hey, B.C.," Franklin yelled through cupped hands. "I got us a job."

"What do you mean?" Brady asked.

"You know . . . working . . . getting paid . . . that kind of a job," Franklin answered.

"Who'd pay us?"

"Mr. Hog would."

"Who?"

"Mr. Hog . . . you know . . . down at the livery?"

Brady looked up. "You mean Mr. Hogue? He said he'd pay us?"

"Yep," Franklin said, looking proud and just a little smug. "We start in the morning. Fifteen cents a day each."

"So what will we be doing?" Brady asked.

"This, that, and the other thing—you know, kind of be in charge when Hog's not there."

Brady shook his head. "Franklin, Mr. Hogue is always there."

"Yeah, well maybe," Franklin said sounding somewhat defensive. "But it don't matter, 'cause we'll be in the money."

"You sure he wants me, too?"

"Uh-huh . . . I, um . . . mentioned there was two of us," Franklin said.

Brady eyed him with a doubtful expression. "What do you mean you mentioned it?"

"Well, I mean I told him. He knows."

"And we start tomorrow morning?"

"Yep," said Franklin, with a grin as he puffed his chest and strutted with his thumbs hooked behind imaginary suspenders.

Brady never knew for sure when Franklin was lying, which was most of the time but, as always, Brady found himself wanting to believe his friend. Whether it was a lie or an exaggeration, one thing was certain, Franklin would see it through to the end. And that meant excitement or adventure—that was good enough for Brady.

Brady grinned. "Knock on my door in the morning."

Franklin wet his fingertip and smoothed his eyebrows and gazed into his palm as though it were a mirror. He raised his eyes. "Try to look good," he said.

THREE

Brady was dressed and waiting when Franklin stepped up onto the porch and tapped on Brady's door just before daylight. "You ready, cousin?" Franklin asked when Brady opened the door.

Brady nodded. "I'm ready."

They could see their breath in the cold air as they walked down the middle of the street and turned at the edge of town along the rutted road that led to Hogue's Livery. A lantern light shone in the barn and, when they stepped through the heavy double doors, they saw Hogue's backlit form bending over a row of grain sacks.

In the darkened shadows of the barn the ominous figure appeared to both boys like some night creature thumping around in the dark. They hesitated and looked over at one another. Franklin nodded them forward. Hogue ignored the boys as they approached him without speaking. He looked larger and more intimidating than Brady recalled. When Hogue spoke his voice boomed and Brady's stomach knotted.

"What do you two piss-ants want?"

Brady looked at Franklin and Franklin continued walking towards Hogue. Brady kept pace and, when they were close enough to discern Hogue's features, Franklin answered.

"Hey, Mr. Hog," Franklin said, as though he and the hulking man were two old friends.

Brady froze. Franklin nodded an acknowledgment to Hogue, which Hogue did not return.

"We're ready to go to work." Franklin looked around. "What can we get started with?"

Hogue stood to his full height. He shifted his jaw. The wet cigar stub he held clinched in his teeth switched from one side of his mouth to the other. He pushed his hat back and scratched his big stomach. He coughed and spat and wiped his mouth on his sleeve. "I don't need no more help."

"Hey, Mr. Hog, it's me. Franklin T. Stilwell," Franklin said. "This here's B.C. McCall. Don't you remember, I talked to you at church Sunday about me and him working for you, and you said, that'd be fine?"

Brady glared at Franklin for the mispronunciation of Hogue's name, and then awaited Hogue's dismissal. Hogue looked at Franklin then over to Brady. He walked up to Brady and lowered his face to the boy's level.

"Yer kindly of a little squirt, ain't ya? How old are you boy?"

Hogue shifted the soggy cigar stub to the other side of his mouth. Brady watched Hogue's lips and the cigar move together, fascinated by his dexterity.

"He's thirteen and a half, Mr. Hog," Franklin lied before Brady could respond.

Brady shot Franklin a devastating look, but Franklin stood firm. Hogue shifted his eyes to Franklin, then back to Brady.

"Can you talk, boy?"

Brady looked back into Hogue's red, watery eyes and lied, "Coming on fourteen, sir."

Hogue straightened up and said, "Well, that's fair enough. Let's get you boys started. You work 'till I tell ye you're done. If you do real good you can come back every Saturday and earn yourselves ten cents."

Franklin looked over at Brady. Brady declined the look and cleared his throat.

"We gotta have fifteen," he said.

Hogue stood his full height again and glared down at Brady. "You what?"

"Gotta have fifteen cents—each," Brady said, his voice steady and clear, but not challenging.

Hogue's eyes narrowed. He looked at Franklin. "You got a opinion on that?" he asked.

Franklin nodded. "Yessir. You said fifteen cents and we took you at your word. You'll get your money's worth."

Hogue pinched the cigar stub and held it between his fingers. He laughed and walked toward the corner of the barn he used as his office. "I always get my money's worth, boy. But, I think I'm going to like you two. You got your fifteen cents. But don't you be no slackers, and you damn sure better take care of my tools."

Hogue waved the boys over to his office—a wooden shipping crate turned upside down and a caneback chair next to it.

"I want you two peckerwoods to sign in and out each day so's we can keep a track a your time."

He scribbled on a dirt-soiled scrap of paper and slid in across the crate.

"You two can read, can't ye?"

Franklin looked at the paper, then over at Hogue. "Yessir, we both read real good. What do we put on here?"

Hogue pulled out his cigar and pointed it at the paper. "Where it says *Start*—write in the time you started. And where it says, *Done*—write in the time you stopped working. There's a clock up there on the wall by the hay hooks. Get yer times offa it."

Brady raised his hand. Hogue and Franklin turned to look at him.

"If we're gettin paid by the day, why are we writing down the hours?"

Hogue pointed at him with the cigar. "Cuz a day's ten-hours. If you cut it short, that ain't a whole day."

Hogue handed the boys each a double-bit axe and two manure forks, then sent them off to clean frozen stalls. By the end of that first day, there was no doubt that Hogue would get his money's worth.

They wrote their names on the paper, filled in the times, and told Hogue they would see him on Saturday. Hogue nodded.

On the way out the door, Franklin punched Brady on the shoulder and laughed.

"Hey, B.C., we're working men now."

The boys worked hard. Each day they tried to get a little more done than they did the time before. But, three weeks into the job, Franklin began to lose interest. He got distracted. He looked for shortcuts and diversions for entertainment. And the less Franklin did, the harder Brady worked to make up for it. By the fifth week things froze up solid. The boys chopped horse manure until noon. The work went slower than ever. For all the work they did that day, there was little to show for it. If there had been any glamour to being employed, it had worn off. Franklin leaned back in the dry hay, crossed his boots and laced his fingers behind his head.

"What are you doing?" Brady asked.

"Thinking," said Franklin.

"C'mon, we still got lots to do."

Franklin set his hat on his knee and scratched his head. He sat up and looked directly at Brady.

"B.C.," he said in a quiet and serious tone. "You know the red-haired lady I was telling you about over at the Silver Star? If I tell you something about her will you promise, on your mother's life not to never tell no one else?"

"Frank, I told you--"

Before he could finish his sentence, Franklin cut him off.

"Franklin." The older boy corrected.

"Okay, Franklin. I told you before don't never ask me to swear on my mother's life. I ain't doing that no matter what, and it ain't right for you to say it. If you don't want to tell me about the red-haired lady, I don't care."

"B.C., I seen her in the altogether," Franklin said.

"What do you mean, in the altogether?" Brady asked.

"I mean in the altogether. Nekkid. Four times." Franklin held up four fingers to make his point.

"You're lying." Brady laughed awkwardly.

He wanted to believe it was true but he was sure Franklin was making the whole thing up to divert his attention away from the job.

"I can prove it," Franklin said.

Brady wanted to believe it was true. With the exception of the one occasion when he walked in on his sister at bath time, Brady had never seen so much as a picture of the unclothed female body. At ten years old, he knew it wasn't happening now.

"Come on, Franklin," he said, "let's just finish up here so we can go."

Brady was disappointed, but he had no desire to indulge Franklin's fantasy.

"Hey, B.C., I forgot to tell you, ol' man Hog said we could leave when this one stall's done."

"You're lying."

Brady knew something was brewing in Franklin's head that would likely get them both in trouble before it was over. It annoyed him that Franklin could stretch the truth and never feel responsible for the consequences. But more than anything, it frustrated him that he always wanted to believe Franklin. Brady recognized Franklin's masterful skill in mixing his lies with the truth to the point it was impossible to tell where one left off and the other began.

The last few hours of the day passed uneventfully as the boys chopped away at the frozen horse manure. Brady couldn't stop thinking about Franklin's detailed accounts of his trip to the Silver Star.

That evening, as the McCall's had just finished dinner, a familiar knock at the door interrupted the quiet family time.

"That's Franklin," Brady said.

Mrs. McCall, nearest to the door, stood up to answer it. She opened the door and there stood Franklin— grinning and as sincere as he could be.

"Evening, Mrs. McCall," Franklin said, nodding to Mrs. McCall as he stood on the porch with his hat held down at his side.

She smiled and he stepped inside without being asked to do so.

"Franklin, please come in," Mrs. McCall said.

Franklin was already in. He grinned at her dry humor.

"I was wondering if B.C. could come help me some with my studies." He shifted from one foot to the other. "I'm starting to get a little behind in my arithmetic."

Mrs. McCall looked over at Mr. McCall, and then at Brady. Brady nodded and pleaded with his eyes. Mr. McCall shrugged. Mrs. McCall hesitated before she answered. She spoke directly to Brady.

"You can go, but be back here by 8:30 and not a minute later," she said.

Brady had his coat on and was heading for the door. "I will," he said, as he shot through the door and joined Franklin who was already outside.

Franklin and Brady crossed the street in the direction of the Stilwell cabin. As soon as they were out of sight of the McCall cabin, Franklin turned and headed downtown with Brady at his heels. Franklin waited for Brady to catch up. He put his hand on Brady's shoulder.

He leaned down close to his much shorter friend and whispered, "Cousin—you ain't going to believe this."

Brady looked at him. For the first time, his stomach knotted with fear. In his heart he knew everything about this escapade was wrong, but now it was here and Brady would have given anything to be back home.

"When we get to the Silver Star we gotta be real quiet. When I give you this sign (*Franklin slashed his finger across his throat and made an awful face*) you can't make a sound—know what I mean?"

Brady's eyes widened. He shook his head. "No, I don't know what you mean."

"It don't matter. It's a Blackfoot sign. All you gotta remember—not a sound." He slashed his finger violently this time.

As apprehensive as Brady was before, he was now absolutely convinced getting caught spying on a *nekkid* woman wasn't worth it. His jaw tightened, his mouth went dry, and his tongue felt twice its normal size.

His voice was weak. "Come on, Franklin. Let's go."

"We're almost there. You'll be glad you did it," Franklin whispered.

They entered the dark alley behind the Silver Star, picked their way over piles of discarded horseshoes, broken buggy parts, and rusty pieces of iron. It looked like a graveyard for every conveyance and farm implement known to man.

Brady's heart pounded. He snagged his shirtsleeve on a nail. He knew his mother would question him about it, and he would have to lie to her. The whole affair made him sick and it was getting worse.

They made their way through the junk pile at the rear of the blacksmith shop and heard the plinking sound of the saloon piano pounding away inside. Brady's heart throbbed in his ears.

Franklin led Brady to an old storage shed at the back of the Silver Star. The door hung by a single hinge. Franklin lifted it and swung it carefully open—this was clearly not his first trip here. Brady watched him, slack-jawed and in awe of his worldly friend. When Franklin disappeared inside, all Brady could do was stand there in the dark and imagine the worst.

Brady heard a soft whistle. Then he heard it again. It came from inside the shed. He waited. Finally, Franklin stuck his head outside.

He motioned to Brady. "Come on in, cuz, but be quiet."

Brady's better judgment told him to leave. His sweaty palms, dry mouth, and rapid pulse all confirmed that what they were doing was wrong. He just wanted to turn and go, but he was committed. Franklin gave him the Blackfoot sign and motioned him to follow. The anticipation and the look on Franklin's face overruled any idea he had of leaving. Brady stepped in behind Franklin. It was cold and damp and Brady shivered.

"Now what?" Brady asked in a voice barely above a whisper.

Franklin whirled and slashed his finger savagely across his throat. Brady felt his heart go cold. His hands shook. Franklin motioned him forward and led him to a boarded-up door that was once an outside entrance for the two rooms at the back of the saloon. A thin beam of light shone into the dark shed from the keyhole of the old door.

On the lighted side of the door, voices laughed and spoke in whispers. A man and a woman laughing, speaking in whispers, then silence.

Brady heard every word. He was mesmerized by the very thought of being so close to something so forbidden. Now it had grown beyond his ability to resist. This was the nature of Franklin's magic. The essence of his persuasive ability to give Brady just enough rope. Brady was just beginning to recognize it.

In the reflection from the light beam Brady could see Franklin had an old anvil stump situated before the door as a seat. The soil around it had been worn smooth. Franklin had obviously given this endeavor more thought than Brady expected. Without another word, Franklin took his seat on the stump, cupped his hands around the keyhole, and pressed his eye to it.

Brady's mind raced as he reflected back on his earlier conversations with Franklin. This was just like Franklin. As often as not, that which sounded like a lie turned out to be the truth. Here was Brady on the verge of his first manly experience and he had no idea what to do next. He just knew the attraction was more than he could deny.

After what seemed a long time, Brady tapped Franklin on the shoulder. Franklin ignored him. Brady tapped him again. Franklin shook him off.

"There she is. I see her. She's got herself a customer."

"Let me look," Brady said.

Franklin slashed his finger across his throat, but didn't budge.

"Her name's Anna Lee," Franklin whispered. He adjusted his eye.

"Okay, get ready. Come on and take a look, quick!"

Brady took his place on the stump. "I don't see anything."

"Get your eye real close, then look off to the right," Franklin said.

Brady drew a sharp breath and pressed his eye to the keyhole. He felt his jaw drop and squeezed his closed eye tighter. "Franklin, she's taking them off," he whispered.

Brady watched as her garments dropped to the floor one by one. He drew in another sharp breath when she exposed the smooth white skin of her shoulders and her large rounded hips. Her hair fell to her back. She whispered to the cowboy, and then turned slowly. There she was—in the altogether, just as Franklin promised.

Brady stopped breathing. His eye strained until it hurt. His imagination ignited as she moved and her large breasts swayed and bounced. He imagined he could smell her perfume. He still hadn't taken a breath. She moved and his eye followed. He couldn't stop staring at her breasts. His face flushed red and hot and suddenly he grew dizzy and lost his balance and tumbled off the stump in a heap.

Franklin leaped past him, took over the position at the keyhole and scanned the room with his eye, hoping for one last look.

The yellow light in the room dimmed, and then went black. "Damn," Franklin said.

Brady leaned against the wall and laughed. "Do you believe that?" he said. "She was *nekkid* as could be."

Franklin turned and leaned back against the door. "See, I told you," he said.

The boys slipped quietly away, left with only their imaginations and the creaking of the old bed. They walked the moonlit streets back toward the cabins, talking and laughing. They stopped for a serious moment still within earshot of the honkytonk piano. Franklin took out his folding knife. They pricked their fingers, pressed the bloody pinkies together and swore never to tell anyone. In a cleansing moment they repented their great sin and vowed never to go back.

One week to the day, after another visit to the peephole, Brady and Franklin stopped on the same corner. This time, in a moment of great reflection and an equal amount of guilt, they rationalized that once committed the sin was cast. They agreed to wait until spring, then ask for forgiveness for the entire affair, including any unforeseen temptations the devil may put before them in the meantime.

FOUR

No two people were any more different than Franklin and Brady, or more alike. They fought and they argued. They stood up for one another. They disagreed on almost everything, but through it all they never questioned their friendship. Franklin cursed and chewed tobacco. His preoccupation with women's breasts made it impossible for him to carry on a conversation without some reference to the female anatomy. As near as Brady could tell, Franklin had no preferences in terms of size or shape. In Franklin's eyes a breast by any description was a sacred jewel to be admired in any setting.

"B.C., did you ever wonder what it feels like to just touch one?"

Brady glared at Franklin and looked away without answering.

"Seriously, did you?"

Brady shook his head. "Not really."

Franklin laughed. "I know you have. I seen you looking lots of times, even in church.

"Yeah, well it's not the only thing I ever think about like it is with you."

Franklin was right, and it aggravated Brady that he could no longer look at a woman without thinking about her breasts. Brady felt guilty about his preoccupation, but not bad enough to discourage him from the weekly pilgrimage to the Silver Star. Franklin, on the other hand, took great pride in his mammary expertise.

Franklin thrived on excitement and the greater the risk the better. Brady loved the excitement, but was bound by a higher level of conventional thinking and a sense of responsibility that never seemed to encumber Franklin. Their five-year age difference was never an issue. Brady looked up to Franklin—fascinated by his older friend's worldliness and his direct approach to reducing every decision down to terms of how much fun it might be.

Franklin admired Brady's sense of obligation and he took special pride in luring Brady off course at every opportunity, as though Brady's fall from grace gave them even more in common. Franklin saw it as his mission to liberate Brady from the constraints of society, but it was not lost on Franklin that grownups trusted Brady and held him in high regard. And, on that rare occasion when they did get careless and got caught, it was a foregone conclusion that Franklin's bad influence was to blame. Their age difference worked in Brady's favor as well. Brady could be excused his indiscretions because of his age; Franklin should have known better.

The job at the livery stable proved to be a good outlet for the excess energy of the two boys. Brady's serious approach to the job began to influence Franklin and, before long, Franklin was working as hard as Brady. Even though he never mentioned it, Hogue was delighted at the transition, but he never expected it to last long with Franklin.

In late January, a storm blew in from the Canadian North Country. It started cold and slow. By mid-morning, the snow began to fall. It was light at first, nothing more than a dusting. Then, the temperature dropped and the wind picked up. The temperature continued to drop and the snowfall became heavy as it drove in crosswise from the north.

The boys, with their backs to the storm, swung their axes hard to break up the ice on the water troughs. They were more than half a mile from the barn and failed to see the big structure disappear behind the wall of blowing snow. The trough lay along the fence line and the fence itself, a sturdy split rail affair, was now covered with drifting snow banked half way to the top rail.

The frozen water in the trough broke into thick blocks as Brady chopped and Franklin lifted the heavy ice and threw it over the fence where it lay heaped in a growing pile.

Then the storm quieted, the wind stopped, the sky darkened, and the temperature plummeted. Brady pulled his collar up and shivered.

Franklin looked up at the sky. "Come on, Brady. Hurry up. We're going to be in for it," he said.

Brady chopped faster. Franklin finally began to slow. He studied the sky again. He stomped his feet and slapped his arms with his mittened hands. Then the full force of the storm cut loose with high winds and whiteout snow whipping everywhere.

"B.C., I can't feel my toes," Franklin screamed over the roar of the wind. "We gotta get back."

Franklin turned to head back to the barn. He leaned into the wind and started across the white, featureless field. Brady caught him by the sleeve of the coat and pulled him back.

"That's the wrong way, "Brady shouted. "We gotta follow the fence."

Franklin nodded in agreement and the two boys plunged into the waist-deep snow. They forged ahead, pushing and lunging and struggling through the snowpack that would not support their weight. Franklin fell, then forced himself up in a flurry of profanity.

Franklin waved Brady on "Keep on going!" He shouted.

Side by side they plowed through the deep snow, following the fence line and finally reaching firmer footing.

"There it is," Brady said. "I can see the barn."

They stomped across the yard and Franklin laughed. "This ain't worth no damn fifteen cents to me."

They approached the barn and the door swung open. Hogue stood there and waited. He brushed the snow from their coats as they stepped past him.

"Ain't you a damn pair to draw to," he said shaking his head. "Git you up next to that stove there and thaw out some."

Hogue reached out and took the axe from Brady's hand. He looked over at Franklin.

"Where's your axe?"

"I guess I left it," Franklin said in a low voice.

Hogue stood to his full height. His expression grew cold. "You left it? This boy here didn't leave his, but you guess you just left yers?"

Hogue's face turned red and his teeth clinched down hard on the unlit cigar stub. "When did you plan on fetching it back here—sometime this spring when it's warm and sunny and you don't have nothing else to do? Or do you suppose it's not your problem?"

"I dropped it. I'm sorry," Franklin said.

Hogue's voice was loud and unreasonable. "Well sorry don't get that axe back here, now does it?"

Franklin gritted his teeth. He weighed his words carefully and, just before he said something he knew he would regret, he heard the door open and slam shut, and Brady was gone.

Hogue glared at Franklin. "I suppose you're going to quit now, too," he said.

Franklin grabbed his mittens and pulled on his hat. "He didn't quit. He's going after you're damn axe."

Franklin didn't wait for a response. He cursed under his breath and, by the time he got out the door, Brady had disappeared into the swirling blizzard. Franklin followed the new outbound footprints rapidly filling with new snow and he called out to Brady as he plunged into the storm. He followed what was left of the fence where the top rail was now barely visible.

Franklin pulled his coat up tighter around his face and he screamed Brady's name, but the wind blew the words back at him and muffled them to the point he could hardly hear it himself. Again and again he called out and again and again the wind blunted the words.

Franklin's stomach turned. He called out until his voice grew hoarse. He pushed deeper into the storm until he wanted to cry. Franklin continued along the fence line, shouting and cursing and watching the snow drift and blow.

"All this for an axe?" He cursed Hogue, he cursed St. Joseph, and he cursed the snow and the cold and the wind.

His legs ached, his heart pounded, and his lungs burned. What daylight there was would be gone soon. The thought of Brady out there at night panicked him. Franklin caged his eyes and squinted into the fading light and shouted until his voice was completely gone. Then he removed a mitten, put two fingers in his mouth and whistled in groups of three shrill blasts, a signal he knew Brady would recognize if he heard it.

Franklin thought he saw movement off to his left. He tilted his head for a better angle and tried to see into the blinding snow. Now it was unmistakable. He stumbled through the snow and he whistled and he shouted a hoarse and raspy shout and the shape moved towards him. Then nothing—no shape—no movement—no sound.

"Brady," he screamed. He cupped his hands to his mouth and his voice was lost to the wind. He stumbled toward the spot he saw movement and squinted into the heavy veil of snow but saw nothing. He had visions of Brady lying face down, snow drifting up around his coat and trousers and silently covering him.

He stopped and he listened, and beneath it all, he prayed. He felt the cold. The wind shifted and the top rail of the fence was all but covered with snow. He sucked in the frozen air and he whistled and he trod in the direction of the movement he knew he saw earlier, and then he saw it again. This time there was no doubt. He plunged through the snow. The dark shape moved and, when it came fully into view, it was one of Hogue's livery mules. The mule stopped and stared at Franklin. Franklin dropped to his knees and the tears that fell down his cheeks froze there.

Franklin struggled back towards the fence. When he got there he sat back on what was left of the top rail. He looked up, and there came Brady shuffling down the fence line, high-stepping through the snow drifts and dragging Franklin's axe behind him.

Franklin seized Brady by the arm. He brushed the snow from Brady's shoulders and away from his face. Now he was mad.

"Why did you do that, B.C.? Are you nuts?"

Brady shifted his eyes, but held his head as though it were frozen in place.

He nodded. "I think so."

They both laughed. Then their expressions grew grave. The light that was dusk now became almost dark and the snow that drifted up against the fence breached the top rail and, if the fence had been there at all, it was no longer evident.

Franklin slapped Brady on the arm. "Come on, we gotta get out of here fast," he said. Then he turned to leave and Brady caught him by the sleeve.

"Wrong way again."

He pointed the axe handle a half-turn to the left. Franklin looked into the whiteout, and then followed the axe handle.

"You sure?"

Brady nodded. "I'm sure."

FIVE

The wind screamed and changed directions, and with the dark came the cold. The effect was disorienting and debilitating and, with each new flurry, the temperature dropped. The frigid temperature slowed the boys to a crawl.

Each step they took felt like the last. Fear gave way to exhaustion and exhaustion gave way to resignation. Brady gave in first. He dropped to the snow face up. Franklin fell to his back next to him.

"I gotta rest," Franklin said. "But just for a minute."

Franklin closed his eyes. Brady rolled over on his back, his eyes closed, snow filling up the folds on his coat.

"I'll be okay in a second," Brady said, as he let out a long breath and the tension left his muscles.

For a moment, just a moment, they would sleep.

Brady felt like he was floating. He smiled. Then, abruptly he was startled back to his senses when Franklin jerked him up by his collar and shook him.

"Wake up, B.C. WAKE UP!"

He jerked Brady up to his feet. Brady stood on wobbly legs and stared out glassy-eyed.

"I'm up. Stop shaking me."

Franklin picked up the axe and drug Brady along as he probed the fence line with the axe handle.

"It's this way," Franklin said, pointing with his frozen mitten.

Ahead, a yellow light swung in the dark. It grew larger as the boys slogged toward it.

It was Hogue on snowshoes carrying a lantern. When he reached them he took Brady's arm then turned and the boys followed him to the barn.

Inside, huddled around the stove, the boys stood shivering. Franklin glared at Hogue and thrust the axe at him.

"Here's your damn axe," he said.

Hogue took the axe and leaned it against the wall. He ignored Franklin's attitude.

"Take this," he said, handing them each a tin cup of steaming coffee.

They held the cups in trembling fingers that shook so bad the coffee sloshed over the rims. Hogue stoked the fire, then slammed the stove door shut. He had something on his mind. He thought about it a long time before he spoke.

"I never meant for you to go back after that axe," Hogue said.

He looked up, first at Brady, then at Franklin. Neither boy responded. They sipped their coffee and crowded the fire. Hogue stoked it again, then cleared his throat.

"That took some grit," he said. He wanted to say more, but didn't.

Franklin stood, reached for the pot and poured more coffee for himself. He offered the pot to Brady. Brady shook him off. Franklin held the pot out to Hogue. Hogue, held out his cup and Franklin poured.

"You was probably right," Franklin said. "I oughtn't to have left that axe like I done."

Brady sat back. The ice was beginning to melt from his eyebrows. His half-closed eyes followed Franklin then they shifted to Hogue. Hogue took the cigar stub between his fingers.

"Look, you're good boys," he finally said.

There was another long stretch of silence from Hogue. The boys waited as though the silence itself demanded their attention. Hogue appeared to be in serious contemplation and Brady could see their careers coming to an abrupt end. Both boys watched Hogue. Hogue cleared his throat and poked the air with the cigar stub.

"Look, I got me a couple a Indian ponies out back."

Franklin nodded. "We know, we seen 'em."

Hogue spat and the boys watched the spittle sizzle on the hot steel stove.

"How'd you boys like to buy them ponies?"

The boys looked at one another.

Franklin shook his head. "We ain't got money to buy no horses."

"No, I didn't reckon you did," Hogue said.

"Well, how much you want for 'em?" Brady asked.

"All I got in 'em is the feed. A Frenchman, a trapper he was, run out of cash and left them Comanche ponies here to pay his feed bill. Didn't do me no favor though."

"How much?" Brady asked again.

Hogue thought a moment. "Tell you what," he said.

The pause took an eternity, but the boys waited him out.

"You work out the rest of the winter—don't take no pay. All you have to do is your work and you have to care for them ponies until you get ready to leave in the spring—feed 'em, care for 'em. I'll throw in a couple of old saddles and blankets and you can make up the bridles from spare parts you find laying around here. After that, them horses are yours free and clear."

"That's it?" Brady asked.

Hogue nodded. "That's it."

If there was a smile on Hogue's face, it only showed in his eyes. The boys grinned and Franklin offered his hand to Hogue.

"You done made yourself a deal, Mr. Hog," he said.

Brady stood, held the blanket around him with one hand and extended the other hand to Hogue.

"Thanks, Mr. Hogue," he said.

"Them's good buffalo ponies," Hogue said. "The Frenchman won 'em from the Comanche in a bet."

Brady looked over at Franklin and Franklin looked back. Franklin grinned and gave Brady his nod of approval. Franklin knew the horses and he knew the story. He was there the day Charles du Mer, the French trapper, shared a bottle of whiskey with Hogue. He listened when the Frenchman bragged in his broken English how he won the horses from a Comanche called Little Crow. And Franklin remembered lying awake that night feeling the wind in his face as he imagined himself riding free and wild across wide stretches of plains and through stands of trees and across creeks and rivers.

Franklin knew these horses. He knew the stout paint gelding with grey eyes and he knew the uncut buckskin with the proud head and tail that flagged when he trotted along the fence line at the sight of new horses being turned out.

The next morning the boys were back at the barn looking at the Indian ponies. Today they looked different— today the boys owned them. They admired the horses a long time before Brady spoke up.

"What do you want to name them?" Brady asked more as a thought than a question.

Franklin looked down at Brady.

"They already got names."

"You mean Indian names?"

"No, B.C., not Indian names. Real names.

"How do you know that?"

"I heard the Frenchman tell 'em to Mr. Hog."

"What are they?"

"That spotted one he called Three Feathers."

"Three Feathers? What's that mean?"

"I don't know, B.C. It's probably something important in Comanche. Like better than One Feather or Two Feathers."

Brady pointed to the buckskin. "What about that one?"

"He called him Buffalo Dancer."

Buffalo Dancer, Brady said to himself. *A perfect name*, he thought.

The buckskin was his horse and he couldn't imagine it any other way. Problem was, Franklin, being the oldest, got first choice.

"Which one do you like best?" Brady asked, trying not to give away his desire for the buckskin for fear Franklin would choose it for himself.

"I don't know," Franklin replied, as though he was ambivalent about the whole deal. "Which one do you like?"

"Don't matter to me none," Brady said. "The paint's nice."

Then, thinking Franklin might take that as a bid, he added, "So is the buckskin."

Franklin walked around the horses eyeing first the buckskin then the paint and back again. He scratched his chin just like he'd seen his father do when he was bargaining. Franklin removed his hat and reset it upon his head, then walked the circle the other direction.

Finally, Brady blew. "Dang it, Franklin, will you just pick one?"

Franklin smiled and looked at Brady from under his hat brim.

"I got a better idea," he said. "Get out your folding knife and we'll play one game of mumblypeg. Winner gets to choose."

Brady shook his head and reached into his pocket. "You can't make nothing easy, can you?" he said.

"This'll be pretty easy if you still throw like a girl, B.C.," Franklin said, then he laughed.

Brady gritted his teeth. "No throw over twelve inches."

"Fine. You go ahead," he said.

The boys faced one another—stood with feet together, then sized each other up. Brady held his knife by the blade and made a solid throw. The blade stuck to the hilt barely less than twelve inches out from Franklin's left foot. Franklin moved his foot next to the blade then pulled the knife from the dirt and looked back at Brady.

"Nice throw," Franklin said, then he stuck his with great authority and Brady moved his foot to the mark and re-stuck his. Franklin moved his foot. Then Brady and back to Franklin. No misses. Soon, Brady was stretched to the point of losing his balance and it was clear that Franklin's longer legs gave him an unfair advantage. Franklin saw the anger in Brady's eyes as Brady realized he'd been cheated. Before Brady could protest, Franklin reached forth and put his hand on Brady's chest and pushed him off balance. Franklin laughed and ran as Brady came for him.

"Take whichever one you want," Franklin said as he ran, "but please don't hurt me."

Brady's anger turned to laughter when he caught Franklin and got him in a headlock.

"Okay, I'm taking the buckskin," Brady said.

Franklin stood up. "The buckskin?" He laughed. "Are you nuts? That buckskin's a stud horse. He'll for sure run your skinny ass all the way to Montana if he don't kill ya first, which he probably will."

"I don't care," Brady said, "that's the one I want." And just like that, it was settled.

The two buffalo ponies took priority over everything in the boys' lives except the standing pilgrimage to the keyhole on Saturday nights. For the rest of the winter they spent every free moment at the livery and worked harder than they had ever worked before. They sat their horses bareback in the barn and talked for hours without going anywhere. They rode in small circles inside and practiced backing and turning. Then, one day Hogue threw two beat up saddles over the top rail of the corral, and hung two pieced-together bridles on the saddlehorns. He dropped two old and worn out wool saddle blankets on the floor below the saddles.

The boys looked across from their bareback horses and watched as Hogue hung his big arms over the top rail and stared in at them.

"Them are good horses," he said. "If you don't do anything else, always ride a good one."

The boys were speechless. Hogue turned to leave. He looked back over his shoulder. His expression was dead serious and there was no humor in his voice.

"You take care of them ponies. Out there your life could depend on them."

SIX

The weather turned and the snow melted. The boys rode deeper and deeper into the wilderness each day, exploring and hunting. Franklin turned out to be a good teacher and Brady learned to track and hunt and find water. Playtime turned serious when the boys began bringing more game home than their families could eat. What was left over they sold to the local butcher. It had been a long winter and it was Bill McCall who suggested the boys give the extra meat to the families around them.

He sat them down one afternoon. "Boy's," he said. "The ribs are beginning to show on your popularity around town, the way you're showing off on them horse and all."

He addressed them both but looked at Franklin. "You might do well to mend a few fences with the neighbors. We got plenty and they could use the fresh meat."

That was all the boys needed to hear. The enterprise was born and Brady took to it as quickly as Franklin did. Selling to the butcher shop was Franklin's idea and the extra money just made it better, but supplying the neighbors began to boost their celebrity around town, and that held more than enough appeal for Franklin.

The two young hunters on their Comanche Indian ponies managed to attain the status of at least minor celebrities, a standing they bore with a complete absence of humility. It was contagious, catching Brady up it its allure as quickly as it did Franklin.

Snow turned to slush, then to mud, and spring was evident everywhere. The transient neighborhood changed with the weather. The men checked and repaired the wagons. They assembled the mule and oxen teams and readied them for the trip. Women packed belongings and removed the children from school.

Garrett, the wagonmaster, inspected the teams and the drivers and their equipment. He organized the last of the new arrivals and, when the roster was full he called for a final meeting of the Third Oregon Expedition as Garrett referred to it. He announced to the assemblage they would depart St. Joseph at dawn the next morning.

Bill McCall loaded the last of his family's belongings on the wagon and walked back to Elizabeth standing on the porch of the cabin that had been their home that winter. He put his arm around his wife's shoulders as they both stood looking back towards the east and the direction from which they had arrived in St. Joseph the previous fall. Elizabeth put her arm around her husband. She looked up at him and smiled.

"This feels so final," she said, "Now I'm anxious to get to our new home and get settled in."

Bill smiled. "Me too, Liz—me too."

She held his calloused hands to her lips and kissed his fingertips. He turned to face her and held her close, and then looked down into her eyes then tilted her head and touched his lips to hers. Elizabeth had her arms wrapped tightly around her husband's neck when Brady came out of the house.

"I'm going to Mr. Hogue's with Franklin to get our horses and say goodbye," Brady said.

Then he looked back over his shoulder. "Hey, Pa" he said. "If you two stand around mooning like that all day we might get left in the morning."

Then he laughed as he ran off.

Bill McCall laughed. "Don't you worry about us. We'll be the first ones there," he said.

Elizabeth smiled at them. It warmed her heart to see the close relationship between Brady and his father. Brady waved and ran towards the Stilwell cabin and Elizabeth shook her head. Then she looked back up at her husband.

"How did that last meeting with Mr. Garrett go this morning?"

"Well, he said the roster is full. We got a total of fifty-three families signed on and all accounted for."

Then he paused and his expression was weighed with carefully chosen words when he continued. "Garrett is concerned about the fact we got so many inexperienced teamsters. He wants our wagon and the Stilwell wagon up front to start out. Seems to think we'll set a better pace."

Elizabeth looked at him with questions in her eyes that did not reach her lips and Bill knew she wouldn't be satisfied with an evasive answer.

"Garrett's real concerned about the Indians, and he's concerned about the Maier family."

"You mean Gustav Maier's health?"

Bill nodded. "Yes, that and them five little children of theirs."

"What did he say?"

"He put it to a vote."

"And?"

"We all voted to let them come. I'm not at all sure we done the right thing."

Elizabeth squeezed his arm. "Everyone has a right to their own dreams."

"I guess," Bill said. "Garrett assigned Brady and Franklin T. to be drovers because of their horses."

"Oh my goodness. That's all those two need."

Bill smiled and shook his head. "You don't suppose they'll be proud do you, Lizzie?"

"Proud?" Then she laughed. "Unbearable is more like it."

That night no one slept much. Franklin and Brady pitched their bedrolls out near the wagons where their horses grazed hobbled and contented. Both boys carried a saddle rifle and each wore a belt knife. Most of the other boys their age walked or shared driving with their fathers. The few that had a rifle kept it packed in the wagon and, of those that had a knife, it was generally a small folding knife tucked away in a pocket.

There was no possession among the boys of the camp to compare to the Indian ponies Brady and Franklin rode. With the mystery surrounding the horses, nothing incited the admiration of the young girls or the envy of the other boys more.

Brady and Franklin settled back on the ground leaning against their upturned saddles, watching the two Indian ponies grazing in the moonlight. Brady's voice was wistful and thoughtful when he spoke.

"You know, Franklin. Them horses of ours probably already been to some of the places we're going."

"Probably," Franklin said. His own voice was also uncharacteristically thoughtful.

Then Franklin turned his head without lifting it from the underside of the saddle. "We ain't never going back, you know?"

"What do you mean?" Brady asked.

"Home. We ain't never going back home."

"I guess I knew that," Brady said. "Just never really thought about it like that."

"Well, cousin, think about it. Once we leave the states, that's it," Franklin said.

Brady shifted his weight and pulled his blanket up. "Does it ever scare you?"

Franklin turned his head to look at Brady who just stared up the stars.

"Does what scare me?"

"Whatever's out there." Brady nodded in the general direction across the river. "And that we ain't never going home again," he added.

"No. It don't scare me none."

Franklin gnawed the inside of his cheek as he thought about it.

"Well, I wouldn't say I was scared but, yeah I do think about it some and wonder."

"Me too, a lot," Brady said.

SEVEN

When the camp rose that morning, it was well before daylight. The emigrants were restless and eager, not well-rested, but tired of waiting for night to end.

Brady and Franklin were the first to arrive at the bedding grounds. Their horses pranced and jigged, and the boys were both animated with nervous energy as they trotted the perimeter of the herd and brought the lowing livestock to their feet as the night sky began to lighten.

Bill McCall and Thomas Stilwell lined their teams out at the river's edge and waited for daylight to blend up grey into the black horizon to the east. Captain Garrett stood his horse knee-deep in the water waiting for enough light to give the signal to move out.

When the black sky turned to grey, Garrett waved the leaders on amidst a chaos of yelps and whistles, creaking wheels and cracking whips, and it appeared as the entire world was on the move.

Elizabeth held her breath as Bill urged the distrustful mules into the swift flowing current of the swollen river. The tongue of the wagon disappeared beneath the surface of the muddy water and the mules snorted and tossed their heads as the cold water inched up over their bellies. The river bottom was firm and relatively flat, and McCall was thankful Garrett had picked a good crossing. Elizabeth turned back in her seat to make sure Rachael and Matthew were bundled up against the cold morning wind that blew through the wagon.

She turned and rose up in the seat to see if she could locate Brady. She saw the herd milling and wagons moving out of sequence, but nowhere in the confusion and the half-light did she see Brady or Franklin. When she looked back at the roiling water eddying up around the mules and tugging at the wagon, she held McCall's arm and he looked over at her.

"Those boys will be all right," he said.

She smiled and it pleased her he understood how she felt. "I can't help but worry. He's still a baby, you know."

"He's closer to being a man than he is a baby," McCall said, his voice more reassuring than his true feelings.

Elizabeth held her breath and didn't exhale until she saw the lead mules step up on solid ground. When the wheel mules emerged and the water drained off the wagon and ran down the sides of the mules, she looked back at Rachael and Matthew

"We made it," she said smiling.

The Stilwell wagon pulled up right behind the McCall outfit. McCall and Stilwell stepped down to survey the progress of the other wagons. Stilwell whistled and shook his head.

"Look at the mess, will you," he said. We're going to be here a while."

Wagons and teams crowded the track to the river and teamsters ignored their line order. Garrett rode up and down the line admonishing first one then another. His face was red and his voice loud. He gestured with his hands and he called forth his trail boss.

"Simpkins, I told you to hold them wagons up. Two at a time is all we can get across. Now get back up there and get them men back in position and keep them there."

Simpkins glared at Garrett. He wheeled about and spurred his horse. Garrett waved his arms and redirected the inexperienced teamsters back into position.

The crossing took all morning, and it took most of the day before the long line of wagons stretched out and assumed a traveling order that would eventually become part of each day's routine.

Brady and Franklin rode day-herd and they rode night-herd and, when they weren't with the livestock, they rode their Indian ponies at the flanks of the great caravan and watched for strays. The horses set them apart from the other boys and freed them from the walking and the dust and the endless hours of being bound to the wagon where each day was the same.

Soon, company began to show some signs of organization. The daily activities established themselves into a routine that gave the travelers some small comfort in the familiarity and the order of things. But, inexperience and poor judgment were commonplace and Garrett found himself challenged time after time by those who would bicker and argue and question his decisions.

Each day, at least one team would buckle under the load of an over-laden wagon, and the owners would be forced to discarded heavy furniture, stoves, and any other thing not absolutely essential to their survival. With each abandoned item represented a lost piece of history no one wanted to forfeit. The women of the expedition looked at the loss of a neighbor's estate today as their own loss tomorrow, and a noticeable depression to begin to set in.

The delicate balance between success and failure hit them all hard. Rather than creating a better sense of community, the settlers became increasingly self-serving and self-focused.

Early into the third week of the journey, Mr. Maier's cough turned to blood. He traveled three more days propped up inside the wagon staring out through glazed eyes, and on that third night he died without making a sound.

Maier's death was the first, and it was the most devastating. For the first time, the severity of what, to some, was nothing more than a grand adventure and the opportunity of a lifetime, had now been defined in clear terms. There was no turning back, no chance to re-think the decision or to reassess the risk. Every family in the company had gambled everything they had. Now they realized the gamble included their lives and the emotional impact created a difficult burden for many to bear.

They slunk away in guarded conversations trying to find someone to blame, some way to mitigate the feelings of regret for even beginning this journey, some way to silence the inner voices that made them want to turn around and go back home, an option they no longer possessed. But it was never said. Instead, an undercurrent of discontent begin to develop.

Standing over the new grave, Mrs. Maier and her children huddled together, the picture of despair. Her slightly built frame draped in a dress too large, her thin arms holding her children to her, and the expression one of complete hopelessness.

She knew her fate rested in the hands of those whose own lives hung in the balance. They avoided her eyes, no one saying it, but all thinking the same thing. Mrs. Maier had no hope to continue and none to return to St. Joseph, much less the home she gave up to make this trip. Her husband's death was the death of the entire family. Every woman watching was Mrs. Maier for that brief horrific moment.

The preacher's wife was the first to step up. She enlisted her husband and together they approached every family for a contribution. Some gave willingly, some gave grudgingly, but all, save one, gave something. When the preacher's wife approached Randolph Osborne, he turned and busied himself at the tool box mounted on the side of his wagon.

"Excuse me, Mr. Osborne." she said when he failed to acknowledge her presence. "Would you like to contribute something to help Mrs. Maier and her children?"

Osborne avoided eye contact with her. "They shouldn't have been out here," he said. "They had no business putting their burden on us. I'm sorry. They'll get no subsidy from me."

The preacher's wife's eyes widened and she glared at him. She turned and hurried away without another word. She knew Osborne was an outsider and a dissenter, but she was not prepared for his cold and vile attitude. Her hands shook as she returned to the gravesite, where the preacher addressed the others in attendance over the austere service.

The preacher asked for help and he asked for anyone willing to take the children in, someone to help drive her wagon. He implored the tiny congregation, but he knew he asked the impossible and it showed in the lack of conviction in his voice. No one raised a hand. Not one person looked up.

The preacher looked over at Mrs. Maier and the children. His voice shook.

"Please bow your heads."

He began the Lord's Prayer.

"Our Father which art in Heaven…"

His voice dropped off as the others joined in.

After the collective *amen*, he raised his eyes to Mrs. Maier. Her expression wouldn't have been more solemn standing at the gallows with a noose around her neck.

He didn't admonish the congregation and he didn't pass judgment. He didn't preach his way into anyone's heart to find a conviction based on faith or poor judgment. But he did wait, and he did weigh his thoughts and his words and, when he spoke, it was a final plea.

"We need a volunteer," he said. "One man to take this family back to St. Joseph."

He looked out over the crowd of downcast eyes. He looked from man to man, from woman to woman. He saw tears and he saw men wringing their hands and others trying to remain inconspicuous. He let the silence touch every man on the shoulder. None acknowledged the touch.

"I'm going to pray one more time," he said. "Then I want you all to join me in a verse of *Just as I Am.*"

They sang and he prayed and no one moved. His voice started out soft and sweet and others joined in, as though the singing exempted each of them from personal responsibility. The preacher looked out over the crowd, his eyes imploring, his arms outstretched to heaven.

"We're going to sing the last verse," he said. And they did. And the long silence that followed that final verse was awful.

Franklin, standing next to his father with tears running down his cheeks, took a step forward and began to raise his hand. Thomas Stilwell reached out and held the boy's arm.

They waited a long time and no one looked up. The preacher refused to give in and he waited. The air was heavy with conviction as Mrs. Maier and her small children awaited sentencing.

Finally, a voice from the back of the crowd rose above the pall hanging over the congregation.

"I'll do it."

The crowd split and stepped back from where the voice originated. There, with all eyes fixed upon him, stood a cowboy few had taken the time to meet. With leather chaps, Mexican spurs and a wide-brimmed hat pulled low over his eyes, he was an unlikely answer to anyone's prayers. His left arm rested over the butt of the pistol he wore cross-draw fashion. His right thumb hung hooked in the front pocket of his trousers. His expression was serious and he had the air of a man who was capable. Who he was and why he was there now seemed like very important questions none had bothered to ask earlier.

"Praise God," said the preacher as he looked skyward then back down at the cowboy. "Amen. What's your name, son?" he asked.

"Travis Kincaid."

Kincaid stood firm and the preacher waited for him to advance. Kincaid held his position and looked down at his boots then back up at the preacher and the preacher stepped into the crowd and approached Kincaid and extended him his hand. Kincaid shook it and the preacher placed both his hands on Kincaid's hand. There were tears in the preacher's eyes. Kincaid diverted his eyes and cleared his throat. He appeared embarrassed by the attention.

"Bless you, Mr. Kincaid," the preacher said in a soft voice. "We can never repay your kindness."

"None expected," Kincaid replied.

The preacher looked about at the congregation that stood silent but relieved. No one spoke and no one moved. Then Garrett stepped forward and joined Kincaid and the preacher.

"Son, we appreciate what you're doing but you know we can't wait for you," Garrett said.

Kincaid nodded. "I understand. I got two good horses. I'm traveling light. I'll catch up."

Less than an hour later, Travis Kincaid tossed his bedroll and saddle into the Maier wagon, tied his horses on behind, and touched his hat as he turned the team about and laid the wheels in the same tracks that had brought them there.

The company stood mute, watching the lone canvas-topped vessel bob and tilt frighteningly insignificant across that ocean of a landscape until there was nothing left to watch. Not a person watching felt exempt from the same fate.

Elizabeth McCall squeezed Emily Stilwell's hand and shook her head. "How arrogant we are to challenge this inhospitable land," she said.

Emily nodded in agreement and said, "I dread to think how many of us would return with her if we knew what lay in store for us."

EIGHT

They followed the Platte west over featureless land that was hypnotically flat. On the best days they covered less than twenty miles—most days not even half that. There were sparingly few good days as the weather was hot and dry and choked with dust.

It rained seldom, but when it did, it rained without warning. The storm clouds blew in suddenly and the ground became a slick mire of clay and mud that stuck to the wheels and to the feet and bogged the wagons until the teams tired and quit. On those days the going was slow and patience ran thin.

The overall dissension among the men lessened as the demands of each day grew, and the routine they settled into became an exhausting list of chores that was never completed. Despite the unending toil, unrest among a few continued to fester.

Brady C. McCall and Franklin T. Stilwell rose above it all. Their horses gave them freedom and independence. They were mobile and exempt from the common chores that kept other boys their age wagon-bound and conscripted into duty as wood gatherers and day laborers.

It was difficult to be inconspicuous and modest, and neither boy tried. Franklin took his arrogance to a whole new level. He accepted his new station in life without a glimmer of grace or humility. Where the young girls gathered at the noon stops he galloped by and touched his hat. When the young girls carried water up from the river he rode through at a deliberately slow walk. And he did the same thing where the boys gathered wood, and then he made sure his rifle was laid cross-saddle and he smiled as he nodded and trotted out of camp with the other men to his herding job.

The attention Franklin received from the young girls was not lost on Brady. Then it was the two of them—galloping through camp and kicking up dust wherever they went. It wasn't long before the horseback duo became more than some of the other boys could bear.

Franklin rode his reckless reputation to the point it crossed Carl Nelson, the blacksmith's son, a thick-chested boy with big knuckles and a short temper. Carl and his friends waited it out, and one evening they caught Franklin alone watering his horse at the river's edge.

Carl called Franklin out, and Franklin met him head on. Carl struck first. He dealt Franklin a powerful blow. Then he beat Franklin to the ground, laid him out, and left him where he fell.

When Brady rode up, Carl and his gang were gone and Franklin was leaning against his horse. His face was bloody, his lips swollen, and his right eye bruised and shut. Brady dismounted and approached Franklin.

"You okay?"

Franklin looked at him with his good eye.

"Do I look okay?" Franklin said, through puffy lips.

Brady looked at him, his expression serious and concerned.

"No."

"Well, I ain't."

"What happened—your horse throw you?"

Franklin squinted his good eye and paused before he answered.

"Carl Nelson jumped me."

"Who?" Brady asked.

"The blacksmith's son. You know, that big-ass kid that's always tight-jawed about we got horses and he don't."

"Oh yeah, him," Brady said. "I'm surprised that's all he done to you."

"Yeah, well," Franklin said. "It ain't over."

"What do you mean?"

"I mean it ain't over—I gotta fight him again."

"Why?"

"I didn't hurt him. Now he thinks he can do this anytime he pleases."

Franklin spat blood and wiped his nose on his sleeve.

"He got the jump on me. Besides, he done this in front of all his friends. If I don't stand up to it, I'll be fighting them all before it's over."

Brady looked up at Franklin. He couldn't decide if Franklin was the bravest or dumbest person he knew, but he felt good for Franklin knowing he was willing to take another beating just to prove a point.

Brady thought about that a long time.

Two weeks later, Franklin rode up on Carl Nelson and his friends away from camp. He swung down from his horse, let the reins drop, and walked into the center of them. The boys looked at him, surprised at his brazenness and curious about his motives.

Franklin stood before the blacksmith's son and smiled a half smile. "Hey," Franklin said.

"Hey," the blacksmith's son said back to him, looking down at him with a questioning expression on his face.

They stood there a brief instant before Franklin drew back a shaking fist with a flat rock rolled up in his fingers and drove the fist hard into the Carl's throat. The boy's eyes bulged and he gasped for breath. Franklin drew back again and fired two awful sounding blows to the boy's eyes. The boy staggered backwards and Franklin followed, delivering blow after blow until the boy's friends pulled him off. Franklin twisted and turned and cursed and fought and, in the short time it took him to break free, Carl Nelson regained his breath and attacked Franklin in a fury. He snatched Franklin around the midsection, wrestled him to the ground, and pounded his face bloody raw. The boy stood and Franklin came up with him. Franklin lunged at the boy and the boy drove his head into Franklin's face, breaking a tooth and lacerating Franklin's lips against his teeth. Franklin staggered and the boy rallied forward and laid his knuckles alongside Franklin's head until his ear bled. He hit him again and Franklin went down. The boy turned to leave and Franklin wobbled to his feet and tottered there.

"This ain't over," Franklin said though swollen and bleeding lips.

"You're crazy," the boy said over his shoulder.

Franklin tried to walk, but stumbled and fell. He sat in the dirt a long time. He finally rose on shaky legs and walked to the river to bathe his wounds and let the cold water run over his bloody knuckles.

A week later, Franklin made his way down the row of wagons at the noon stop looking for Carl. He found him and, when their eyes met, the blacksmith's son stood and his face went white and he watched Franklin boldly stride toward him. Carl's face drained. He took a step back. Franklin stopped directly in front of the boy and the boy stood his ground. Franklin opened his mouth to speak and he grinned a broken-toothed grin and stuck out his chin.

"I'm ready to pick it up anytime you are," Franklin said.

Carl shook his head. "I'm good with it like it is if you are."

He extended his hand and Franklin shook it. They never fought again.

After that the days all seemed to roll together. Each one was like the day before. Soon the pattern became a routine that never changed. At four each morning the night guard woke the wagonmaster, who in turn woke the camp. People emerged from tents and from under the wagons where they slept. They tended the stock and hitched the teams. Small cook fires lit up throughout the camp as the smell of breakfast mixed with the smell of woodsmoke. A baby cried. A dog barked. Harnesses rattled and men's voices carried through the darkness.

When the wagons rolled out, drivers argued and bickered. Garrett mediated meaningless quarrels and shouted directions at inexperienced drivers whose teams were fractious and disruptive. By seven, the caravan had formed into a moving tangle of disorder that eventually righted itself into a convoy.

The wagons inched along, the steel tires of the wheels cutting into the virgin earth with what would become the beginning of a Westward migration that changed America's destiny forever.

By midday the earth lay before them parched and dusty. Heat waves shimmered up from the horizon. Mothers tried in vain to keep wet rags on the faces of their children to ease the burnt skin and swollen cheeks.

Garrett scouted ahead. When he returned, he rode the line of wagons and spoke to each he passed. "Cool water and shade another mile ahead."

They watered up from an artesian well where they pulled the wagons up into a stand of cottonwoods and scrub willow bordering the banks of the Platte. The spring water they filled the barrels with was sweet and clear. They all drank what they could and replaced the muddy river water they had carried since they struck the Platte. They pressed on, and the weather, which in the beginning had been unstable and cold, was now unbearably hot. With the heat came short tempers and a growing swell of criticism of Garrett's leadership.

Osborne, who resented Garrett from the onset, grew more irrational and critical as he found others who were equally dissatisfied with the way Garrett commanded the company.

The previous night, Garrett had stopped the convoy early to camp without water and with no shelter from a dust storm that developed and drove the immigrants to their wagons with no fires and little sleep. By dawn the wind subsided. Garrett woke the camp early to travel in the cool pre-dawn while it was still dark.

The stock needed water and grass. Garrett knew they could not travel another day without it. His maps and charts were more misleading than helpful. This was his first trip as a wagonmaster. The restrictions facing an expedition of this size were far beyond anything he had experienced as a trapper. He now realized he had only his own resources to rely upon and he resisted the temptation to simply ride out and leave the whole mess behind.

Osborne complained to anyone who would listen and, after the dry camp and poor shelter, more listened than didn't. They whispered in the shadows and there were those among them who shared Osborne's misgivings.

Now, less than three miles from last night's dry camp the caravan arrived at a grassy site with good water. It was protected from the wind by a dense stand of trees and brush.

Instead of being thankful for the find, many were criticized Garrett for stopping short the night before. Osborne gloated. Had Garrett scouted three miles further, this would have been last night's camp.

Most agreed with Osborne. Garrett's credibility began to erode and by the end of the following week the attitude of the malcontents bordered on mutiny.

Garrett warned of hostile Indians and admonished the men for their careless manner and lack of readiness. Over the next week they were approached on three separate occasions by Indian hunting parties who came and traded fresh meat for cloth and buttons and trinkets of little value.

They came childlike and almost shy. They made no demands and turned their eyes to the ground when addressed. The immigrants regarded the Indians as ignorant and harmless. Nothing Garrett said dissuaded them from that opinion.

Talk of Garrett's weak leadership grew to the point of raising doubt among those who supported him. Garrett sensed the problem, but chose to deal with it in his own quiet way by not dealing with it at all.

Thomas Stilwell approached Bill McCall as McCall fed the small cook fire near his wagon.

"Hey, Bill," Stilwell said. "Got another cup there?"

McCall looked up and nodded. "Sure do," he said.

McCall tapped the tin cup against his trouser leg, righted it and poured hot coffee from the pot hung over the edge of the fire. He handed the cup to Stilwell and offered him a seat at the log laying like it had fallen there for that purpose.

"How you all making it, Tom?" McCall asked.

"Good as can be expected, I guess." His expression was somber and McCall could see he didn't come just for the coffee and company.

"You concerned about this thing with Garrett?" McCall asked.

Stilwell looked over his cup, a little surprised at McCall's directness.

"Matter of fact, I am," Stilwell said. "How 'bout you?"

"I'm real concerned," McCall said. "If Garrett don't do something soon, he's flat going to lose control of this outfit."

Stilwell took a slow draw on the hot coffee and nodded.

McCall shook his head. "I don't know about you, Tom, but good or bad, I don't see how we can make it without Garrett." Then he added, "Besides, I ain't sure all this is his fault anyway."

Stilwell stood up, tipped the last of the coffee down and looked over at McCall. "It ain't his fault. He's doing what he knows to do."

He paused, then splashed the last few drops from his cup into the fire. "What worries me," Stilwell said in an uncharacteristically soft voice, "is what happens when we do hit Indian Territory."

McCall nodded and started to comment as Garrett stepped into the light of the fire.

"Coffee?" McCall asked as he offered Garrett a cup.

Garrett nodded. "If you got extra."

Garrett took the cup and looked first at McCall, then at Stilwell. "I couldn't help but overhear you," he said and there was no malice or apology in his expression.

McCall began to speak but checked himself. Stilwell looked down at his boots then his eyes rose to meet Garrett's.

"It's not a secret we got a problem," Garrett said. "Look, I'll do what I can, but when it comes right down to it every man's got to decide for himself where he stands."

Stilwell nodded. McCall pondered a thought, and Garrett waited.

"Seems clear to me," McCall said, "that the big issue is the Indians."

"That and clearing the Sierras before the first snowfall," Garrett added.

Stilwell looked at Garrett. "How serious is it with the Indians?"

Garrett shook his head. "I don't know how to tell you how serious it is. But don't let what you saw the other day fool you. Them Gros Ventres weren't here just for the buttons and mirrors and pretty ribbons."

"What do you mean?" McCall asked.

"I mean, they were sizing up our outfit," Garrett said.

"What do you think they want?" Stilwell asked.

"Pretty much everything we got," said Garrett. He stared into the fire and the flames reflected in his eyes that appeared tired and troubled.

Then, without looking up he said, "I'm a trapper. I know the mountains, I know the weather and I know Indians—but I don't understand farmers. I can tell you what I know. I can get you across them mountains. But, I can't make no one do anything he chooses not to do."

There was a long silence. McCall weighed every word Garrett said. It was clear to McCall that Garrett knew his business. The Gros Ventres treated him with respect. On the trail he never lost his bearings. He was a loner, but he took his job seriously and he never avoided an issue. Garrett had good judgment and he made good decisions. But he never pretended to be what he wasn't. McCall knew when he signed on, just as did the others, that crossing the frontier was a gamble. There would be casualties—that was a guarantee. Everyone understood it. McCall wondered how many believed it.

What they didn't know was that Garrett was not the first choice for the job. With no previous experience, he was selected on the basis of his knowledge of the mountains when the man hired as the original wagonmaster declined the job. The company needed a wagonmaster, Garrett needed the money. Most critically, Garrett was the only applicant for the job.

Garrett was handed a few crudely drawn maps, the company roster and a handbook of vague rules of conduct that detailed things like the weather, the terrain, and a short section advising on how to negotiate with the Indians.

McCall drew his own conclusions about Garrett's capabilities, but most agreed he was a good guide. McCall and Stilwell reckoned it was all the years hunting and trapping alone in the wilderness that accounted for the lack of leadership skills he demonstrated.

But more concerning than Garrett's lack of leadership was the deep realization that most of the men in the company were not prepared, and they unanimously refused to believe the Indians were a threat at all. When the doubters became vocal and challenged Garrett's decisions and leadership, both McCall and Stilwell grew troubled over the divisiveness that weakened Garrett's control and influence.

Finally McCall spoke up. "You know, Jim, there aren't more than a dozen men in this company going to be ready for any kind of trouble if it starts."

"If that," Stilwell said, looking up at Garrett.

"I know," said Garrett pushing his hat back and staring into the fire.

"So, what do you think?" Stilwell asked.

"You mean about the Indians?" Garrett said looking over at him.

Stilwell nodded.

"Here's how I figure it," Garrett said. "Them Gros Ventres is a long ways from home. I expect they'll be back looking to run off some of our livestock—try to pick up a few horses—maybe catch a wagon or two straggling behind."

Garrett stopped talking and a long silence followed. He looked back up at McCall and Stilwell.

"They won't think twice about killing anyone," he said. "Best thing we can do is not give them an opening."

Garrett nudged a half-burned limb further into the fire with the toe of his boot. He pulled his hat down tight and stood up. He tipped his hat to McCall and Stilwell.

"Appreciate the coffee and the talk," he said, as he turned and strode off to the center of the camp.

He stood near the big fire. The flames caused shadows to flicker across his face as he stood there. His silence commanded the attention of those near him and soon all eyes were upon him and he began to speak in a voice soft but firm and cold.

"I got a few things I need to tell you all. I signed on to get you all across the mountains alive. I'm not sure I can do that," he said.

Not a soul moved. Not an eye left his. "If we do everything right, some of you are going to die. That's a fact. What I can't do, is allow you to keep going the way some of you are. Sickness and misfortune are beyond my control—being prepared for Indians ain't."

Garrett surveyed the gathering and they grew uncomfortable. He let the words sink in. Then he addressed the unarmed man nearest him.

"Where's your rifle?" Garrett asked.

The man looked down. "In my wagon."

"Where abouts in the wagon?" Garrett asked.

"Somewhere in the back."

"Is it loaded?"

"No sir, it ain't," the man answered.

Garrett picked another man, asked him the same question and got the same answer. He asked three more and of those only one was armed and ready.

"The Gros Ventres will be back. When they do come back, it won't be for ribbons and beads. They'll want horses and cattle and maybe a white woman or two."

At first no one responded. They all stared up at Garrett. Then they started buzzing among themselves.

Garrett raised his hand and the talking stopped.

"Starting tonight we'll double the guard. Every rifle will be loaded and where you can get to it fast. And I don't mean just for tonight," Garrett said.

"How do we know there's anything to worry about?" Osborne asked from the shadows of the camp.

Two more voices seconded Osborne's question. Then another and another echoed the first. Garrett raised his hand again—again the men fell silent.

"Because we're interlopers here. It's not our land and they don't want us here. These Indians have been here since the beginning of time. They fought for this land and the right to live on it. They ain't going to stop fighting for it just because you have some dream of taking just a little here and a little there. It's an Indian's nature to protect his land from interlopers. We have things he doesn't have. Out here they take what they want. But mostly, Mr. Osborne, they don't want us here. We have every reason to be worried."

NINE

With no sign of Indians and no other mishaps, Garrett lost control over the company of immigrants one day at a time. Nothing he said or did could have changed that. Those who opposed him resented his threats and discounted his warnings. Those who sided with Osborne did so openly, and the camp began to split. Garrett couldn't see he was on a collision course but, by his own nature, he knew he couldn't adjust his thinking to that of the inexperienced dissenters he commanded. He also knew he lacked the ability to force them to his way of thinking.

The diseased organization consequently began to consume itself. They fell further and further behind schedule until Garrett's plan became no plan at all. He cursed the maps provided to him, not so much for their poor rendering which made them crude in scope and scale, but for their absence of reliable detail. There was no water where water was promised, distances were neither accurate in terms of mileage or travel time. Landmarks appeared where none shown on the charts and those that were shown on the charts were inaccurately placed.

Finally, the wagonmaster put away his navigational aids and trusted his instincts. He considered the odds of engaging the Sierra's late in the season. He worried about the weather. A September crossing was a gamble, but a gamble with fair odds. He would risk that. An October crossing was a fool's wager he sensed he may be forced to take.

Early snows came regularly in the Sierra and, when they did come, they came with frightening speed. No contingency plan could offset a late start and an early snow. Garrett felt himself cornered by the impossibility of his circumstances.

Each night he closed his eyes and vowed never again to captain a foolish mission, but each day he arose determined to get this company of ill prepared easterners delivered as promised, whatever it took to do so.

He gave up explaining nature's unalterable timetable and simply pushed the immigrants as hard as he dared, pursuing the trail like a man possessed. They stopped twice a day. At midday they rested the stock. At night they collapsed into their bedding. All but a few of the settlers degenerated into a contingent of detached beings sleeping in their clothes and eating cold meals. The women were the last to give up but, when they did, they lost the energy to keep their children clean or to maintain any family life beyond that which was required to manage through each day.

Then, sickness beset them. They buried first one, then another. Some fell to cholera, others to consumption, and some to misfortune until burial ceremonies became perfunctory exercises—funerals devoid of all but the briefest religious observance over shallow graves presided over by hard faces and expressionless eyes gone beyond the capacity for tears.

Garrett ran out of things to say to those who ceased trying, so he said nothing at all. He could scarcely contain his anger as he watched the men in the families put away their weapons and resign themselves to whatever consequences befell them. His stomach twisted at the thought of his own fate tied to theirs.

On a dry morning three hours past dawn, the temperature rose to stifling levels. Garrett and his scouts preceded the dust-embroiled wagons, riding into the sun, tentatively aware of two horsemen approaching. The shapes of the horsemen shimmered up with the heat, barely discernible from the scorching landscape. Garrett stood in the stirrups. Then, he swung down from the saddle, dropped to one knee, and then skylighted the riders as they topped the next rise in the trail before they disappeared in the swales only to re-appear, faceless silhouettes.

Garrett declared them peaceful and stepped back up into the saddle. He kept his eyes fixed on the riders and signaled a scout rider back to alert the wagons, and then he waited. Peaceful or not, Garrett quietly slid his rifle from its beaded scabbard and ratcheted the hammer back two clicks. He laid the long gun across the saddle in front of him and traced the curve of the trigger guard with his fingertip. His eyes never left the approaching horsemen.

He nudged his pony to the top of a brushy knoll and stood the horse among the cover of stunted scrub willows and buck brush and gazed across the void whereupon the two horsemen advanced. He knew they saw him and he knew they could see the dust cloud raised by the wagons. But still they closed the gap and their pace was neither urgent nor reticent, and by nothing more than their sunlit forms he reckoned them to be a white man and an Indian. A trapper and a squaw, he concluded.

Garrett relaxed some. When the riders were close enough he could discern the features of their faces, the man held up a hand and smiled a toothy smile.

"Hey," the trapper said, his voice resonating deep from within his big chest.

"Hey, yourself," Garrett said, regarding the trapper with a sideways look.

"Mathias Melzer?" Garrett asked.

"Yes, sir," the trapper said. He squinted and looked at Garrett, then he grinned and nodded.

"Well, bless my heathen ass—Jimmy Garrett, how are ye, son? I thought sure they'd of buried you by now."

Garrett shook his head and the two rode forward and shook hands.

"No, not yet," Garrett said.

"I see that," the trapper said laughing. "What business do ye have with them folks?" Melzer asked, pointing with his thumb at the cloud of dust inching up on them from the east. Garrett rubbed his eyes as though the act itself was an expression of some implied absolution.

"Trapping wasn't working out. I figured I'd try my hand at this," Garrett said. "Winter of '36 and I just up and quit the mountains."

Melzer nodded. He understood.

"What about you?" Garrett asked.

"Oh, I still trap some," Melzer said. "You know, enough to get by is all. Mountains is in my blood. I don't know nothing else."

Garrett said nothing for there was nothing to say, but in his eyes resided a distant reflection of an ancient calling both men had answered a thousand years before they were born. And by their silence they acknowledged an unwritten pact of brotherhood, a fraternal covenant of misfits rendered in a deviant language known only to those who found solace in the absence of people.

Melzer let the silence run over past the point of social comfort. "Pardon my lack of manners," he said. "Jimmy, this here's my wife, Kit-ah-lay."

Garrett touched his hat and said good morning. She smiled but said nothing.

"She's a good woman, Jimmy." Then he laughed. "She don't say much, but she speaks pretty good English when she's mad," he said.

Garrett recognized her Nez Perce outfit. He spoke to her in her native tongue. He said it was nice to meet her, and she replied back that it was nice to meet him too. She was not shy but had the reserve common to her people in the company of strangers.

The three dismounted and took up a place in the shade of a thin row of cottonwoods clustered at the runoff trickle of an artesian spring that surfaced from a rocky ledge above them. It wet the ground where grass grew thick, and trees grew as though to have come there for the water as the remainder of the landscape around them lay barren and parched.

Garrett had spent two winters on the Bitterroot with the Nez Perce, he told Kit-ah-lay. He asked if she knew his friend, Spa-wa-khan, a Nez Perce shaman. Her eyes sparkled and she covered her smile with her hand. Yes, she knew him. He was her uncle she said. She spoke first in Nez Perce, excited and animated and mixing in English words among the lilting and guttural sounds of her own language.

When her speaking slowed and calmed, she spoke of her tribe, and her family, and of her homeland. It pleased her that Garrett knew of the places she knew and knew of the people she knew. She stood and talked with her hands. She asked many questions and told stories as though they had been a long time waiting to be told.

Garrett asked them to stay the night. Melzer hesitated then deferred the decision to Kit-ah-lay who said yes they would stay. Melzer laughed and said he guessed they would be staying.

The trapper and his Indian bride were honored that night as the entirety of the camp turned out to see them. Whether they were a good omen or an oddity, or both, everyone wanted to see a trapper and a real Indian up close.

The men gathered wood and built a large fire in the center of camp. They ate together and after they ate they talked. Then two men with fiddles tuned up and were joined by a five-string banjo player and a man with a Jew's harp.

One man sang. His voice, a sweet tenor, hauntingly out of place in this frontier outpost, was clear and perfect. When he sang no one sang with him, so enraptured were they. The music transported their thoughts out of the wilderness and back to a civilization many would gladly have returned to if that choice had still existed.

For that brief interlude there was no dust, no doubt, no regret and no fear. It was a magical reprieve like a cool fountain from which they all drank freely. A full moon rose amidst a sky thick with stars. The night air grew cool. The heat of the fire made the children yawn. Some slept in their mother's lap. The fire burned down. One by one, the women and children retired to their beds. The night guards excused themselves and retired as well.

More than a dozen men remained. They stoked the fire and a whiskey jug of uncertain origin circulated among them. There was small talk and there was man talk. There was talk of the past and some talk of the future, but there was no talk of substance as far as Melzer was concerned. He stood and refilled his cup. Facing Garrett, he corked the jug and put one foot up on the log he used for a seat. He made no bid for the floor, but the talking stopped and Garrett and the others regarded him as though he had.

"We seen sign of thirty, maybe forty Gros Ventre on the trail the two weeks past," Melzer said. "Heading your way. They split up and sent ten or twelve of them your direction. You should have met up with them a while back."

"We did," Garrett said. "Looked like a hunting party near as we could tell. We traded them some and they left."

Melzer took a pull on his whiskey cup and nodded. "Figure they was just sizing you up?"

Garrett nodded back. "I figure they was."

Melzer took a seat nearer the fire. "They'll be back," he said.

Garrett nodded.

An uneasy silence ensued and the men watched Melzer. It was not lost on Melzer that he had the full attention of the tiny congregation gathered about him. He spoke in a low, almost reverent voice.

"Ever seen a man scalped?" he asked slowly of no one in particular.

He looked around at the men over the rim of his cup and took another pull. No one responded.

"It ain't a sight you'd soon forget."

He wiped the whiskey from his moustache with the back of his buckskin sleeve and continued.

"One time, me and a couple a them young heathens from the Northern Cheyenne was packing a muley deer back from a hunt. We broke a clearing and run up on a Crow boy all by hisself with his plaited hair greased and his face painted up. Him being no more than sixteen or seventeen and kneeling down and drinking from the river alongside a stole Cheyenne pony. He seen us and he run. They caught him, 'course. Took him down. Jerked his head back and cut his scalp right off a his head. I never heard so much screaming. Blood running in his eyes—his head bone showing through. Him, red with blood and no hair, stood up pounding his chest and cussing them Cheyenne."

Melzer paused and stared into the fire. He looked about and his voice dropped to a whisper.

"They took him down. Spread him out like this. Made him watch. Then they cut that poor bugger's pecker off. He begged for his life like nothing I ever seen."

Melzer stood and traced an imaginary line with his knife from rib to rib across his stomach.

"Then they cut him like this," he said. "Not too deep. His damn innards dropped out. It was just plain awful. He didn't beg for his life no more. This time he begged to be killed."

Melzer took another pull on the whiskey cup and cleared his throat.

"Did they?" someone asked.

"Did they what?"

"Kill him?"

Melzer shook his head. "No. They left him. Down on his knees in the dirt. His blood running out. His insides falling out of his hands. We rode off and left him like that."

He tipped the cup again and sat down. No one spoke and he continued.

"Gros Ventres will do you the same way they get a chance," he said, nudging a stick back into the fire with the toe of his moccasin.

"It don't seem right I know, but it makes good sense to a Indian," he added.

No one spoke and no one wanted to be the first to move. Garrett eyed the men, each of whom seemed to be trying to sort out what Melzer had said as though he might find exemption for himself.

McCall and Stilwell carried on a brief, private conversation. They waited and looked to Garrett but he also waited. McCall then stood and contemplated his words before he spoke. All heads turned toward him and their shadows wobbled in the light of the flame.

"I'll say it straight out," he began. "I don't doubt what there's more that Mr. Melzer hasn't told us. And I don't doubt for a minute that we'd be easy pickings for an Indian war party. Excepting for Mr. Garrett here, and Travis Kincaid, who ain't even here, I don't think there's another man among us who's fought Indians before or much understands their ways."

McCall gestured toward Garrett. Heads bobbed in agreement. "I think it's time we let Mr. Garrett here do his job."

Melzer nodded, but he had his say and that was that. McCall looked about, searching the shadowed faces for some sign, some righting of reason, but there was none. Not a whisper. They looked pitifully like the farmers and merchants and civilized citizens they were, ill prepared to defend their lives and feeling terribly threatened by the images of scalped and brutalized human bodies.

The circle of men drew in tighter. Some threw out what liquor remained in their cups, others took in deep breaths, but none spoke and all eyes fixed on Garrett.

Despite his lack of leadership skills, Garrett appeared confident and convincing as he stood straight and addressed his grave and uncertain congregation.

"Well, I didn't plan it this way, but we are where we are and there ain't two ways about that." Garrett's eyes sought out those he could see directly and a few heads nodded in agreement. He let an uncomfortable silence make his point, then he continued.

"Look, "he said. "You can choose not to follow my orders—that's up to you. But this ain't no place to argue about who does what. I'll say what and I'll say when. If that ain't good enough for you, I'll ask you to leave camp and you're on your own. I'll do my best to get the rest of you where you're going alive. That's my part of the bargain."

Garrett motioned the men in closer and snapped out orders to those he picked out of the group as he outlined his plan. Then he tossed the stick he used for a pointer into the fire and sparks crackled and the fire flared and flaming cinders rose up into the black sky.

"The easiest part of this trip is pretty much over," he said. "Here on out you got to assume everything wants you dead."

TEN

Garrett sat alone by the fire with Melzer and Kit-ah-lay. He pushed another log into the coals and the three of them talked into the night. They spoke of the mountains and of the rivers where the beaver and the muskrat and the mink and otter filled their traps—places they had been, places still not on any white man's map.

Garrett and Melzer respected the Indian for his ability to live at peace with nature. And they admired the way nature provided for the Indian in ways that would leave a white man lost and wanting. Melzer could not understand and Garrett could not explain how he found it in himself to guide a caravan of would-be landowners into the midst of a people who could themselves not conceive of the principle of land ownership. In their hearts, Garrett and Melzer were more Indian than white man and, while they believed philosophically in the Indian way of life, they were part of a culture that found them belonging to neither the Indian nor the white man. They were caught in the opposing evolution of the two lifestyles.

Neither man realized it, but both were trying desperately to adapt, each in his own way. Neither with any hope of success.

"You know," Garrett said. "My last winter on the Musselshell with the Piegans was the worst year I ever had."

His eyes seemed to age as he spoke. "I remember the last trap I ever set just like it was yesterday. Me and three of them Piegans was working a trap line and we seen this old Pend d'Oreille warrior dressed in his best war shirt. His hair was greased up and he was sitting a warpainted pony by himself on a rocky ridge high above the river. He was calling on the spirits. It made my hide crawl to hear him chant and sing like that."

Melzer listened quietly and sipped from his whiskey cup. Garrett shook his head slowly.

"I rode on up to him thinking it would be all right," Garrett said. "He looked at me like he couldn't see me. If I didn't see him move I'd swear he was dead. I spoke to him. He just kept on with his chant like I wasn't there."

Garrett stared off into the night, then back at the fire. "It was like he knew the end was coming. That was the worst winter I ever had and I ain't never been back."

Kit-ah-lay listened to Garrett's story, but she neither spoke nor gave any indication she understood any of it. This dark-eyed daughter of the earth, whose destiny was forged in ancient teachings whispered down from one generation to the next for more than a thousand years, was of a culture that stood teetered on the brink of extinction. And though it was never spoken, in her heart she understood and ventured forth into the white man's world alone and searching.

"Jimmy," said Melzer in an uncharacteristically subdued voice. "Sometimes I get to thinking and I just don't know where this world's goin'."

They stared at the fire a long time. An owl glided quietly through the trees, a coyote yipped at the moon and, somewhere a long way off, a Gros Ventre warrior prepared himself for battle.

At daybreak, the trapper and his dusky bride stopped at the crest of the trail and turned back long enough to see the last of the wagons lurching and creaking along deeper into Indian Territory.

Over the weeks after the visit from Melzer, Osborne quietly refocused his attention on one or two remaining dissenters once it was clear most of the settlers had reinvested themselves in Garrett's leadership.

Mr. Dixon, an unusual man not unlike Osborne himself, gravitated to Osborne and together they shared embittered criticisms and fed off each other's negative sensibilities, departing further and further into the darkness of irrationality.

"Garrett put me on night guard tonight," Dixon complained to Osborne as they unhitched their teams at the end of a long day. "I got two spare horses not worth ten dollars in that herd. They're not worth getting killed over and I, for one, don't plan on losing sleep over someone else's livestock."

"I understand," said Osborne. "It's your right to do as you see fit. If Garrett had his way we'd all be bowing down to him. He might think he is almighty important, but you damn sure don't owe him a thing."

At midnight, Dixon failed to report for his shift. Garrett waited twenty minutes. When Dixon did not arrive, Garrett headed back to Dixon's wagon. Garrett found Dixon asleep in his bedroll beneath the rear axle of the wagon. He nudged the end of Dixon's bedroll with the toe of his boot.

"Wake up," he said.

Dixon did not reply. Garrett reached down and grabbed the end of the bedroll and dragged Dixon and his bed out from under the wagon.

"Get up."

Dixon came to life in a fury and he threw off his bed covers and jumped to his feet. He drew his belt knife and charged Garrett.

Garrett stood firm. Dixon stopped face-to-face with the unflinching wagonmaster and shouted, "You no good son-of-a-bitch. Get away from my wagon."

The knife trembled in Dixon's hand. Garrett didn't budge. The savage look in Garrett's eyes caused Dixon a brief moment of self-doubt. Before Dixon could slash out, Garrett slammed the barrel of his pistol hard against the side of Dixon's face, causing his jaw to shift and his teeth to grind.

"Don't make me take your head off," Garrett whispered. "I'll be back in five minutes and you best be mounted up and on your way out to relieve your man."

Dixon trembled with fear and anger. His eyes went wild and he pursed his lips and set his jaw. He threw down the knife and left it where it lay and glared at Garrett. His expression reeked of frustration and confusion. He knew if he spoke, his words would be vile and inside he wept.

Garrett gave him the room he needed to make the right choice and, as he walked back into the night, Garrett turned and looked Dixon in the eye with neither hate nor malice.

"You got the one chance to do this right," he said.

In the next wagon, Osborne lay in his blankets and listened, quietly pleased with himself. Others overheard the incident and many thought Garrett harsh and unreasonable, but no one challenged him and none comforted Dixon.

Dixon's wife watched from inside the wagon, horrified and unwilling to interfere. Dixon saddled up in silence, never acknowledging his wife and her not asking to be recognized by him. Dixon reported as directed and rode his post alone and brooding.

Before first call the next morning a wailing cry came from the Dixon wagon. Garrett was the first to get there. He found Mrs. Dixon staring out at her husband mounted on his horse where it stood tied to the rear of the wagon. Dixon's head hung over his bloody shirt and his legs were bound to the saddle with rawhide strings. His throat gaped and his eyes lay fixed and hollow in their cold sockets.

Others came running, screaming hysterically and cursing and grumbling and speculating. Their rage spewed forth vile and contemptible. They blamed the Gros Ventres. All the evidence was there—the rawhide lacing that lashed Dixon to his saddle and his missing knife and pistol belt. They insisted Garrett dispatch a search party, but Garrett waved them off. He studied Dixon's outfit before McCall and Preacher Baldwin covered the body and carried it off.

"No Indian did this," Garrett said. "I can't tell you for sure what happened, but I can tell you this wasn't the work of the Gros Ventres."

"How can you be so sure?" A voice asked from the crowd of faces pressed around Dixon's wagon. Garrett looked to be sure Mrs. Dixon had been taken to another wagon.

"He still had his scalp," Garrett said. "This isn't the way an Indian works," he added.

"Well, then who did do it?" the voice asked.

"I don't know, but it wasn't them," Garrett said.

They buried Dixon that morning. The preacher spoke over him amidst an undercurrent of dissension that made it clear to Garrett he hadn't been convincing. He offered no further explanation and instead put the camp on full alert and doubled the guard.

For all the complaining and disagreement on the subject, the McCall's and Stilwell's and the majority of the others sided with Garrett. Osborne and those he influenced grew increasingly outspoken. The camp, divided and distracted, drove on into the wilderness more vulnerable than ever.

ELEVEN

Three days after they buried Dixon, just as the sun inched up over the ridgeline, Brady McCall exploded into camp at a full gallop, his coat blowing and his eyes streaked with tears, kicking and whipping the buckskin. The horse's nostrils flared, his ears lay pinned to its head and its hooves pounded the dry dirt up into clouds that flew about its legs.

"Indians," Brady screamed. "Hurry! They're killing everyone. Come on, you gotta help."

Brady charged recklessly into the throng of men and women and spotted his father among them. Bill McCall grabbed the reins and stopped the buckskin as it blew and pranced and tossed its head.

"Brady, are you all right?" he asked, his voice shaking.

"I'm okay pa—but I don't know what happened to Franklin. We gotta go back and help him. Please hurry," Brady pleaded.

"Get to the wagon now and look after your ma and the kids," McCall ordered. "Mount up," he shouted to those around him.

Two dozen armed riders fell in behind McCall, whooping and yelling as they galloped wildly out of formation along the river, up through the brush, and into the breach of battle with gunshots echoing all about them and no sense of who the enemy was or where they were. When they broke out of the trees and onto the grazing site it was a confusion of horses and men out of control.

When the men from camp rode onto the grazing grounds, they scattered what livestock remained. They rode up on four night guards defending positions in a deep ravine above the river and located three others firing from positions in the rocks at the mouth of a small clearing. Five Indians and a riderless Indian pony escaped into the cover of the woods north of the trail and disappeared into a coulee where the brush grew thick.

Cattle, mules, and horses stood scattered for three or four miles throughout the trees and it was impossible to make any sense of the confusion. What Indians they could see were out of range and had too great a lead for any of Garrett's riders to overtake them.

McCall located Stilwell. He could see by the expression on his face that he had not yet found Franklin. They spread out and searched frantically for Franklin. Stilwell turned his horse and rode into a thicket of trees. No sign of Franklin. He emerged from the brush onto the shoulder of a clearing gently sloping away to a granite escarpment at the distant edge of which lie a crumpled body clad in dark trousers and pull-on boots.

Stilwell paused. The fletching's of two arrows waved from the man's back. Stilwell spurred his horse and dismounted on the fly at the foot of the corpse. He prayed to himself. *Please don't let this be Franklin.*

He gently lifted the man's head. "Barnett," he said aloud.

Stilwell pressed his fingers to Barnett's jugular, then laid the colorless face back onto the cool grass. He remounted and followed the hoofprints of cattle and horses across the clearing and into the brush.

While Stilwell searched the low meadow, McCall circled high up into the rocks. He spotted Franklin's horse picketed in the thick brush, but he saw no sign of the boy.

"Hey, Mr. McCall, up here," Franklin shouted from his granite fortress.

"Franklin, are you all right?" McCall asked, as he dismounted.

"Yes sir, I'm fine. But I think they done got Mr. Barnett. I seen them run him yonder down into them trees."

Franklin reloaded as he talked.

"They almost got B.C.," he said.

"What happened?"

"Me and him was riding together over there. Mr. Barnett was over there by them trees. Some of the horses started acting funny, but not ours. We figured it was Indians so we started for these rocks."

He reached into his pocket and continued talking fast.

"We told Mr. Barnett we thought there was Indians but he didn't believe us. Then a arrow got him and he rode off with it stuck in his back. I told B.C. to head for help and he lit out. I was up here. Then I saw a Indian going after B.C. I yelled, but he didn't hear. So I shot him—the Indian I mean."

McCall looked at Franklin. He wasn't sure how much of all that to believe, but he put his arm around Franklin's shoulder.

"I'm just glad you're all right. Let's go find your pa. He's mighty worried about you."

They mounted their horses and rode together down into the meadow that was a battleground already buzzing with flies. Dead cattle lay about in disarray, among them a saddle horse with his lifeless legs sprawled out before him. A mule stood gazing glassy-eyed with an arrow wobbling halfway through the crest of his thinly-maned neck.

McCall and Franklin leveled out on the trail and turned toward the east. In the tall grass at the edge of the path lay a copper-skinned body with plaited hair adorned with otter fur and eagle feathers, his finely beaded buckskin shirt violated by a red hole in the back the diameter of a man's thumb.

"That's him. That's the one that was going after B.C." Franklin said, his voice apprehensive and uncertain. "Is he dead?"

McCall dismounted and knelt beside the body, his back to Franklin.

"Yes he is, son."

Franklin dismounted, but wouldn't look at the body.

"I didn't have no choice, Mr. McCall. He was after B.C."

"You did the right thing, Franklin. That took some courage."

McCall stood and led Franklin to the edge of the brush. He looked back up to the spot in the granite outcropping from which Franklin fired the fatal shot.

"That was close to a hundred yard shot," he said. "That took a steady hand and a sharp eye."

"Yes sir," said Franklin.

Franklin was expecting a speech or at least a few words of fatherly advice, but none came. Franklin began to feel more like a man than a boy and the feeling suited him. He chanced a closer look at the warrior on the ground and nothing he could think of made him feel good about that.

"Franklin!" Mr. Stilwell yelled, as he rode up. "Franklin are you okay?"

He swung down before his horse, stopped, and then grabbed Franklin and held him tight in his arms. Franklin hugged him back.

"I'm okay, pa."

"You had me worried."

"I'm fine."

Garrett rode up, followed by half a dozen others. They milled around trying to assess the damage and sort out the details of what happened.

"Who shot this one?" Garrett asked, as he walked over to the warrior's body.

"Franklin T. Stilwell here," McCall said, nodding toward the boy.

Thomas Stilwell looked amazed. "Franklin, you shot him?"

Franklin nodded.

"He got a clean shot from up in them rocks," said McCall, pointing to the spot, a hundred yards from where they stood. "He was after Brady and Franklin stopped him."

Garrett shaded his eyes with his hand, looked back up the hill and then to Franklin. "That was a hell of a shot."

Garrett stepped past Franklin and bent down on one knee next to the warrior's body. He loosened the warrior's knife and slipped it free. He stood and pulled the wood-handled blade from its beaded sheath, and then slid it back in as the men watched in silence.

He offered the knife to Franklin. "This is yours. A Gros Ventre reminder for you."

Franklin hesitated. Then he reached for the knife, almost afraid to touch it. He held the knife and looked at the bloody body. It was real now and he wanted to cry. He broke the sixth commandment, killed a man, and here they were congratulating him, glorifying him.

Franklin felt ashamed. He tried to swallow, but couldn't. He looked at his father for reassurance, but his father had no encouragement for him. Franklin tucked the knife in his shirt and swung back up into the saddle without using the stirrups. He touched the horse with his heels and started back to camp alone.

Half a mile from camp Thomas Stilwell caught up with his son. He looked straight ahead when he spoke.

"Look, son. You should never feel good about killing a man. There ain't nothing good about it, but what you did was the right thing to do." They rode on in silence.

TWELVE

Brady met Franklin and Mr. Stilwell as they rode into camp. He waved and rode up next to Franklin. He sensed Franklin's somber mood.

"Hey," he said.

"Hey," Franklin said back.

"You okay?"

"I guess."

Brady looked over at Franklin. Franklin did not look back.

"I kilt one of 'em," Franklin said.

"You did not."

Franklin stared straight ahead.

"You didn't kill no Indian."

Franklin handed Brady the knife. Brady was surprised at the heft of it.

"That was his," Franklin said.

"Is that true, Mr. Stilwell, did Franklin really shoot one?"

"Yes he did, Brady."

"Was it the one that was coming after me?"

"Yep," Franklin said.

"Franklin, I seen him. I thought I was a goner for sure. I turned to look at how close he was and I seen him fall off a his horse."

"I seen he was going after you when you lit out, so I drew a bead on him," Franklin said. "When I could see past the smoke he was down and his horse was a running loose by hisself."

"Well take a look at this," said Brady, pointing down to the rear of his saddle.

Franklin looked at the painted arrow buried deeply between the two layers of saddle skirting leather behind Brady's left leg.

"That's how close he came to getting me," said Brady, wide-eyed and indignant.

"That sombitch," Franklin said. He caught himself and looked over at his father.

"Sorry," he said.

"They would have kilt us all," Franklin said, looking up at his father.

Mr. Stilwell touched his son's shoulder, "I know, son," he said. "No question about it."

Franklin began to feel a little less guilty and a little more vindicated.

"Pa, what I done, I mean shooting that Indian and all—was I wrong for doing that?"

"No, you weren't wrong. It's just, we brought you up to believe in the Bible and God's word, and nowhere does it say killing is a good thing. But, what you done—saving the life of your friend and protecting what's yours—that's a different story. What you done today was not an easy thing to do, but you done the right thing."

"Yeah," said Brady, confirming Stilwell's approval, "I'd be right there with Mr. Barnett if it wasn't for you."

Franklin smiled. He began to feel a little prideful.

"Well, I did get a nice knife out of the deal," he said.

"Are you going to wear it?" Brady asked.

"Yeah, I'm gonna wear it. Why wouldn't I?"

"Well, what if they come back and see you with it?"

Franklin gave that one some thought.

"I don't mean I'll wear it all the time. I'll just wear it when I want to."

Brady handed the knife back to Franklin. Franklin ran his fingers over the fancy beadwork.

"Look at them beads," he said. Then he leaned over closer to Brady and whispered. "This knife probly scalped many a white man."

Brady felt a chill run down his back. His face drained of color. The knife, so big and heavy, now carried with it a magical quality, like it had a power of its own that both boys recognized. Like some forbidden treasure that Franklin possessed that made him special because of it.

Franklin whipped the knife from its scabbard and slashed the air in a reckless manner, then drew the flat of the blade across his pant leg and tested the edge with his thumb.

"No Gros Ventre's getting this back without a fight," he said with growing self-confidence.

They rode the rest of the way in silence and it was uncertain which of the two boys held Franklin's heroics in higher regard.

THIRTEEN

The overhead sun burned high in the sky by the time Preacher Baldwin had said his piece over Barnett. When the wagons rolled out, they left behind a freshly turned mound of earth that would be gone by the time they made camp that night. For Dixon and Barnett the journey was over, but for their families the ordeal had just begun.

What Garrett failed to achieve in unifying the immigrants, the Indians accomplished with amazing efficiency. The men looked to Garrett for leadership and found him to be direct and unwavering. Even Osborne became less antagonistic and limited his criticisms of Garrett to private conversation unlikely to draw Garrett's attention.

Each day broke hot and dry and the wagons pushed steadily onward as Garrett worked under pressure to make up lost time. He called stops only to water the stock and force-marched through the midday breaks. If there was a common sense of urgency it was motivated more by the settlers' desire to leave behind the battleground than it was to make up for any time lost.

Despite the dust and heat, the wagons traveled in close formation, banded together like buffalo falsely secure by their numbers and the proximity of one to the other. The dust that rose about them obliterated the sun and obscured their visibility and, though they saw no further sign of Indians, they chose the tightly clotted formation instinctively and would not deviate from it. Behind the first rank of wagons that made up the forward contingent, the secondary ranks were manned by teamsters covered with tarps and rag-covered faces and hats lowered against the dust amidst a cloud that hovered over them and extended for miles and hung in the air to the east long after they had passed over the land to which it eventually returned.

Drivers lurched hacking in their seats, coughing mute coughs while their children huddled blanketed in the heat with dry tears on their cheeks and their sweaty little faces red and parched. Mothers rationed water and passed wet rags up to their husbands and attempted to keep their babies cool and dampened their dry lips with spit-moistened fingertips, none of which offered any lasting relief.

At noon the McCall wagon rotated to the front rank. Bill McCall mounted his saddle horse and scouted forward with Garrett while Elizabeth took up the double-reins and clucked the mules forward into the clear sunlight. The breeze that passed through the wagon was hot, but clear and breathable. Elizabeth felt privileged and grateful to be out of the dust.

McCall and Garrett rode five or six miles ahead of the wagons and found no sign of Indians. They relaxed some, but Garrett's eyes never stopped moving. He noticed everything.

"You know, Bill," Garrett said. "Them Gros Ventres was mainly only after horses. If they was after scalps, ain't none of us would be here."

He stopped, dismounted and examined a slightly turned track Bill missed.

"Coyote," he said.

He stepped back up into the saddle and touched his horse forward.

"I don't know if them Gros Ventres will be back or not," he added.

"If you had to say, what would you say?" McCall asked, not meaning the question to be taken lightly.

"I wouldn't say—but I'd be ready just the same," Garrett said.

McCall nodded and they rode for the better part of an hour before they spoke again.

"When do you expect we'll reach Fort Laramie, Captain?"

"Two weeks, give or take," Garrett replied.

A small spring bubbled up at the base of a stand of cottonwoods, a welcome alternative to the muddy river water in their drinking barrels. They pulled up and watered the horses, filled their canteens, and drank their fill. McCall was quiet. He pulled his hat off and ran his thick hair back with his hand, then pinched his hat back on.

"How much stock you put in Mr. Melzer's talk of Comanche up this way?"

"Quite a lot."

"How so?"

"Well, for one thing, I heard them Texas Rangers is running the Comanche pretty hard. And maybe it's justified and maybe it ain't—all the same they're stirring up a hornet's nest and it don't make it any easier on folks up this way."

"This is a long way north for them, ain't it?"

Garrett thought a moment. "Well, I don't know a lot about 'em first-hand, but I do know this is a long way out of their territory. There's always a chance they could get this far. Not likely, but a chance. I reckon we'll know more when we get to Laramie."

It was sunset when Garrett and McCall turned back toward the wagons, and it was full dark when they got them circled for the night. A breeze picked up and cleared the dust that followed the wagons into camp. They watered the dray animals and loose stock and re-filled water barrels by the light of the moon.

The river water was cool and some stood belt-deep in it for a long time while the gently flowing river slowly soaked away the heat and the dust. Brady and Franklin rode their horses up to their saddles into the river to let them cool and drink. Both boys floated and splashed in the water while their horses took the cool water as a reprieve from the flies and the heat.

Despite the earlier attack and the concerns of their mothers, Brady and Franklin left their names on the night guard roster and, when they pulled their blankets around themselves shortly after supper, both boys fell into an exhausted sleep.

At midnight the air was cold and Franklin kneeled beside Brady, careful not to wake the rest of the family lying nearby.

"Hey, B.C., come on, it's time to go," Franklin whispered.

Brady sat up and shivered and rubbed his eyes.

"Hand me my hat," Brady said to Franklin, as he pulled on first one boot then the other.

"It's cold," he said, reaching into his bedroll for his jacket.

"It ain't bad once you been up."

"How come you're wearing that knife?" Brady asked nodding toward it.

"Ain't you scared some Gros Ventre will see it?"

"I thought about it."

"And?"

"If we do see any Indians, it probably won't be good, so it probably doesn't matter none anyway."

Brady pulled on his jacket and admired Franklin's trophy knife as he slipped his own old skinning knife on his belt. In the low light from the campfire Franklin looked like one of the men standing there. He was almost as tall as his father and his shadowed silhouette was muscular and broad in the shoulders.

Twice Brady caught Franklin shaving with his father's razor, practicing, and laughing in a voice that had grown deeper over the winter. Brady liked the way the Gros Ventre knife hung recklessly at Franklin's side and he liked the way the fringe and the beadwork attracted attention to it. His own knife, by comparison, seemed insignificant, but he wore it like Franklin wore his and, in some ways, it made him feel more prideful for having it.

As he buckled his belt and pulled on his hat, Brady felt like a little boy next to Franklin, who stood six inches taller and out-weighed him by forty pounds. Five years difference in their ages never seemed like much to Brady until now. In Brady's eyes Franklin couldn't have been a bigger hero. An Indian fighter at fifteen with a story to tell that he was asked to repeat over and over again to grown men who listened in awe and nodded to him when he rode past, or when they chanced to meet him walking through camp.

Franklin bent down and picked up Brady's rifle in one hand as he carried his own in his other.

"Ready to go?"

Brady reached over and took his bridle off the wagon wheel hub. "Yep," he said. "I'm ready."

The boys caught their hobbled horses and led them to the picket line where they brushed them and saddled them in the lantern light. Other riders approached the picket. Some coming off, others going on. There was little talk and what talk there was came brief and strained.

They drovers rode out together under a moon that was full and a clear sky. The shadows in the bushes moved on an intermittent draft of cold air that settled in the meadows and rolled softly up from the river. The air smelled of damp grass and wet dust and everywhere the riders looked they imagined Indians harbored by the darkness and bent on revenge.

The relief riders banded together as they rode out, making nervous talk. Turning in their saddles at the sounds in the night and carrying their rifles across in front of them, cocked and ready.

The livestock grazed a high meadow bordered by the river to the north and lined with cottonwood trees and buck brush on the southern and western perimeters. The captain of the guard avoided riding into the exposed clearing on the tree side of the meadow where he ordered Brady and Franklin to take up their posts without a word of advice or caution.

Three Feathers and Buffalo Dancer stood calm and relaxed as the boys sat their horses side by side, facing in opposite directions, watching each other's back as they whispered.

"You know we'll be splitting up when we get to the Snake River, don't you, B.C.?"

"Yeah, I know."

"We probably won't ever see each other again."

"I know that too."

"We sure did have us some good times," Franklin said.

Brady laughed quietly and nodded. "The saloon was the best."

They fell silent. Franklin leaned forward, his arms resting on the saddlehorn.

"You could come on to California with us."

Brady looked at him. His eyes reflected the moonlight. He crossed his arms.

"I can't."

"Well you could, but I know you can't," Franklin said. Then he leaned back and put both hands on his horse's rump.

"Anyway, we'll still be blood brothers no matter what." he said.

Brady smiled. "Yep, we'll always be blood brothers."

They rode on until they came upon the other night guards they were to relieve, they found them bunched in small groups huddled and waiting out the night.

Franklin leaned over to Brady at the sight of the night guards hiding out in fear. "That ain't right."

Brady looked up at him. "They're supposed to be spread out," he said.

Franklin seemed truly disappointed. "It's just plain cowardly."

"Ain't you a little afraid, yourself?"

"Yeah, a course," Franklin said. "But being afraid and being cowardly is two different things."

Brady sat up straighter in the saddle. Just before they split up to take their posts, Franklin spoke over his shoulder. "We ain't never gonna be like that."

If Brady's hero-worship for Franklin ever needed any confirmation, it was settled that night as he rode off into the dark alone and unafraid.

FOURTEEN

The night passed without incident. The next two days were dry, hot, and uneventful. By noon on the third day the sun bore down upon the shadowless earth until not a living thing save the immigrants and their livestock chose to stay out in the heat of it. When the wagons rolled to a stop, the small shadows they cast were crowded with camp dogs and children and elderly men and women, all competing for a chance to get out of the sun.

Brady rode up from the north side of the river. His face flushed red and the crown of his hat soaked through with sweat. Trail dust clung to the buckskin's legs as high up as the river was deep, and flies swarmed about its face. Brady swung his leg over the saddle and dismounted.

"Is that wheel broke, pa?" He asked, pointing to the massive rear wheel leaning against the sideboard.

"It just needs a little grease. It started squeaking some after we crossed the river," his father said, holding up the grease pot to make his point.

"Where's ma?"

"She's bringing up water. She'll have something for you to eat here shortly. You hungry?"

Brady smiled. "Starved," he said.

"Here, hold this for me." McCall handed the grease bucket to Brady. "You mind checking them single-trees and taking a look at that kingpin while I grease this up?"

"Sure, Pa."

Brady handed the bucket back to his father, tied off Buffalo Dancer, and loosened the saddle cinch. He crawled under the front part of the wagon where the tongue meets the kingpin and checked it all around.

"Hey, Pa. You want to take a look at this?"

"What is it, son?"

"I don't know. It looks like a crack in the sand bolster."

McCall's expression was serious. He slid under next to Brady.

"Where?"

"See right there?" Brady said, pointing to a hairline fracture that ran half the length of the bolster.

"Sure enough. Good eye, son."

McCall ran his fingers down the crack and inspected the backside of the bolster.

"It don't go all the way through, but I best wrap it just the same. It'd be a long walk if that broke down."

Brady smiled.

McCall wiped the area clean with his big, rough-skinned hand and wrapped it meticulously with wire in smooth, even turns which Brady admired for their symmetrical perfection. He wondered how men learned to do things like that so well.

"Pa?" Brady said quietly.

McCall looked over at the boy as they both lie on their backs in the dirt.

"When do you think we'll get to the Snake River?"

"Oh, five maybe six weeks if we keep going like we been. Why?"

"Well, no reason really."

"What's bothering you, son? You starting to think about leaving ol' Franklin when we split up there?"

Brady smiled a weak smile. It always surprised him when his father seemed to know what he was thinking.

"Yeah, I guess," Brady said.

McCall stopped what he was doing. They slid out from beneath the wagon and sat across from one another on the ground. He was quiet and gave Brady time to think.

"Franklin's the only best friend I ever had."

"I know. That's a gift not everyone gets."

He pushed his hat back and patted Brady on the leg.

"Your ma will keep in touch with Mrs. Stilwell—I expect you two ain't seen the last of each other yet. Things happen and good friendships endure," he said.

His eyes were confident and the corners wrinkled when he smiled and that was enough for Brady. He tried not to think about it past today, and having it officially on record with his father gave it a sense of reckoning and credibility of a higher order that made it better.

Brady saw his mother and sister back at the fire. He grinned at his father.

"Thanks."

He stood at the side of his horse and dug into his saddlebags. Whatever he pulled out, he hid behind his back, and then approached the fire.

Rachael saw him first. "What you got, Brady?"

Brady smiled. "What to do you mean?"

"You got something behind your back. You're not very tricky."

Brady pulled out a small bunch of wildflowers. He divided it into two, and handed one to his mother and the other to Rachael.

"Oh Brady, they're beautiful," his mother said. "That was so thoughtful. Thank you!"

Brady blushed. Rachael had her nose buried in hers. She looked up at her big brother, gave him a tight hug.

"These are the first flowers anybody ever gave me," she said with an adoring smile.

Brady hugged his little sister and smiled down at her. "When the next boy gives you some, he's gonna have to talk to me first."

They all laughed. For a few moments, life wasn't about the trail, and all three seemed to feel it.

Back on the trail and less than three hours later, the terrain began to change. Trees and brush appeared scattered before them and the flat plane became hilly. An hour after that the wagons spread out and stopped along the cut of a violent river. Its banks denied them access and its current spit and swirled in contempt as it crashed through rocks and boulders and carried with it debris and whole trees uprooted and turning slowly like prehistoric carcasses of unknown origin.

Garrett held up the wagons. The teamsters crowded their rigs in closer. Tempers ran short as the men contemplated the treacherous crossing and waited for Garrett and his two scouts to search up and down stream for a safer place to enter.

Osborne strode through the clutch of men gathered at the river's edge, ranting and cussing. And, while some thought him irrational, others nodded approval. Half a dozen men avoided the gazes of the others as they slunk about and drew into a delegation with Osborne presiding over them, his eyes consumed in hatred and his expression restrained but malevolent. He reckoned Garrett to be an Indian sympathizer and he said so, and others concurred. From there it was a small step to condemn Garrett's actions as those of a man in whose judgment they had grave misgivings.

By the time Garrett and his scouts returned, the mutinous deputation had adjourned and only Osborne remained at the meeting site. Garrett assembled the drivers and addressed them from atop his lathered mount.

"Boys, we've been up and down this river four miles in each direction, and there ain't but one place to get these wagons across. But it ain't gonna be easy and it ain't gonna be fast. The river is higher than it's ever been the last three times I come through here. The bottom is loose rock and sink holes that'll swaller a wagon. We got no choice but to float 'em, and it'll take the better part of a week."

Garrett sat up straight in the saddle and waited for a response. People grumbled and shook their heads. There wasn't much talk, but the talk there was bordered on dangerous. Garrett chose to disregard it. He could never reconcile his thinking to the arrogance he saw in some. He had no tolerance for complainers and whiners, but the well-intentioned he knew among the others were a dilemma for him. They listened and worked hard. They learned and tried to improve but, for all their good intentions, they were no better off than those who refused to learn.

The weak delegation of would-be adventurers bent under the load. Less than halfway through their journey they had travelled for over two-months and the road back was no longer an option. It showed on their faces and their hands and the way they shuffled along. It showed in their dress and it showed in their disregard for cleanliness and conversation.

There were a few among them who held up, but even they lost the will to carry the emotional load of those who broke early. But, for all their failings and misgivings, the inexperienced travelers were remarkably resilient.

The women of the company bore the greatest burden, for their lot had been cast by their men and was not a thing of their own doing. They tended the morning fires and they tended their thin and raggedy children. They stoked the evening fires. They were the first to rise, the last to rest. When they had nothing left to give, they gave more. Their skin, blackened by dirt and sun, was rough and their hands looked like those of their husbands. Vanity and fastidiousness died early. Then the smiles disappeared. And, when the women began to withdraw for their own self-preservation, the vitality of the company bled into dust.

James Garrett felt like an observer of a great pantomime in which the players deteriorated before his eyes. He saw it in them all, but he saw it in the women in a way that was disturbing. The fair-skinned ladies who joined the company in St. Joseph had about them a delicate manner and refined appearance.

He now saw before him hollow-eyed creatures, one indiscernible from the other, who seemed to have mutated into leather-skinned beings of uncertain age mechanically moving through each day. Most made no attempt at changing into fresh clothes. Many slept in the clothes they wore. The men walked and rode. At night they collapsed onto their blankets, some without removing a boot.

Garrett never expected the news of the week-long river crossing to be received well, but he was unprepared for what followed. A voice, loud and irrational, exploded from the fringe of the crowd. It was Osborne, spittle dribbling from the corners of his mouth, his fist pounding the air. He railed at Garrett. Nothing he said made sense, but his words were vile and accusing and, in the end, it was his fear of dying on the trail that pushed him past his limit.

He stood silent and surveyed the crowd, then he looked up at Garrett.

"Garrett, you misfit, heathen, son-of-a-bitch," he said calmly. "You just wouldn't listen. Because of you people are going to die."

There was a frightening presence about this inconsequential man that made it personal for Garrett.

"Dixon should have killed you when he had the chance," Osborne added in a soft voice.

Garrett dismounted and started for Osborne. McCall pushed his way through the crowd and wrestled Osborne out of the crowd and dragged him back to his wagon. Osborne did not resist. Three men intercepted Garrett.

"Hold on, Jim," one of the men said. "He doesn't know what he's saying. It was just too much for him."

Garrett was calculatingly well-controlled. The atmosphere was explosive and everyone was fearful that Garrett would not be as forgiving with Osborne as he had been with Dixon. The strained anticipation was unbearable. Finally Garrett defused the tension.

"Let's get these teams moving. Two miles upstream we'll make camp and ready the wagons. We'll start across as soon as we get the first one set up."

Garrett remounted and turned his horse upstream where they prepared for the crossing. When the first of the wagons was in position, Garrett barked out orders to the four drivers in the lead.

"You men, start unhitching them teams and start unloading them wagons. We're going to float 'em."

Garrett tied the end of the rope to his saddlehorn, plunged his horse into the swift current, and started for the other side. A dozen feet into the current, both horse and rider disappeared below the surface. The men on the bank froze. The two men holding the loose end of the rope watched as Garrett's end drifted downstream underwater. They leaned back against the pull and set their heels as Garrett and his horse bobbed back to the surface.

The horse, in a panic, snorted and pawed the air wildly with his front feet, fighting to get to solid ground. Garrett was swept from the saddle. He gripped the horse's tail with one hand as he reached for the rope with his free hand.

Every eye in the camp watched until the exhausted horse reached the river bank, emerged from the water with Garrett in tow, and stood there shaking. The horse's sides heaved as he sucked in air.

Garrett came out of the water at the same time. He caught his breath, and then untied the rope from the saddlehorn and tied it off to a sturdy tree near the water's edge.

He shouted across the river. "Tie on two more like this one. I'll drag them across."

Once all three ropes were in place, Garrett returned to the wagons without mishap. He proceeded to get the four teams across, then had the first wagon stripped of its wheels and pulled down to the water. One rope, secured to trees on both sides of the river, ran through the center of the wagon to keep the wagon body from drifting downstream. They tied a second rope to the front bolster. Garrett hitched the other end to a team on the far side of the river. Using a tree as a fulcrum, the team strained in the traces as the first wagon entered the water. When the floating wagon was in the mainstream of the river the force of the water pushed it heavily against the center rope, but the pulling power of the team moved it easily across with its load of two men and the wheels from two wagons.

The first wagon made several trips back and forth, transporting people and belongings, until the entirety the four lead wagons had been deposited on the western side of the river. The first wagon was then pulled out of the water and reassembled.

This process was repeated until darkness made it too dangerous to continue. By nightfall, five wagons had been taken across.

"Mr. Garrett," said Preacher Baldwin, as the men and women gathered on the east bank of the river to assess their progress, "How long do you think it will take for us to get the rest of the wagons and the livestock across the river?"

"Maybe four days," Garrett said. "Right now our camp is split and in no position to defend ourselves if we need to."

Garrett turned to address the men waiting. "By the time that sun cracks up in the morning I want you four wagons unloaded. Don't leave nothing inside but the wheels and jacks."

Garrett continued with his orders for the next day's work and assigned men on both sides of the river to work the ropes and help with the heavy work of dismantling and reassembling each of the wagons. It would take the better part of a week to move the company less than a mile closer to Fort Laramie. With time beginning to run out, concern for beating an early winter in the Sierra's weighed heavily upon all.

FIFTEEN

The river crossing was a delay no one had planned on. Most expected to replenish supplies in Fort Laramie before then. The overlanders had lost almost a week—a week beyond their most cautious estimates. Now essentials like flour, beans, and bacon were running out, especially for the larger families who simply couldn't carry enough surplus for extended contingencies. The most important relief point in the trip lay ahead and, in many wagons, the food shortage caused more stress than the company could bear.

After the river crossing, Osborne became reclusive and stopped his campaign against Garrett altogether. On this particular night he had taken refuge in his wagon and did not come out to unhitch his team. It was well after dark when McCall walked by Osborne's wagon, noticed the team in its traces, and heard Osborne inside engaged in what sounded like a muffled conversation with someone whose voice McCall did not recognize. He resisted the urge to tell Osborne to turn his team out for feed and water and debated whether or not to stop at all.

He continued on past the wagon, but was struck by the peculiar sound of Osborne's voice and by the fact that there was no light in the wagon. Contrary to his nature, he decided to go back closer to the wagon to try to hear what Osborne was saying. Osborne spoke in a voice that at times sounded like the voice of a child and at other times was deep and angry.

McCall listened but never heard a response to the one-sided conversation. Then the voice changed, and it was neither that of Osborne nor anyone McCall recognized. He listened and chills ran down his spine when he realized that Osborne was alone. McCall resisted the urge to throw back the canvas fly at the back of the wagon. Then, the voices stopped. McCall held his breath and listened. Then the softer of the two voices hummed a lullaby. Then silence.

McCall reached for the canvas at the same time a bright flash of light lit up the inside of the wagon and an explosion from a shot being fired rattled the framework. White smoke belched out of the small opening at the rear of the wagon.

McCall threw the canvas back. He stared into the darkness until his eyes adjusted and he saw in the reflected light of a nearby campfire, Osborne leaning up against the sideboard with a gaping red hole in his forehead and blood splattered across the canvas side.

They wrapped Osborne's body in a sheet and laid him out on the ground. When McCall reached back inside the wagon for a blanket to cover the bloody sheet, he found Dixon's knife and pistol belt and strings of rawhide, the same as those that bound and tethered Dixon to his horse.

Garrett waited for the protests, waited for the accusations, and waited for the gasps of disbelief, but as he looked out upon the downcast eyes of the company before him, all he saw were men and women exhausted of energy and drained of emotion. Standing with expressionless faces, they were no longer willing to invest in the right or wrong of Osborne or Garrett, or even the loss suffered by Dixon's wife. They had nothing left.

They dug the grave that night. They buried Osborne and bowed their heads with open eyes while the preacher said words no one heard. They returned to their blankets and, in the morning after they allocated Osborne's provisions, they turned his team in with the free stock and never moved his wagon from where it stood near his grave. His name was never mentioned again.

SIXTEEN

The morning after the last wagon was across the river, Garrett rode out at daybreak. It was after noon when he returned. He rode up and down the line of slow moving wagons, waving his hat and stopping at each one just long enough to say they would reach Fort Laramie by mid-day the next day. There was great whooping and hollering as the news passed down the line.

That night they built a large fire and they ate together, sharing what food they had and serving portions without limit. It was a feast of abundance that dried up the larders of all but the most conservative among them.

The men wore clean shirts and the ladies wore fresh dresses. Young girls tied their hair up in ribbons and young boys gathered around the fire with hair combed and parted wet and left to dry in place.

They ate and they visited and the men passed a whiskey jug. Preacher Baldwin played the fiddle while some danced and others repaired to small groups to talk. Talk had been spare for a long time, but tonight they put aside their concerns and their differences. For tonight there was no journey—upon that there was unspoken and unanimous agreement.

Bill McCall and Tom Stilwell shared a cup of whiskey. Neither spoke much, but when they did it was of what lie ahead. It was hopeful talk, but it was uncertain talk. They left their doubts unsaid in the unspoken understanding that they were well beyond any option of turning back.

Bill passed the jug to Tom and, in that brief meeting of their eyes, a pact was drawn and agreed upon that they would press on at all costs.

No such covenant existed between Elizabeth McCall and Emily Stilwell. When they spoke, the conversation was of home and friends and lives given over to the kinds of dreams men dream. Both women, each in her own way, looked back at what they surrendered with a divine strength and a resolution to go forward, which they did on faith alone.

Fort Laramie was a milestone, the first real measure of success—an outpost once thought remote and distant, unreachable when calculated by the progress of each day's journey, but now it was there. Less than a day's ride. The thought of it renewed their spirits and brought light back to the eyes of those now gathered about the campfire.

Tom Stilwell raised his eyes and looked to the shadows at the center of the clearing where the preacher stood and tapped his foot and played the fiddle to a group of young people gathered around him.

He looked back at McCall, half smiling. "Wonder where them boys of ours got off to?" he said.

McCall nodded in the direction of the music. "Looks like them over yonder drawing straws to see who asks that pretty little Granger girl to dance."

Stilwell laughed. "Yeah, sure enough," he said. "At the rate they're going about it, this could take a while."

McCall smiled and shook his head. Franklin and Brady stood off to the side, just at the fringe of the firelight but near enough the center of the activities to be easily noticed. They wore their shirts tucked in and buttoned to the top. Both boys combed and slicked back their hair—Franklin's suggestion and his first order of business in explaining to Brady how to impress the girls.

"Girls like boys with smooth hair," he said.

Franklin moved into the perimeter of the firelight. He slid his Indian knife more towards the front of his belt than he normally wore it and turned to Brady.

"How's it look, B.C.?"

"How's what look?"

Franklin pointed impatiently at the knife.

"It looks good," Brady said. Then his expression clouded.

"What's wrong with you?" Franklin asked, as though he didn't care if he got an answer or not.

"Well, are you going to ask Allison to dance or ain't you? She keeps looking over here," Brady said.

"I ain't decided if I want to ask her or the other one," Franklin said. "If I ask Allison, the other one will be disappointed and if I ask the other one, Allison will be."

Franklin looked at Brady and Brady tightened his jaw and fumed, but didn't say anything.

"It ain't easy deciding," Franklin said.

Just as Brady was about to respond, Allison and her friend approached the boys.

Allison smiled at Brady. "Would you like to ask me to dance?"

Brady felt his face burn, and his mind raced to find the right thing to say. While he fumbled for the right words, Franklin stuck out his arm. Allison's friend hooked her hand in it, and off they walked laughing and talking as they headed into the dancers' circle.

Brady looked down at his boots then back up to Allison, who stood there smiling and waiting.

"Umm, well, yeah I would," Brady said softly.

Allison smiled and waited. "Well?"

Brady laughed. Then he smiled. "Would you like to dance with me?"

Allison took his hand. "Yes, of course."

Brady had never heard anyone his age say *of course*. He couldn't have been more impressed or intimidated.

They danced and they laughed, and every time the couples passed, Franklin tipped Brady's hat or pushed him off balance. The longer they danced, the more the boys disrupted the patterns, until the square dance became a pushing contest between Brady and Franklin, much to the annoyance of the two girls.

Emily and Elizabeth watched their sons from their seats at the far side of the fire. Both women smiled as they talked.

"Will you look at those two boys of ours," Emily said. She laughed. "Sometimes I don't know whether to be embarrassed or grateful."

Elizabeth shook her head and laughed. "I'm sure there is much we don't know that would justify the embarrassment. But I can't imagine a deeper friendship."

"No," Emily said. "It's a rare gift those two have. They argue all the time, but I've never seen two boys look out for each other like they do."

"Yes, I think it's wonderful they found each other," Elizabeth said. "I'm just worried what will happen when we go our separate ways."

"I think about that every day now that we are so close," Emily said.

They fell silent, then Elizabeth spoke. "We will only be in Fort Laramie long enough to get supplies and repair the wagons. But I hear there will be hot baths available." She smiled at Emily.

"Oh, I can't wait to sit and soak in a steamy hot bath." Emily said. "And, if I'm not out by the time you all get ready to leave, just leave me there." She laughed and Elizabeth nodded in agreement.

Elizabeth looked down at Matthew sleeping in her arms and Rachael nodding off at her feet. She stood slowly.

"I think I better get these two off to bed," she said to Emily. Then she bid Emily and the others goodnight and walked back to the wagon.

One by one the lanterns went out at each wagon. Tree frogs and crickets answered one another's calls, and somewhere deep in the night an owl called out. A hawk screeched from somewhere very high overhead, and the soft breeze that floated across the plain carried with it the lonesome sound of a distant coyote. The flames of the campfire slowly subsided until only the glowing embers persisted, and the camp slept.

SEVENTEEN

Brady, wake up," Bill McCall whispered, as he touched the boy's shoulder. McCall stood in the light of the moon that hung bright and low, and the boy raised his head from the blankets and looked about. He watched his breath as he spoke.

"What time is it?" he asked in a voice still husky from sleep.

McCall smiled. "About two hours before dawn. You said you wanted to get up early."

"Thanks, Pa," Brady said as he shivered and dressed and saw the camp was busy with people already up and readying themselves for an early start.

Elizabeth had breakfast ready by the time Brady pulled on his last boot. She looked up from the cook fire as he ran around the end of the wagon on his way to catch up his horse.

"Brady McCall, you hold it right there young man," she called out in time to stop him before he was out of earshot. Brady turned and walked slowly back to the fire.

"Yes, ma'am," he said, shifting impatiently from one foot to the other.

"Brady you have to sit down and eat breakfast. You can't expect to be out there all day on an empty stomach."

"But I ain't hungry," Brady pleaded. "Everyone else will get the good spots and I'll get stuck in the back again."

He looked up at her from beneath the brim of his floppy hat with pleading eyes.

"Well, all right," she said, "but you take these along to eat on the way."

She handed him two hot biscuits. He stuffed one into his mouth and the other into his pocket. Then he turned on his heel and ran off.

"Thanks ma," he called back, his voice muffled by the biscuit held between his teeth.

Late in the afternoon, Garrett's scout rider trotted his lathered horse among the wagons and announced Fort Laramie lay just over the next set of hills. Judging by the tracks of many horses and wagons, this was a much used roadway, and that alone gave cause for excitement and anticipation.

Drivers clucked their teams up, tightened the formation of the wagons and hurried along, eager to see anything that even remotely resembled civilization.

The first wagon was close behind Brady and Franklin as they crested the last rise and saw the timbered structure of the fort. They stood in amazement at the activity in and around the compound that was neither as large nor as elaborate as either of the boys imagined. It was not a city or even a village, and whatever military value the place had was lost on the boys. But the number of horses and riders and men walking about was far beyond their expectations. The sight of tipi's grouped around the stretch of plains to the west left them staring wide-eyed as they sat their horses and watched without speaking.

Finally Franklin stood up in his stirrups for a better looked and whistled as he exhaled to make a point.

"Damn . . . I mean dang, B.C. Look at all them Indians."

Brady stood in his stirrups as well and then sat back down and looked over at Franklin.

"What if they're Gros Ventres?"

"What do you mean?" Franklin asked.

Brady nodded toward the beaded knife on Franklin's belt.

"One a his relatives could be among 'em," Brady said.

Franklin unbuckled his belt and slid the knife off as Brady spoke. He reached back and tucked it deep inside his saddle bag. Then he smiled at Brady.

"I ain't worried about it, cousin," Franklin said. "Then again, there ain't no point looking for trouble neither."

Brady laughed. "They probly already heard a you by now, anyway," he said.

Garrett halted the wagons and rode on in to the fort alone. When he returned he waved the drivers on and led them to a bivouac area in a grove of sparse cottonwoods at a broad and grassy bend in the Chugwater River, a mile or so west of the fort.

As the last of the wagons pulled into camp and formed up, a committee of curious Indians and an Army captain and his sergeant rode up and asked the whereabouts of the wagonmaster.

Garrett rode out and presented himself. The captain saluted, then dropped his hand crisply to his side without dismounting his horse. The sergeant sat his horse straight-backed and unsmiling.

"I'm Captain John Lewis. Welcome to Fort Laramie." His expression was friendly and his manner easy, but beyond the outward appearance of professionalism lay a sense of fatigue in his bearing. His eyes were the eyes of a man aged beyond his years.

"Captain," Garrett said, as he nodded in response to the officer's salute.

The captain anticipated the next question and said, "We got plenty of hot water for baths, the quartermaster's stores are full and the blacksmith can fix you up on wagon repairs."

Then he added, as though it were a necessity and not an option, "You'll want as much ammunition as you can handle and the armory has a few good rifles for sale if you're interested."

"Much obliged, captain," Garrett said as he looked across the faces of the drivers and their families gathered and standing within hearing distance.

If they had a response to the captain's suggestion it did not show in their expressions, and Garrett dismissed it at that. The captain paused as though expecting questions and, when none came, he continued.

"After you folks get settled in, General Gibson would like to meet with you in his quarters—say five o'clock?"

"That'll be fine," Garrett said. "It will be me and a few of the men."

"Very good, sir," the captain said. "Enjoy your stay and let me know if there is anything I can do for you while you're here."

He snapped another salute and turned his horse back through the line of Indians who had followed him there.

That evening Garrett and a group of men that included McCall and Stilwell rode back to the fort and found their way to the general's office. General Gibson greeted them and invited them to sit. The general was pleasant, but short on words, and his patience balanced between obligation and intolerance. His voice was heavy with the responsibility of his station while his manner suggested he had spent too much time assigned to wilderness outposts like this one.

Gibson carried an unlit cigar between his fingers as he paced back and forth across the room. He surveyed the company of civilians assembled before him. His eyes were alert and hard and filled with authority. He gazed from one man to the next, not at all uncomfortable with the direct eye contact and lack of dialogue. The civilians grew ill at ease and some shifted in their seats while others diverted their eyes.

"This is the Wind River Mountains, and this is South Pass," the general finally said, pointing to a spot on the large map that dominated the wall behind him.

He used the cigar as a pointer and didn't look too check for accuracy as he tapped the spot on the map with the end of the cigar.

"And here," he said, moving the cigar eastward, "is where we are."

He waved the cigar over a large expanse of the map.

"The rest of this is Indian Territory."

His eyes moved from man to man, examining them one at a time as though he was searching for something or waiting for a response, but none came. He stood with his cigar hand in front of him and rolled the cigar between his fingers. The men watched the cigar.

"For the most part these are hunting grounds to the Crow and the Blackfoot and some of the Sioux tribes."

He paused again. Then he snuffed the cigar vigorously into a tin ashtray and there was nothing left to watch but him. He moved a step closer to the assemblage.

"They tolerate us," he said. "But they don't change their ways to accommodate us. See, they don't know what to make of all these white people and their wagons, yet. We've not had much trouble with them, but it is coming."

He touched his forehead and his voice softened, and the men sat up and raised their eyes to him.

Garrett stood to speak. The general ignored his motion for the floor. He walked back to the map and Garrett sat as though commanded to do so. The general turned to the map. He ran his finger along an area southeast of the route between Ft Laramie and South Pass.

"We have information that a war party—as many as two-hundred give or take, renegade Comanche are on the move north of here. The Army has yet to engage them anywhere, but this is, as near as we can tell, a loosely organized band of young warriors out killing just for the sake of killing."

He stopped and contemplated some private thought.

"Normally, the Comanche never come this far north. But, we believe they are here somewhere."

He tapped the map, stopped talking, and looked out at the small gathering of expressionless faces.

Any relief the settlers felt at reaching this stage of the journey now hung like a millstone on the backs of each man in the room and, after a long silence, Garrett once again took the floor.

"General," Garrett said, with an air of directness that caught the general off-guard, "we couldn't be less prepared to defend ourselves against twenty, let alone two-hundred. We don't have the arms, the ammunition or the experience."

He let the declaration hang out there a moment, and then continued.

"What are the chances we'll encounter that war party?"

The men looked up at Garrett, silent and staring, most now moved up to the edge of their seats.

The general thought before he answered.

"Look, I can't tell you for sure what they'll do or where they'll go, but I can tell you, an outfit like yours would give them young bucks bragging rights for a long time."

Garrett waited.

"I would expect them to turn back south at some point, but they shouldn't be up this far in the first place, so there's no guarantee they won't keep coming."

The general looked over at Captain Lewis. If the captain had an opinion about the situation, it did not show in his expression.

"What are chances of getting an Army escort through South Pass?" Garrett asked.

"I'm prepared to offer you some help, but I can't spare enough men to do you any good in the event you encounter hostile activity from a bunch this large."

"We'll take what we can get," Garrett said with genuine gratitude in his voice.

The general nodded as though to acknowledge the implied thank you. Then he waved the captain over to his desk.

"Captain Lewis," he said, as he wrote out a brief set of orders and handed the document to the young officer. "Select fourteen of your best men and draw mounts from the stock we've had under training."

"Yes, sir," the captain said. He stood erect and held a sharp salute until the general returned it, then his hand cut away smartly. He immediately turned and walked briskly out of the room.

The general's expression was grave. He turned to Garrett. "I would strongly advise that you lay in whatever ammunition and rifles your company can afford to properly arm themselves. In the meantime, we do have plenty of provisions available and we'll do all we can to get you all back on the trail as quickly as we can."

He offered his hand and Garrett shook it.

The layover at Fort Laramie took eight days—five more than Garrett planned on. Now, the prospects of an early snow troubled him as much as the thought of an encounter with the Indians. When they departed the fort and their last link with civilization, Garrett set about pushing the company at a grueling pace.

Behind them, wheel ruts lay across the plains and converged on the horizon, where they disappeared and made their homes seem impossibly distant. Before them lay the foothills and beyond that the mountains. The closer they got the further they seemed to have to go. Garrett grew unrelenting in his efforts to drive them onward.

EIGHTEEN

The configuration of the Platte River began to narrow. It flowed faster and deeper. The terrain transitioned from sandy loam to rocky hardpan. The going became increasingly inconsistent, and the livestock showed the strain of the extra effort required to traverse it. The pace slowed and wagons queued up two and three abreast from the broader formation allowed on the flat plain.

They left the Platte and followed the Sweetwater. Each day the going grew a little more difficult and each day the range of mountains and its intimidating peaks grew more prominent. They camped in a high meadow at the base of the mountain, and the mountain itself stood before them, and the trail they saw etched upon the ground rose up and into the high ground. When they saw the full magnitude of the mountains before them, they struck with an awful sense of impossibility that left no man among them untouched.

After supper, Garrett stopped by to talk to a small group that had gathered near the campfire where the McCall's and the Stilwell's ate together.

"Evening folks," he said. "You all ready for the big climb up them mountains?"

The question came in the form of small talk, but his tone suggested an underlying concern and a seriousness that did not invite a rhetorical response.

Bill McCall looked up at Garrett's sun-darkened and deeply lined face. He forked in another mouthful of beans and swallowed slowly before he spoke.

"Jim, my mules are dog-tired. We're working em into the ground."

"That's a fact," Stilwell added. "Most of these teams are running thin, mine included. We either got to slow the pace a bit or give them a day to rest up."

Garrett nodded as though he understood. "Simple truth is, we can't rest or slowdown, neither one."

He paused, looked up the trail in the direction of the mountains, then back at the fire.

"You never seen it snow up there. If we ain't over when the snow comes, that's all there is. It ends right there."

Emily and Elizabeth listened and, though neither spoke, they were both thinking the same thing. If the teams didn't keep pace the loads would be lightened and that meant more valuable keepsakes would have to be discarded. Stoves, bureaus, chairs and all but the barest of essentials would be sacrificed first. The trail below them was littered with the reminders of those who preceded them—furniture, heavy cookware, stacks of books, things all believed essential in St. Joseph, now a testament to the lengths to which they would have to go to get up the mountain.

The men talked and the women silently prayed. When McCall looked over at Elizabeth he saw in her eyes a willingness to do whatever had to be done, and he knew he could not ask her to sacrifice even one more piece of what little she had left. Their eyes met in mutual understanding of a situation they both knew was beyond their control.

Garrett reached down and peeled a piece of bark off the log and threw it into the fire as if to emphasize his point.

"We got no choice," he said, shaking his head and staring into the fire. "Every day we use up on this side of the mountain we'll pay for on the top."

Garrett's words shot through the heart of the matter. No one argued, no one offered another point of view. The expressions looking back at him were those of resignation more than determination. He excused himself and walked on.

For the next three days the wagons inched slowly up the eastern side of the pass. Behind them the trail lay littered with furniture, trunks, and equipment, discarded as the first of the weaker teams began to fail. Up ahead the trail narrowed. On the north side a steep, rocky cliff formed a rough wall reaching nearly two- hundred feet to the top. The south side was boxed in by a thick stand of aspen trees growing so closely in formation that a man on horseback could not navigate a direct route through any part of it.

The trail snaked its way through the narrow passage between the rock wall and the trees and the wagons were forced into a single file for the better part of it.

Garrett sent extra scouts out, and Captain Lewis deployed his men front and rear. His instincts and military training converged in a chilling realization that their position was not only un-defendable, but it compromised every advantage they might make for themselves. He watched his forward contingent ride up then drop over the first rise before them, disappearing from sight as though the mountain itself had taken them.

The captain ordered his men to seek the high ground wherever they could, but there was none to be had, and they pressed on against every instinct he possessed as a man and a soldier.

Storm clouds gathered and rolled over the highest granite peaks to the west. The sky grew dark and overcast and the air was sultry. The earth took on the musty smell of new rain. The darkness of the sky hung low over them like a premonition of something uncertain and every man, woman and child of them felt its cold presence.

The women bundled and tucked the babies deep inside their blankets like fragile porcelain dolls and the children gathered about their mothers without being asked to do so. There were no sounds save that of the wind and the creaking of the wagon wheels. The unnaturalness of it all weighed heavily on man and beast.

McCall's mules crowded the steep north side wall with their ears cocked forward, their heads tilted and their nervous eyes fixed on the dark, shadowed trees. The mules mouthed their bits and tossed their heads and refused to settle into their normal rhythm.

"I don't like the feel of it, Elizabeth," said McCall, as he jumped back onto the moving wagon and climbed into the seat beside his wife. "Check them rifles and make sure we got plenty of shot and powder close by."

McCall had felt trapped and exposed from the time they were forced to run the wagons into a single line. Elizabeth looked shaken.

"What is it, Bill? Did you see something? What's wrong?"

"I ain't sure. I didn't see anything, but I've got a real uneasy feeling I can't explain. Maybe it's just the weather or this crowded trail we're on. I don't know for sure."

McCall watched the mules. He trusted their sixth-sense ability to detect danger, but nothing he could see or hear justified their nervousness. He knew it was probably just the change in the weather, but he couldn't help feel there was more to it than that.

For the next three hours the wagons slowly penetrated deeper and deeper into the confines of the pass. The aspens bent in the wind, the dark clouds tumbled lower and dropped down to treetop level. The air turned cold.

Captain Lewis stopped to talk to each of the drivers as he made his way back along the trail from the lead wagons. He approached the McCall wagon and drew his horse in closer. McCall handed the reins to Elizabeth and leaned over to hear what Lewis had to say. The captain's troubled expression betrayed his professional demeanor and McCall could sense the anxiety in the soldier's voice.

"Mr. McCall, no cause for alarm, sir, but we're pretty spread out on this trail, and I want to make sure you have your firearms ready—just in case."

McCall reached down and lifted the barrel of his rifle.

"Good," the captain said. Then he looked across at Elizabeth. "Ma'am, if you got anything inside you can use as cover against this side canvas, you should get it moved right away. Anything that will offer a little protection would help."

McCall looked at the captain and his voice was noticeably uneasy when he spoke.

"Captain, you seen any sign of Indians since we been up here?" McCall asked impatiently.

"No sir, we haven't. But if they're out there, we couldn't have picked a worse place to. . ."

The captain's voice trailed off. He sat there with no expression on his face, and then began to list from side to side. His eyes dropped to the arrowhead protruding from his shirt and dripping blood onto his saddle. Bubbles frothed at the wound site and, as the young officer pitched from the saddle, he appeared apologetic.

NINETEEN

The McCall's stared in stunned disbelief. They watched the
captain's body drop to the ground. As quickly as McCall
began to climb down to go to the aid of the captain, the
dreadful sound of screaming warriors reverberated up from
the darkness of the trees like come great cataclysm of
smoke and fire with the whining of bullets and the sizzling
sound of hundreds of arrows buzzing through the air.
Women screaming, babies crying, and the savage war cries
coming from the shadows.

There was no plan and there was no organization.
Men died watching without ever raising a rifle or lifting a
hand to come to their own defense. Confused horses took
flight, crowding the narrow trail in a milling mass of
congestion as the bodies continued to drop. Riders fell like
shooting gallery targets with every flight of arrows and
volley of rifle shot that came up out of the trees.

The wagons stood in disarray. In those few brief
moments, death and disorder spread from the lead wagon to
the last wagon. Panic set in. The company of settlers fired
blindly into the trees, and most never got an opportunity to
reload.

Then, the unthinkable.

Swarming up out of the trees came a terrifying
swarm of painted warriors brandishing war axes and bows
and rifles of all description. Their eyes were on fire behind

the warpaint and their fury every bit as evil as anything conceived out of the inferno itself.

Another black barrage of arrows and McCall's mules dropped as one, their legs buckled, and their heads rested on slack jaws with eyes that looked ahead with no movement to them.

"Elizabeth, get under cover," Bill shouted, as he pushed her back into the wagon.

In the same motion he brought his rifle up to his shoulder and looked down the barrel at a warrior running straight at his wagon. He squeezed the trigger and the lead ball tore a path through the Indian's chest, catching him mid-stride and taking him off his feet. He exchanged rifles with Elizabeth who handed him a loaded one. She slammed powder, shot, and wadding down the warm barrel of the first rifle and held it ready for the next exchange.

A young boy warrior, no more than fifteen, noticed movement through the rear canvas of the Baldwin wagon marooned just ahead of McCall. McCall thought briefly of his own son and hesitated to fire. The youngster motioned to another his age with blood up to his elbows and they descended upon the wagon and disappeared inside. McCall heard screams from both Mrs. Baldwin and her husband.

McCall's stomach turned when he watched the two drag the lifeless body of Mrs. Baldwin over the tailgate by what was left of her hair and drop her to the ground pounding their chests with their fists.

McCall took aim, squeezed the trigger, and watched the skull of the first boy shatter and spew blood and gore over the bare skin of the second boy. He was unprepared for the reaction that came next.

The young warrior turned, glared at McCall, and then drug his fingers across this chest. He shouted some abomination at McCall, and then licked the blood of his comrade from his dripping fingers, charging the McCall wagon and waving a bloody knife over his head as he did so.

There was no time to wait for a reloaded rifle. McCall unsheathed his knife and stepped forward to meet the warrior who lunged up onto the wagon tongue and was at the front foot board when a rifle shot boomed from inside the wagon. A cloud of white smoke followed. The warrior crumpled to the ground and McCall turned to see Elizabeth lower the weapon from her shoulder and sit back down to reload.

Behind Elizabeth, Matthew and Rachael huddled together, shaking and sobbing. McCall saw the terrified expressions, his stomach knotted and he felt ashamed. For the first time he could remember, he felt fear. Elizabeth looked over at him as she slammed the ramrod down the bore of the rifle. He prayed Brady was safe, but he knew better. His hands shook. Elizabeth screamed. McCall turned to see another warrior halfway up the front of the wagon.

McCall's fear turned to rage. He met the warrior at the foot board. He reached forth, took a handful of the greasy hair, and jerked the warrior inside the wagon. Elizabeth screamed. The children screamed. The warrior groaned when his chest crashed against the seat. In one swift motion, the warrior plunged his knife its full length into McCall's groin.

Elizabeth and the children watched in horror. McCall showed no reaction to the knife, as he mechanically raised his own blade over his head with both hands grasping the wooden handle. With his full force he drove the blade deep between the shoulder blades of the young warrior. He withdrew the bloody blade then slammed it home a second and third and fourth time.

The warpainted body went limp. McCall pushed it back over the side, then slumped to his knees on the floor of the wagon, his trousers soaked with blood and hemorrhaging from a severed femoral artery. He looked up at Elizabeth. His eyes apologetic, his expression helpless and ashamed. She reached out to him but they never made contact. An arrow, silent and errant, ripped through the canvas and lodged itself deeply into her back. The impact took her off her knees and she stared at her husband as she fell forward and she watched as another arrow tore blindly through the canvas and struck him squarely in the chest.

William and Elizabeth McCall died before the savages overtook the wagon and dispatched the two children.

In the confusion of the attack, Thomas Stilwell was able to get Emily out of the wagon and near the cover of the trees when the attackers over-ran them. Stilwell fired his last shot, stood between Emily and the warriors converging upon them and took the barrel of the rifle in his hands and swung viciously at the first of the Indians to come into range. The warrior fell and behind him a flurry of arrows hissed through the air and left Stilwell and his wife standing there momentarily stunned at the number of feathered, wooden shafts protruding from all parts of their bodies. They collapsed to the ground and Stilwell hovered over Emily's body as he felt a knee driven into his back. Stilwell reached behind him and grabbed a handful of hair and pulled his attacker over his shoulder and pinned him to the ground before him. His hands clinched around the warrior's throat and the warrior twisted and writhed and fought for his release until he could fight no more, and his eyes rolled back and he lay calmly in Stilwell's grasp.

Stilwell's head snapped back, and he felt the weight of a man upon his shoulders and felt his hair being pulled. He struggled, but had no strength. Blood ran into his eyes and he could smell it and taste it on his lips. When he sensed his scalp lift away in a violent ripping sound, he felt the earth grow quiet and dark. He died before he felt the burn of the knife on his throat.

A Comanche warrior stood. His victory cry rang out loud and he held his trophy high, blood running down his bare arm and his eyes filled with hatred and triumph.

TWENTY

Brady and Franklin rode a narrow draw to the upper trail shortly after they left camp that morning, leaving the scouts and other outriders to the trails below. High on the upper rim they rode undetected leaving a good view of the lower trails much of the time. They rode carefully through the brush and granite boulders, and they rode slightly back from the forward positions of the two army scouts, staying concealed in the brush near the ridgeline.

When the weather turned and the dark clouds rolled in, the electric smell in the air was unnerving. Both boys felt uneasy, but neither mentioned it to the other. They ventured out upon a lightly treed escarpment to check their positions. Two army scouts sat their horses far below them. They appeared to be extraordinarily occupied with the forested area below them.

"What do you suppose they're doing?" Brady asked.

Franklin stood in his stirrups for a better look, then replied in a soft voice that made Brady uncomfortable.

"They see something . . . I don't know what."

The boys heard no sounds and they saw no movement below them. Then, as though it were being played out in slow motion, the two scouts lurched convulsively in their saddles, and slumped forward, both with arrows ruffled up to the feathers in their backs. Blood ran from both the entrance wounds and the exit wounds, pumping from the holes in their shirts until their hearts stopped and they fell silently to the ground. Their horses sidestepped them but did not bolt. There was no other sound and there was no other movement—two arrows, two dead men, and everything else as though nothing had happened.

Brady and Franklin looked at each other in absolute shock. Franklin slashed his finger across his throat, then pointed back up the side slope to the cover of the brush and boulders. They wheeled their horses about and hid out in the brush out of sight from the trail below. Franklin drew his rifle.

"What are you doing?" Brady asked.

"We gotta warn the others," he said.

Before the last word was spoken, the awful sounds of gunfire and war cries and screaming echoed up the canyon. Both boys sat momentarily frozen in the saddle.

Panic gripped them and Franklin screamed. "Let's go!"

Brady looked down the steep trail and spurred his horse out of the heavy brush in the direction of the gunfire, Franklin right behind him. The sounds resonating off the canyon walls painted a horrible picture in the boys' minds. Brady's hands shook uncontrollably and Franklin cursed and pounded the horse's sides with his heels and fended off the brush with the hand that carried the rifle.

The trail was narrow and in places the gravel so loose the horses slid on their haunches to stay upright. At a wooded bend, Brady pulled his horse up abruptly and turned to Franklin, his eyes wide, as he signaled Franklin to get off the trail and into the brush. Brady jerked his horse's head around. Franklin did likewise. Their horses stood with sides heaving and gasping for air. Brady dismounted, and Franklin swung down beside him.

"What's wrong?" Franklin asked, his chest pounding.

Brady looped his reins around the stalk of a tall bush and dropped to his knees. He motioned Franklin to follow and crawled out to a rock outcropping where Brady pointed out a Comanche warrior standing his post mounted on a painted horse blocking the trail not a hundred yards before them.

"What are we gonna do now?" Brady asked, in a voice shaken with childlike uncertainty.

Franklin put his index finger to his lips to signal Brady to silence. He paused for a moment, then handed his hat to his young friend. Franklin cradled the rifle in his arms, dropped to his belly and snaked his way thirty yards closer. He rose partly up to look over a fallen tree, then lowered the rifle down to the dry bark and rested it against the notch of a broken limb. He set his sights.

Brady was mesmerized and barely breathed as Franklin slowly drew back the hammer. It seemed an eternity. The warrior turned his horse, exposing the broad view of his back to Franklin, and Brady saw Franklin's jaw tighten and saw his finger apply pressure. Franklin held his breath and, when the shot exploded, he flinched and his eyes widened at the big, red hole gaping along the warrior's spine as he lifted from the horse's back and lay in a grotesque heap on a twisted leg, with an arm turned up behind him.

Franklin rose to his feet and took a final look at the dead warrior. He stood there for a moment like he was going to speak, then a second warrior rode out onto the trail, reining his flighty horse with one hand, brandishing a bloody war axe in the other.

The warrior spotted Franklin and let out a horrifying war whoop before Franklin could take cover. The warrior whipped his fiery mount up the trail at a gallop. The awesome spectacle of the painted warrior on his painted horse destroyed Franklin's confidence. He stood locked in fear as the warrior bore down upon him.

With no time to reload, Franklin looked back at Brady. Franklin's eyes widened as he watched Brady brace his rifle against the side of a slender pine tree. Brady pulled back the hammer and waited. Franklin watched like a sacrificial lamb as the shrieking warrior bore down upon him.

Franklin turned to run, slipping and scrambling to get up the incline. The Comanche brave covered fifteen more yards. Brady didn't move a muscle. Ten more yards and Franklin broke for cover, yelling at Brady as he ran.

"Run," he shouted.

Brady could now see every detail in the warrior's face. The dark Indian pony never broke stride as he closed the distance on the stumbling Franklin. Moving in for the death blow, the warrior raised the long-handled axe over his head.

Brady closed his eyes and squeezed the trigger. White smoke and fire belched out of the muzzle of Brady's rifle, and the deafening roar of the shot reverberated through the trees. The Comanche brave's head twisted violently when the shot ripped through his cheekbone. The impact of the big gun blew the warrior off the back of his horse as the heavy, lead ball tore the flesh away from his face.

His war-painted horse bounced to a stop, then calmly walked a short distance away and quietly dropped his head to graze.

Franklin ran back to Brady. He picked up his hat and he motioned to Brady. Brady nodded back and his expression was hard. He set the rifle on its butt plate and packed in another load.

"Reload and let's go," Brady said hoarsely.

Tears threatened to betray Brady's manly demeanor, the little-boy look in his eyes was that of a lost child and Franklin patted him on the arm.

"Thanks," Franklin said.

With their rifles reloaded, the boys mounted up and made their way slowly along the rim of the trail, careful not to reveal themselves and watchful to avoid another surprise.

The going was slow and the sound of the battle in the pass below raged at a feverish pitch. The boys both knew that as long as there was gunfire there was hope. The game trail they followed turned and dropped sharply down to the right where the boys began the final descent.

War cries and anguished screams and rapid fire gunshots were close when half a dozen mounted warriors caught sight of the boys and opened fire on them. Bullets chewed up the ground all around them and arrows hissed overhead. Neither boy was hit.

The frenzied Comanche whipped their horses up the hill. Brady and Franklin spun their horses around and lunged back up the mountain. A quarter of a mile up the granite break they left the trail and took cover in a tangle of heavy brush among the boulders where their horses left no sign.

The boys breathed heavily as they moved deeper into the concealment of a narrow ravine. They listened intently, gasping for air and shaking involuntarily. The warriors clattered by in the rocks below, whooping and yelling until their frightening voices faded beyond the next crest in the trail.

The boys dismounted, tied off their horses and slipped into a long narrow rift between two granite outcroppings with only one way in and one way back out. They rested and they waited. Smoke columns rose high into the air overhead from the killing grounds below, and the sounds of gunfire and war cries became more sporadic.

Now only an occasional shot cracked the still air, and the voices they could hear were voices of the warriors speaking a language they didn't understand.

They looked at each other and began to weep.

For the third time, the searchers rode within fifty yards of their position without detecting the location where the boys had left the trail. The Indians' voices were loud and angry as they rode back in the direction of the wagons.

When night came, the smoky air turned cold and the only light in the rift came from the stars and a full moon.

The boys lay huddled and waiting. Not a shot was fired for more than two hours and not a word was spoken between the two boys, but both understood the only thing left for them to do was to try to stay alive.

When they dared go out for a look, they crept out on a ledge where they could see down into the clearing half a mile below them. Burning cinders rose up from the massive fire in the Indians' camp and twisted skyward until they burned out.

Below, the Indian camp turned into a celebration as the warriors gathered up bags of sugar and jugs of whiskey and sat about the fire licking the sugar off their wet fingers and drinking the liquor that made them vomit and want more as they became rapidly intoxicated.

The boys couldn't see well from their position, but they could hear the screams of many women. With only their imaginations to suggest the terror, they secretly prayed their own mothers were granted the better option to die in the battle.

Brady cringed each time a female voice cried out. The boys felt sick and empty.

Long into the night the cries continued until one by one they too were silenced and the only sounds were those of the warriors who argued and fought among themselves. Eventually even those voices stilled as the whiskey took effect, and then there were no sounds at all.

Brady stared into the darkness. He tried to remember exactly how his mother looked when he last saw her. He remembered his father's smile and his big strong hand on his shoulder. He saw clear images of his sister and his little brother, and tears swelled in his eyes.

Franklin sat with his head in his hands. His face was streaked with tears. He looked over at Brady.

Brady looked back at him with an almost pleading expression. "You think they killed them all?" he asked quietly, slightly shaking his head from side to side as though to prompt the right answer.

Franklin nodded. "I think they did."

Franklin choked back the tears and stood up. Brady stood with him. He put his arms around the boy and held him like a father holds a son, and they both cried.

Brady cleared his throat, then pushed himself away.

"We can't let 'em get away with this," Brady said, as he wiped his arm across his nose, and dug his knuckles into his eyes to clear away the tears. He picked up his rifle, made sure it was loaded, then reached down to check his knife.

Franklin spoke through gritted teeth. "We'll leave the horses and go on foot."

They stayed close to the rocky path in the darkness and picked their way toward the spot where the renegades had dragged their prisoners. The wind had scattered the cloud cover and small patches of moonlight broke through, giving the boys enough visibility to see the trail and to see the shapes of several warriors stretched out in the dirt near the campfire.

Franklin assessed the situation as best he could. He took Brady by the arm and whispered.

"B.C., all we can do is get as many as we can before they get us."

Brady nodded in agreement and they sat to wait out the cloud cover for better light.

TWENTY-ONE

The moon slipped in and out between the thin clouds, casting long shadows across the camp when it did. In the shadows lay warriors, some in their own regurgitation and others on the bare dirt. A few others sat tilting over whiskey jugs between their legs, talking in subdued voices as the last of the liquor took its toll. For all they could see, the boys knew there were far more scattered undetected throughout the camp.

Brady and Franklin waited quietly, searching the dark ground and hoping to find a way to catch this small detachment of warriors by surprise. Brady's heart ached with loathing and anger to the point he could barely contain himself. Franklin was unusually calm. Neither was prepared for what they had to do next.

Brady grew impatient and inched forward for a better look. As he did so, he momentarily lost the grip on his rifle and caught it just as the steel-plated butt struck loose rock.

The seemingly insignificant sound occurred when all else was silent, and the three sentinels heard it. They fell dead silent and listened, tilting their heads.

Brady held his breath. Franklin froze in place. The loose rocks tumbled down the granite face picking up more debris on the way down until everything dropped over the edge and clattered to the trail below.

The warriors, now on their feet, scrambled upwards toward the source of the sound, hoping to add the scalp of a straggler to their string.

Franklin was halfway back up the escarpment. He whispered in a loud voice. "Brady, up there," he said, pointing to a small cleft in the granite boulders.

They concealed themselves as best they could among the large rocks, invisible from the downward side of the trail, but partially exposed if the braves passed abreast of their position.

The boys backed into the cleavage and steadied their weapons on the opening. Their hands shook as they heard the sentinels pounding up the steep embankment toward them.

For all they had to drink, the Indians moved quickly. They split up just before they reached the boys' position, and then everything went silent.

Brady stood fast with his rifle trained on the narrow opening, his heart hammering and his chest heaving. They waited there a long time.

Then, a painted face filled the opening, its black eyes like those of a devil. So close Brady could smell his liquored breath.

Terrified, Brady pulled the trigger. The shot exploded into the throat of the warrior, tearing out a fistful of bone and gore where it exited at the back of his neck. The muscular body dropped backwards, out of sight.

"Over there," Franklin shouted, as a second warrior swung his rifle around the far side of the rock and ratcheted the hammer back.

Franklin fired without aiming. The shot ricocheted off the face of the rock and buzzed out into the open night air then made a splattering sound when it tore a ragged path into the renegade's mid-section. The warrior spun off his feet, dead.

Brady was trying to reload, but was shaking so badly he was unable to line the ramrod up with the bore of the rifle. Franklin's hands shook. He dropped his powderhorn and looked up at Brady, who was also struggling.

"B.C. There's still one more out there. Hurry."

Their nervous hands made a mess out of reloading and, as they slowed down, the boys heard the unmistakable double click of a rifle hammer above them. Franklin felt a chill and the hair on the back of his neck raise up as he anticipated a shot ripping into his back.

Brady whirled and looked up as he jammed the ramrod to pack the shot. There above them stood a warrior, his legs braced and his rifle pointed down at them. For a moment the moon shone from behind the dark clouds and the light reflected off the barrel of the warrior's rifle.

There was no hurry about the intruder. Franklin heard the last click of the hammer, saw the executioner shoulder the butt of his weapon and, just before he pulled the trigger, Franklin pushed Brady out of the line of fire and the bullet cracked against the rock behind him.

Franklin looked up in time to see the warrior drop back out of view and his rifle slide down the rock face into the breech. He and Brady exchanged puzzled looks.

Franklin grabbed Brady by the arm. "Let's get out of here," he said, as he turned to retreat through the narrow passageway.

Franklin led the way, squeezing between the rocks. As he approached the opening, the dark outline of a man stood across the exit. The dark figure moved toward him. Franklin drew his knife and stood his ground, prepared to die if it came to that.

Then, a voice in English. "Hold on, I'm on your side."

Brady and Franklin looked at each other and took a step back. The man slipped in beside them.

"It's me, Travis Kincaid."

Brady and Franklin were stunned. Both boys started talking at the same time. Finally, Brady stopped to let Franklin continue with the questions.

"How did you find us?"

"It's a long story," Kincaid said. "Right now we got other things to think about."

The boys agreed.

"What are we going to do?" Franklin asked.

"Look, I'm real sorry," Kincaid said. "But there's not much chance they left anyone alive down there, you know that don't you?"

They nodded again.

"They ain't getting away with this," Brady said.

Kincaid stared at the gutsy boy. "What are your names?"

Franklin looked at Kincaid, anxious to get the formalities out of the way.

"I'm Franklin T. Stilwell. This here's Brady McCall."

Kincaid stuck out his hand and they shook.

"All right, listen to me," Kincaid said. "It's not likely we're getting out of this alive."

"What do you mean?" Franklin asked.

"These Comanch' been pushed hard."

The boys held their heads down.

"I don't blame you for wanting revenge."

"How much of what happened down there did you see?" Franklin asked.

"Not much. I saw the smoke from way down the trail. Saw Indian sign early on. By the time I got close enough to see anything it was almost dark."

"And?" Brady asked.

"It was never their plan to leave anyone alive."

TWENTY-TWO

Dawn was less than two hours away. The camp lay dead quiet with only the sound of drunken sleep. The wind had died down to a soft shifting of the air currents and, for that moment, the world seemed at peace.

Peace was the last thing on the minds of Kincaid and the boys as they crept single file back up the narrow trail. Kincaid sensed the boys' uneasiness and turned to speak over his shoulder as they continued silently through the brush.

"Don't let the quiet fool you. It won't take much to set them off again."

When they passed the spot where Buffalo Dancer and Three Feathers stood tied, Kincaid tied his horse off with them. The boys followed close behind Kincaid as he led them away from the direction of the wagons and the main war party to within a hundred yards of the forward camp.

Young warriors slept where they fell. There was no sign of any white captives if they had taken any.

The three crept cautiously through the tangled brush. A few yards in front of them, one warrior lay apart from the others, wheezing and sleeping deeply. Kincaid drew his knife and motioned for Franklin and Brady to stay under cover. He handed Franklin his rifle then dropped to his belly and snaked his way into the enemy camp.

As he made his way through the brush, a bleary-eyed warrior they had not seen sat bolt-upright directly in front of Kincaid. Kincaid made no sound as he raised himself and pulled the warrior back down and drove his knife upward between the soft V of the Indian's rib cage. Kincaid held the muffled and writhing warrior until he stopped struggling. He twisted the knife and drove it home twice more before he gently lowered the body to the ground.

Brady and Franklin looked at each other nervously. Kincaid crawled back to them. He was all business now, with no emotion on his face or in his voice.

"I'm not sure how many of them are out there," he said. I'm going to try to slip into camp without waking anyone."

If Kincaid had a plan, it seemed to be a loose one.

"I'll try to get across to the other side. If they did keep anyone alive, I'll find them."

Kincaid began inching his way down into camp. Brady and Franklin trained their rifles his direction to provide what cover they could.

Brady spoke without taking his eyes off the sights of his rifle. "We only got time to get off one shot each if something goes wrong. Then what?"

"Just make sure we don't miss—the rest is up to him."

Kincaid closed in on the position of the nearest drunken renegade, stalking him with the lethal precision of a big cat. Brady and Franklin watched in awe. Without a sound or so much as a scuffle, Kincaid hunkered over the warrior and, in one smooth motion, covered the Indian's mouth, and then plunged his knife blade deep into the center of the warrior's chest. He eased the body to the ground, and then worked his way towards the next one.

Brady's mouth went dry. He could hear his own heart pounding. The moon slipped from behind the clouds and cast its silvery light onto the clearing, exposing Kincaid as he continued methodically on in the direction of the three other warriors.

When Kincaid was within striking distance his stomach knotted. Their hands were covered with blood dried to a black stain. The nearest one lay with two blonde-haired scalps laced to his wrist.

Less careful now, Kincaid rose up and drove his knife violently into the chest of the sleeping Indian. With his last breath the Indian groaned loudly, waking the warrior next to him. Kincaid was caught off-balance. The groggy Indian rolled sideways with great swiftness, leapt to his feet and stood facing Kincaid who was still on his knees.

Franklin saw Kincaid's predicament and raised his rifle looking for a clear shot. Kincaid was in the line of fire. Before Franklin could set up a shot, Kincaid lunged toward the warrior. His quickness caught the young warrior off guard. Kincaid laid him open with a violent slash across the abdomen that spilled the warrior's intestines out at his feet.

Franklin watched the horrified expression on the young warrior's face and, in a moment of misplaced compassion, he squeezed the trigger.

The warrior dropped. The report from the rifle echoed off the canyon walls.

Kincaid rose to his feet and shouted, "Get out of here."

Kincaid ran into a previously passed-out warrior who rose to his knees. He drew his pistol from its holster and fired a round into him without breaking stride.

When he reached the boys, Franklin shook his head. "Damn, Travis, I'm sorry. Everything happened so fast."

Kincaid grabbed them both and spun them around.

"Don't worry about that now. Back up into the brush."

No sooner had Kincaid said that, then the fury of hell broke loose back in the direction of the wagons. War whoops and loud angry voices echoed up the pass. Then came the steady pounding of the horses' feet galloping up the trail towards them.

"Get up that hill under the brush," Kincaid ordered.

All three dove for cover. The ground shook and it sounded like every warrior in camp was mounted and charging after them.

The warparty searched in vain. They rode the trail up and back, and they tended to their dead. They milled around within feet of the boys' position.

When the skyline began to change from black to a dull shade of grey, Kincaid told the boys to remain quiet. All night long the boys had prayed for daylight. It couldn't have come at a worse time.

Travis and the two boys lay hidden less than twenty feet from the trail. Their cover was thin but, with no time to move into a better position, they knew their only chance was to remain absolutely still and to hope the Comanche would move through fast enough not to notice them.

There was much confusion in the camp as the warriors tended to their dead and argued about what had happened. Dust billowed up from the hooves of scores of horses when the main party trotted onto the crowded trail. War whoops and loud voices mingled with the sound of the horses as they drew nearer.

"Don't make a move, and don't make a sound," whispered Travis. "Even if they look you right in the eye, stay still. If they do spot us, wait for me to make the first move, then make your shots count."

The boys' eyes filled with terror. They nodded. Brady was emotionally drained. Fear, guilt, uncertainty, hate, and sorrow numbed his senses.

The first of the riders passed directly in front of them without slowing. At this point the trail was narrow and, as the warriors filed past, Brady was sickened by the blood spattered bodies and the many scalps he saw hanging at their sides. Brady counted silently to himself and tried to remember the faces as they passed. He stopped counting after a hundred—and still they came.

Kincaid watched as the warriors rode by in many groups of half a dozen or more.

They carried their dead and wounded with them and Kincaid realized they were leaving. They were not looking for them. He prayed neither of the boys would give their position away.

Then, a cluster of five warriors riding apart from the rest pulled their ponies to a halt and stopped directly in front of Kincaid and the boys. They were so close Brady was sure they saw him. He held his breath and waited with his eyes riveted to the faces streaked with war colors and sweat. The warriors talked loudly to one another.

Brady's rigid muscles ached. He sat frozen in position trying to memorize every feature of the faces before him. These five were different from the others. Even Brady could see it. Their hair was not the same. Their headdress was different. They wore beautifully decorated deerskin shirts, unlike the bare-chested majority who were far more primeval in appearance. Brady tried to remember the horses and the painted marks they bore.

He listened to their voices, the unintelligible guttural sounds. He hated their careless demeanor and their casual regard for the slaughter they had committed.

One of the five spun his high-stepping grey horse around and stood facing Brady. From his neck hung a locket. It reflected in the morning sunlight. Brady could not stop staring at it.

And then he recognized it—it was his mother's. Franklin recognized the locket at the same time. Brady tensed. His expression turned reckless and vengeful. Franklin pleaded with his eyes for Brady not to do anything. Brady half rose and Franklin stopped breathing. Kincaid touched Brady's leg with the toe of his boot and the boy let it go.

TWENTY-THREE

The five warriors argued back and forth, and then they dug in their heels and loped off. The morning sky began to blaze with color and the sun warmed the chill off the air. Ground squirrels scampered across the trail and birds twittered as though nothing had changed for all the killing that went on there.

In the serenity of that majestic mountain morning, countless blood-stained horsemen rode away celebrating a brutal victory. They carried with them worthless treasures and trinkets and left the livestock of the overlanders to fare for themselves. Behind them two young boys contemplated revenge.

It was a long time before Kincaid gave the boys permission to move. He sat back and looked at Brady. His demeanor clam and unusually unbothered by the events that took place the night before.

"Did that gold necklace belong to your mother?"

Brady stared blankly at the ground and nodded. His lip quivered and a tear fell, wetting the back of his dirt-stained hand as it made a tiny trail across his knuckles and dripped down onto the wooden stock of his rifle.

"Yeah, it did. I'll get it back," Brady said, looking up at Kincaid with a cold expression.

Franklin stared into the dirt. His eyes narrowed. He looked up at Brady.

"I'll help you," Franklin said.

Brady stood and Kincaid stood in front of him and placed his hand on the boy's shoulder. "Some things are better left alone."

"Not this one. It ain't even my choice to make, Travis." Brady nodded towards Franklin. "He don't have no choice neither."

"Why's that?" Kincaid asked.

Brady looked up at Kincaid from beneath the brim of his hat. "We're blood brothers."

Kincaid nodded. "I'm just asking you to think about it, that's all."

Kincaid and the boys had their horses and belongings collected. They stood in the warm morning sunlight soaking in the heat before Brady and Franklin mounted up.

They were tired and wrung out and the thought of returning to the site of the massacre hung heavily over them. With one foot in the stirrup and the other still on the ground, Kincaid hesitated. He stepped back down.

"Why don't you boys ride on up the trail and water your horses? Give them a chance to graze some? I'll ride back to the wagons to get a look at things first."

Travis knew it was a weak attempt, but he hoped he could save the boys from what he knew awaited them.

"Forget it, Travis," said Franklin. "We're going with you."

Brady nodded his agreement with Franklin.

Kincaid spat and pulled his hat down as he stepped back up into the saddle. "I figured as much," he said.

TWENTY-FOUR

Kincaid and the boys descended the rim in silence. The hoof prints of many unshod ponies lay before them where the trail had been ridden to dust. All along the trail, the personal treasures of those in the Garrett Party lay strewn recklessly; clothes, books, pots, dishes, shoes, and a child's doll. Further down, a broken rocker and a twisted steamer trunk and, for the next two miles, pages from Bibles and old pictures, all slung about with great disregard. A mile more and the woods were thick with debris that, a few hours earlier, seemed so valuable, yet now so worthless.

They walked their horses. No one spoke. Brady's face was pale and drained. Franklin's eyes were red-rimmed, his jaw clinched. Kincaid rode two horse-lengths ahead of the boys. The trail rose, then fell and turned at a shallow bend.

Kincaid raised his hand. "Looks like the lead wagon up ahead."

He looked back at the boys. Brady nodded him onward. They rode together. When they approached the wagon, it buzzed with hordes of flies and the gut-wrenching odor of death assaulted.

They came to the oxen first, grotesquely tangled in their bloody harness, their bodies bloated and pockmarked with bullet holes and pin-cushioned with arrows. The wagon rested on its side, the canvass burned away and the contents strewn about from both ends.

Kincaid dismounted and checked inside. The boys waited. Kincaid stepped back into the saddle and shook his head. They rode on.

The next wagon was the same story—another dead team with eyes gone and buzzards tearing flesh from the empty sockets. The birds hissed and gorged themselves, tearing at the bullet holes and spreading their wings but not leaving.

Kincaid checked inside the second wagon then, before they reached the third, he pulled his horse up. "Wait there," he said over his shoulder.

He dismounted and moved down into the brush below the trail where several bodies lie. The boys waited, their faces ashen, their eyes dark and hollow. Kincaid was gone a long time. When he climbed out of the ditch he dropped his eyes and shook his head.

"I think it's the Turners and the Eastman's and some I don't recognize.

"Dead?" Franklin asked.

Kincaid nodded. "Nine including the babies."

Franklin dismounted.

"Don't," Kincaid said. "They're scalped and cut up bad. You don't need to see that."

"You sure they're all dead?" Franklin asked.

"They're dead."

Kincaid remounted and Franklin followed suit. They rode slowly. More bodies appeared. First a few here and there then more until they had to dismount and walk so littered was the trail with human remains and debris.

From a slight rise in the trail Franklin recognized his family's wagon. Four of the six mules stood waiting as though nothing had happened. The two wheel mules lie heaped in dark pools of dried blood.

"You don't have to do this, Franklin," Kincaid said.

He held the boy's arm. Franklin jerked free. Brady stood beside him.

"I'll go with you," Brady said.

Kincaid let the boys go ahead. They found Emily Stilwell first. The wide skirt of her dress fluttered in the wind and she lay face down, her arms twisted behind her and her feet turned at unnatural angles. Her dress was soaked in blood. When Franklin saw her he collapsed to his knees before he could approach her. He dropped his head and wept.

Brady stood next to him with his hand on Franklin's shoulder and he cried.

"I'll get her a blanket," Kincaid said.

He found a quilt near the wagon and before he covered her he straightened out her arms and fixed her feet.

At the edge of the trail he found Thomas Stilwell, his scalp torn away, his shirt gone, and his body cut many times with gaping slashes. Kincaid wrapped him in a cotton sheet and placed his body next to that of his wife.

Franklin and Brady watched and sobbed.

Kincaid returned and stood over the boys. There was no give in his voice this time.

"You two go back down the trail to one of them other wagons and fetch us three good shovels. Do it now."

His voice was firm, and the boys did not question him.

They returned with the shovels, their faces streaked and all the fight whipped out of them.

"Yonder's a clearing," Kincaid said, pointing to a small meadow off the trail. "Go on down there and start digging."

"Travis," Brady said. Travis cut him off. "I know Brady . . . you go on and help Franklin with the digging. I'll let you know what I find."

Kincaid located the McCall's where they fell. He wrapped Bill McCall in a canvas wagon sheet, found a quilt for Elizabeth and blankets for each of the children. He wrapped them and laid them out in a line. He fashioned a travois and began dragging the bodies to the burial meadow.

The boys stayed at the meadow digging graves. Kincaid found bodies everywhere he looked and hauled them one by one back to the grassy clearing. By the end of the day they had buried twenty-three bodies and marked each grave with a board and a name. The remaining bodies they couldn't name and couldn't bury.

Kincaid built a great pyre of sideboards, wooden furniture, and dry lumber. Upon it they placed the bodies, each one wrapped and soaked with kerosene.

They caught up their horses and Kincaid sent Franklin and Brady on ahead. He returned, said a prayer over the massive arrangement and set it afire. He waited until the heat and stench of burning flesh drove him away.

He circled the graveyard meadow and saw wild flowers on the graves of the McCall's and the Stilwell's. The McCall grave markers were carved with a knife point, *Love Brady,* they said.

Brady had retrieved the McCall family Bible and his spare clothes from his wagon. Franklin did likewise. They rode with their Bibles clutched beneath their arms and tears running from their eyes.

They waited up the trail, turned back in their saddles, and watched the massive billow of black smoke rise from the forest until it formed a column and the flames followed it skyward.

TWENTY-FIVE

They rode in silence for the better part of an hour, each leading a pack horse and not a word exchanged as they plodded along the trail inching their way to the summit. Behind them, a column of smoke rose up from a distant place in the forest that would forever remain fixed within the minds of two young men if they lived through it.

It was Kincaid who finally broke the silence.

"I don't like to be the one who brings this up, but you boys are going to have to give some thought to what you want to do next," he said. "I'll get you to Fort Hall, but after that I leave the trail and head north from there."

"What are me and B.C. supposed to do?" Franklin asked.

Kincaid hesitated. He thought of his own circumstances and could find no way to include two young boys in his plans. He looked over at Franklin.

"Look," he said. "You boys are in a fix, but I'm just one man living in a shack so poor the dog won't stay in it. Every dollar I had is in a bunch of Texas cattle that may not even make it through the winter. I ain't no help to you."

"We can work," Franklin said.

"Yeah, we can help out and we ain't that much trouble," Brady said.

"I didn't say you were any trouble, I just don't have any way to take care of you."

Both boys stared at the young cowboy.

"At Fort Hall you can ride with an Army patrol back to Fort Laramie. There should be someone at Laramie that can help you get back home," Kincaid said.

Brady and Franklin continued to stare.

"We got no home to go back to," Franklin said.

Dead silence. Brady was thinking.

"I got my pa's place in Montana. It's on your way. Help us get there, then me and Franklin can figure something out."

Kincaid's frustration was beginning to show. "Figure what out?" He waved his arm across the broad landscape of untamed wilderness. "Montana ain't no different than all this."

Kincaid's resolve was final.

"You know what, Travis? Forget it," Franklin said. "Me and B.C.'s going after them Indians anyway. And when we get done with that we're going to live on our own ranch. We don't need your damn help anyway."

Brady spat off to the side and nodded. "Yeah, we don't need anybody's damn help." He turned his horse and jerked the lead rope of his pack horse. "Let's go, Franklin."

Franklin turned his horse up the trail. Kincaid watched them leave.

Just before the got out of earshot, he called out to them. "How do you expect to take on two-hundred Indians?"

Franklin shouted back over his shoulder. "We ain't. We're just going after one."

Kincaid spat. He pulled his horse up, looped the pack horse's lead rope around the saddlehorn and stepped down from the saddle. He paced back and forth, kicked the dirt every time he turned and spat again. The boys saw him get off his horse. They turned and rode back to him.

"That might work, but you're running out of time."

Brady looked down at Kincaid. "Will you help us find the one who killed my family?"

Kincaid threw his hat in the dirt. He leaned over the saddle, draping his arms across the cantle. He looked sideways at Brady and then over his shoulder at Franklin.

Two dirty-faced boys looked back at him.

"Dammit all to hell," he said. "I'll do it on one condition—we find him and whatever happens, happens. If we don't get killed, which we probably will, we part company and you two are out of my life forever. You can go to Montana or Pennsylvania or where ever the hell you came from and I'm done with you."

Brady grinned and Franklin smiled. Franklin stuck out his hand.

"Deal," he said.

They shook. Kincaid picked up his hat and remounted. They started up the trail behind the unshod hoof prints they followed. Kincaid was quiet. The boys rode one on either side of him and neither spoke.

"For starters," Kincaid said. "The one we're looking for is a Sioux, not a Comanche."

"How do you know that?" Franklin asked.

"Their dress, their ponies, the way they did up their hair and war paint. Then we heard 'em talk. I don't know the language much, but it was Sioux . . . no doubt about that."

"Think we can find them?" Brady asked.

"Finding them is the smallest part of the problem."

The talk stopped and they were barely away from the killing ground when Franklin bristled and gave Brady the Blackfoot high-sign. He pointed to a spot in the brush just off the trail.

"Something's down there."

Kincaid nodded. He saw it at the same time. He swung swiftly down from the saddle and circled the brush with his pistol drawn and cocked.

Franklin and Brady held the horses and stood by with their rifles ready. Suddenly a scream ripped through the afternoon quiet and the boys swung their legs over their saddles, hit the ground, and ran for cover. Kincaid lunged into the brush and his muffled voice drifted forth.

"Hold your fire boys."

Kincaid pushed the branches aside and emerged with a tattered white girl and a ragged woman in a blood-soaked dress.

"It's Allison," Brady said. "And her mother."

"B.C., get me a blanket off my bedroll," ordered Franklin, as he rushed out to assist Mrs. Granger.

The young girl appeared unhurt, but the woman had lost a lot of blood. When they laid her on the blanket she looked at them through glazed eyes, then collapsed into unconsciousness.

"Franklin, bring me the canteen off my pack horse," Kincaid said.

He stripped the scarf from around his neck. Franklin returned with the water and waited while Kincaid checked the woman for injuries.

"Bullet went clean through her arm. Missed the bone, but she's been bleeding some."

Allison sat blank-eyed and still, her focus somewhere inside her for she regarded neither her rescuers nor her surroundings. Franklin draped his blanket over her shoulders but she gave no sign she noticed or cared.

"We can't stay here," Kincaid said. "There's a place back the way we came, about a half a mile. Let's get these two back there before it gets dark."

Kincaid gestured off towards a thin stand of new growth pine.

"Franklin, you go cut two strong saplings about fifteen feet long. We're going to have to make up a travois for that pack horse of yours. Brady, you get a rope out and then repack as much of Franklin's load onto your trail horse as you can and leave the rest."

The boys hurried about while Kincaid tried to speak with Allison, who refused to say anything or to look directly at him. He checked to make sure she wasn't injured then left her to help the boys get their outfit together.

It was near dark when they settled into camp among the trees, out of the wind and at the edge of a small mountain stream. Kincaid insisted on a cold camp on the off chance the renegades left behind a diversionary contingent of warriors who would surely have seen the funeral fire.

Kincaid daubed Mrs. Granger's wound with a wet rag, treated and bound it, and then let her sleep.

When she awoke hours later, it was dark and the night air was cold. He offered her water from a tin cup. She drank and coughed then drank again.

"Not too fast." Kincaid said, steadying the cup in her hands. "How you feeling, ma'am?"

She looked up at him, her eyes glazed and darting. "Allison?" she said, her eyes flitting across the shadows.

"She's right here," he said pointing to the girl sitting off in the shadows.

The woman calmed and she drank again. "My husband and my boys?"

Kincaid shook his head.

Mrs. Granger, unusually stoic and distant, pushed herself up and managed to get to her knees and slide over closer to her daughter. She reached across and pulled her daughter into her arms. She turned Allison's face up to hers and their eyes seemed to communicate some unspoken message as the young girl's expression softened and the tears trailed down her cheeks.

Mrs. Granger held her daughter tight in her arms and then Allison's arms embraced her mother and they both began to weep.

"It's all right, sweetheart. It's okay now," she said. "We're safe."

Allison buried her face in her mother's matted hair. "Who's here?" she asked, still not fully aware of her surroundings.

Her mother patted her back and rubbed it and spoke softly. "It's Brady and Franklin, and Mr. Kincaid."

Allison pulled back and looked around, still groggy, but less detached. She saw Brady first, then Franklin, and then Kincaid. She reached an arm out without releasing her grip on her mother. They each hugged her in turn.

Brady's mind was numb. Neither he, Franklin, nor Kincaid had slept in the last thirty-eight hours. It was all he could do to manage a clear thought. He looked at Allison feeling envious and a bit jealous. At least she still had her mother. He had no one. It was a fleeting thought and he was ashamed for thinking it.

Brady moved around to sit in front of Allison. He touched her hand and looked into her eyes. He spoke to her in a slow, gentle voice.

"Are you all right?"

She nodded. "I'm okay," she said in a whisper so soft Brady could barely hear it. "Do you know if my father and my brothers are all right?"

Brady looked at Kincaid. Kincaid gave him a nod. Brady's eyes were red-rimmed and his soft voice cracked when he tried to speak. She looked at him and he wanted so badly to tell her they were fine. He cleared his throat and spoke with such a tender manner she began weeping before he finished.

"We found a nice sunny place and put them there next to mine so they'd all be together. We put up grave markers for them and Travis prayed some."

Mrs. Granger listened and her body lurched as she held herself back. She held Allison and they both wept until there were no more tears and exhaustion overtook them. They made their beds and, as they all slept, Kincaid walked to the edge of the clearing. He sat with his back to a tree and his mind racing. He crossed one boot over the other and looked up into the night sky, clear and ablaze with stars. Of all the stars in the sky and all the people on earth he wondered about the order of it all. He stared a long time contemplating the circumstances that had beset him.

TWENTY-SIX

Kincaid let everyone sleep more than an hour past daybreak. He had a fire blazing and a hot pot of coffee hanging. He knelt at the stream cleaning half a dozen trout he caught while everyone slept.

He had the fish sizzling in the pan. Brady stumbled to the fire, his hair matted, his face puffy, carrying his boots in one hand and his hat in the other.

"Morning," Kincaid said.

"Morning."

"Sleep good?"

"I guess—I don't remember."

"Still sleepy?"

"Uh-huh."

Kincaid handed the boy a cup. "Hold this, I'll pour you some coffee."

"Thanks."

"Are you going to be like this all day?"

Brady smiled. "No, I'll probably get worse."

Brady appeared contemplative. He sat back and sipped the hot coffee.

"You know, Travis, I feel like I just dreamed all this. It feels like we can go back to the wagons and everything will be like it was."

Kincaid turned the fish and nodded. "Yeah, I know," he said.

"It wasn't no dream, was it?"

Kincaid looked up from the fire and studied the boy's expression. "No, it wasn't. Go on and wake the others. We got a lot to do." Kincaid said.

They ate breakfast. Talk was spare and Franklin was unusually quiet. Kincaid stood and scraped his plate into the fire.

"Mrs. Granger, do you feel like you're strong enough to travel?"

She didn't answer immediately. Kincaid hoped her spirits were in better shape than the rest of her. He remembered her from the first few weeks on the trail. She had fine features with sunshine eyes and a friendly smile. To look at her now it was impossible to recognize her as the same woman.

She looked at him. Her face swollen and cut, her eyes dark and lined, and her hair matted with blood. She tried to smile.

"Yes, I think so," she replied. "But we have to go back to the wagons."

Kincaid knew that was coming. "Yes, ma'am, we will," he said, knowing it would do no good to try to dissuade her. He dreaded the thought of how she and the girl would react when they came face to face with the massacre site.

"Thank you Mr. Kincaid. I don't mean to be a burden."

"It's no burden, ma'am."

She stood slowly and moved nearer where Kincaid busied himself packing up the camp. She spoke quietly, hoping to be out of earshot of the youngsters.

"What will become of Allison and myself?"

She appeared, for all appearances, to be piteously destitute.

"We can't possibly finish this trip all the way to California alone, and going back is out of the question." With that, she began to cry.

Travis resisted the temptation to take her in his arms and to comfort her—to be her protector. Instead, he stumbled over his thoughts.

"Do you have family in California?" Kincaid asked as he began to lay the groundwork for what he knew to be a thinly constructed solution that absolved him of any future responsibility for her well-being.

"Yes, my sister and her husband. We had planned to stay with them until . . ."

Tears ran down her cheeks. She paused to compose herself.

"Until John could find work and we could get our own place."

She took in a deep breath, held it for a moment then exhaled as she closed her eyes. Looking back up at Kincaid, she said, "I'm sorry."

"Ma'am, you've been through a lot. Nothing to be sorry about."

Kincaid endured the long awkward silence that followed, and then got to the business at hand.

"If we push steady we can make it to Fort Bridger in a couple of weeks. I passed two other companies coming up behind us on my way back from St. Joe. They should both be through Fort Bridger within a week or two of the time we get there. Maybe you can join them and go on to California like you planned."

Diverting to Fort Bridger was not what Kincaid wanted to do, but Mrs. Granger and her daughter were a new set of obligations he hadn't counted on and he knew he had to get them to Fort Bridger or he might find himself promising to take them all the way to California.

Mrs. Granger insisted on going back to the wagons, and Allison and the boys unanimously said they were going as well. Kincaid tried to dissuade her, but to no avail.

Heading back down the trail to the site of the killing was as chilling a prospect for Allison and her mother as it was a dreaded reminder to the boys of the horrific nightmare that had played out there.

Allison rode double with Brady on Buffalo Dancer. Mrs. Granger refused to be carried on the travois and chose instead to ride one of the pack horses.

The trail, fresh and dusty from the unshod hoof prints of many Indian ponies, descended the high ground to the narrow pass below that reeked with the heavy stench of death that carried up on the soft uplift of the slight breeze that blew there.

The thought of the renegades traveling here only a day earlier un-nerved Allison. She clung to Brady and he patted her hand where it gripped his shirt.

They passed an upper meadow scattered with loose stock, oxen, mules, milk cows, and horses left behind by the Indians. The animals grazed there with no sense of the danger that lurked around them, placid as the farm stock they were.

They came next to the first carcass, a bloated oxen lying stiff-legged and pocked with bullet holes. When Allison saw it, she turned her head and buried her face into Brady's back.

Brady looked back at Mrs. Granger as they rode past the stinking oxen, and came upon the first of the scattered effects and clothing strewn about the grounds. She covered her mouth with her hand as they approached the first battered wagon where half a dozen hissing buzzards stood gorging themselves.

For all the animal carnage that lay rotting in the sun, Kincaid had done a good job of removing all the human remains. One of the horrid birds stretched its wings to lift off, barely able to do so as it came clumsily to rest upon the ground where it stood and watched them pass by.

The air was still. The smell of rancid flesh and evacuated bowels hung over the area, gagging Allison, who held her hand over her nose as she complained to Brady.

Brady reached into his back pocket and withdrew a dirty rag.

"Put this over your nose."

Allison cringed at the sight of the rag. "Brady, this is awful," she said, as she shook her head and covered her nose with both hands instead.

At that point they turned off the trail, passed the burned out funeral pyre, and followed Kincaid through the trees. The smell of death was now downwind from them, and they entered the welcome shade of the tall aspens. They continued through a break in the woods and emerged onto the graveyard meadow.

Kincaid dismounted. The others did likewise. The sun crossed the trees at a mid-morning angle casting long shadows across the clearing and lighting the makeshift wooden markers at the end of each fresh grave.

Kincaid showed Mrs. Granger and her daughter to the Granger markers, then nodded and returned to where the boys stood with their horses. Franklin handed Kincaid his reins. He took off his hat and walked to the far end of the meadow where he stood at the foot of the graves he had dug earlier for his parents. He bowed his head and his body shook. He stood there a long time, then walked off into the trees to be alone.

Brady, who the night before appeared so much older to Kincaid, looked like a little boy kneeling and crying on the graves. Kincaid watched the boy praying or speaking to the graves, but was unable to hear him. Kincaid watched as the boy dropped onto one of the graves and wept, his tiny body convulsing with each breath. Kincaid turned away and ran his sleeve across his eyes.

Brady stood, wiped his nose, and thumbed the tears from his eyes. He walked to the sunny end of the meadow where he picked an armload of wildflowers. He returned to the graves and stopped, first at his mother's, then his father's, then those of his sister and brother and laid fresh flowers on each one. Then he did the same for the Stilwell's and the Grangers. He turned to leave, but the graves with no markers stood lonely and unattended, and Brady returned to the meadow where the wild flowers grew and collected a great many of them and distributed them to each of the anonymous burial plots and said something over each one before he returned to the horses.

Brady and Franklin stood by the horses with Kincaid for more than an hour before Kincaid went into the graveyard and convinced Allison and her mother it was time to leave.

They rode in silence to a grove of trees where a creek ran through. Kincaid made the ladies comfortable and instructed them to wait while he and the boys made a final trip back to the wagons.

They located the Granger wagon, righted and reloaded it as best they could. They caught up a mule team and hitched it up, then employed a team of oxen to clear the trail to allow the wagon to pass.

Kincaid and the boys with their well-stocked outfit re-entered the grove by late afternoon.

Clouds piled against the mountain peaks. The sun disappeared and the air grew cold. Mrs. Granger shivered as she and Allison climbed up into the wagon. She recognized the wagon, but not the team and, apart from a weak smile, she showed no interest in the contents nor the order in which she found things.

Mrs. Granger held her arm around her daughter while Kincaid climbed up onto the seat beside them. He clucked the mules on. When they passed the grazing livestock, the animals slowly milled and fell in behind them as they had done every day since they left St. Joseph.

Franklin and Brady rode a mile ahead watching the trail and sharing no talk. What was on their minds was private and neither would breach the privacy of the other.

For the next two weeks the solitary wagon tilted and bumped along like a ship lost at sea. On the fifteenth day the tiny surviving remnant of the Garrett wagon train limped into Fort Bridger.

TWENTY-SEVEN

At Fort Bridger the heavy gates stood open and the single wagon proceeded through, attracting more attention for the oddity of its singularity than had it been a full company.

Kincaid led his party across the parade ground. A solemn reception of soldiers and on-lookers could only imagine what had befallen this unlikely arrival. Kincaid located the post commander and made a full report of the massacre. He secured accommodations for the Grangers and made provisions to sell the extra livestock on their behalf.

He told the boys they would layover one day, trade what stock and provisions they had for those they needed, and then they would set out after the Comanche war party. The boys settled in as best they could and, just before dark, a trapper trotted his pony and packhorse through the gates. Brady and Franklin watched from the quartermaster's doorway as the trapper greeted first one then another and another of those he knew by name. He seemed to know everyone as he rode across the grounds and stopped at the hitch rail where the boys stood.

He touched his hat. "*Garcons,*" he said.

They touched their hats.

"Sir," Franklin said back to him.

Brady nodded.

The trapper dismounted. "They call me Charles Du Mer," he said, in a big but gentle voice.

"I'm Franklin T. Stilwell," Franklin said, as he stuck out his hand.

"My name's Brady McCall," Brady said, and he too stuck out his hand.

The Frenchman smiled. He shook hands first with Franklin and then with Brady.

"So, what brings two *bébés* like you to this *Dieu a abandonné la place*?"

Franklin furrowed his brow. "Huh?"

"What brings you to this God forsaken place?" Charlie repeated in English.

Franklin nodded towards the lone wagon conspicuously out of place among the military and trade wagons.

"We come out from St. Joseph," Franklin said.

"Part of the Wind River incident with the Garrett outfit, eh?"

"Yessir," Franklin said.

The trapper turned and undid the first knot on his pack load. "A sorry shame . . . you lads are lucky to be alive."

The trapper unlashed a worn Hawken rifle from his pack. He held it out to Brady. "Hold this for me."

Brady took the long gun, handling it with great reverence.

"Life can be hard on a man out here," he said. "But if you got it in you, there ain't no better life anywhere."

He set his pack down and reached for the rifle. He tied the rifle onto his saddle and then turned to face the boys.

"What now?"

Brady spoke up without hesitation. "We're going to kill the Indian who killed my ma."

Charlie continued working. "Ever kill a man?"

Brady and Franklin looked at each other. Franklin looked down at his boots then looked the trapper straight in the eye.

"Yeah, we both did," he said, his eyes unflinching and no brag or regret in his voice.

The trapper looked them both over, looked at Brady, then at Franklin.

"It's no concern of mine, but revenge can get control of your life."

"Well, that's fine for you," Franklin said. "But you ain't us."

"No, I know I ain't. But if you're dead set on it, maybe I can help some."

"How can you help us?" Brady asked.

"Well, I can tell you where to start looking for the ones you're after."

Brady's eyes widened. Franklin asked the trapper to wait and ran off to fetch Kincaid. When they returned, Kincaid introduced himself and told the trapper what he knew. The trapper put that together with what he saw and concluded the war party he encountered was the same one.

"They was packing dead and traveling slow when I came up on their camp at Sandy Creek," the trapper said. "Maybe half a dozen Sioux rode with them. Renegades for certain by my calculations."

"How much of a lead do they have on us?" Kincaid asked.

"Maybe a week," the trapper said. "But three men traveling light could make that up. If you was to take the June Pass, which is rough going, you could maybe catch them on the Ottertail."

Can you tell us how to get there?" Kincaid asked.

"Yeah sure. I'll draw you out a map."

Brady watched the trapper talk and looked at the broken fingernails and rough hands and buckskins and moccasins. The trapper's blue eyes shone from skin darkened by the sun. When he smiled, deep creases made them come alive. Brady couldn't figure him out, but he was mesmerized. When the trapper left to tend to his other business, Brady followed him.

"Mr. Du Mer?"

"My friends call me Charlie."

"Charlie?"

"Yes, Charlie."

Brady smiled. "Okay, Charlie. What's it like up in them mountains where you trap?"

"Sit down," Charlie said, pointing to the bench on the plankboard walk in front of the commander's office. They both sat. Charlie seemed to be pleased to have someone to talk with. There was a reverence about the way in which he referred to the land and the people.

"Up in them mountains is places no white man has seen. It's like it was when the good Lord left it. Lakes blue and clear so's you can see clean to the bottom. Every manner of game and fish . . . if you take to fish, which I seldom do."

"What about the Indians?"

"Some's good, some's bad . . . pretty much like folks everywhere. I always found them to be fair and generally they treat you like you treat them."

Brady looked up at him with a skeptical expression and anger stirring in his eyes. "Not always," he said.

"Don't hate them all because of what happened. If you got to hate someone, which I don't recommend, hate the ones that did it, but don't hate everyone because of it."

They talked of the weather, and Charlie made the weather come to life as though it were a person, and Brady understood the meaning of what he said. He talked of nature and creatures and freedom, and Brady asked many questions.

They talked late into the night and Brady's head was filled with grand images and a longing planted like a tiny seed waiting for the right time to germinate.

The next morning, Kincaid and the boys stood their saddle horses and well-provisioned packhorses at the livery where Amelia and Allison Granger met them to bid them farewell.

The post commander assured Kincaid the Grangers would be looked after and would join the next wagon train bound for California.

Amelia looked longingly at Kincaid and the boys with great concern in her heart for what she feared awaited them.

"Travis," she said. "Please be safe."

Kincaid nodded and he smiled slightly. "Yes, ma'am, we'll try."

She smiled back and they both knew the smiles were like some secret code for unspoken words that would remain unspoken.

"I cannot tell you how indebted Allison and I are to you and the boys. We owe you our lives and I will never forget your kindness. I sincerely hope we meet again someday."

Mrs. Granger hugged the cowboy, then she thanked Brady and Franklin and kissed each of them on the cheek.

Franklin pulled down his hat, "You take care, ma'am," he said.

Brady just blushed.

Allison thanked Kincaid and threw her arms around him. He wrapped her up in his arms and said, "Maybe we'll see you in California someday."

Allison grinned. "I hope so."

Then she and walked over to Franklin. She stood there a moment, looked up at him, and then gave him a hug.

Franklin grinned back at her. "Don't worry, you ain't seen the last of us," he said.

Allison got to Brady. He braced himself for a hug. Allison took his hand and held it to her cheek. Her eyes welled with tears.

"I won't ever forget you . . . ever," she said.

Brady felt a knot in his throat. He clinched his teeth and swallowed. He touched her face with his fingertips, then withdrew his hand in embarrassment.

"I won't forget you neither."

When Kincaid and the boys rode out, Brady looked over his shoulder a long time and watched Allison standing there waving and he watched until he could no longer see her. He wasn't sure what the feeling was in his chest, but he knew it was good.

TWENTY-EIGHT

They left Fort Bridger with Travis Kincaid dogging the trail of the renegades at an exhausting pace. With a singularity of purpose as lethal as that of a timber wolf on a blood scent, he located and pursued the tracks of the war party with relentless determination. His eyes missed nothing and what talk he did make was spare and he made no concessions to the inexperience or age of the boys.

Kincaid was frighteningly somber. Every ounce of his energy was drawn together and focused on the task of reading the trail left by the Comanche.

The longer they went, the more distant Kincaid became. He was like a man the boys no longer knew, and neither boy dared question him or divert his attention away from the signs of the renegades as they bore deeper into the wilderness.

They watched him with sideways glances. They strained to see the invisible signs that caused him to drop unexpectedly from his horse to the ground, where he would examine bent grass, an overturned stone, or an obscure impression in the flinty earth.

Then, with no noticeable reason for his action, he would stand and he would raise his head and look about. Without uttering a word he would remount, and they would be off again. Each day the pattern was the same. The cold, lonely nights were spent in restless sleep with meager sustenance, and before dawn they were mounted and waiting for daylight.

On the sixth day they rode high where the air was thin and the timberline was a clear demarcation between the forested slopes below and the barren granite summit above. The trail turned sharply up along a rocky butte where the aspen trees grew thick, then it dropped abruptly down into a high mountain meadow and onto a trail that showed evidence of having been trodden by the hooves of many unshod ponies as it disappeared into the shadows of the close growing pines.

Beyond the stand of Ponderosa pines lay Sandy Creek, a snow-fed flow deceptively gentle with treacherous holes and poor footing for the horses.

From Charlie's description, Kincaid recognized the broad meadow where the river widened and formed a clear, deep pool. The river tumbled gently over the rocks, and green grass grew up to the water's edge. Kincaid raised his hand to signal the boys. They halted and held the horses. Kincaid dismounted.

"This is it," he said, his voice barely above a whisper. "This is where Charlie saw the war party."

His eyes searched the trees below. The late afternoon shadows stretched across the clearing, making it difficult to distinguish the real from the imagined.

"The old Frenchman must have been back up in there," Kincaid said, pointing to a thin line of trees high above the clearing that angled off back to higher ground to the southwest.

"By the time he got from here to Bridger it had to have been a week or better," Kincaid said, thinking aloud. "We gained some ground on them."

Brady's heart pounded in his chest. He was preoccupied with vengeance. The consequences of what may happen when they did overtake the renegades never occurred to him. His stomach churned. Charlie's warning rang in his ears.

"Always keep the edge in your favor. If you lose that out here, you're as good as dead before you start."

Brady wasn't thinking about the consequences of what they were doing, but Charlie's warning and Kincaid's caution made his nerves come alive, and he leaned down from the saddle and tilted his head toward Kincaid who had already dismounted.

"Do you think any of 'em's still around here?"

Kincaid shrugged. "Not likely. You boys stay put. I'll go down for a look."

He handed the reins to Franklin and made his way down through the brush.

Kincaid was gone almost an hour. The sun dropped behind the jagged peaks that rimmed the western edge of the meadow and the air turned cold. The bright colors that surrounded them turned to grey shadows before Kincaid walked out from the lower stand of trees. He approached with his rifle resting in the crook of his arm.

"They were here all right. Just like Charlie said. They rode out heading due north, and they aren't more than two, three days ahead of us," Kincaid said, catching his breath.

"We'll rest the horses and be on our way at first light."

Franklin hobbled the horses while Kincaid set up camp and started a fire.

Brady stood knee deep in the numbing-cold creek poised with a spear he had cut from a nearby willow. He plunged the makeshift lance into the water and lifted out a glistening rainbow trout. In one easy movement he cast the fish up onto the grass and plunged the spear back into the water. He lifted another from the water and lay it next to the first. He lay down the spear and hefted both thrashing fish with his fingers through the gills as he turned and headed for the fire like some primeval hunter lumbering up through the darkness.

That night they sat hunkered and staring, silently eating with their fingers before a fire that cast their gaunt shadows against the trees behind them.

For the next three days they followed the trail from Sandy Creek until they found the place where the Indians changed course and headed east just as they old trapper predicted they would with no concern for covering the trail they left behind them.

Kincaid knew they would detour South Pass, cross the summit through the rugged mountains on treacherous game trails, and then exit the eighty-mile long bowl at Muddy Gap.

The fresh tracks of the renegades hammered the ground into a clear path that headed in a direct line up the western slope of the Divide. The three searchers swung their horses out onto the trail in pursuit.

Sweat foamed on the breast collars of the pack animals, and the headstalls of the saddle horses ran wet and shiny. The horses' sides heaved as the fagged animals sucked in the thin air and plodded upward. Kincaid gauged the spent horses' stamina and finally pulled off the trail and dismounted.

"Get off and let 'em blow," he said.

Franklin drank from his canteen and wiped the back of his hand across his mouth to catch the dripping water as it ran down his chin. He offered the canteen to Brady. Brady shook him off.

Standing next to Buffalo Dancer, Brady loosened the stallion's cinch, then walked him in the shade to cool out. The buckskin snorted as it dropped its head to nip the tops off the tender clumps of grass that grew where the sun warmed the ground between the thick stands of trees. Brady moved slowly around, checking his horse's feet and legs, then did the same with his pack horse. The load was secure, there was no galling from the rigging, and both horses were now breathing easier. He re-tightened the cinch on his saddle and looked impatiently over at Kincaid.

"Travis," he said, with annoyance in his voice. "Can we get going?"

"Brady look at these damn horses. They're plum wore out."

Brady's impatience showed in his expression.

"I know what you're thinking," Kincaid said. "But these horses need to rest, just like those Indians do. They don't know we're after them, so it ain't like they're trying to outrun us. If they did know, they'd likely as not turn back and take care of this little business just for the amusement of finishing off what they started in the first place."

Kincaid was right and Brady knew it, but that didn't make it any easier.

By nightfall they had climbed to a point just below the summit when darkness forced them to stop. They made no fire. They had no supper. When they wrapped themselves in their thin blankets, all three shivered and tried to sleep with hunger gnawing at their insides, while they waited for morning.

An hour before daybreak Kincaid had the pack horses loaded and his own mount saddled when he woke the boys. The moon hung low in the sky, inviting only the slightest suggestion of dawn at the rim of the sharp ridge to the east.

They rode out in the dark urging the worn out horses up the steep grade. The horses plodded and their breath smoked out in front of them in great plumes in the frigid air. Brady's teeth chattered. He held his arms tight against his chest and looked over at Franklin. If Franklin was cold, he didn't show it, and Kincaid seemed impervious to every discomfort, including starvation.

They hadn't eaten in more than a day. Their thin packs now deplete of all but a partial sack of salt and a handful of beans. As the sky begin to light up in the dim glow of dawn, Brady was on the lookout for anything that might make a meal, but saw nothing.

Gradually the sun shone in their faces from an oblique angle and the horses lunged up the last brutal uplift of the steep grade where they emerged from the dark forest to gaze down onto the Great Divide Basin below.

The air was cool and the rich colors of morning brushed across the landscape in spectacular shades of blue and green and ochre. In the shade of a spruce a young buck raised its head, on high alert, sniffing the air and switching its tail, scanning the highlands with nervous, darting eyes.

Kincaid hushed the boys, raised his rifle, and squeezed the trigger. The buck fell where it stood.

He looked across at the boys who watched him with wonder in their eyes, no longer surprised at anything he did.

"Fetch the two hind quarters and leave the rest. That shot could be our undoing."

By day's end, with their stomach's full and their packs loaded with venison, Kincaid and the boys exited the east end of the basin and followed the trail north where it crossed Muddy Gap. They forged the Sweet Water River following the tracks leading them ever eastward and deeper into Indian Territory.

The trail skirted the north bank of the river for nearly three miles before Kincaid pulled his horse up and cursed.

"Damn it. I knew it."

"What?" Franklin asked, his voice nervous and uncertain.

Kincaid swung down from the saddle and led his horse behind him as he studied the tracks that appeared no different here than they did earlier as far as the boys could see. Kincaid knelt and traced a series of prints with his fingertips. The he stood and gazed out across the rolling hills of the grassy prairie.

"What?" Franklin asked again.

"They split up on us."

"What do you mean?"

"Twenty or thirty of them never came out on this side of the river."

"Where'd they go?" Franklin asked.

"I should have caught it sooner. I just didn't figure it out until we got to this stretch of softer ground."

Kincaid remounted.

"Brady, you stay with the horses."

Brady nodded as he took up the lead ropes of the pack horses.

"Franklin, you come with me."

"Where we going?"

"Back to the river. We got to find where the rest of the war party came out and where they're heading."

"You thinking they're on to us?" Franklin asked.

"Could be."

They rode the riverbank, Kincaid downstream, Franklin upstream.

Thirty minutes later, Kincaid came galloping back bouncing to a stop where Brady stood with the horses. He swung down from the saddle with great urgency to his voice.

"They used the river to cover the tracks where they split up. Get Franklin back here. We got to move fast here on out."

Kincaid reset the loads on the packhorses while Brady galloped out after Franklin.

Kincaid and the boys sat their horses overlooking the spot where the second set of tracks came out of the water and headed north.

Brady's expression was one of anger and frustration. With two trails to follow, they would have to pick one or the other. Either they had been outsmarted by the warriors knowing they couldn't follow both sets of tracks, or the renegades were on to them and this was a trap. Either way, Brady knew this was the end of the trail for them.

TWENTY-NINE

As Kincaid and the boys stood at the river's edge contemplating the departing set of new tracks, Brady exploded.

"What now, Travis? I know you're gonna say we can't follow 'em both."

Kincaid turned to regard Brady as he let the outburst hang there before he responded.

"The fact is, we can't follow them both."

"Well, we ain't quitting." Brady snapped back.

Kincaid ignored the outburst and nudged his horse in the direction of the new tracks. Franklin followed and Brady sat there undecided before he fell in behind Franklin and soon they rode three abreast following the new tracks into unknown territory.

Brady rode alongside Kincaid a long time before Kincaid spoke.

"I'm betting the Sioux went with this bunch," Kincaid said, nodding toward the tracks on the ground. "They're heading east toward Sioux country. If I'm right, the big part of the war party will turn south and start back to their own country once they reach the flatland."

Brady clinched his jaw and gritted his teeth. "Well, that's a lot of tracks and we didn't see that many Sioux with the Comanche. Why would they all leave and go this way?"

"I don't know," Kincaid said.

They descended the mountain and crossed the foothills. The smaller war party made no effort to cover their tracks, but as the land leveled out it was dry and hard and rocky and the trail became more difficult to follow. When sign was clear it showed the tracks of twenty-three, maybe twenty-four horses, all headed east and moving at a brisk pace. Not hurried, but deliberate.

The temperature at the lower elevations turned hot. Kincaid and the boys tied their coats on behind their saddles, squinting into the sunlight with sweat running down their backs.

The treed foothills flattened into a broad plain of golden grass, and the only trees that grew were those at the creek banks and springs. The trackers pressed on, stopping only to rest the horses or take water when they could. They ate dried strips of venison and never made a fire. Rest came only as a necessity, and they did not stop long in one place.

Kincaid rode ahead. Brady and Franklin followed with the packhorses. At the top of a shallow bluff Kincaid waited and surveyed the terrain. The boys approached and Kincaid walked back toward them, leading his horse.

"Well boys, looks like this is it," he said, as he paused and looked over the broad expanse of earth that lie before them.

Travis' voice sounded resolute, and he looked over at the younger boy.

Brady bristled. "What do you mean this is it?" He shook his head. "We ain't quittin'," he said, setting his jaw and glaring back at the cowboy.

"Yeah, come on Travis, we done come too far to give up now," Franklin added.

Kincaid looked up at the boys and shook his head. "We're not quitting. Get down off your horses, I want to show you something."

With puzzled looks on their faces, the boys followed Kincaid to a nondescript patch of bare ground.

The hard, red, dirt was rocky and dry, but it didn't look any different than a hundred other places they passed that morning.

"See them brush marks?" Kincaid said, pointing out barely visible lines among the many sets of hoof prints.

As they walked on, Kincaid showed the boys where, one by one, five sets of brush marks left the trail in a northerly direction.

"What does that mean?" Brady asked.

"Well, it looks like the Sioux are heading home, and the Comanche are covering the trail for them."

"Travis, that don't look like nothing," Franklin said. "All them horse tracks go this way," he said, whipping his hand straight down the trail.

"That's how they want it to look," said Kincaid. "It's an old Comanche trick. The lead riders tie onto loose brush and drag it behind while the others ride over the trail. When the brush-draggers pull out they don't leave a mark, and everything else looks pretty much the same. Next thing you know, there's one less set of tracks in the bunch and a fella won't even miss them in the count," Kincaid said.

"Now, look at this," he said, walking along an invisible line where he claimed the brush-dragger rode.

"This one got a little careless, or maybe the brush rolled over, but he left a mark."

Sure enough, one unshod hoof print stood out just as clear as if someone had left a road sign.

"These marks are your Sioux heading for home. The rest of these tracks will head straight down the trail far enough to cover the cut-offs, then they'll turn south to join up with the rest of the band."

Kincaid counted five sets of brush tracks he knew belonged to the Sioux. The prospect of catching up with five Sioux renegades was far more reassuring than the long-shot odds of surviving another encounter with a full war party.

"Boys, it looks like things are starting to fall our way," Kincaid said. "We got a chance if we can catch up before they run in with the rest of their tribe," he added, with a broad sweeping motion that took in thousands of miles of prairie.

THIRTY

Five proud young warriors rode the Medicine Root River deep into their home country. Three beleaguered white riders followed.

The victorious ones carried scalps and trade rifles and rode with patchwork quilts laid across the backs of their ponies. In a few days, they would be welcomed home, bragging late into the night of their great battle and showing off the prized yellow-haired scalps dried with the blood of their victims. It would be a time of celebration and a joyful reunion for the warrior-boys who, in their arrogance, inadvertently left a clear trail behind them.

Kincaid and the boys pushed their horses unrelentingly through the heat of the day. By late afternoon, Franklin's packhorse pulled a tendon. They stopped, unpacked the panniers, stripped the horse of his rigging, pulled its shoes, and turned it out to fend for itself. Cursing their bad luck they rode hard to make up for the delay.

At dusk the trail turned and headed out across a rocky, alkaline flat. The hard ground and long distance finally got the best of Kincaid's packhorse. The poor beast stopped and hung its head, unable to go any further. Kincaid split up the ammunition and venison between the saddle horses and Brady's one remaining packhorse. What they couldn't carry, they left behind.

They traveled until Kincaid signaled for a stop where they dismounted near a small spring. Kincaid studied the area in the light of a full moon. The soft moist ground near the water had been walked over by the tracks of unshod ponies and moccasins.

"It's them," he said. "And they ain't more than a few hours ahead of us."

Brady and Franklin exchanged hard looks. There was no quit in either of them. They were tired and they were hungry, but when Kincaid said *mount up*, they watered the horses and remounted.

This was it. As much as Kincaid wanted to see things go another way, he knew they had to overtake the five renegades before the rejoined other members of their tribe.

The boys watched him in the moonlight, their eyes tired and red-rimmed. Their horses lumbered along sore and stiff-legged, but even they seemed to know this was a do-or-die mission for all concerned.

Moon shadows were sharp and the extra light gave Kincaid the advantage he needed to stay on the trail and shorten the lead the Sioux had on them.

Brady and Franklin watched carefully for the signs that led Kincaid through the rocks and over the hard ground. Brady dropped back and pulled his horse in close to Franklin. He looked across at his friend and whispered.

"How does he know where he's going?"

"I don't know," said Franklin. "I reckon it's something he learned from the Indians. He's acting strange, ain't he?"

Brady didn't reply. He just watched as Kincaid leaned low over the side of his horse's neck focused on the tracks he followed. The Big Dipper rotated to a vertical position in the northern sky.

In the light of the bright moon, they could see the trail continued due east, and then took a sharp turn that dropped off a precipitous slope strewn with granite scree. They stopped their horses and looked down the impossible incline.

Kincaid studied the slope. "They made it, we can make it. he said.

Brady pointed out a more gradual route that circumvented the slope. "Maybe they went that way."

Kincaid shook his head. "That's another hour we don't have."

Kincaid started down first. The going was treacherous. Kincaid let the horse have its head. A few more tentative steps, and then the loose rock gave way. The horse's front legs slid out from beneath it, and it plunged downward headfirst, rolling, sliding, and tumbling, end-over-end with Kincaid flopping in the saddle like a ragdoll.

The horse rolled over on top of Kincaid. He managed to kick free of the stirrups, but could not avoid the horse as it crashed over him a second time, coming to rest at the bottom of the slope with the horse pinning him to the rocks.

Brady and Franklin watched as the scene seemed to go on forever. When it stopped, both horse and rider lay motionless in a bloody heap at the bottom of the washed-out draw.

The boys swung down from their saddles and slid down the loose scree in their heels. They got to Kincaid lying face-down in a puddle of blood. The horse, lying ten feet away, was alive, but unable to stand. In the bright moonlight they could see Kincaid's face covered with blood. There was no sign of life as Franklin pulled him up by his shirt and shook him. "Travis!

Kincaid hung limp and unresponsive. Franklin pressed his fingers to Kincaid's carotid artery alongside his neck.

"Brady, get me a canteen," he shouted to his young friend, who knelt beside him. Brady scrambled up the hill.

Franklin held Kincaid and watched Brady taking forever. Then Kincaid moaned, and blood oozed from his mouth when he tried to speak. Kincaid's glazed eyes stared into the darkness, unfocused and darting. He did not try to move as he struggled to regain his senses.

Brady returned with the canteen and a rag.

"Is he alive?" Brady asked.

"He's hurt bad, but he's alive. Give me that water," Franklin said, as he reached for the canteen.

Franklin poured the water over Kincaid's face. The cowboy pulled himself up slowly into a sitting position. Diluted blood ran freely from his nose and mouth. Kincaid reached out and clutched the canteen. He took a small amount of water into his mouth, then spit it out, thick with blood. He tried to blow his nose, but it was swollen and painful and plugged with broken cartilage and bloody mucus.

"Son-of-a-bitch broke my nose," Kincaid mumbled through puffed lips.

"It looked like that horse killed you," Brady said.

Kincaid seemed to be recovering. "Did he get back up?"

"No, but he ain't dead," Franklin said, nodding toward the bottom of the draw.

Kincaid looked up at Brady.

"Take your knife. Go down and check him out. If he's still alive, cut his throat."

Brady looked at Kincaid. He hesitated, hoping Kincaid would reconsider and send Franklin.

"What if he's okay?"

"He ain't."

"Can't we just shoot him?"

"We're too close. We can't risk a shot. Go on now."

Brady started down the steep incline. At the bottom of the ravine he approached the downed horse slowly, talking softly to him. He moved in closer, hoping the horse would be dead.

When he knelt at the head of the horse, it turned a big eye toward him. Brady never felt more helpless.

The horse lurched, but was unable to stand. When the horse dropped its head and its legs ceased thrashing, the boy sat and rested the horse's head on his lap. He looked into the trusting eye of the big animal, covered it gently with one hand, then thrust the knife deeply into the big jugular vein and wept while the warm blood ran out onto his trousers and pooled where he sat.

The horse flinched. Brady felt the blood pouring across his hand until the animal began to relax. Brady held the head and whispered to the horse long after the eye closed and the air expelled from its lungs.

Finally, Brady lay the head down, put up his knife, walked a few steps, and then vomited.

He spat and wiped the tears from his eye. He couldn't look at the horse's face when he returned to it and stripped it of its saddle and bridle.

He drug Kincaid's gear to the top of the escarpment, and then returned to help Franklin get Kincaid up to the camp they made for the night.

They rested until morning, taking turns watching over Kincaid.

In the light of day, Kincaid looked far worse than he did the night before. Aside from the broken nose, the cuts, and abrasions, he survived with no broken bones.

When they rode out at just after dawn, they traveled light, carrying only what food and ammunition would fit into their bedrolls and saddle bags. Kincaid rode Brady's packhorse. He was miserable. Both eyes black, his nose battered into a shapeless, purple bulb, and the skin from his eyes to his upper lip stretched tight from the swelling.

For the first half of the day, Kincaid snorted and spat gagging wads of mucus and coagulated blood. With his eyes puffed to the point the narrow slits barely let in enough light for him to see, Kincaid struggled to stay upright.

Franklin rode point and studied the tracks as carefully as did Kincaid. He took on many of Kincaid's mannerisms, none of which Brady missed.

They followed the tracks that the Sioux warriors now made no effort to cover. Then, somewhere in the shadowless heat of midday, the additional tracks of two unshod ponies joined those of the five Sioux warriors.

THIRTY-ONE

The endless flatness of the country converged with gently rolling hills barren of trees and woody vegetation except where a creek ran or a spring surfaced. Kincaid and the boys rode up out of a long ravine. Franklin pointed off in the distance and pulled the grey-eyed paint up sharply.

"Travis, ain't that a fire up yonder?"

Kincaid tilted his head back and squinted through puffy eyelids.

"It's them," he said. He thought a moment before he spoke again. He looked at the boys. They stared at him.

"We could leave it here," he finally said.

Brady's expression hardened and Franklin's jaw clinched.

"Evening up one killing with another ain't always the right answer."

The boys looked at him a long time. Kincaid coughed, snorted, and spit out a bloody wad.

Brady seemed to be softening. Franklin waited. Brady was expressionless when he responded. He looked Kincaid directly in the eyes.

"This time it is," Brady said.

Franklin nodded. "Let's do what we came to do."

Kincaid drew a deep breath.

"Well, all right then," he said. "Only chance we got is to take them by surprise."

He dismounted, tied off his horse, and motioned the boys down. He nodded to a low spot in the ravine before them.

"Tie off them horses. We're going on foot from here."

The boys tied off the horses, and took stock of their weapons. Each carried a rifle, a handgun, and a belt knife. They checked the weapons.

"Won't be no time to reload," Kincaid said. Then he stuck out his hand to Franklin.

"Whichever way it goes, you boys done your families proud."

Franklin shook his hand and Kincaid turned to Brady. They shook hands.

"We won't know what to do 'til we get there," Kincaid said. "So stay low, keep quiet, and shoot straight."

They skirted a shallow draw into the trees, then followed a slow-moving creek in the direction of the campfire smoke. Further down in the meadow beyond the campfire, stood seven Indian ponies hobbled and grazing in the tall grass.

Kincaid and the boys inched up through the tangled brush to the edge of the shaded clearing where the Sioux lie spread out in the camp to sleep through the heat of the day.

Kincaid signaled the boys, pointing and holding up three fingers. As Kincaid searched the camp with his eyes, Franklin held up two fingers and pointed to a partially concealed spot in the brush where one of the braves and a young girl lay together bare-skinned.

Brady spotted the other two nearby in the brush to his left, not far from where the horses grazed. A copper-skinned Indian girl lay peacefully in the arms of her young warrior. Their eyes closed and their bare bodies in a deep sleep on a settler's quilt spread out on the ground.

Kincaid signaled to Franklin to cover the pair nearest him, and then made his way to an advantaged position over the three sleeping warriors. He signaled Brady to cover the sleeping girl and the brave on the quilt.

From where he stood, not ten yards away, Brady had a clear line of sight on the girl and her sleeping warrior companion. Brady's heart pounded, his mouth went dry and his breathing was short and rapid. His hands shook. He checked his handgun and looked down to make sure the hammer was cocked on his rifle.

One of the hobbled ponies raised its head and tested the air with flared nostrils. Then another raised its head. The first pony pawed the ground and snorted and, when it caught the full scent of the white men, it tossed its head and whinnied.

Everything happened at once. Brady heard gunfire echo out in volleys from downstream where Kincaid and Franklin were positioned. There were too many shots fired. Brady knew the renegades were returning fire. Instantly, all the memories of the long night of the massacre came back to him, and Brady seethed with fear and anger.

He stepped into the clearing and screamed at the warrior and the girl as they sat rigid and stared up at him with terror-stricken eyes.

"Stand up!"

Brady hesitated. Before him sat a young girl, not much more than a child. Her face was one of innocence and she covered herself and, for a moment, Brady felt embarrassed.

Without his war paint, the warrior looked like a schoolkid, no more than fifteen or sixteen years old. The boy's terrified expression was nothing like the vile image Brady carried in his memory from the morning after the massacre.

The Indian boy looked up at Brady with the same soft-eyed innocence he saw in the girl.

They're just kids, Brady thought to himself. He had second thoughts and relaxed his grip on the rifle, but stood unmoving. Two more shots cracked in the brush.

Franklin's voice followed. "B.C. where are you at?"

"Over here." Brady yelled. "I got two of 'em."

Franklin crashed his way through the brush and into the clearing. When he beheld the unclothed pair, he tilted his head in the direction from which he had come so as to avoid looking directly at them.

"Travis wants you to bring them two over to the fire." He pointed in the direction of the smoke.

"What happened?" Brady asked.

"They fired on us, and Travis got all three of them."

Franklin glanced at the boy and the girl, and then continued talking. "Travis is holding the other one with his girlfriend over there," Franklin said, nodding over his shoulder.

Brady motioned with his rifle for the boy and girl to stand up. When they did, the boy stepped out to the side in full view, covering himself with his hands. Brady's expression ran cold and his hands trembled. Franklin looked at Brady then back at the boy. The young brave's face drained of all expression and his eyes filled with fear. He reached to his throat and tore away the gold chain and locket and dropped it at Brady's feet.

The girl recoiled and held her arms tight around herself when the boy began pleading for his life. The girl sobbed and held her hands to her mouth, and she too pleaded over and over again.

"Come on B.C., let's get them back to Travis," Franklin said in a soft voice.

Brady relaxed his grip on the rifle, and tears threatened his red-rimmed eyes. The warrior made a sign of gratitude with his right hand and, when he brought his left hand up to his face, Brady recognized his father's wedding band on the boy's thumb.

A deafening report caused Franklin and the girl to recoil and the fifty caliber ball from Brady's rifle split the boy's chest and sent him twisting to the ground. Brady lunged forward, straddled the boy's back, jerked his head back by the hair, and then reached for his knife.

"No," Franklin screamed as he wrestled Brady off the warrior's back. "He's dead. That's enough."

Franklin stood back. He looked at Brady. There was no remorse or regret in Brady's eyes and Franklin knew not to push the issue. Brady sheathed his knife. Franklin picked up the locket and removed the ring from the dead hand.

Brady stood over the body and glared, his breathing heavy, his heart full of hate. The girl wailed hysterically and stood quivering with her hands covering her mouth. Franklin, himself visibly shaken, took pity on the girl and handed her the deerskin dress at her feet.

"Come on B.C.," he said, as he led his friend and the young girl back to the campfire.

When last Indian boy saw only the girl and realized he was the only one of the war party still alive, he panicked and bolted, disappearing immediately into the heavy brush along the creek with Franklin right behind him.

Kincaid waved his arm in the direction of the trail to where the Indian ponies grazed.

"Brady, cover the trail. I'll get the other side of the creek," he shouted as he splashed across the water and into the heavy brush along its banks.

Franklin crashed through the brush blindly, right on the heels of the young Sioux, who quickly disappeared.

When he lost sight of the renegade, Franklin stopped to listen. All he heard was his heart pounding.

His eyes darted back and forth. He stood in the eerie stillness and waited. Suddenly, he felt his head snap back, an arm across his eyes, and the impact of the Indian's knee against his spine as he was driven to the ground. Franklin attempted to scream for help but a berry vine across his throat cut his air off.

Franklin's lungs burned, his face flushed red. He worked the fingertips of one hand under the vine and clawed frantically at it. The warrior pulled it tighter. Franklin dropped his pistol and, with his free hand, grappled for the knife at his side. His fingers found the handle. He jerked the knife out and slashed wildly at the boy behind him. He felt the knife penetrate and he slashed again and again.

He reached over his head, took a handful of hair and pulled the warrior up and over his shoulders, driving him to the ground. Franklin stopped, gasping for air and, when he turned to the warrior, the renegade held Franklin's handgun. He took aim, but his hands faltered, and in that moment of hesitation Franklin set upon him with the knife in a wild frenzy until the young warrior lay limp and bloody at his feet.

Franklin staggered to the creek. When he reached the water he dropped to his knees. He submerged his hands and watched a long time as the water ran red with blood. He stayed like that until the water ran clear and sat there starring after Kincaid walked in beside him.

Kincaid laid his hand on Franklin's shoulder. "You okay?"

Franklin looked up at him. His expression was old and ancient. He shook his head.

"No, I'm not," he said.

Kincaid understood.

They walked back to the camp where Brady stood over the two young girls who huddled together trembling— neither girl able to comprehend the brutality they had just witnessed.

Brady and Franklin stood mute with blank expressions waiting for Kincaid to tell them what to do next. Kincaid became more authoritative than they had ever seen him.

"Fetch their horses . . . all of them."

Brady appeared resistant. Franklin saw it and he braced for trouble. Kincaid saw it too, and he pushed past it.

"We did what we came to do."

Brady looked over at Franklin for confirmation. Franklin nodded.

Kincaid indicated the dead. "We'll wrap them in their blankets and tie them on their horses so these girls can take them home and give them a proper burial."

While the boys caught up the horses Kincaid bundled each of the bodies in a blanket. He tied them off, and when the boys returned they secured each of the lifeless bundles to an Indian pony and handed the lead ropes to the girls.

Hatred burned in the eyes of the girls but fear kept them from speaking out. Kincaid tried to explain to them in his stilted Lakota tongue, but he didn't have the words, and they didn't have the inclination to listen. He stopped mid-sentence and waved them off.

The young girls swung up, one leading two ponies, the other leading three. When they set off across the shifting grasslands, neither looked back. They would return to their camp and tell of the lustful savagery of the whiteman and his taste for mindless violence.

Kincaid and the boys watched them until they disappeared into the horizon.

Finally, Brady looked over at Kincaid.

"Why did it have to be like that?"

Kincaid just shook his head. "It's been like that since the beginning of time."

THIRTY-TWO

Kincaid and the boys never spoke again of the massacre or the bitter revenge they wrought upon the five young Sioux warriors whose blood stained the sand at an un-named creek in a place they would never see again. There was no pride in what they had done—no satisfaction and no remorse. They let the nightmare end there.

Now, as they rode the trail back toward Fort Bridger, there was an absence of purpose. For Franklin and Brady there was nothing left but uncertainty. Kincaid sensed it. He felt it himself. But Kincaid was overdue to get on with his own life and in no position to further burden himself with two boys he was convinced would be better off in California.

Kincaid knew he could arrange accommodations for their trip once they reached Bridger. He would return to Montana and the boys would manage on their own.

The sun was full-up when the boys awoke the next morning to the sound and smell of their first campfire in more days than either could recall. Franklin and Brady pulled on their boots and stood next to Kincaid where they all three stared into the fire.

"Morning."

"Morning, Travis."

"Morning, Travis."

"I worked out a plan last night," Kincaid said.

"So did we," Franklin said.

Kincaid ignored Franklin.

"I'll get you to Fort Bridger, get you lined up with someone heading to California, and that'll be it," Kincaid said, as he splashed the last of his coffee into the flame.

"And that'll be what?" Brady asked.

"My obligation to you two."

Franklin stood up to his full height and looked Kincaid straight in the eye.

"That ain't a good plan, Travis."

Franklin spoke in his most responsible sounding voice. "We can't just up and leave you to fight it out on the rundown place a yours on your own after all you did for us."

"We're coming with you to Montana to help you get your ranch going," Brady said.

"Like hell you are."

Franklin was firm. "We already decided."

"Well, it ain't up to you," Kincaid said.

"We ain't dumping you like that," Franklin said.

Kincaid laughed. "You dumping me?"

"Come on, Travis. You don't have no one either," Brady said. "We'll be good help. You know we will."

Franklin looked at Kincaid. His expression softened, and he smiled that rogue smile of his.

"Try it for the winter, Travis. If it looks like you're going to be okay, or something goes wrong, me and B.C. will line out for California come springtime."

Kincaid took off his hat. He wrung his face in his hands and slapped the dust off his trouser leg with the hat as he shook his head.

"Look, it's hard work. It gets lonely . . . and damn cold. There ain't even a decent place to live in there. The answer is no."

Brady watched Franklin's expression turn to the whipped puppy look he was so familiar with when Franklin would find himself with his back against the wall.

"Okay, we understand," Franklin said softly.

"I'm sorry, boys. There's just no other way."

"You know we got no one and nothing waiting for us in California? Right?" Franklin asked after a long uncomfortable silence.

Kincaid didn't respond. He studied the two young faces. *These boys have already seen the bottom end of it*, he said to himself. He turned, packed his cup in his saddlebag, and then looked back over his shoulder.

"I ain't gonna be your momma," he said.

Franklin grinned.

Kincaid turned to face the boys. "Let's give it a go. If it works, it works. If it don't, it don't"

The three riders sat their horses at the tree line looking down upon a vast parkland. It wasn't much of a ranch. A one-room cabin stood at the far end of the valley against the base of a gentle-sided mountain. It was built sturdy but the chinking was in poor repair and it needed a door. In the wide meadow a river split and made up two sides of a small pasture fenced with lodgepoles and thick with grass.

The grass grew green and tall in the valley laid at an east-west tilt, protecting it from the prevailing north wind and lending itself to mild winters. Kincaid defined the ranch in terms of the area it covered from one mountain peak to another, and it covered an area more than a man could ride in three days.

The first day at the ranch Kincaid stood on a flat area of clear ground and used a pointer he carved from a pine bough. He sketched his vision for the layout of the place as he drew the lines in the soft dirt for Brady and Franklin to see. He showed them winter pastures and summer feeding grounds and corrals and barns and he filled it in with cattle and good horses and, when he had finished, his vision was etched into the imagination of both boys.

Then Kincaid smoothed a spot in the dirt with his boot. He used the stick to draw three circles at the corners of an imaginary triangle.

"This will be our brand," he said. "We'll call it the Triple Dot and burn it into the hides of the best cattle and the best horses in the territory."

And so it began, a magnificent dream larger than life itself. For the next six years they put all their time and energy into building one of the largest cattle operations north of the Canadian River. With windfall profits from army contracts and the cooperation of the Blackfoot Indians, the three cattlemen were able to expand the ranch, which included two divisions: the Gallatin, and the Ennis Lake Ranch.

With a growing demand for broke horses as the military expanded into one outpost after the other, Kincaid brought broodmares up from Texas and crossed them on Brady's stud, Buffalo Dancer. Soon, the buckskin and dun-colored offspring of Buffalo Dancer established a reputation for speed and stamina that made them the most sought after horses in the territory.

Only Triple Dot mares were bred to the buckskin sire. No outside mares were covered and only mares and geldings were sold off the ranch, insuring that the topside bloodlines would remain within control of the Triple Dot Ranches.

When the boys decided to stay on after that first year, Kincaid promised them each a one-third share of every new calf and every foal that hit the ground from that day forward. A nod and a handshake cemented the partnership.

Cold Montana winters and short mountain summers forged the boys into men. Travis Kincaid galvanized their youthful minds with a discipline for hard work, a sense of honor in their business dealings and more horse and cow knowledge than most men learn in a lifetime.

Franklin and Brady threw themselves into the business and, when he was fourteen, Brady was sent by Kincaid to negotiate an army beef contract, which he was sure they had little or no chance of getting in the first place. Brady, more out of naiveté than good business skill, brought back an agreement to supply not only beef, but horses as well and at prices that virtually guaranteed the success of the ranch.

By the early spring of '47, the boys could no longer deny their restlessness. Franklin was almost twenty-two, and Brady had just turned seventeen. It was time to see what the rest of the world had to offer.

It was an agonizing decision for both the boys. They owed everything to Travis Kincaid. Their love for the man and the ranch they grew up on pulled at them with a force so strong neither boy could be the first to verbalize the feelings that now ran deeply in both of them.

Brady and Franklin sat in the mid-morning shade near the corrals where they had been since daybreak, branding, castrating and doctoring the new crop of calves.

While they waited in the shade for the cowboys to bring in the next bunch of cattle, Brady put his hat on his knee and wiped the sweat from his forehead with the back of his gloved hand. He kept his head down, but directed his eyes toward Franklin.

"You'll be about twenty-two here in a few weeks won't you, old-timer?"

"Damn sure will. What's it to you?" Franklin said, sticking his chin out defiantly.

"Oh, I was just thinking," Brady said, leaning back against the tree.

Franklin refused to give him the satisfaction of his curiosity. Brady finally broke the silence again.

"I'd sure like to see some of them places Charlie talks about, where he traps up north."

"Not me," said Franklin. "I'm more inclined toward a little more civilization. Eating fancy food off real plates where the women smell good and someone else washes the dishes, if you know what I mean."

"Like what Travis tells us about San Francisco?"

"Exactly. Or something close to it."

"Do you think we'll ever do any of that?" Brady asked in a serious tone that told Franklin this was more than one of their wishful-thinking discussions.

"You never know," Franklin said with a look that suggested he knew something Brady didn't know.

That conversation was the beginning of a major turning point for the boys. They talked about it a lot. Then they began making plans and setting deadlines for themselves. Finally, they acknowledged the last obstacle and decided it was time to tell Kincaid.

At the supper table one night in late summer, Kincaid pushed his empty plate away, got up, walked over to the big, stone fireplace and retrieved three long cigars from a tin on the mantle. He handed each of the boys a cigar and sat back down.

Brady and Franklin looked at each other in confusion. This was not like Kincaid. He would occasionally enjoy a cigar himself, but early on he laid down the law and absolutely forbid the boys to smoke or chew.

Kincaid passed the candle around then leaned back in his chair and let a billowy, blue cloud drift up toward the massive logs that made up the cross beams in the ceiling.

"You boys got anything you want to tell me?"

They shifted in their seats while they blew the smoke away from their faces.

Brady relit his cigar and cleared his throat.

Franklin took a long drag, made a circle with his lips and then, with his natural flair for showmanship, blew a thick lopsided smoke ring that floated irreverently across the room.

Brady kicked him under the table, and Franklin looked back at Kincaid.

"Actually, we do," Franklin said.

Brady watched the two, apprehensive and wishing they had left the topic for another time, but Franklin was not to be deterred.

"We always come out and say what's on our minds, right?" he said.

Kincaid nodded. "That's right."

"Well . . ." Franklin appeared to stall.

Kincaid smiled. "You boys thinking about seeing a little more of the world?"

Brady looked up at Kincaid, and then over at Franklin.

Franklin stood. "Well, things are caught up pretty good around here. We got help, so's it's not like you'd be left high and dry. We'd expect the cost of the help to come out of our shares."

"Franklin, you know it's not the money. Hell, we got more than we ever figured on anyway."

Kincaid moved near the fireplace, sat on down in his big chair, crossed his boots on the hearth. He took a draw on his cigar.

"What are you figuring to do?"

Franklin nodded to Brady.

"Well, I was thinking to do some trapping with ol' Charlie. He said he would help me get started."

Kincaid flicked his ashes into the fireplace. "There's a lot to be said about trapping. Some good, some bad, but I think it's something you'd be good at."

Kincaid took another drag. "You given any thought to what it will take to get started?"

"According to Charlie, it will take about $200 to get set up. And, I'll need a packhorse and a good saddlehorse."

"You thinking about taking Buffalo Dancer?"

"If you don't think it will hurt our breeding program."

Kincaid smiled. "He's ready to go. We got good sons of his working, so it won't hurt to take him out at all."

Kincaid could see Brady was still a bit uncertain.

"I trapped some when I was about your age, Brady. Best decision I ever made. I learned a lot and don't regret a minute of it."

Brady deferred to Franklin. Kincaid turned his attention that direction in time to see Franklin loft another smoke ring into the air.

"Something tells me trapping isn't in your plans."

Franklin uncrossed his boots from the hearth and leaned forward in his chair.

"No sir. I'm thinking a man of my proclivities is better suited for a more cosmopolitan lifestyle than that to which I was born."

Kincaid laughed. Brady stared in wonder.

"Where in the world did that come from?" Kincaid asked.

Franklin grinned. "I been reading them books you gave us. *The Cricket on the Hearth* made me think of that."

Brady was amazed. He read most of the books as well, and couldn't remember much from any of them.

Kincaid's tone took a serious turn.

"You thinking about going back east, then?"

Franklin shook his head. "San Francisco. Just something about what you told us appeals to me."

Kincaid sat back to take it all in. "There's no good time to do what you boys need to do . . . and I guess there ain't no bad time either. But you know this is your home. Don't lose sight of that. And don't feel like you ever drifted so far or so deep you can't come back."

Both boys stood and moved to the fireplace to stand near where Kincaid sat.

Franklin spoke first. "Travis, we owe you everything. We know this is home. The three of us are the only family we all got. That won't ever change."

He reached out and squeezed Kincaid's shoulder.

"We'll be back, Travis," Brady said. "You pretty much raised us to be how we are, so you're stuck with us."

Kincaid laughed. "I been trying to get rid of you two since the day we met. It just took a lot longer than I expected."

Kincaid pulled his feet down and leaned forward. The boys sat on the hearth. Kincaid took a pull on his cigar.

"So, tell me about your plans."

"Well," said Brady, looking over at Franklin for reassurance, "I'll be heading out soon with Charlie so's we can get setup before winter sets in."

Kincaid turned toward Franklin. Franklin looked up at the ceiling beams doing a calculation in his head. "I figure it'll take me about eight-hundred dollars in cash. I'll need, a pack horse, that stripped-legged mule and, a course, I'll stick with Three Feathers for my saddle horse. He's still got some good miles left in him."

"Good as done," Kincaid said. "Any idea what you'll do when you get to California?"

"I can't rightly say that I do, but I figure that'll work itself out when I get there."

From there, talk ran late into the night. The lantern wick was burning low when the three friends finished their reminiscing about the past six years together.

A week later the boys were packed. They shook hands all around. Outside the gate Franklin turned his outfit to the southwest, while Brady and Charlie took the trail north.

Just before the trail dropped away toward the river Brady turned in the saddle and waved for the last time to Travis, who now stood barely visible alone on the porch of the cabin.

Brady was quiet. He felt an emptiness settle over him. He wondered if he would ever again see Franklin and Travis. His thoughts were filled with a mixture of anticipation and apprehension. This was a glorious turning point in his life, yet he felt he was riding away from the closest thing he may ever have to a family and a home. He turned to Charlie and nodded up the trail, and then they were off.

Suddenly, the frantic sound of hoof beats pounded up behind them. Brady and Charlie turned their horses, puzzled and a little unnerved. Charlie swung his rifle to the other side of his saddle in the direction of the approaching horseman.

Through the intermittent breaks in the trees, Brady could make out the unmistakable sorrel and white markings of Three Feathers. Franklin waved his hat and yelled as he galloped toward them.

"B.C., hey B.C., hold up."

Franklin was out of breath when he bounced to a stop alongside Buffalo Dancer.

"Give me your knife."

"What?"

"Just give me your knife."

Brady slipped the knife out of its sheath and started to hand it to Franklin.

"No, I mean the whole thing," Franklin said. "I need the sheath too."

Brady handed it to him. Then Franklin reached inside his shirt and pulled out the prized Gros Ventre knife with the beaded sheath.

"Here," he said. "I want you to have this."

"I can't take your knife," Brady said, trying to pass it back.

"Yes, you can. It'll bring you good luck and I'd feel a whole lot better if I knew you had it. Besides, I like yours better anyway."

Franklin slid Brady's knife under his pistol belt, turned back down the trail, and waved his hat as he called back over his shoulder.

"Charlie, you take care of B.C. or you're going to have to answer to me." Then he laughed a big laugh like his father used to and disappeared into the trees.

THIRTY-THREE

Charlie and Brady trapped and hunted the mountains and streams in an area that ranged from the Musselshell River in Montana Territory to the tip of the northern Rockies in the Canadian Territories. It was a time of magnificent discovery for Brady. Under Charlie's subtle guidance he learned how to find food and shelter in a land that appeared to be inhospitable. He learned how to read the signs of nature and how to anticipate and adjust to the ever-changing weather. He learned to balance the brutal necessity of survival with the gentle tranquility of the unspoiled wilderness. He learned to take nothing for granted except his own insignificance.

Most importantly, Charlie helped Brady to understand the close relationship the Indians had with the earth, and he taught Brady the delicate balance that existed in their way of life.

The old trapper held a high respect for the Blackfoot, Nez Perce and other tribes that allowed him to hunt their lands in peace, and Brady soon developed his own high regard for these people who accepted him, gave him a place by their fire, and shared their last food with him with the feeling they were honored to do so.

Brady adapted quickly. Their first year of trapping together was good. He loved the solitude of the wilderness and eagerly looked forward to the time he spent with his friends in the Blackfoot tribes. In quiet, thoughtful moments, Brady could not imagine himself living his life any other way.

Charlie knew when to push the boy and he knew when to let him succeed or fail on his own. And, just like Kincaid, Charlie was quick to recognize Brady's gentle heart and his independent spirit.

Their second winter blew in early and as brutal as any could remember, stranding the boy and the old trapper for days without letup. On the morning of the 11th day of the unrelenting storm, Charlie laid out their circumstances for the boy.

He stood at the door, swung it open and faced a wall of snow halfway up the opening.

"*Sacré bleu*," he shouted as he forced the door closed against the pressure of the snowbank and the howling wind.

"I tell you, boy. . ." He looked around the small room of the trapper's cabin. "If we don't get some meat back here now, we ain't getting out as long as this storm keeps up."

Brady knew that was coming.

"Let's go hunt us some meat," Charlie said.

Minutes later, they stood outside in the blowing snow, wrapped in skins, outfitted with snowshoes, and their rifles tied across their shoulder with a rawhide lace.

Charlie looked at the determined boy. "Get a beaver if you can, but anything will do."

Brady nodded. He understood. Charlie directed the boy upstream, and he set off snowshoeing the opposite direction.

On the second day, the snow stopped and Brady shot a 45-pound beaver coming out of the water near a willow break. He gutted the animal, sucked the warm blood pooled in the chest cavity, and headed back to the cabin with the frozen carcass slung over his back.

When he got there, Charlie was still out, but that wasn't unusual.

By the fifth day Charlie, the consummate hunter, had not yet returned to the cabin. Brady, fearing the worst, set out downstream in search of the old man. The drifts of fresh snow and the frigid temperature made the going slow.

Six miles downstream, no sign of Charlie, but the weather took a bad turn and it began to snow. Light flurries at first, and then heavy flakes floating down softly until the wind picked up, the light faded, and visibility began to diminish.

It was not unusual for Charlie to be a few days late, but this time Brady had a bad feeling—a premonition like the ones the Blackfoot medicine men claimed were a message from the Great Spirit.

Brady reached the bend in the river where Charlie had a trap line set. He searched for signs of his friend but the snow-covered ground showed only the disappearing footprints of an errant snowshoe rabbit.

Further downriver he found Charlie's mittens hanging from a tree branch near the water's edge, swinging by the rawhide thong that lashed them together.

Brady slogged another half mile downstream where he found a string of Charlie's traps piled in a reckless heap near the water's edge.

The sky darkened. Ahead, at a wide turn in the river, the water eddied into a pool around an ancient aspen shrouded in ice where it lay bent over the water and embraced in its bony branches, the frozen body of a man.

Brady stopped to stare. His heart pounded. His hands trembled. He stopped at the base of the giant tree, removed his snowshoes, and then crawled out to retrieve the unidentifiable body frozen to the branches. He struggled a long time to hack away the ice to free the body, praying it was not Charlie.

When Brady hauled the body to the bank, laid it on its back, and brushed the snow from its face, the crystallized eyes were those of a stranger and the frozen skin distorted the features, but the grey beard was that of the old trapper and, when he saw it was Charlie, Brady broke down.

He felt empty. He said a prayer, built a travois, then rigged the ice-covered body to it. Brady lifted the drag poles to his shoulders and set out upstream in the direction of the cabin.

He trudged through the deep snow until nightfall, and reckoned he had barely covered a mile. He built a shelter in the snow and slept. When he awoke it was still dark, blowing snow and frigidly cold. He huddled in his snow cave and looked upon the out-stretched arms and bent legs of the frozen body now covered in a thick blanket of white.

Brady waited until daybreak. When he stepped out of his cave, the wind had subsided, but the temperature remained unbearably cold.

He brushed the snow from the frozen body, hooked up the makeshift harness, and pressed on. He stopped only to drink. On the second night, he fashioned another snow cave, but never slept.

Three more days Brady inched his load forward. His strength gave out, and his reason for hauling the body was no longer clear to him. His determination drove him until he had nothing left to give.

He sat in the snow and fought to keep his eyes open. He stood and fell. He stood again, and drug the body forward a step—then another and another. This time he went down and did not get up.

Brady crawled to the leeward side of the frozen body and hunkered down behind it for protection from the wind. He did not remember going to sleep.

He awoke rudely to a fierce storm and a hand shaking him by the lapels of his coat. He sat upright, unaware of where he was or why he was there.

His snow-blind eyes did not recognize the blurred images of the Blackfoot hunters, but when he heard their voices he recognized them. He struggled to his feet, gestured toward the frozen body. The hunters shook their heads, urging Brady to leave the body.

Brady refused. They argued. Brady was unyielding.

When the hunters finally set out, they did so with Brady riding double with one, and the other with the travois lashed to his horse.

A day later, the superstitious Blackfoot left Brady inside the trapper cabin with the frozen body propped up outside the door.

Brady covered the cadaver with a tarp and spent the next ten days snowed in until the storm finally broke. That morning, the sun shone and the world outside the cabin was a crystal palace of ice and snow. Brady knew his trapping days were finished.

He gathered up what he could carry, set it outside, then dragged Charlie's body inside. He gathered dry brush and piled it high around the cabin. He said a prayer and then ignited the kindling.

He stood and watched the cabin burn a long time. The cinders flared and rose high into the cold air. Ash drifted on the gentle breeze. When the smoke rose high into the clear sky, Brady fell to his knees. For the second time in his life he watched the dark column of a funeral pyre carry his dreams away.

Brady's reign over this wooded kingdom trapping with his old friend had come to a close.

From the corral, Brady watched the fire until only the ashes smoldered. He saddled Buffalo Dancer and patted the neck of the old buckskin who seemed to sense their journey was far from over.

They traveled deep into Blackfoot country, Brady as lost as he had ever been. Brady crossed the Cut Bank River and rode up out of the water into the camp of the Blackfoot, he met with a mixed reception. Many were skeptical of the white man's presence in their camp.

After much consultation with the ancient shaman of the tribe, Brady won the confidence of the old man who blessed him and informed the chiefs that the boy was sent to them as an omen of good things to come. Brady vowed to earn their trust and to live up to the promises made by the shaman.

Brady spent the winter hunting with the Blackfoot and joining them in their battles with other tribes. He learned their ways and he learned the language. His hair grew long, his skin darkened by the sun, and his manner of dress became that of his warrior brothers. He greased and plaited his hair. He wore the trappings of his tribe and fell in with their nomadic ways.

For all appearances, Brady was as much Blackfoot as any of the young men his age. He was more Blackfoot than white, but an invisible line existed that he was never invited to cross. He was excluded from tribal rites ceremonies of a high-religious order and forbidden access to the medicine lodge.

His closest friends, two young warriors near his age, Shy Wolf and Otter Tail, embarrassed at Brady's obvious exclusion, made attempts to minimize the importance of the rituals. But it was not lost on Brady that Shy Wolf and Otter Tail took great pride in the scars they carried upon their chests from the rites of passage in the medicine lodge.

Late in the spring of 1850, when the weather was warm and dry, the tribe followed the buffalo to their summer feeding grounds along a grassy stretch of Birch Creek.

It felt good to be on the move again, to be on the hunt, to be out of the grip of winter. Women and children scurried about camp making preparations for the night-long celebration that always followed a successful harvest of the buffalo.

Outside the tipis, buffalo ponies stood painted and feathered. They pawed the ground and waited impatiently. Inside, the hunters passed the pipe and the medicine man prayed for a safe and bountiful hunt.

Brady sat with the hunters, his first ceremonial participation among the elders of the tribe. He drew from the pipe, exhaled the smoke and watched it drift upward, slowly spiraling toward the slash of daylight where it exited at the top of the lodge.

The strong tobacco dizzied Brady. He heard a far off rumbling. The ground beneath him shook. He looked about and the elders smiled. They paused momentarily. The rumbling intensified. The hunters rose as one to their feet and scrambled for the opening.

Outside, the horizon rose and fell like a giant ocean of black hides as an unending mass of thundering buffalo, like some apocalyptic dream, swarmed across the earth beneath a cloud of dust so immense it blocked the sun. So massive was the herd that it lacked all discernible definition as to its size.

Mothers panicked as a mass of stragglers turned in the direction of the camp. Dogs yelped. Horses tore loose from their tethers. Children scattered out of control as the people scrambled for safety across the creek to higher ground.

The massive black herd bore down upon the camp. There would be no turning the blindly stampeding herd. No stopping it, and no way to save anything in its path. The dust cloud closed on the camp at a frightening speed.

A mother's voice screamed. Her baby, a child of three or four years of age, stood crying, left behind in the path of the charging buffalo.

Brady and three other warriors looked across to see the stranded child at the same time. All four ran to their tethered horses, the panicked beasts pulling back and fighting their picketed lead ropes. The unmanageable Indian ponies bucked and circled. Buffalo Dancer calmed when Brady reached his side, freed the tether, and swung his leg over the buckskin's back.

Mothers watched and screamed. Old men and horseless warriors stood helpless. No one attempted to cross the creek. Brady turned Buffalo Dancer to face the child and the charging herd. The stallion pranced, tossed its head, and flagged its tail. Brady dug his heels into the horse's sides and he exploded across the creek, splashing water and riding headlong into the shaggy herd.

He engaged the outer edge of the buffalo herd and rode hard to outrun it to the spot where the child stood. The still powerful buckskin threw itself against the first heavy-bodied buffalo to gain position, then lightly switched leads to slip out of range of the curved, black horns. The Comanche buffalo horse sidestepped the lethal horns, its hooves floating over the ground where they seemed to touch down only long enough to launch each powerful new stride.

They cleared the herd. The leaders were as near the child as Brady, bearing down on it with terrifying speed.

Brady kicked Buffalo Dancer with both heels again. The stallion lunged forward, eating up the distance in great strides. Brady was barely able to stay ahead of the herd. He could hear their heavy breathing and smell the musky odor of their sweat-drenched bodies.

Less than twenty yards ahead, the ground dropped away into a steep-sided draw. In seconds, the horse plunged down the embankment and across the narrow ravine, never breaking stride. Brady laced the fingers of his right hand into the thick mane hair of the horse, gripped tightly with his legs, and leaned low to the ground as he thundered towards the boy.

The crying boy saw him coming and took two steps backward, then a third, and Brady nudged the horse closer with his left knee. Brady's mind raced. He knew if the boy sat or fell or stepped back, he would have no second chance. The boy wept and Brady prayed he would not move. The noise of it all was deafening, the speed overwhelming, and the intensity pounding like a hammer in his chest. Brady could feel the hot breath of the buffalo at his back.

He closed the distance. The boy stood firm, faltered and stood, then raised his arms. Brady stretched as far as he could. The horse corrected and when he was upon the boy his hooves missed him by inches. Brady leaned further outward and caught up a great handful of the boy's thick hair. With one quick motion he snatched the child up off the ground and carried him crosswise as he nudged the horse with his heels praying for one more burst of speed to outrun the terrible beasts that closed in around him.

Brady lost his balance and he lost his grip on the boy. The child slipped from his grasp and slid off the side of the horse. But when he dropped, Brady caught the fold of the boy's shirt and swung him back up and laid him across the horse's neck. He held him tight and looked back. Off to his right and to his left, buffalo stretched like an endless stream of ghostly images that appeared to go on forever. It was impossible to outrun the herd.

Brady took the only chance he had and set the buckskin on an oblique course in front of the charging herd. The buckskin gasped for air but refused to slow. They pounded up a round hill that flattened to the creek then he followed the contour of the land where it bent away to the right. Brady counted on the buffalo following the creek. He turned the buckskin hard to the left and down across the water. He kicked the horse onward. He didn't look back until he heard the rumbling subside and he knew the herd had turned.

It was a time of rejoicing in camp that night. The buffalo had come to them. The hunt was good, and many believed the shaman's prophecy had been answered. He encouraged those who remained reticent to embrace the white man among them. Some were hesitant and some were doubtful, but none questioned that McCall was good medicine.

As the tribe celebrated, the medicine men secluded themselves in the vision pit. They stayed there for three days seeking guidance and illumination. When the eldest and most respected among them told of his dream, he told of a white eagle and where the white eagle flew there were buffalo, and he also believed the white man among them was a good omen.

The elder shaman then caused much concern among the other warriors when he told his people the white man must be given the opportunity to prove himself in the ritual of the medicine lodge, the final test from which all doubt would be settled.

The chiefs and great warriors of the tribe deliberated throughout the night. Some protesting, others uncertain. They passed the pipe and by the early hours of morning agreed that if McCall was the good omen sent to them by the great spirits, he could prove himself worthy in the sacred rituals of the medicine lodge. If not, his failure and his banishment from the tribe would settle the question.

For weeks McCall prepared himself. He saw the scars and pride worn by those who had succeeded before him, and he saw the shame and disgrace suffered by those who had tried and failed.

From what he could learn from those who would speak to him, there were many mysteries associated with the secret rites. Otter Tail confided in Brady. He explained the most difficult part of the ritual was the one in which those who succeeded took the highest level of pride. He showed Brady the massive chest scars he carried above his breasts and showed Brady how skewers pierced the heavy muscle there, one on each side. He demonstrated how the skewers were secured to long rawhide thongs hung from the reinforced braces at the top of the tall lodge. He tried to explain the pain and the need to block out all conscious thought as the lashings were drawn tight. He would be raised high above the floor of the lodge and suspended there until the muscles ripped free, or he begged to be let down. And he told of how he endured and how Brady must endure as well.

Brady remained apprehensive. This was the Blackfoot way of life. The boys spent all their waking hours developing and preparing themselves to become warriors. Their games were games of war and hunting and weapons and bravery. From childhood the boy children prepared for the rituals in the medicine lodge, each believing he would not fail.

Then Brady was told it was time. He readied himself. He entered the dream pit. If he were to be chosen for the ordeal of the medicine lodge, the great spirits would come to him in a dream. The shaman would interpret the dream. If it was a good dream Brady would be considered.

For three days and three nights he hunkered without food or water or light and for the first day he had no dream. On the second night his dreams were nightmarish images with no connection or meaning. They appeared randomly throughout the day and night and next day.

When he emerged from the dream pit on the fourth day, Shy Wolf, Otter Tail, and the elder shaman awaited him. The shaman led him to his lodge and told him not to speak. Inside he prepared Brady a strong tea and lit the pipe. They drank and smoked and, eventually, the shaman asked the boy to tell him of his dream.

Brady told him he dreamed of a bird with no wings abandoned on a cliff high above a great river inhabited by ravenous creatures with dripping jaws that awaited its wingless flight. Then he told the shaman he dreamed the dream from inside the bird's body, for when it stepped off its high perch he felt the wind in his face as he plummeted earthward into the waiting jaws below.

Then Brady stretched out his arms to demonstrate. He said to the shaman that the bird grew wings and he could fly. With each new stroke of the wings, the bird flew higher and higher until the earth appeared far below him. From that great height he saw buffalo and deer. He watched the movement of people and rivers. He experienced a new vision of the world and a freedom he had never known.

After he spoke he watched the old man who nodded but did not speak. The old wise one built a small fire. In the fire he placed leaves and grasses and colored powder. The fire smoked and the old one waved the smoke about the darkened interior of the lodge with the wing of a hawk, and then he chanted low and haunting.

Then he became still and appeared to have left his body. When he returned he sang and chanted again. He told Brady his dream was a good one.

"I do not know why the Great Spirit blessed you with this power," he said. "You will rest, and at the next new moon you will be tested."

Brady McCall left the lodge of the shaman to be alone. He did not return to his own bed, but secluded himself away from the others to wait.

The night of the new moon McCall, looking older and walking as though a heavy weight lie upon his shoulder's, approached the shaman's lodge. The shaman was waiting.

He motioned for McCall to follow him.

Inside the dim light of the massive medicine lodge, stood nine young men stripped to their breechclouts with their skin painted, trepidation on their faces, and acolytes attending to each.

The elder shaman motioned a hideously decorated man to attend to McCall. Soon enough, McCall was stripped and painted and stood with the others.

All ten stood and waited. There was no bravado about them. No fear. But, when the ritual began there was a great amount of wailing and the night wore on with no reprieve. The day came and passed, and the second night came. McCall remained among the six who persevered.

Throughout that night McCall quit many times in his mind, but he would not give in. When they hoisted the six into the air and he could feel the muscles detach from his bones, he forced his mind to exit his body. If there was pain, he felt none.

When the first glimmer of sunlight shone through the smoke hole and they lowered the boys, McCall did not remember the pain, the blood, the moaning, and the pounding drums that never stopped beating. But, for the rest of his life he never forgot the faces of Shy Wolf and Otter Tail when he stepped out of the medicine lodge into the daylight and they addressed him by his Blackfoot name.

THIRTY-FOUR

By the time McCall turned nineteen he had ridden with the Blackfoot so long he could scarcely remember when he hadn't. His friends, Shy Wolf and Otter Tail, had taken wives and began to change as they started families and had less time for him. McCall felt like an outsider again.

He spent more time with the Pend d'Oreilles, who sometimes hunted with the Blackfoot. It wasn't that the Pend d'Oreilles accepted him anymore freely than the Blackfoot, but he was able to move among them with more anonymity, and he grew to feel more comfortable as a loner.

He met among them a young girl with a bashful smile and a playful manner. Her carefree nature was tempered with a serious side that reminded him of Allison and he was drawn to her.

Otter Tail, who knew her family, said her name was Little Deer but cautioned McCall.

"Do not take lightly the smile of a woman or your desire to be with her. Their people, like ours, have no tolerance for a man whose intentions are untrue."

He paused and looked at McCall, reluctant to say more. McCall sensed it.

"Especially for a white man?"

Otter Tail nodded. "Even a white man who has proven himself as a Blackfoot warrior.

"But you do know her?"

"Yes. And her family."

Eventually McCall convinced Otter Tail to introduce him to Little Deer. It was an awkward affair. McCall stumbled with the unfamiliarity of the Pend d'Orielle language. He scrambled English and Blackfoot words along with the few he had learned from Otter Tail. He was painfully uncomfortable in her presence but he felt warm and good when he was with her. When he was not, she was in his thoughts constantly.

McCall asked Otter Tail for advice. Otter Tail asked him if he intended to court Little Deer, a commitment to marriage. McCall wasn't sure. All he knew was that she stirred feelings deep inside him and he wanted to spend time with her. After much prodding, McCall told Otter Tail he was ready to court Little Deer.

"Then you must talk to her father," Otter Tail said.

McCall went to her father with two good horses and a Henry repeating rifle. Her father was pleased, and Little Deer and her sisters stood outside and giggled. They chided Little Deer because McCall was a white man but, they whispered that he was very handsome and rode a magnificent horse.

That afternoon McCall called on Little Deer for the first time. They walked to the river with her steely-eyed grandmother for a chaperone. They sat in the grass near the water, the grandmother watching and listening the whole time. She never spoke but she remained consistently vigilant, staring McCall down every time he stole a glance her direction.

That night McCall sought out Otter Tail and Otter Tail assured him it would not always be so. But each time it was the same. When it wasn't the grandmother, it was the mother or an aunt.

After McCall and Little Deer began to feel comfortable with one another, they would steal off and meet in some secluded place where they could be alone and spend many hours talking and lying together in the tall grass high above the encampment.

Little Deer, propped up on one elbow, would stare at McCall and touch his face with her fingertips as he lay on his back with his fingers laced behind his head trying to pronounce the Pend d'Oreille words she taught him. She would then lie in his arms and slowly repeat the English words she learned from him. She was captivated by her white warrior and he hungered for her attention. In her presence he was calmed and gentled. But, below the idyllic contentment ran an unsettling sense in McCall that troubled him. A feeling he could not explain and that he could not discuss with Little Deer.

By the end of summer McCall couldn't remember ever being happier. Little Deer had grown more beautiful and she carried herself with grace, the envy of every young girl in camp.

They spoke of marriage. The grandmother no longer accompanied them. McCall was welcome in her father's lodge where he provided much game and ate many meals. In the spring they would talk of marriage, McCall decided.

Fall came quickly and by late September the snow came and cold settled over the harsh land. The Blackfoot people departed for their winter camp and McCall stayed on with the Pend d'Oreilles. The days grew short. Game was scarce. McCall was gone for weeks at a time with the men of the tribe to hunting grounds far from camp.

After a prolonged absence in which the hunters traveled many miles and spent many weeks on the trail, McCall returned to find Little Deer weak and coughing. When McCall asked her about it, she said it was nothing. The cough gradually worsened. Little Deer struggled to keep up appearances while each day her condition deteriorated.

McCall stayed with her, but each day she seemed to weaken. One morning she was unable to rise from her bed and, when McCall arrived at the lodge of her father, he found her attended by her mother, her grandmother, and the shaman.

"Will she be all right?" McCall asked.

"I think so," said her grandmother. The shaman was less sure. He chanted and prayed over the girl. McCall sat in the shadows and watched.

For six days she lay, unable to rise, and McCall never left her side. He spoke to her and held snow packs to her fevered head. She smiled at him and spoke softly. McCall held her hand and lay his head on her breast, and they talked of spring. She squeezed his hand and told him she would be very proud to be his wife. She laced the fingers of her other hand in his hair and rubbed his head weakly as they talked into the night.

McCall told her to rest and sleep some, and she said no. She asked him if he would like a son, and he said he would. She asked if he would like a daughter, and he said a daughter would make him very happy.

In English she said very softly, "I give you my heart. And every star that is in the sky that is mine to give, I give to you."

McCall rose to look into her eyes and tell her how much he loved her, but when he looked down at her, she was gone.

McCall mourned for Little Deer a long time. He watched them offer her to the heavens and he wept. He watched the smoke of her funeral pyre lift skyward and thoughts of the killing field gripped him in anger and hatred.

When his time of mourning passed, McCall lashed out in anger. Hatred seethed within him and he sought someone or something upon which to wreak revenge. He returned to the Blackfoot and rode with their warriors against their enemies. He painted his face, greased his long hair, tied it up and adorned it with eagle feathers. He painted his body and when he rode into battle he did so with a vengeance and a self-destructive disregard for his own life.

In time, the blue-eyed warrior and the fiery buckskin horse became the subject of many conversations whispered around campfires in both the Blackfoot camps and those of the enemies who came to know him. Both he and the horse carried the scars of many battles. He distanced himself from those close to him.

When Shy Wolf or Otter Tail tried to talk to him he shook them off, for he harbored a lifetime of hatred not even he understood.

At twenty-one he was a seasoned warrior—more Blackfoot than white. His three-year quest for vengeance no longer had meaning. He thought often of Little Deer, but in his heart he knew the demons he fought were not the ones who had taken her.

He watched Buffalo Dancer grazing, always alone and never with the other horses. The buckskin was badly scarred. His gait showed some stiffness, especially on cold mornings when he hadn't been ridden for a few days.

Spring came and the snow began to melt. McCall announced it was time for him to leave. They understood. That evening they passed the pipe and celebrated. Otter Tail, Shy Wolf, and McCall talked well into the night. They had grown up together and, as close as McCall felt to Franklin, he shared similar feelings for these two.

When McCall stepped out of his lodge the next morning, the entire tribe awaited him. Broken Wing, the wife of Otter Tail stepped up first. She held his hands. She embraced him and she presented him with a deerskin pouch which she placed about his neck.

"This will protect you," she said.

One by one they came by him. They stood quietly as he swung easily up onto the buckskin's bare back. McCall had earned the respect of the Blackfoot people, both as a warrior and a man of honor. He rode out with grave misgivings.

Young men on horseback solemnly rode alongside McCall on his way to the river. Each touched him on the shoulder as they peeled off to make room for the next rider. At the water's edge, McCall turned to take a long, last look. He wanted to remember forever the friendship and acceptance he had experienced with the people who he respected and loved.

He turned away. The buckskin plunged into the fast moving water. They rode for many miles before Brady turned his head to look back.

THIRTY-FIVE

Buffalo Dancer sensed this journey would be different. There were no other warriors with them, no hunting party, and none of the wild energy he had come to expect each time they rode out of the Blackfoot camp. Instead, the man on his back was quiet and subdued. There was no urgency this time.

McCall took a deep breath and tried to remember the day he and Charlie pulled out from the Triple Dot. He glanced at the Gros Ventre knife that hung at his side. He thought about the old trapper. Back in the far reaches of his mind he remembered two young boys he was no longer sure ever really existed.

McCall was tired. He wanted to hear English words. He wanted to see Kincaid and he wanted to hear how Franklin was doing. He wanted to see the ranch and smell the hay and drink strong coffee. He wondered how Kincaid looked. *Would his hair be grey? Did he ever marry? Was Franklin back yet? Was Franklin still alive?* His mind wandered and his thoughts began to gradually make the transition to the life he knew before the Blackfoot. A lot had changed. McCall had changed—he hoped Kincaid had not.

He traveled south warmed by the sun with a sharp north wind at his back. He dropped down into the valley at the tip of Flathead Lake, then crossed over and followed the South Fork of the Flathead River until it petered out.

When he crossed the Madison Mountains and looked down into the green Gallatin River Valley, he knew he was home.

Brady McCall pushed Buffalo Dancer to a trot as they turned up the long, narrow road leading to the ranch house.

Before he realized it, Brady stood apprehensively on the porch of the log house he and Franklin had helped build. It appeared as he had remembered it and it felt good to be there. But, he felt like a stranger with no right to enter freely.

He knocked on the heavy wooden door. There was no answer. He knocked again. Kincaid swung the door open. Both men stared. Five years had made a lot of changes. Each waited for the other to speak.

Summer sun and the winter winds had etched deep lines at the corners of Kincaid's eyes. Grey showed through his hair and he appeared smaller than Brady had remembered. Kincaid's eyes narrowed and he gawked at the young man standing before him.

"Brady?"

"Hey, Travis." He smiled a weak smile.

Brady offered his hand. Kincaid grasped it with his knotted fingers and squeezed hard. He looked Brady up and down.

"Well, look at you."

He laughed and hauled the rugged looking young man into the cabin.

Brady grinned. He loved hearing the English language, and he especially loved hearing it spoken in a voice so vaguely familiar. Kincaid studied the moccasins and the long hair. Brady had filled out. His shoulders and chest showed great strength. His manner was shy and Indian like.

"Look at you. If we weren't standing face to face, I'm not sure I'd recognize you, Brady . . . but you look good," Kincaid lied.

Brady looked down at his feet then back at Kincaid. He smiled.

"You ain't a very good liar, Travis."

Brady then threw his arms around Kincaid and held him tight. Kincaid put his arms around Brady and they stood that way a long time.

"It's so good to be home," Brady said, still holding Kincaid, not wanting to let go, not sure if this was real or a dream.

Kincaid patted him on the back grabbed the back of his head and pulled it to him.

"You're home now. That's all that matters."

Then they pushed back and stood at arm's length, their hands still on one another's shoulders, as if both thought the other would somehow disappear if he broke contact. A knot swelled in Brady's throat as he looked Kincaid over. He tousled Kincaid's hair then ducked back and laughed.

"You don't look bad for an old man."

Kincaid took a swipe at him.

"You might have been some kind of big deal with the Blackfoot, but you're still a snotty-nosed kid around here."

Brady looked around the room. His eyes took in all the changes he could see in Kincaid's appearance. The years had treated him well and, even though there was some age showing on him, Kincaid hadn't changed much.

"I sure missed this place," Brady said. "Even thought about you a time or two, Travis."

He paused. His tone took a more serious tone. "I wasn't sure you'd remember who I was."

Kincaid understood. His expression showed it.

"Well, I'll have to admit you have changed some since the last time I saw you," Kincaid said, as he laughed and shook his head. "Come on and sit down."

"It's real good to be here," Brady said.

There was a long silence as both men let it all sink in.

Finally, Brady spoke. "Have you had breakfast yet?"

"No, I was just fixing to though. You hungry?"

"I can't remember the last time I wasn't."

Kincaid busied himself over the stove, banking it with more wood and shuffling the frying pan over the heat.

"Pour us each a cup of coffee and I'll heat this skillet up."

The two men had a lot to catch up on. Brady listened intently to every word Kincaid said and, in his excitement to tell Kincaid of the events of the past five years, he found himself using Indian sign language and substituting Blackfoot phrases for English words that didn't come readily to mind.

"Whoa, slow down," Kincaid said. "My Blackfoot's a little rusty."

"Sorry, Travis. I guess my mouth's outrunning my brain."

Kincaid laughed. He refilled their coffee cups. The fresh smell of biscuits drifted over from the stove and two huge steaks sizzled in the frying pan. Brady's stomach rumbled.

"What do you hear from Franklin?"

Kincaid laughed.

"That kid," he said and shook his head. "He's real good about staying in touch."

He looked askance at Brady. Brady smiled and shrugged his shoulders.

"He owns a big hotel in San Francisco."

Brady laughed. "Franklin T. Stilwell owns a hotel?"

"That's what he said. He started with a used up gold mine he won in a faro game. Struck a fair vein the second week he was in it, figured that was too much work for him and traded it to two Irishmen for the hotel."

Kincaid set the steaks on the table, then took the biscuits out of the oven.

"The first thing he did was change the name of the hotel to the Gold Nugget . . . for good luck I guess."

Brady laughed.

"I don't know, Travis. I can't picture Franklin running a hotel."

Kincaid smiled. "Neither can I."

"Have you been to see him?"

"No, never have," Kincaid said.

They ate and talked and, when they finished and sat back, Brady smiled at Kincaid.

"Let's go see him."

Kincaid looked over his coffee cup at Brady. He appeared to contemplate Brady's suggestion with some serious consideration.

"I'll make you a deal, Brady," he finally said. "You stick around here long enough to help us get through the spring branding and drive a small bunch of army cattle over to Fort Smith, and you and me will head out to California."

Brady toasted the idea with his coffee cup. "You got yourself a cowboy."

The following day, Kincaid, Brady and three ranch hands set out for what should have been an easy gather. By evening bad weather set in, and the cattle scattered.

It was four weeks before they got them gathered, and two more weeks before they delivered the herd to Fort Smith.

The calves had been branded, the herd was delivered to the army and things were back in order at the Triple Dot. With nothing left to delay them, Kincaid and Brady packed their saddle bags and turned in right after dark to get a good night's rest before they set out on the journey to California.

By the time the sun was high enough to cast a shadow the next morning, Kincaid and Brady had already put ten miles behind them.

THIRTY-SIX

San Francisco: 1853

When they crested the last of the hills overlooking the bay, the San Francisco fog had cleared and the sun shone cool and bright over the picturesque stands of Eucalyptus trees, red-barked manzanita brush and endless fields of golden poppies that colored the landscape.

They rode bayside and both men stood awed by the activity of the embarcadero, where ships docked, cargo lined the wharf, and bobbing vessels rocked empty, riding high on the tide while their crews holed up in the bawdy backrooms of dark establishments presided over by women with no last names.

Kincaid inquired of a local businessman of the whereabouts of the Gold Nugget Hotel. In minutes, they stood beneath a sign that read, *Gold Nugget Hotel and Saloon.* From its outside appearance it was more saloon than hotel.

Located at the corner of an alley that looked as uninviting in the daylight as it must at night, the place occupied a section of a partially cobbled street down from which lay the bay, an easy walk for even a drunken sailor. From where Kincaid and Brady stood, they gazed out across the water at two islands floating in the lingering haze that clung to the water and obscured the view to the Pacific.

Brady and Kincaid climbed the steps at the entrance.

"After you," Kincaid said, holding one of the two doors open.

Brady stepped inside. Kincaid followed. They saw two men sitting at the bar. By the looks of them, they had not succeeded in drinking off last night's drunk and were well on their way to a long day.

The bartender busied himself behind the mahogany bar. In the bar-length mirror the reflection of a once stunning woman smiled back at Kincaid and Brady, neither of which could keep from staring. She tucked a wisp of hair behind one ear, smoothed the front of her dress. And then stepped out from behind the bar to greet them.

"First time in town?" she asked, smiling pleasantly and assessing them both with her intense gaze.

Kincaid removed his hat and nodded. "Yes, ma'am, it is."

He nudged Brady and Brady removed his hat, and when he did, the woman regarded him with a surprised and curious expression that begged some sort of explanation. Both the look and the explanation escaped Brady. She looked up at Kincaid.

"We're from Montana Territory, ma'am. Not much need for city clothes where we come from."

She smiled and Kincaid stuck out his hand. She took it in both of her hands, an overly warm response that caught Kincaid off-guard.

"I'm Travis Kincaid and this here's Brady C. McCall."

Her eyes widened. She dropped her hands and covered her mouth. For a moment she was speechless.

"Oh my gawd," she exclaimed. "B.C?" She looked back at Kincaid. "Travis?" Then she laughed and put her arms around them both.

"I cannot believe it. Franklin is going to be so surprised to see you two."

She walked them to a table. "I've heard so much about you two I feel like I've known you all my life."

She looked at Brady and winked. "In your case, all your life."

Brady and Kincaid looked at each other and smiled.

"Franklin had to run an errand, but he'll be back soon. There is no way I'm letting either one of you out of my sight before then."

She sat them at a table in the corner with a view of the bay and introduced herself.

"I'm Maggie," she said. Her face glowed and the beauty of her youth shined brightly in her eyes.

"Pleased to meet you, Miss Maggie," Brady said, as he stood and smiled.

"Here, sit down, sit down. We're not at all formal here."

She took Brady's hand as he sat and looked back at Kincaid, who remained standing.

"And you," she said, "are the handsome devil I've been dying to meet."

Kincaid beamed. "Well, Maggie, if I'd known you were here, I wouldn't have waited so long to make the trip."

Kincaid sat. Maggie stood over them scarcely able to believe her eyes. She caught herself staring and appeared to be embarrassed.

"What can I get you?"

She pointed first at Brady. "Beer?"

Brady nodded. "Yes ma'am.

Kincaid shot Brady a skeptical look. "You ever had a beer before?"

Brady grinned and shook his head. "No sir. This'll be my first one."

Kincaid turned to Maggie. "Same for me, Maggie."

Maggie hurried to the bar and returned with two beers and a cup of coffee for herself. She sat next to Kincaid with her eyes looking directly into his.

"So how long are you here for?" She asked.

Then she gave Brady a courtesy look to include him in the conversation.

Kincaid's eyes sparkled and Brady smiled as he watched the two.

"Well," Kincaid said. "I'm thinking from what I've seen so far, we may be around a while."

He winked at Maggie and she seemed to blush, although Kincaid knew better.

"I would just love to show you around anytime. Both of you," she said with a genuinely friendly smile that couldn't have uninvited Brady any more quickly.

They talked while they waited. Maggie served them lunch and they had another beer.

She was alive with enthusiasm and wit and soon all three were laughing and talking like old friends. She apologized for Franklin. They both assured her they understood.

Outside someone thumped around and banged against the doors and shouted out, "Hey, someone give me a hand with these doors."

It was Franklin's voice. Brady held his finger to his lip and motioned to Kincaid. Together they rose, and each held one side of the doors open while Franklin backed in with his arms loaded down. He was dressed in a striped suit and wore a bowler hat tipped back on his head.

"Thank you gentlemens," he said, as he nodded to Brady and turned towards Kincaid on his way to the bar.

He stopped mid-stride and turned back to do a double-take on Kincaid. Franklin stared a long time, and then he Franklin grinned and slapped the bar top with both hands.

"Travis! What the heck are you doing here?"

He laughed and advanced toward Kincaid as Kincaid smiled and reached out for him. Franklin picked the old cowboy up and spun him around, ignoring the stranger who stood quietly and said nothing. Both Franklin and Kincaid laughed.

"Just came to check up on you," Kincaid answered to the question that seemed like it had been asked too long ago to still be relevant.

"Man, you look good, Travis," Franklin said, pushing himself back and taking a long look at the cowboy.

"You look pretty fancy yourself," Kincaid replied, snapping the brim of the bowler with his finger.

"So, what do you hear of B.C.?" Franklin asked with some concern to his voice.

Kincaid shook his head. Maggie could barely contain herself and Brady stood like an invisible cigar store Indian looking at Franklin expressionless and dying to say something.

"Last I heard he was in San Francisco," Kincaid said.

Franklin's eyes widened. "He was here? In Frisco? When? What was he doing here?"

"You should ask him," Kincaid said, nodding toward the stoic figure to his right.

Franklin turned his head and stared. He stood immobilized and couldn't speak. Tears welled up in his eyes. He took a step toward Brady and all he could do was cry.

Brady moved forward and they embraced in a rough bear hug. There were no words spoken. Tears ran down their faces and neither man made any attempt to conceal the fact.

Maggie held her hands to her mouth and she shook with emotion, her makeup running down her cheeks in dark streaks. Kincaid's throat tightened and all he could do is watch the two boys.

Brady was the first to stand back.

"You sure don't look like no cowboy I know," he said, grinning at Franklin.

Franklin laughed and slapped Brady on the shoulders. He flipped Brady's long hair with his fingertips.

"Look at you. Ol' Charlie turned you into some kinda heathen."

They looked each other up and down, making note of all the changes, seeing the toll the past few years had taken on them both.

They laughed and both began talking at once.

"Speaking of Charlie, how is that Frenchman doing?"

Brady dropped his eyes. "He froze up our second winter out."

"Sorry to hear that. He was a good man."

"Yeah, he was a good man."

One of the drunks at the bar slammed his fist down, his voice loud, his words slurred. He glared at Brady.

"There ain't no good Frenchmen . . . or Indians neither."

Franklin rushed to the bar, grabbed both drunks by the collar and hustled them to the door. He pushed one then the other out into the street.

"You ain't welcome back in here."

Maggie took Brady and Franklin by a hand and led them to a table at the far end of the room.

"Here, you two sit down and visit," she said. "I'm going to show Mr. Kincaid around town."

She deposited the boys and stood close at Kincaid's side.

"Mr. Kincaid," she said as she took his arm. "How would you like to see San Francisco?"

"That would suit me just fine, Maggie."

As the couple left arm in arm, Maggie stuck her head back in the door and whispered to the boys.

"Don't wait up for us."

Franklin and Brady visited through most of the night, and the next morning at breakfast Kincaid sat between the two boys with a smile on his face.

"Good morning," is all he said.

Franklin smiled. "Well, Travis, I hope you're proud of yourself, keeping my help out all night like that."

Brady laughed. Kincaid raised a hand in protest but didn't argue the point.

"There's lots you didn't tell us about you, Travis," Brady said.

Kincaid grinned. "Maggie was just showing me the sights—there's a lot to see in San Francisco."

Franklin looked at Kincaid then back at Brady. "He raised us right, but nobody raised him right."

They all laughed.

The next evening, Kincaid and the boys stood on the cliffs watching the moon float at the end of a bright silver trail leading out across the breaking waves of the ocean. Franklin turned the conversation, and thought he saw Brady's face flush.

"You all remember Allison Granger?"

Brady nodded and Kincaid said, "Yeah, how could you ever forget her and her mother. Two of the toughest women I ever met."

Brady waited, his heart racing, and his curiosity almost uncontainable.

"I see them from time to time," Franklin continued. "They stop by every now and then, and I call on them whenever I'm down their way."

"How did things work out for them?" Kincaid asked.

Brady felt the warmth rise in his face and he felt confused. He wanted to hear more about Allison, but at the same time he did not want to learn that she might be married and have a family of her own. He wasn't sure why, but he felt like she owed him some loyalty, or at least the first-right-of-refusal if she wanted to take a husband. It was nonsense and he admonished himself for thinking it.

"Mrs. Granger, her name's Mrs. Hayes now, got married. Her and Mr. Hayes run a dry goods store about a half a day's ride south of here," Franklin explained.

"What about Allison?" Brady asked impatiently.

"I'll tell you straight away B.C., she ain't the same kid you remember," Franklin said. "She turned out pretty good. In fact, she turned out real good."

Brady gritted his teeth. "What do you mean *real* good?"

"Don't tell her I said this, but she's about as pretty as they come. She works down there with her folks. They got a nice place and she learned to speak a little Mexican and she's real smart.

Franklin paused. He was torturing Brady and Brady knew it.

"Damn it, Franklin will you get to the point? Is she married or ain't she?"

His words echoed back to him in the silence that followed, and Brady would have given anything to have not said them. His frustration and embarrassment exposed, Brady stuck out his jaw defiantly, and his expression dared one of them to say a word.

Kincaid casually threw down his cigar stub and kicked sand on it as he turned away to look up the coast line, struggling to suppress the laughter building up inside him. Franklin grinned. The moonlight lit up his mocking smile. When Brady realized how much fun Franklin was having with him, he laughed.

"No, she ain't married and she asks about you every damn time I see her," Franklin said.

"She does?"

"Yeah, I don't know what she ever saw in you anyway, but she drives me crazy."

"She asked about me?"

"Yeah, but don't ask me why," replied Franklin. "You never let me know nothing, so I never had much to tell her."

Now, Brady was excited.

"How about the three of us taking a ride down to see them?" Brady asked.

"I think that's a fine idea," said Kincaid. "It would be nice to see them again."

"I don't know," Franklin said, hesitating. "That might not be a good idea."

"Why not?" Brady asked.

Franklin shuffled uncomfortably from one foot to the next. His demeanor took a serious turn.

"Well," Franklin began, "I never thought in a hundred years you'd ever come to California and I was getting tired of never having anything to tell her, so I figured I needed to find a way to get her to let it go once and for all and, uh, well, you know."

'No, Franklin, I don't know. What?"

"I think I told her you got sick."

"What do you mean, sick?"

Franklin searched for the right words. "I didn't want her to think you just forgot about her, so I told her you were. . ." he paused.

Brady waited. Kincaid watched, slack-jawed.

"I was . . . ?"

Franklin held up his hands. "Look, B.C., I was in a tight spot here."

"Franklin?"

"All right, all right. I told her it had been just you and Charlie alone together for so long, you both just got to where you preferred it that way."

"What does that mean?"

"You know."

"No, I don't know." Brady looked at Kincaid. Kincaid just shrugged.

"That was pretty much it. It don't matter now that you're going to see her yourself."

"Was that it?"

"There might have been some other things, I don't recall for sure."

Brady sat on a sawed-off tree stump and slumped.

"Tell it all to me."

"I don't remember it all. I do remember about you getting snowed in and running out of firewood and you and Charlie sharing a buffalo hide when you slept together."

Brady exploded to his feet. Kincaid caught Brady and stood between him and Franklin.

"Easy, easy, easy boys," he said. Then he chuckled. "I'm sure we can get it all straightened out tomorrow."

Brady's expression eased. "Just let me shoot him once, Travis."

Kincaid laughed. "I don't think that's a good idea."

Franklin looked at Brady in his most innocent of expressions. "I don't know what you're getting all huffy about," he said.

They walked back along the dark streets that dropped sharply to the embarcadero and the smell of the ocean and the cool air seemed strangely out of place to Brady and Kincaid.

By morning the foggy streets swirled in a misty haze of damp air that, in the half-light of dawn, gave an eerie cast to the place. The clatter of the horses' feet on the hard road echoed into the empty corners of the alleys they passed.

Kincaid and the boys rode south on a well-travelled road that skirted the ocean on the right and the sandy upslope of the coastal hills to the left.

Brady had thought about Allison off and on over the years, and now the prospect of meeting her again rekindled boyhood memories as vivid as though they occurred yesterday. Somehow, in his mind, the image of her as a child matured with the years and he could see her as a woman, but her features were unclear, and all he recalled with clarity were her eyes.

His thoughts drifted aimlessly, but always returned to Allison and, the more he thought about her, the more apprehensive he became.

He rode up quietly alongside Franklin.

"You suppose there's somewhere along the way we can stop and get me a haircut?"

Franklin looked at him. "I don't know, cousin. We can keep an eye out for one of them cantina's where you might could talk someone into taking a shot at it, but I wouldn't count on it."

Brady nodded and dropped back. Kincaid fell in beside him but didn't speak.

"Hey, Travis."

Kincaid turned his head.

"Shouldn't I maybe a get a new shirt in town before we go visiting?"

"Don't you like the one you got?"

"I like it fine."

"Then why get another one?"

Brady laughed. "Come on Travis. I haven't seen Allison in a long time. I think I ought to look decent."

"You look just fine."

"Are you sure?"

"I'm sure."

"All right. I just don't want to be embarrassed."

"Brady, you look fine."

Brady felt uneasy. What if she didn't remember him? What if she was simply indifferent and this entire unspoken bond between them was all in his head? Exactly what did he expect from a woman he last saw as a child?

The more he thought about it, the more he regretted the entire idea. He watched Franklin and Kincaid riding ahead, talking, enjoying the trip, laughing.

It was all too complicated. Finally, Brady resigned himself to his fate, whatever it may be, and settled into the rocking rhythm of the saddle.

The trail led through dark-green forests of broad-leafed ferns and tall redwoods and stands of eucalyptus with bark shredded and hanging. Occasionally the thick vegetation opened up onto wide expanses of windblown sand where the damp breeze carried in off the Pacific Ocean, and waves crashed against the shore and rolled up on the beaches. Then the trail turned inland and dropped down into a valley protected on two sides by the rolling hills of the coast range.

They encountered two vaqueros riding high-stepping horses of good breeding and, when they were within talking range, Kincaid touched his hat and said, "*Buenos Dias.*"

The vaqueros returned the greeting and all five horsemen stopped mid-trail while Kincaid carried on a brief conversation in Spanish and then they rode on.

"Well, damn, *Señor* Kincaid. I didn't know you could talk Mexican. What'd they say?" Franklin asked as he looked over his shoulder to watch the two riders disappear up the trail. Brady listened curiously.

"They said there was a fiesta tonight in San Gregorio. Said we'd be welcome there."

"Ain't we the fortunate ones?" Brady said, grinning widely.

"We'll see about that tonight after you wash down some tortillas and beans and a couple shots of *mescal,*" Franklin said, with the authority of previous experience.

Kincaid laughed. "If *mescal* is the only word you boys learn in Spanish, I'll guarantee it won't be one you soon forget."

They rode for the better part of an hour then the road turned eastward. They reached the top of a low round hill and looked down upon a storybook *Puebla* in the distance.

"There it is, gentlemens. San Gregorio."

The earth-colored adobe buildings with red-tiled roofs looked oddly foreign. From their position overlooking the small valley stretching to the south, the three horsemen could see people moving about the *zócalo,* around which the town was built.

In the center of the *zócalo* stood a fountain. Around it, the plaza was cobbled and trellises shaded the tables. On the east end of the square, outside an adobe cantina, a charred beef lay on a bed of hot coals. In the fire pit in the corner grease dripped and sizzled from the hides of several pigs attended by young, dark-skinned girls in colored dresses. The grease flared on the hot coals, and the flames scorched the slick-skinned carcasses hung there with gaping mouths and beady eyes bulging from the heat.

Kincaid and Brady followed Franklin into town. They dismounted near a well-kept store with a neatly painted sign that read, *Hayes Dry Goods &Freight Co.* Franklin stepped down and the others followed suit. They wrapped the reins around the hitch rail and loosened their saddle cinches.

Franklin and Kincaid stepped up on the wooden sidewalk. Brady remained at Buffalo Dancer's side. The door exploded open and a woman's voice caused the surprised horses to set back. Franklin and Kincaid whirled toward the sound and Brady looked down at the leather latigo still in his hand, not daring to look up.

"Franklin T. Stilwell," Allison said, as she ran up and threw her arms around him.

"Allison T. Granger," Franklin said, holding her at arm's length to get a better look at her.

"Don't they ever feed you? You're skinny as beam."

Then he smiled. "Hey, I want you to meet someone," he said, as they turned toward Kincaid. Allison smiled but did not recognize him. She stuck out her hand.

"Hi, I'm Allison," she said.

Kincaid smiled.

"Travis Kincaid," he said.

Her hand covered her mouth and tears streamed forth.

"Oh my gosh. Travis."

She threw her arms around his neck and squeezed him tight. "I didn't recognize you—I'm so sorry. I can't believe it's really you."

She stepped back, but held his hand. She smiled.

"You're even more handsome than I remembered," she said.

Kincaid smiled.

"I'm not so sure about that," he said.

Her eyes were bright and still teary. She finally managed to compose herself and stood with an arm around each of them.

"What are you two doing in San Gregorio?"

Before Kincaid could answer Allison's excitement and curiosity got the best of her.

"What about Brady? How is he doing?"

Travis smiled and nodded toward the horses where Brady stood half hidden by the big buckskin.

"You can ask him that one."

Brady stepped out from behind the horse. Allison let out a shrill scream.

"Brady!"

She ran into his arms laughing and crying at the same time. He held her close and smelled her soft hair as it pressed against his face. His emotions whirled and his senses converged in confusion. The years rolled away.

Brady laughed with relief. He had dreaded and looked forward to this moment with so many misgivings and now he held her in his arms and any doubts he had disappeared.

Allison breathed in the earthy smell of Brady's buckskin shirt. She squeezed her arms around his well-muscled back and buried herself next to his chest. She raised her face to look up at him. Her eyes explored his features. Her fingers gently touched an old scar that had healed roughly along his jawbone.

His skin was dark, his eyes intense, and there was an unmistakable seriousness about him that were not there as the boy she remembered. But the gentle look in his eyes was still there, and the soul-revealing smile that she remembered in him from St. Joseph was still there.

He spoke softly. "I know we were just kids when all that happened to us, but after we all split up there was hardly a day went by that I didn't think about you," he said.

He looked down into her eyes and his face flushed as he turned away.

She looked up at him, surprised at his quickness to express his feelings.

"Brady, that day you left us at the fort I prayed so hard that you would come back someday."

Her smile took the edge off the awkwardness he felt.

"Now here we are all back together again. It's so wonderful to see the three of you."

Allison wiped the tears from her cheeks, looked over at Franklin and Kincaid, and then took Brady's hand and put her other arm around Kincaid.

"Mother will be so surprised to see you. Come inside, I can't wait to see the look on her face. And I want you to meet my step-father. He's been so wonderful to us," Allison said, as they walked together.

Allison reached over and tipped Franklin's hat over his eyes.

"Stilwell, I'll get even with you."

"For what?"

"You know for what—for all those things you said about Brady."

Brady laughed. "He already told me most of it. I hope you didn't believe anything he said."

Allison feigned a serious look and spoke in her best southern belle voice. "I must admit I was just a bit skeptical in the beginning, but I believed every word of it."

Franklin shook his head in his own defense. "You did not, you just wanted to have a reason to talk about B.C."

Kincaid watched the three of them like a father proud of the way his children had grown.

THIRTY-SEVEN

By early evening the *zócalo* was crowded and noisy. Young vaqueros outfitted in finely tailored jackets and tight pants studded with silver conchos salted their hands and traded tequila shots, man for man. Their eyes were red and they became loud and reckless over the course of the evening.

The smoky smell of hot tortillas, roasted beef, and pork hung over the square in the still air of the night. Old men talked and dipped tortillas in plates of refried beans and ate hot peppers until their eyes watered. They quenched their thirst with beer from bottles with no labels and watched with desire the young girls who danced before them and flirted with the young men, who passed the tequila from one to the other.

The young ladies taunted and teased the young vaqueros with their eyes and their flagrant smiles as they raised their skirts and flaunted their bare legs while they danced. The vaqueros competed for their attention, taking straight shots and addressing the ladies with lewd remarks and obscene gestures that made the girls giggle and carry on as they encouraged the young men.

Kincaid and the boys said goodnight to Allison and her mother and her step-father when they left their table to return home. Kincaid and the boys returned to the *zócalo*. They walked through the narrow streets crowded with Mexican soldiers and many vaqueros, who eyed them darkly and disparaged them with quiet remarks among themselves.

They found a table outside a crowded cantina where music played and intoxicated young ladies danced and attracted a gathering. Franklin stepped into the cantina and returned with six bottles of beer he placed on the table before them.

"Welcome to California," he said as he raised his bottle and touched it to the bottles raised by Kincaid and Brady. They drank and talked and watched the young ladies. When the beer was gone, Brady went inside for more.

When he returned, a beautiful young girl sat in his place. She held Franklin's hands as she kissed his face and whispered to him and laughed, her eyes mocking a young vaquero who watched with a hateful expression and clinched teeth.

She sat back in her chair. Brady set the beer on the table and stood away. She leaned forward, whispered to Franklin, then leaned back and slowly unbuttoned her blouse. First one button then another and another. Franklin smiled. He reached forward and let his fingers trace a line from her throat to her cleavage. She caught his hand there and brought it to her mouth and pressed his fingers to her lips.

Brady slipped back into the shadows, uneasy and on edge. Franklin took another pull on the beer bottle and Kincaid turned to address the two ladies who pulled their chairs in next to his.

Kincaid danced with one, then the other, and he bought them beer and laughed and they made suggestive advances toward him, playful and teasing, and very noticeable. Kincaid spoke to them in Spanish, and they laughed and giggled. One wore his hat, the other whispered to him and asked him to dance again.

Brady watched Franklin as his young lady moved to his lap and kissed him while his hands openly explored her bare breasts beneath her loose blouse under the darkening gaze of the young vaquero she taunted.

Brady looked at Kincaid, but Kincaid seemed unaware of anything beyond the two young ladies he entertained. It disturbed Brady that Kincaid let himself become distracted.

Franklin was loud and reckless, and it was his recklessness that ignited the passions of the young girl with him. Her teasing began in fun, but in the arms of this handsome gringo cowboy it became more than that, and now she was as void of caution as he.

Kincaid laughed and carried on with the girls at his side. But he never lost sight of the festering circle of intoxicated vaqueros, whose expressions grew grave and dangerous as they watched Franklin openly challenge their pride.

Kincaid saw trouble coming and looked over at Brady. Brady nodded and shifted over to a better position near the arched adobe wall. Kincaid reached across and loosened the revolver hanging at his left side. He excused himself abruptly from his surprised female companions, then stood with his back to the cantina wall.

Half a dozen drunken vaqueros pushed through the crowd, advancing on Franklin's table. Kincaid saw them and called to Franklin, his voice drowned out by the loud music and drunken singing.

Kincaid turned and Brady was gone. Kincaid pushed and shoved through the mass of people, trying to reach Franklin before the vaqueros did.

The vaqueros rushed Franklin, waving their pistols and cursing him. An explosion and the fire of a bright muzzle flash in the dark lit up the place.

By the time Brady and Kincaid pushed their way through the crowd, Franklin lay on his back bleeding from the head, his legs twisted grotesquely in those of the chair from which he fell.

The girl stood, her dress splattered with blood. She screamed. A second shot cracked and she stood motionless a moment as a boutonniere of red blossomed across her back before she fell.

A third shot rang out and the vaquero with the smoking gun in his hand fell beside her, his tailored jacket wet with blood and his eyes gazing empty and skyward.

Brady got to Franklin the same time Kincaid did. He holstered his still hot pistol and dropped to his knees at Franklin's side. Franklin lay on his back, his eyes closed, and his expression vacant and bloody, his legs twisted beneath him. Brady looked up at Kincaid.

"He's still breathing."

Kincaid knelt next to Brady and held his fingers to the arterial groove alongside Franklin's neck. He turned Franklin's head gently in his hands and examined the wound.

"The bullet just took off some skin and part of his eyebrow," he said. "Hand me that bottle."

Kincaid tipped his head in the direction of a half-empty tequila bottle on the table next to them. Brady handed him the bottle.

Kincaid then turned Franklin's head and splashed tequila on the wound. Franklin jerked his head, and his eyes opened. They darted about wildly. He shook his head and tried to sit up. He rolled his eyes, and stared up at Kincaid. When his eyes focused, he lay back down and tried to put his hand to his head.

"Who hit me?"

"No one hit you. You been shot," Kincaid said.

"Who shot me?"

"That fella over there."

Franklin sat up and looked at the bloodied vaquero whose lifeless body lie at the feet of those who attended it along with that of the young girl lying dead beside him.

"Is he dead?"

Kincaid nodded.

"What happened?" Franklin asked.

"Things just got out of control too fast." Kincaid motioned toward the dead vaquero. "This one was watching you and the girl, and I guess he didn't like what he saw. He came at you and got off one round, then hit her with the second before Brady stopped him."

Franklin looked up at Brady with an eye bloodshot and discolored from the impact of the bullet. He held his finger over the bloody patch where half an eyebrow once resided.

"Sorry, B.C. I never meant for anything like this to happen," Franklin said, with as much sincerity as Brady had ever heard from him.

The law came. The vaqueros were ushered out of town to the south and Kincaid and the boys were escorted out of town to the north and told not to return. They rode two hours in the dark and followed their moon-cast shadows up the coast trail. They looked for a place to sleep and, when they decided on a sheltered cove where the ocean waves could be heard in the distance, Brady did not dismount his horse.

"I'm going back," he said.

Franklin looked surprised. "What for?"

Kincaid looked up from the spot where he had thrown down his saddle and bedroll. He smiled at Brady.

"Leave too many things unsaid with Miss Allison, did you?"

Brady nodded. "Yeah, I did, Travis. I promised myself I'd never do that again. You boys be okay without me for a few days?"

Franklin touched the edge of his missing eyebrow. "We'll try to manage," he said. Then he stuck out his hand and Brady shook it.

"I owe you one, cousin."

"Take care, son," Kincaid said, his tone one of deep concern.

Brady looked at Kincaid, then at Franklin. "I'll catch up with you as soon as I get this sorted out," he said, then he turned his horse and rode south in the moonlight.

For the next two weeks Brady and Allison spent most of every day together. In the beginning, their conversations were congenial and guarded. They had both grown from children to adults only in the mind of the other. While they shared a deep and enduring part of their lives together, they found they no longer knew the person each had become. Their common bond—a nurtured memory that continued to grow into something neither was sure how to transition into reality.

It was difficult for both. They had feelings too complex to express, and neither had a vision for their future.

Their relationship was natural and warm but it confused Brady. He knew how he felt, but he was unable to put those feelings to words. He was, at times, sure she had strong feelings for him as well, but other times he wasn't sure. In the end he just left it alone.

One afternoon they walked on the sand of a quiet stretch of beach. Allison put her hand in Brady's as they walked barefoot at the water's edge. The touch of her hand felt electric but Allison made it seem very matter-of-fact. She talked as they walked.

"Have you thought about the Wind River Mountains much?" she asked.

Brady looked at her, stunned that she was the one to bring up what he regarded as off-limits.

"I think about it all the time," he said.

So, here it was. The one thing in his life he never shared with anyone. In the silence that loomed between them, both Brady and Allison shared a hunger to find intimate common ground and there was none more personal or more private than that nightmarish day.

They found a quiet place and stopped to talk. It felt right and Brady opened every wound for her. She shared hers with him. They spoke in great detail of their nightmares and fears and regrets. They relived that wonderful winter in St. Joseph and they shared stories of the months on the trail after St. Joseph. They shared their feelings and, when Brady spoke of his baby brother and his sister and his mother and his father and their graves, he wept. And when he did, Allison wept as well. They held each other a long time, two lost souls bound by tragedy.

Finally, after a cathartic and long talk, Allison looked up at Brady and wiped the tears from his cheeks with the backs of her fingers. She touched his scars and traced the long one along his jawbone.

"You know I love you don't you?" she whispered.

Brady smiled. He felt he had always known Allison. He felt at peace when he was with her. When he was alone she was always in his thoughts. When they were together he found himself falling in love with her all over again one feature at a time. He loved the profile of her face, her high cheekbones, and her soft smiling lips. He loved the curl that fell loosely in front of her ear and her strong feminine hands. But most of all he loved the way she looked at him, as though no one else in the world existed.

Allison accepted Brady for everything he was and was not, and hers was an unselfish love that she expressed freely and openly. She never questioned her love for Brady and never thought for a moment that he could love her any less than she loved him.

Brady held Allison's face in his hands and spoke to her in a language she did not understand. She smiled.

"What does that mean?" she asked.

"In the Pend d'Orielle language, it means . . ." He paused to think of the right words. "Your smile is my sunshine." He touched her lips. "Your tears are my tears." He placed the tip of his finger below her eye. Then he placed her hand over his heart. "You are forever in my heart."

Allison was overwhelmed with emotion. She could not take her eyes off this rugged young man with his long hair, tattered buckskins, and scared face she last saw as a child full of innocence in what seemed to be a lifetime ago in a universe she felt she had invented as a child herself.

"That is beautiful, Brady."

He brushed her hair back from her face.

"I am so in love with you," he whispered.

She lay in his arms for a long time. Her expression turned from one of contentment to one of concern. She sat up and looked directly into Brady's eyes. It was everything or nothing for her, and Brady could sense it in her tone.

"I was almost married four-years ago."

Brady rolled onto his side looking up at her.

"Almost?"

"Yes. To a very nice man who owns a bank in San Francisco. I met him through my step-father."

"What happened?"

Allison struggled. She chose her words carefully.

"His name is Waddell Stuart. He offered me everything, Brady. A nice home, commitment, security—everything."

She dropped her eyes. "I don't know what happened. I let us get all the wedding plans made, he bought a house for us. It was all set."

"But you didn't do it," Brady said as a matter of fact, but it sounded like a question.

"I couldn't. I was waiting for something and that wasn't it. I didn't know at the time what I was waiting for. I just knew I couldn't go through with it."

She smiled and her eyes shined.

"Now I know what it was."

Brady touched her face. He smiled, but his eyes were sad.

"What's wrong?"

Brady looked away. He agonized over his words.

"I was in love once with a girl I would have married," he said softly.

Allison felt a shudder course through her.

"Who was she?" Allison asked delicately.

"Her name was Little Deer. She was a Blackfoot—a Pend d'Orielle actually."

Allison took Brady's hand. "Tell me about her," she said.

Brady took a deep breath. "She made me feel like I was worth something. Our life was simple—hard, but it was simple. I had this hole inside me that I couldn't fill. It's like part of me was always empty. No matter where I went or what I did, I couldn't fill it. And I did things I'm not proud of. Little Deer made all that go away for me."

Allison rubbed his hand between hers as he talked. Her eyes never left his, and she neither passed judgment nor asked him to explain. Then he got very quiet and she sat with him without speaking. He put his arms around her and held her tight and kissed her hair where it brushed his lips. He felt her arms around him like she never wanted to let go.

She closed her eyes and smelled him and touched him. She kissed him with great passion and held his face and finally looked at him. She detected a distance in him— some primeval calling she knew she could not reach.

"You're not staying, are you?" she asked, her eyes wet with tears.

"I can't," he said.

He pulled her close. He wanted to absorb every memory of holding her in his arms. Allison's confusion and frustration gripped her in disbelief.

"What are you looking for, Brady? We're not enough? I'm not enough?"

"It's not that."

"What then? Please tell me so I can at least try to fix it."

Brady was at a loss. He had no answers. Whatever it was that drew him away from everyone and everything he loved made no sense, not even to him. His heart ached and everything that was good urged him to stay.

"Why? Why are you leaving?" she asked.

He searched her eyes with his. He searched his heart for an answer she would understand but, in the end, he didn't have an answer even he understood. He held her hands tight in his.

"I don't know who I am, Allison," he said. He swallowed hard.

"I just feel so lost inside. I don't even remember being a kid. Every time things start to feel comfortable to me, I feel like I need to move on. I won't be any good to you or anyone else until I can settle these feelings up."

"And you think running away will do that?" she asked, her eyes soft and her expression one of delicate concern.

He shook his head. "I don't know. I hope so," he said. "I don't want to lose you."

He looked away. His voice was barely a whisper. "Everything good around me dies."

Allison was devastated, but her voice was more encouraging than Brady felt he deserved from her.

"Brady, I can't make you any promises, but you do what you need to do."

She kissed him and they held each other a long time. When he left, neither understood why.

Kincaid had left for Montana by the time Brady rejoined Franklin in San Francisco. Before he left, Kincaid told Franklin he didn't expect Brady would be coming back to the ranch for a while. He asked Franklin to look out for him where ever he went. Franklin promised Kincaid he would.

Franklin could tell Brady was uneasy as they sat at a corner table in the hotel and talked that night. Finally, setting aside the small talk, Brady stood up looked over at Franklin.

"I'm going to Texas," he said. "You coming with me?"

"Texas?" Franklin scratched his head. "Texas."

Franklin stood up and shook his head.

"No, I ain't. B.C. There ain't nothing in Texas. Nothing I'm interested in, anyway."

"I'm looking to join the Texas Rangers," Brady said.

Franklin laughed. "The Texas Rangers," Franklin said with a sarcastic tone in his voice.

"Why the Texas Rangers?"

"It's something to do," Brady answered.

"There's lots of things that are something to do, but they don't all involve getting shot at," Franklin said.

"I know, but it would be like old times, Franklin. You and me. A new place every day. It beats sitting around a hotel counting your money."

Franklin surveyed the place with his eyes and with a broad sweep of his hand said, "I happen to like this hotel, and I don't having nothing against counting money."

Brady didn't respond. Franklin sat back down, leaned forward on his elbows, and thought for a few moments.

"It's respectable," Franklin said, then he was quiet. "But you know, a man of my proclivities does require a certain amount of adventure to stay properly stimulated."

Brady laughed.

Franklin waved at Maggie.

"Can you bring us two more beers and come sit with us a minute?"

Maggie returned with two mugs of beer and turned to leave.

"No, sit down here with us a minute. We need to talk something over with you."

Brady was as puzzled as Maggie was.

"Maggie, how'd you like to buy The Gold Nugget?" Franklin asked.

Maggie smiled. "I would like that just fine, Franklin. I'd like to be twenty-years younger too, but that's not likely to happen."

She stood and Franklin caught her arm.

"I have a proposition for you," Franklin said.

"Well I am flattered dear but I am old enough to be your mother."

Franklin smiled. "I didn't mean it like that," he said.

He looked over at Brady and grinned.

"Me and B.C.'s going to Texas and I don't know when we might be back."

Brady looked at Maggie and shrugged.

"Look, Maggie," he said. "I've got more than enough money to take care of my needs."

Maggie sat down. Her expression was hopeful, but doubtful.

"This is a good place," he said gesturing broadly. "It makes money and you already run it top to bottom."

Maggie listened. Brady pushed his chair back and watched Franklin's familiar logic unfold with no idea of where it was going next.

"You set aside ten percent of your profits at the end of the year, after you pay all the bills. Deposit it in my bank account each month and, when it gets to ten-thousand dollars, the place is yours. I'll sign the deed and leave it with the bank."

"Franklin, this place is worth a lot more than that and you know it."

"Maggie, you were the first friend I met when I got here. You put me up, fed me, and never asked for a nickel," Franklin said.

Maggie's eyes lit up. She pinched his chin and laughed. "How could a girl turn down a face like this," she said. "I did that as much for me as I did for you."

Maggie leaned back in her chair. "Say we do make a deal. How much are you going to need for a down payment?"

"Sweetheart, you just give me a big ol' hug and pack me and B.C. a lunch. That's all the down payment I need."

Maggie stood and Franklin followed suit. She threw her arms around him.

"I knew you were a good bet the day you walked through that door and announced to all the drunks in here that Franklin T. Stilwell of Montana had arrived and San Francisco was now your new backyard."

THIRTY-EIGHT

Austin, Texas: December 19, 1853

The cold wind that followed them across Texas carried dust devils down the street in Austin where Brady and Franklin stood outside the poorly kept Adjutant's office of the Texas Rangers.

They exchanged *last chance* looks. "What do you think?" Brady asked.

Franklin shrugged. "Let's go in and see what they have to say."

An hour later, they stepped out of the building holding their Texas Ranger badges. "So, we get paid the last of every month, provide everything for ourselves, try not to get killed and, in exchange for that, we get these," Brady said, holding out his badge.

Franklin shook his head and spat. "It ain't much of a step up from working for ol' man Hog," he said.

They walked down Congress Street and stopped at the Continental Saloon. They stood at the end of the bar where three other young men covered in trail dust and wearing Texas Ranger badges celebrated. Brady looked at Franklin and, without a word exchanged, they pinned on their badges.

One of the three celebrating rangers noticed Brady and Franklin. He raised a glass to them, and then sent the bartender down with two beers on him.

Several beers later, the five rangers had commandeered the place. By the time they closed it down that night, Brady and Franklin were officially indoctrinated into the new brotherhood and, any second thoughts they had about their decision to join were dispelled by the contagious pride the veterans took in the Texas Rangers.

The shortage of manpower in the politically ignored Rangers made it almost impossible to stay ahead of the unrelenting pressure from the Comanche, the Lipan Apache, and the Mexican raiders, all of whom still regarded the recently formed state of Texas as the fair game it was prior to joining the Union.

Brady and Franklin thrived on the high action, fast-paced life style. They lived from day-to-day and didn't see the changes coming as Texas began to bend under the weight of growing involvement from Washington.

For nearly two years Brady and Franklin hunted down and brought in wanted fugitives, they led retaliatory raids into Mexico against border outlaws, and it wasn't lost on either of them that, in many ways, the Texas Rangers were little more than organized outlaws themselves.

Eastern politicians and local officials tried unsuccessfully to control the reckless style of the rangers. But Texans rallied around their Rangers, a wild and unruly law enforcement agency that managed to get things done the Army couldn't. They operated in a swift and decisive manner carrying out justice in the field rather than the courts. While this vigilante practice went against the grain of justice and legal deliberation, it was an efficient way to deal with crime under the frontier conditions that existed across most of Texas.

The reputation of the Rangers along the Texas-Mexican border became legendary and every Ranger worthy of the badge did everything he could to perpetuate the legend.

Like the American cowboy, the Texas Rangers had a low image in the eyes of many, but they caught the attention of writers and artists who began romanticizing them in their work. There was a perceived glory and pride about them that created a mounting wave of public admiration. It was just a matter of time before local politicians began to use the Rangers' successes to promote their own agendas, and that's when the myth collided with reality.

Brady's skills as a scout and tracker put him at a level above all others. No one could pick up a trail and follow it like he could. His days with the Blackfoot taught him things few white men knew. His ability to function under impossible condition and his understanding of Indian ways set him apart from the others and he found himself leading missions that engaged the hostile Indians from one end of Texas to the other, often working alone.

In the meantime, Franklin's recklessness and courage earned him a wide-spread reputation throughout the border towns, where he was assigned to cases dealing with the worst of the criminal lot. His mind worked like theirs. He was uncanny in his ability to locate and bring to justice, any way he could, outlaws so corrupt even the Army had given up on them.

Franklin did everything with style and to excess. He refused to compromise any assignment and his ruthless pursuit of bringing criminals to justice at any cost narrowed down the number of those who would ride with him to but a handful of men no less impassioned than himself. Franklin operated at a level beyond even the most dauntless of the lot.

Fourteen months after he and Brady were sworn in with the rangers, Franklin was promoted to captain. He led an elite squad of eight Rangers considered no less dangerous than the outlaws they pursued.

The Mexicans called them *Los Tejanos Diablos* and, while they were loved by some and feared by others, even those they protected regarded them with caution.

The territory they policed was governed by violence and ruled by violent men, the most violent among them, Miguel Zaragoza. For a year and a half, Zaragoza and his men rode up from Mexico, eluding the army and raiding at will along a stretch of border one hundred and fifty miles long. He stole horses and cattle and killed indiscriminately and, when he returned each time to Mexico, he was harbored by his people.

When neither the army nor the rangers could effectively protect ranchers from Zaragoza, Captain Stilwell was asked to lead an illegal operation across the border into Mexico to pursue the outlaw where he least expected it. There were no rules. No restrictions. If killed or captured, the U.S. government would disavow any knowledge of the operation, and Stilwell would be on his own.

Franklin gathered up his men, explained the mission he described as a *suicide operation*, and then asked for volunteers. All eight men stepped forward and, by midmorning, wearing no badges, they splashed up out of the Rio Grande River onto the shores of Mexico riding hard.

They crossed the dead landscape of rocky, treeless ground, passing villagers and travelers who eyed them with grave doubt.

Zaragoza knew of Stilwell's presence before the end of the day. The *federales* knew of the breach of jurisdiction a day after that, and both Zaragoza and the *federales* sent men to intercept Stilwell.

Stilwell and his men, who made their presence known that first day, spent the night in a remote village where they traded clothes and traded horses. The next morning they split up. Stilwell rode alone. The others rode out in ones and twos, disappearing into the countryside regrouping only long enough to execute Zaragoza's men one at a time where ever they found them.

They haunted northern Mexico like ghost riders leaving no trail and only whispered references to who they were from the mouths of peasants and farmers they encountered along the way. But, what the people knew, Zaragoza knew. His continued evasion of the Rangers emboldened him and he grew more reckless as the months passed.

On a moonless night following a raid into Texas, Zaragoza and a dozen of his vaqueros crossed back into Mexico with over eighty-head of Texas horses. Stilwell and his men were waiting for them.

The Mexicans made camp for the night on some unnamed river in steep hill country. Four vaqueros made up the night guard while the rest slept. Stilwell split up his company, sending four men in to quietly dispatch the guards while the other four positioned the herd to move north in a hurry.

Stilwell spotted the last of the guards, dismounted, and slunk through the night to surprise the unwary sentry who sat his horse and smoked a cigarette, appearing to be half asleep.

Stilwell held up his hand. He and the Ranger with him, Sergeant Roberts, stopped to study the situation. Stilwell slipped his belt knife from its scabbard and nodded for Roberts to do likewise.

"You catch up the horse. I'll take the rider," Stilwell whispered.

"Hell of a way to make a living, Captain."

Stilwell kept his eyes on the guard. "Stealing horses or killing people?"

Roberts shrugged. "Both, I guess."

Stilwell made a motion toward the guard with his fingers pointing that direction. When they were within twenty yards, Roberts hooked a spur and went clattering to the ground at the same time the guard fired a round and sent a bullet ripping through his throat. Stilwell drew and fired and the vaquero tipped back with hole in his chest before he slumped forward and died in the saddle.

The camp erupted with gunfire. The horses broke and ran, stampeding north in the direction from which they had come.

When it was done, Zaragoza and the others lay dead. The Rangers packed up their two dead and rode out following the horses to the border.

Brady McCall was on a quest of his own. In October of 1854, McCall stood before his commanding officer in a field outpost in the southwest.

"The Burnett place is here," he told McCall, pointing to a remote location on the wall map. "And that's where they took them two girls from."

"They sure it was the Lipan Apache?"

The officer nodded. "Mr. Burnett watched them ride off with both of them slung across the backs of their ponies."

McCall studied the map a long time before he responded. Then he looked up.

"I'll do what I can," McCall said.

"You can take your pick of the men you need from Company C."

"I'm going alone."

"You're going to need some help."

"I ain't looking to start a war. I'll do better by myself."

McCall rode out the next morning in the half light of a predawn moon that shone down on the single rider who appeared a ghostly image.

News of the kidnapping reached Washington swiftly as politicians capitalized on the event to publicize attention against the Apache and in favor of the extreme measures they proposed to eradicate the Indian threat to citizens of Texas. Undue political pressure was brought to bear upon the U.S. Army and the Texas Rangers.

McCall had picked up the trail of the Apache at the Burnett Ranch. He rode day and night, stopping only long enough to rest his horse. He remembered the single-mindedness of Travis Kincaid, and pushed on until he was at the base of the Peloncillo Mountains. He crossed the Gila River and followed the tracks that confirmed the shoe prints of the two white girls. McCall dreaded the thought of the fate that may befall the girls and pushed his horse harder as the country became rougher.

Late in the evening of the tenth day, as McCall sat overlooking the Apache camp below, thoughts of the Wind River massacre ran through his head. His heart was heavy and his anger seethed as he relived that awful night.

He watched when they tethered the girls. He made note of where they hobbled the horses and then, late into the night he stood when the last of the warriors hunkered down to sleep. It was a simple plan—steal into camp, free the girls, catch up an Indian pony for them, and then disappear quietly into the black of night.

He made his way past the hobbled Apache horses, he picked out a young branded gelding, and bridled it with a rawhide lace. He slunk into camp and waited outside the sleeping circle.

The two captive girls huddled white-eyed, and recoiled when he approached them and the restless warrior to which they were lashed. He hushed them with a finger over his lip.

McCall fell upon the sleeping warrior, muffling his scream and cutting his throat in one swift motion as the terrified girls lay petrified. He held the warrior pinned to the ground until the body stopped thrashing, and then he cut the girls' tether.

They followed him out of camp to the waiting pony. McCall set first one, and then the other upon its back. He lashed their feet with rawhide laces running under the horse's belly, and led the horse out of camp.

As quietly as he had come into camp, McCall was gone with the children.

Days later, McCall rode into the outpost with the two children in tow, much to the surprise of the commanding officer and the New York reporter who was prepared to return to his newspaper with the final disastrous outcome of the kidnapping already written and ready.

Ever a publicity opportunist, the reporter scrapped the failure angle and went to work fabricating details of the rescue to a level that embarrassed McCall, but elevated the Texas Ranger mystique to the point the outlaw image they originally endured began to transform into something humanly impossible to live up to.

News of the rescue traveled with blinding speed and, before McCall and the Rangers could comprehend what was happening, the entire affair developed into a major political event. Aspiring politicians drew in reporters and writers, all clamoring for McCall's story and attempting to share the glory by association.

The details of the rescue had been told and retold so many times by so many different people, each adding his own embellishments, and making McCall an overnight celebrity. Franklin, not to be outdone by any eastern Johnny-come-lately reporters, fueled the fires of fiction with stories of McCall's exploits that challenged the imaginations of even the most eager writers. So engaged were they with his tales, they followed him all over back in

Austin, furiously taking notes and asking questions of their own.

In the beginning, Franklin would humor himself by telling brash lies, not really expecting anyone to believe them. When he realized the entourage of journalists took him seriously, he gave them plenty to write about. They gathered around him and he leaned back in his chair and rattled on as they wrote.

If the legend of the Texas Rangers needed a lift, it got it. Deep down, Franklin felt satisfied with himself. He knew he had left his mark.

The next couple of months passed quietly. The excitement of the rescue had run its course and the politicians had milked it for all it was worth. McCall's life, much to his relief, had returned to normal.

THIRTY-NINE

McCall and Stilwell stayed with the Rangers three more years, but things were changing. It was progress, the commanding officer told them.

The job was evolving quickly as the state grew and local law enforcement and the military grew with it. Regulations and paperwork choked the fun out of the job as McCall and Stilwell spent more time indoors than out in the field. It was no longer a job, it was a career.

The old days were gone. McCall and Stilwell thrived in the unstructured operation where rules were made up as they were needed and changed as often as the situation demanded. Now it was different. The rules were printed and posted, there was a standard operating procedure for everything. The Rangers were coming of age.

The days of three or four rangers cleaning out a town full of outlaws on their own were gone. The raids into Mexico had ceased altogether. The reputation of the Texas Rangers would live forever, but the excitement of the early days had been consumed by progress.

Their boot heels struck the wooden sidewalk of Austin in cadence where McCall and Stilwell walked together one warm summer evening. Brady looked over at Franklin with that same expression that crossed his face every time he had an idea.

"I been thinkin'," he said.

Franklin listened and waited.

"All this progress, as they call it, is wearing a little thin on me."

Franklin nodded. "I don't know what it is about progress that everyone finds so damn appealing, but I got it up to here." He waved his fingers across his chin.

"And whatever you been thinking, B.C., it can't be any worse than what this is, so just spit it out. I ain't saying I'm for it, but I will hear you out."

They continued walking. Brady paused while he formulated his thoughts.

"I've been thinking a while about us getting out of the Rangers."

He looked at Franklin expecting a protest.

Franklin laughed. "You are the thinker, B.C., no doubt about that. But, it don't take no genius to figure out we overstayed our usefulness here."

Brady shrugged and grinned.

"So, what are you thinking we do?" Franklin asked.

Brady turned and regarded the setting sun a long time before he answered.

"Let's follow that," he said.

El Paso, Texas: January 1857

McCall and Stilwell wandered across Texas and in and out of Mexico half a dozen times before they ended up in El Paso sitting in a decaying cantina. They had no concern for where they were going and none for where they had been, but Brady had a growing restlessness about him that was not lost on Franklin.

"You look like you got a little girl on your mind, cuz."

Brady looked up from his *cerveza.*

"I got one letter from her in Austin two and a half years ago, Franklin. I ain't heard another thing since."

"You been writing to her?"

Brady shook his head.

"Then, what do you expect?"

"Just what I got, I guess."

"I'd say that was about right."

This time, Franklin got *that* look on his face. "I got a idea," he said.

Brady stared at him.

"You know, we could join the army," he said.

Brady thought about it.

"I think we can take our rank from the Rangers and both start out as officers," Brady said.

"You sure about that?"

"No, I ain't for sure sure."

Franklin tipped back his beer and slammed the glass down on the table.

"I say we do it."

Brady grinned. "All right, but how about we go back to California first? I can't leave everything undone like it is—I need to know one way or the other."

Franklin looked down at his boots. "You know it's going to be the other, right?"

"I reckon I do."

Brady had a faraway look in his eyes. Franklin waved the bartender for two more beers. They sat that way a long time before either spoke again.

"We ain't heard nothing from Travis," Brady said.

Franklin grinned. "No, but I bet Maggie has."

"We haven't heard from her, neither," Brady said.

Franklin brushed it off. "No need, I guess. We never been in one place long enough to have an address."

They rode west with no particular hurry about them. The army was a plan but it was not a priority and, for now, they were content to be free of obligation and under the authority of no man.

They arrived in San Francisco and tied their horses at the rail of the Golden Nugget. The town had changed. It was busier, more crowded, and showing signs of growth with many new buildings and a harbor more congested with ships than ever.

The meeting with Maggie was a joyful affair. She had kept her word and banked Franklin's money as agreed. After a long dinner, Brady, Franklin, and Maggie were caught up on the news. Kincaid was doing well, she said, but she didn't expect he would be coming back to San Francisco again. She bought the place next door a year or so back, and turned it into a café serving meals to the crews who worked the docks through the night.

Brady appeared restless. Both Franklin and Maggie saw it. When he pushed his chair back and prepared to excuse himself, they both smiled.

"I think I'm going to take a ride down to San Gregorio," he said. "How about if I meet up with you back here in a couple of days?"

"I'll be here," Franklin said, grinning.

Brady stood. Maggie stood with him. She wrapped her arms around him.

"You tell Miss Allison she better not let you go again."

Brady smiled. "I will. Thank you, Maggie."

Franklin didn't stand. He just looked up at Brady and nodded.

It was late when Brady followed his moon-cast shadow into the small village that looked no different than it did the last time he was there. He pitched his bedroll at the edge of town and lay on his back gazing at the stars most of the night without sleeping.

The following morning, he visited with Allison's mother a long time. They sat in her kitchen and talked over coffee. She felt bad for him and agonized over how to tell him Allison had married Waddell Stuart and they had a daughter together.

But, she did, and he took it hard.

"Where do they live?" He asked.

"Brady, it's not in anybody's best interest for you to see her."

"I know. I was just wondering."

"They live in San Francisco."

"What's her daughter's name?"

Mrs. Hayes's eyes reddened. She wiped away the trace of a tear on her handkerchief.

"Elizabeth."

Brady's eyes watered up.

"That was my mother's name."

Mrs. Hayes nodded. "I know."

Brady slumped back in his chair. The he stood. She followed him out to his horse. Mrs. Hayes stared at the old battle-scarred buckskin.

"I got something here," Brady said.

He fumbled around in his saddlebags, pulled out a deerskin sack, and pulled from the sack, a silver and turquoise bracelet and a woman's ring, also of Navajo turquoise. He thought of the many times in his mind he played the scene in which he would present them to Allison. In none of them did he envision the situation in which he now found himself.

Brady handed the bracelet to Mrs. Hayes and tucked the ring back into the sack.

"If you wouldn't mind, Miss Hayes, could you give this to Allison for her little girl?"

Mrs. Hayes hesitated. She saw the pleading in his eyes and acquiesced.

"Yes, of course. Thank you, Brady. It's lovely."

She stood back, crossed her arms, and watched him swing up into the saddle. He looked down at her with so much he wanted to say, but he just touched his hat.

"Ma'am."

Mrs. Hayes felt the ache in her heart, but she stood strong.

"It's for the best, Brady."

She watched him cross the square, turn up the road traveling north out of town, and simply disappear from view.

He came to a crossroad and sat there at a point of indecision for a long time. He chose to go back to the only place he knew as home, with Montana drawing him back with a power he couldn't deny.

FORTY

Brady McCall set out with a cold heart and dark thoughts.
He rode empty. Devoid of purpose. He had no idea what he
expected to find at the Triple Dot, and he had no concerns
for abandoning Franklin or their plans to enlist in the army.
His life was nothing more than a series of losses—he
expected nothing more. He had no one and nothing to strike
out at, so he just rode.

Whatever he expected to find waiting for him at the ranch,
it wasn't there. It felt like home, but Kincaid had changed.
He was married to Laura Spaulding, the widow of an army
officer in charge of procuring horses for the Fort Smith
remount program. After her husband was killed, she and
Kincaid became close friends, eventually fell in love, and
in the spring of 1858, they were married.

Kincaid did everything he could to make Brady feel
at home, but Brady knew he could not stay. He would have
left sooner, but Laura and he developed a close friendship.
He valued her advice and she seemed to understand his
unsettled soul better than anyone. She treated him like a
son. He confided in her and trusted her with his deepest
feelings. Both Laura and Travis went out of their way to
help him feel comfortable, but Brady could not get on even
terms with his feelings.

He never questioned why Allison didn't wait for
him. He understood that. He replayed his decisions over

and over in his mind and wished it would have been different. He wanted to blame someone or something, and every time he tried it came back to him and he was the worse for it.

Late one night after the others had gone to bed, McCall sat outside on the porch, staring out at the darkness. The door behind him opened and closed softly. He turned expecting to see Travis. It was Laura. She smiled and handed him a cup of coffee then sat down on the step beside him without speaking.

They sat like that a long time. Finally, Laura put her hand on his arm and spoke very softly.

"You know, Brady, love can be a hurtful thing sometimes. We never know for sure what God has in his plans for us. You just have to do the best you can."

Brady didn't look at her, he just nodded his head in agreement.

"I'll tell you what I do know," she said. "I know that you must be careful not to let that hurt get in the way and make you do things you know are not right."

Then she put her arm over his shoulder and, just for the moment, he let himself feel like a small child. With all his heart he wished it was Bill McCall asleep in the house and his mother here with him on the porch. He closed his eyes and wished it hard, and when he opened them, Laura smiled gently and patted his back.

"Miss Laura," he started, then caught himself. He cleared his throat and collected his thoughts.

"I just feel like I'm going out of my way to give up everything that means anything to me, and I just can't seem to do anything about it. I don't understand why me and Franklin are left and everyone else is gone."

Laura wanted to cry, wanted to comfort this small boy, but all she could do was pray for the right words, and she knew there were none to be prayed for, and that alone made her feel empty and helpless. If Laura had any strength to offer this boy it was gone, and she crept quietly over her next words.

"You've lost more in your young life than most ever do, Brady. But, you're a wonderful young man with so much to offer and so much to look forward to."

She cried when she looked into his eyes.

"You have a good heart. Please listen to it."

Brady looked over at her and smiled. He turned and hugged her and thanked her.

The next morning, Brady went to the barn before the sun came up. He gave Buffalo Dancer an extra ration of grain. He spent a long time brushing the buckskin. His fingers touched the roughly healed scars that reminded him of so many places they had been together. He thought of the boy the big horse carried to safety at South Pass, the battles, the buffalo hunts, riding through the prairie grass with his Blackfoot brothers. He wondered where all the years had gone since the young buckskin buffalo pony splashed across the Missouri river with a ten-year old boy on his back.

Brady felt more alone than he ever had in his life. His heart was heavy as he spoke to the stallion, who flicked its ears and seemed to understand.

Buffalo Dancer raised his head, stopped chewing, and watched Brady intently as the cowboy continued talking. The proud, old buckskin seemed to know something was different this time.

Finally, McCall slipped the halter up over the buckskin's head and led him out to the gate of the big, tree-shaded brood mare pasture. McCall dropped the halter from the buckskin's head and stood there holding the slack lead rope. The horse stood without moving. Then he sniffed McCall's shirt and snorted. He raised his head. Trotted off a distance.

Brady watched the stallion strike a noble pose then thunder majestically off to claim his mares.

"I owe you everything, old friend," McCall said, his cheeks wet with tears. He felt insignificant and alone as he watched the horse disappear over the ridge. He stood there a long time staring out across the meadow waiting for the buckskin to return, but it never did.

McCall left Montana and drifted for the sake of drifting. He traveled south. By the time he reached Arizona Territory, he had attracted trouble in more places than he could remember. He didn't consciously look for trouble, but he went where trouble went and something inside him began to feel comfort in conflict. Soon enough he gravitated closer and closer to those things that allowed him to feel pain or to inflict pain, until it became his nature.

On an evening in late July, McCall sat alone at a small table at the back of a smoky saloon in Tucson. He started to get up to leave when the doors flung open, and three buffalo hunters pushed their way to the bar. McCall poured himself another drink and sat back in his chair.

He reached across and laid his pistol in his lap. The loudest of the three was a slightly built man, whose courage was re-enforced by the two well-armed friends who drank his whiskey and laughed at his crude badgering of the bartender as they took over the place.

McCall's heart pounded when he recognized the face of Willie Stokes, the last man he and Franklin were assigned to bring in the day they turned in their badges.

Stokes was wanted for the murder of a desperate young boy whose father hired him out to skin for a company of travelling buffalo runners.

McCall sat back and watched as Stokes and his cohorts ran two old men out of the cantina. Stokes was looking for his next victim when his eyes stopped on McCall sitting alone. Stokes stood staring while he tried to figure out whether or not he recognized McCall. McCall made it easy for him.

"How's the buffalo business, Willie?" McCall asked.

Willie Stokes, caught off-guard, recognized McCall and his hand dropped to the gun at his side. He drew. The shot went wild, tearing into the wall behind McCall.

McCall fired. His shot caught Stokes in the jaw and sent bone and teeth flying, twisting Stokes off his feet where he fell at the foot rail of the bar.

The two liquored-up wretches with Stokes unholstered their pistols and hesitated while each gauged his odds of being shot first.

"This ain't your fight," McCall shouted.

Before the words were fully spoken, bullets whined across the room, carelessly drawn and off-target. McCall dropped to one knee, fired twice in rapid succession, and watched his bullets rip through the shirts of both men. They were dead when they hit the floor.

The spectators in the bar stood gawking. No one came to the aid of the buffalo runners and no one addressed McCall.

The next morning McCall saw the sunrise through the bars of the Tucson jail. He was later that day absolved of any criminal wrongdoing, but the judge advised him he should consider moving on.

Outside the courtroom, McCall stared blankly at the distant mountains. There was nothing about himself he was proud of—no redeeming quality to balance against the men he killed and those he knew were yet to be killed. If he had thought of Allison, he would have been ashamed. But as it was he felt neither guilt nor shame.

That night, McCall lay in his hotel room bed with his fingers laced behind his head trying to piece the loose ends of his life together.

He had gone from one odd job to another, finding trouble wherever he stopped until that was all he knew. He avoided people altogether and turned to crossing the border into Mexico stealing a few horses at a time. He sold them in Texas knowing the horses he stole came from Mexican outlaws who had stolen them in the first place. It gave him a degree of satisfaction, but he took no pride in it. It was simply a game he played better than most.

He had seldom thought of Franklin and only rarely let his mind wander back to Kincaid and the Triple Dot.

He knew it was anger that drove him and a dark soul that sustained him. His aimless existence asked nothing of him, but the brooding violence that festered within would be his undoing and he knew that too.

Every memory he made was black and malignant. He had reached a crossroads but had no idea what to do next. He knew he had made his last trip across the border and he knew there was nothing for him in Montana or California.

The next morning, McCall stood looking up and down the street, watching people move about with a purpose. The only choice he had was to decide which way to ride out of town. Knowing one direction was as good as the other was a hopeless testimony to what he had become.

From across the dusty street, a soldier in a blue officer's uniform walked his direction. The soldier called out to him.

"Captain McCall."

The soldier approached him and extended his hand. "Captain, it's me, Clayton Parmelee. I served under you in the Rangers."

McCall stuck out his hand, happy to see a friendly face for a change.

"Clay, it's good to see you again."

There was a moment of awkward silence as they looked each other over. McCall noted the oak leaf rank on Parmelee's lapel.

"It appears they call you Major Parmelee these days," McCall said, nodding toward the gold insignia.

"Yes sir. Has kind of a nice ring to it compared to some of the things they called us in Texas."

"How do you happen to be in Tucson?" asked McCall.

"Well sir, we're down here on a little Apache business. I heard you were the main attraction here yesterday so I thought I'd see if you might be interested in a job."

"What kind of a job?"

"We need scouts."

"We?"

"The army. The pay is good. You'd operate with a fair amount of freedom—not like it was in the end with the Rangers."

"I don't know Clay. I'm not really looking for anything too structured right now. And, truth is, I've pretty much had my fill of killing."

"As a scout, your only job would be to locate the troublemakers. The army takes care of things from there."

"I appreciate the offer, but no thanks."

"Look, Captain, you have skills not many men have. We got innocent folks out there dying. It doesn't have to be long-term—just long enough for us to get those renegades off the backs of those families trying to make a go of it out there."

Parmelee struck a chord that sent McCall's mind reeling back in time. He nodded slowly.

"For a while, I suppose."

"You'll do it?"

"I'll do it."

McCall paused a moment.

"There is one thing, though."

"What's that, Captain?"

"I work alone."

Parmelee didn't seem surprised. He extended his hand again.

"Agreed."
They shook on it.

McCall adjusted to Army life slower than he expected. But, for all that was in him that resisted the structure of an obligated existence, he found solace in the sense of purpose the military gave him. Discipline was rendered equally and, despite the immunity he had as a military employed civilian, they called him on his infractions and showed no tolerance for his disrespect for convention. But, he adapted.

The military redirected his aggression and frustration to a common enemy, and McCall took to it with a great vengeance. Mescalero and Chiricahua Apache raiders felt the wrath of a new breed of army scout. McCall was a patient hunter—a relentless tracker who took his prey one at a time. If they saw him he, was a shadow, if they heard him, he was a whisper. But, mostly they never saw him nor heard him and that made him a force more feared than the army itself.

McCall respected the Apache. They were tough and elusive and able to survive in a land never meant for the living. In them resided an instinct for cruelty and an endurance for hardship unlike anything McCall had ever seen before. He knew them as a young Ranger and he knew there was no give in them. He had no personal hatred for them, nor they for him, but both understood there was no negotiation for an accord between them.

In due time, McCall took one, then another and another of them, until the offenders retreated further and further into the wastelands of the high desert, where they vanished without a trace or any sign they had ever existed in the first place.

McCall felt a familiar pattern in his life repeating itself. Scouting had run its course. He lost his taste for that which had driven him there. He found himself thinking more and more of the road he traveled and those whose faces now seemed like the faces of strangers he dreamed in a dream.

He sat alone at a dark table with the glass of whisky he never touched and said to himself, *"If I could go back and change any part of my life, what would I change?"* He had no answer.

The next day he quit the Army.

Brady C. McCall stood his horse at the edge of the world and gazed out at the end of it where it must surely have dropped off and nothing beyond it was visible. Like a small ship with a tattered sail and no rudder, he set forth upon that shimmering sea of grass, bobbing and waiting for the current to push him along.

There he was. Twenty-nine years old and he felt as though he had already lived two lifetimes. Allison Granger remained his greatest regret and the one failure for which he could find no way to forgive himself. He carried three month's pay in his saddlebags and rode north, only because Mexico was to the south and he had no reason to go there. He skirted the tall mountains to the east and set a course which was no course at all, but it took him onto the prairies that stretched before him. He measured his own insignificance by his smallness in comparison to it all.

The air smelled sweet and for the first time in as long as he could remember nothing hung over his life. No obligations, no responsibilities. When he came to a fork in the road, he gave the horse its head. He ate when he was hungry, slept when he was tired, and each day was a magnificent reawakening in which he was thankful to be a part.

At day's end he stopped and watched the sun set in a resplendent red sky, like a prairie fire at the edge of the world. He couldn't remember ever feeling more alive. He listened to the leaves of the cottonwood trees whisper in the wind. He heard a multitude of bird sounds he didn't remember hearing the day before. The water in the creek tasted cool and sweet and not since his days with the Blackfoot people had he felt so close to the earth.

At night, when he pulled his blanket up to sleep, the sky was crowded with stars. Owls called gently to their mates, and McCall could close his eyes and rest. When the moon was up, coyotes bent their heads heavenward and called out to it. In those moments of consummate solitude, Allison Granger never failed to slip into his thoughts.

FORTY-ONE

Kansas: 1859

The open land before McCall stood empty and the vastness of it gave it a sense of foreboding. But to McCall it represented freedom. Freedom from obligation and freedom from his memories and, he hoped, freedom from himself. He rode easy in the saddle, and the horse he rode stepped out at a relaxed pace that suited him. Neither the man nor the horse saw anything before them but more of the same and there was no hurry about them.

In the early morning hours he could smell the sweet smell of fresh dew on the buffalo grass that grew where he lay. At night the sky seemed to move further away to make room for the stars that shone, and he remembered the Blackfoot names for many of them. He watched the stars move, and he lie there breathing slowly.

"If I could," he said to himself. *"I would change a few things. There would have been no killing. There would have been no move from Virginia."*

Then it occurred to him there would have been no Franklin and no Allison and no Kincaid. Nothing that was part of his life would have existed. No Buffalo Dancer. No Little Deer. There was more of him on this side of the Wind River Mountains than there was on the other. He tried to imagine his father and his mother growing old, and he couldn't.

For all he had become, good and bad—for all he had seen and done, he couldn't imagine it any other way. For as many times as he had wished it different, he had no picture of how it should have been.

He lay there a long time before he completed the thought. *"You can't change one thing without changing the rest—that's God's plan."* He smiled.

He looked skyward and imagined the stars were angels. In his mind, he reconciled himself to a universe of a much higher order than man alone. He didn't name it, he just accepted it as a reaffirmation of his own insignificance, and he understood.

"Maybe where you're going and how you get there is all that matters. Where you've been is gone, and there's no way to change that," he said to himself, or maybe it was to the horse or to the stars, but when it was said, he left it at that.

By the time McCall reached the Arkansas River he began to encounter other riders. They traveled in ones and twos and in large companies. Some looked to settle. Some pressed on. Those that came to settle did so in unlikely places. He wondered which of them had stopped and settled where they did because they had nothing left in them and stopped because of it, and which stopped because their dream was small and they accepted the first offering presented to them.

"Do they have any idea what's on the other side of them mountains?" He asked himself. *"And if they did, would they move on or stay?"* He knew they would stay just as easily as he moved on.

He came upon signs for towns with splendid names like Emporia and Great Bend. When he passed through them, they were small clusters of modest buildings presided over by visionaries who planted the seeds of civilization just as the farmers who followed them planted seeds of corn and wheat. And together they stood waiting and hoping that others would follow. It looked to McCall as a futile effort born of vanity and nurtured by arrogance. He continued riding. He saw farmsteads carved into hillsides with roofs of sod and no tree about for as far as the eye could determine. The ground was dry and parched, and the raggedy families stood in doorways waiting for the rain which never came. But still they stayed and waited. It was their lot, and they had cast their fate to it.

Some would hold their hand up to him, and he to theirs, but he rode without stopping, and he wondered if they knew more, would they pack up and leave or hunker down and wait for the rain. He knew they would wait.

One evening, at the gentle cusp between sundown and darkness, McCall turned his horse toward a brilliance of lights that rose up from the dark prairie like a great beacon that beckoned him. When he reached the outskirts of the town, he stopped at a painted wooden sign. LAWRENCE it read in the hand-rendered letters of a skilled scrivener.

He stood his horse where the sign was and regarded both the town and the open plain before he touched the horse with his heels and rode toward the light.

He came first upon two saloons situated on opposite corners of the street. Both busy. Both loud. Yellow light filtering through dirty windows onto the street casting long shadows of the horses tied at the posts out front. He heard a piano and then he heard loud laughter. He heard the sounds of loud whisky voices coming from both places.

Too crowded for his taste. Too high a price for the hot bath, the big steak, and the cool beer upon which he had his mind set.

Then the sweet laughter of a woman's voice lifted across the soft evening air drawing McCall in like some lost sailor at his first sight of land.

In the morning McCall sat in the hotel dining room over a plate of steak and potatoes. He watched a portly man approach the desk clerk. They spoke a few minutes, and then together the portly man and the clerk walked over to McCall's table, where the portly man interrupted McCall's breakfast.

"My man here tells me you could be someone he believes he recognizes as a Texas Ranger of some reputation."

McCall continued with his breakfast without responding. The portly man offered his hand.

"I'm sorry. My name is Luther Wainwright and I'm the mayor here. I do apologize for my rudeness."

McCall shook his hand.

"Brady McCall."

"That's him," the clerk said.

The mayor dismissed the clerk. "Thank you, Hugo. That will be all."

Hugo returned to the counter. The mayor took a seat across from McCall.

"I don't mean to impose, but I have an opportunity here that might benefit both of us.

McCall listened as the mayor explained that the town was looking for a new sheriff. In the last three years, four men had held the job. All four lay side by side in a small cemetery just outside of town.

The town's citizens were prepared to pay whatever it took to restore control and order to the lawless place Lawrence had become.

McCall heard him out. He was tempted.

"A man could build a nice nest egg for himself here," the mayor said. "There's a spot for the right man on the city council and enough enterprise here to make a generous long term contribution to the man who has the ambition for a political future in an up and coming center of commerce like we envision here."

McCall pushed his empty plate forward, finished the last of his coffee, set the cup down, and looked the mayor in the eye.

"No, thanks," he said as he stood and walked out of the place.

McCall continued to drift and wander. He watched the months slip away. He had time to think, and he realized Allison was on his mind every day. He crossed the border from Arizona into California, crossed the desert to the coast, and then continued riding north.

The day he rode into San Francisco he had a plan. He knew Allison had a new life and he knew he would never be a part of it, but he wanted her to know how he felt—to clear the air—to set things right. His mind was made up. He needed that to move on. He needed to know she was where she wanted to be so he could go on about finding where it was he needed to be.

McCall stood outside a stylish emporium waiting for it to open. Covered with trail dust and wearing a hat that he had worn since before Texas, McCall presented a derelict image to the surprised shop owner when he raised the shade on the door and saw McCall standing there.

An hour later, there stood McCall ready to embark on the toughest mission of his life. He was dressed in a new wool suit with a high-button vest, a linen shirt, a black tie, and a stiff pair of new boots. He stopped and turned to assess his image in the window glass. Except for the old hat he refused to part with, he appeared the proper gentleman.

That evening, he invested in a hot bath, a shave, a haircut, and a splash of lilac water before he set out to find the Stuart residence. Polished and dapper, he strode proudly across the uneven cobblestone street. His jacket bunched up awkwardly where it hung on the protruding bulge of his sidearm.

McCall couldn't have been more pleased with himself as he gazed approvingly at his handsome reflection in the store windows and tipped his hat at those he passed along the street.

A merchant who knew Waddell Stuart provided McCall with the address and directions to the Stuart residence in a posh neighborhood nearby.

McCall paused at the gate before proceeding up the long walkway leading to the massive pillar-supported front porch of the Stuart house. He started to knock with the back of his knuckles but noticed the ornate brass knocker, and gently lifted it and let it fall softly against the backing plate. It elicited no response, so he tried again. Again no response, and the third time he banged it forcefully and began to repeat the action when the door swung open and a formally attired, elderly gentleman stood before him.

"Yes?" the gentleman asked stiffly.

"My name's Brady McCall. I'm here to see Allison Granger . . . I mean Allison Stuart," Brady said, as he removed his hat.

"I am terribly sorry sir, but the Stuart's are no longer in residence here."

"They're not?"

"No sir. Mr. and Mrs. Garrison bought the entire estate more than a year ago."

McCall looked questioningly at the gentleman. "The estate?"

"The house and the property," the doorman said smugly.

"Can you tell me where the Stuart's went?"

"I have no idea. They were gone sometime before the Garrison's took possession of the place."

McCall was crushed. He returned to his hotel room. He was angry, restless and unable to sleep. He could not calm his thoughts. He knew Waddell Stuart was a successful banker and an important man in financial circles. He also knew Stuart would not leave San Francisco unless it was for a bigger opportunity somewhere else, the kind of opportunity that lures ambitious men to odd places all over the world. They could have gone anywhere.

He knew he may never see Allison again, but wherever she was, McCall had to know. He pulled on his boots and, with the night half over, he set out for San Gregorio.

The sun was high in the sky when McCall rode through the familiar town square in San Gregorio. As he approached the store he saw Mrs. Hayes sweeping off the wooden walk out front. Nothing seemed to have changed much. Mrs. Hayes was a little heavier but still looked trim. Her hair was mostly grey, and she showed her age. She glanced up at McCall sitting silently on his horse and, not recognizing him, shifted her eyes back down and continued sweeping.

McCall stepped down, wrapped the reins around the hitch rail, and then walked up behind her.

"Mrs. Hayes," McCall said apprehensively.

She recognized the voice and she spun around. She stared at McCall with a stern look.

"Brady McCall," she finally said. "My word, what are you doing back here?"

Her tone was more accusative than curious.

"Ma'am, I don't mean no harm," McCall said defensively. "I just came to see how Allison and her family are doing. I stopped by their place in San Francisco and found out they don't live there anymore."

Her expression softened. She put her arm around McCall and led him into the store.

"Come inside. We must talk," she said, as she closed the door behind them.

She looked up at McCall and for several moments did not speak. McCall shifted uncomfortably from one foot to the other. They sat at a small table.

"Brady, you broke my daughter's heart," she finally said. "She waited for you and sent letters everywhere she thought you might be and never heard a word from you."

McCall lowered his head. "Ma'am, I'm truly sorry for that. I always meant to write but never seemed to be in the right place at the right time, and never was in one place for very long. Next thing I knew, a lot of things had got away from me."

"Brady, I never saw a person hurt for someone like Allison hurt for you. It took a long time, but she got over it. She doesn't need any more complications in her life right now."

"Mrs. Hayes, I know you're right, and I don't want to do anything to make her feel bad, but I just want you to know, I never meant to hurt Allison."

"I'm sure you didn't, Brady, but I think it is for the best that you forget about her so she can get on with her own life."

Mrs. Hayes hugged McCall. "She always loved you, Brady. I'm so sorry things didn't work out differently."

They exchanged a long silent gaze.

"You better go now."

She kissed him on the cheek. McCall turned and walked out the door. He stood with the reins in his hand as he slumped against the hitch rail staring vacantly down the street that led out of town and out of Allison's life. He stepped up into the saddle and moved his horse slowly along the dusty street.

In the center of the square an old Mexican man leaned over the fountain and splashed cool water on his face while his burro drank. Several small children played near the water. Their laughter and squeals caught McCall's attention, as he found a spot to water his horse. The sorrel gelding thrashed at the water with his muzzle before settling in for a long drink.

McCall watched the children play while the mothers busied themselves under the shaded arbor at the edge of the square. A little golden-haired girl stood out from her dark-haired friends as they chased each other around the adobe-edged fountain.

When she passed in front of McCall, he saw that she wore a silver and turquoise bracelet on her left arm. At the same instant he recognized the bracelet, he heard a familiar voice call out from the arbor.

"Elizabeth. Come on, sweetheart, it's time to go."

McCall's heart pounded and he looked away to avoid being recognized. He hesitated, aware that Allison was looking at him and slowly walking his direction. An eternity passed and McCall turned his face toward her, as she approached with uncertainty. When their eyes made contact, his throat tightened. He watched her, but could not speak.

"Brady? Brady McCall, is that you?" she asked, in disbelief.

McCall stepped down and dropped the reins. Allison continued walking toward him.

"It's me," he said, barely able to get the words out.

He took an unsure step in her direction and she ran to him with her arms outstretched. Brady wrapped his arms around her and swung her off her feet. He buried his face in her sweet smelling hair and held her tightly. Their faces touched and her tears wet his cheek. They held each other without speaking. Finally, Allison pushed herself away from him. She touched the tears away with a ruffle-edged handkerchief and looked up at him.

"Damn you Brady, why did you have to come back now? I needed you so many times and you were never there. Why now?"

Brady looked down at her. The expression in his eyes was confident, but uncertain. All he knew was how he felt and he tried to tell her.

"Because now is all I got. I had to see you again no matter what."

"But you knew I was married. Why did you come back?"

"I have so much I need to tell you," he said. "I did everything wrong. I see that now. I couldn't leave it like that between us."

Allison turned and walked over to the wide glazed-tile edge of the fountain and sat down. Brady followed and sat beside her. She looked at McCall a long time before she began speaking. McCall could tell she was weighing her thoughts carefully, and he gave her time as he waited in silence. She took a deep breath—let it out slowly.

"Brady, you never made an effort. You never even asked me to wait for you."

"Would you have waited this long?"

"No. But you could have at least asked."

"It wasn't like that."

She looked away, then turned back and stared into his eyes to make sure he understood every word.

"I married Waddell because I wanted a family. He did everything for me, but it was never about the money."

She dabbed a tear from her cheek.

"I thought about you every day and I always felt so guilty. When we made love, I was never sure who I was with because you were always in my thoughts and afterwards I would feel so ashamed. Eventually I put you out of my mind. But, when my daughter was born, I named her Elizabeth after your mother—just so you and I could have some unbroken connection between our lives."

Allison held her head down and took a slow, deep breath as she gathered her thoughts and tried to bear up under the embarrassment.

"A little over a year ago, Waddell was thrown from his horse. He hit his head on the cobblestones and spent almost two months in a coma before he died. Then things got worse. He and his partner had borrowed heavily against all their personal and business assets to invest in a mining operation in South America. After he died, the deal went bad and we lost everything. It was terrible, but Elizabeth and I have our lives back together now. Brady, I loved Waddell and I lost him, just like I lost you earlier. I can't go through that again."

Brady put his arms around her. He pulled her close to him and she wept. With his hands gently cradling her face, McCall kissed her on each closed eye, then softly wiped the tears from her cheeks with the back of his finger.

McCall felt another presence. He looked out past Allison to see the old Mexican still sitting there, tears running down his brown, wrinkled face. The old man looked over at McCall and he nodded his approval. McCall flushed. He held Allison's hand. She laid her head against his chest.

He whispered to her.

"I promise you on my life no one has ever loved you more than I do. I don't want us to be apart again."

Her face shone, and her smile was radiant.

"McCall, what are you trying to tell me?"

She laughed as he fumbled around with the words.

"I know I could never take Waddell's place, but I'd be a good father to Elizabeth."

She nodded and waited.

"We won't ever be rich, but I'll always be there for you."

She nodded again, "Uh-huh."

"Well, I'm trying to tell you I want you to be my wife—if you'll have me."

Allison looked up at Brady. She wiped his cheek dry. She wept and couldn't answer. McCall waited. Finally he put his finger under her chin and tilted her head up. His eyes asked the question again. Allison trembled, and the tears continued to fall.

"Yes, yes of course I will," she said, half laughing and half crying.

FORTY-TWO

Brady and Allison stayed in San Gregorio long enough to help get Mr. and Mrs. Hayes accustomed to the idea that Brady would be their new son-in-law. It was not an easy adjustment for either of them. When Allison announced they would be leaving for Montana after the wedding, it became a time of serious counseling, but Brady weathered the storm with Mrs. Hayes.

Allison reassured her mother and, while nothing Allison could say would ease her mother's concerns, her daughter's rekindled happiness convinced her she must give her blessing. With great reservations, she conceded. Privately she promised McCall she would personally track him to the end of the earth if he ever hurt her daughter or grand-daughter, and then she hugged him and welcomed him into the family.

Brady and Allison shared their wedding vows at the foot of a massive, carved crucifix in the old Spanish mission in San Gregorio. When the padre told them their marriage would endure throughout eternity, they never doubted him.

Allison prepared for the journey to Montana with the same determination that got her across the frontier, through the massacre, and over the worst that life had to throw at her.

McCall and his new family made it to Montana. They moved into the old cabin Brady and Franklin had helped Kincaid build years earlier. With the help of Kincaid and Laura they got it patched up the best they could before the snow fell.

That first winter was one of fond memories for Brady, Allison, and Elizabeth. On stormy nights they listened to the raw wind whistle through the cracks in the walls and they listened to the mournful cry of the wolves howling at the frozen moon, while Allison read to Elizabeth before the warm light of the fire.

McCall would smile contentedly as he watched Elizabeth's innocent eyes when she asked her mother to explain the words she didn't understand. He was as happy as he had ever been.

If McCall had a regret, it was looking at Elizabeth and knowing she would have been his daughter had he been a better man.

One night, as a brutal storm slashed through the valley driving ice and snow against the glass near Elizabeth's bed, Brady comforted her and told her stories. He held her until her sleepy eyes began to close.

"Sleepy?" He asked.

She nodded. He pulled the buffalo robe up around her. She reached out from beneath it and wrapped her arms around his neck.

"Night, sweetheart," he whispered, as Allison looked on from across the room near the fire.

Elizabeth smiled and kissed him on the cheek.

"I love you, daddy," she said.

Allison held her hand to her mouth. It was the first time Elizabeth had ever called him daddy.

"I love you too," he said, his voice barely audible as a lifetime of doubt was lifted from his shoulders.

Allison stood weeping.

When spring arrived, Allison announced that she was carrying McCall's child.

In the fall, John William was born. John for her father and William for Brady's father.

News traveled slowly in this part of the country but, when South Carolina announced its secession from the Union and Jefferson Davis established the new capitol of the Confederacy in Montgomery, word spread into the Gallatin Valley with awesome swiftness. By June of 1861 the capitol of the Confederacy was moved to Richmond, Virginia and the Civil War was brought to the doorstep of the McCall's home in Montana.

Brady was certain his kin in Virginia would rally beneath the Confederate flag, not so much in support of slavery, but rather in defiance of any political imposition of Yankee will on southern morality.

Montana Territory was not a part of the United States, and McCall outwardly refused to feel any responsibility toward the fight between the north and the south.

Inwardly, McCall was torn. Allison continually reassured Brady that it was not his war, but he was unable to convince himself, and he grew more and more restless as the army of the Union took the battle lines deeper into the south.

On a pleasant fall evening Brady returned home from the upper summer range of the Triple Dot. Allison's hand shook when she handed him the wrinkled letter from Virginia. Brady's expression darkened as he read it.

Dear Captain McCall,
Having resigned my commission in the Union Army, I have, in good conscience, pledged my support for Jeff Davis in defense of the new Confederate States of

America. As you are of Virginia stock and the confederacy has a great need for your services to aid in the protection of the capitol in Richmond and to assist in the preservation of the Virginia homeland, Col. Jackson has authorized your services, with full officer's pay as a civilian scout and reconnaissance leader. Your support and employment as such are hereby requested by my personal recommendation and under special signed order of Pres. Davis, in Richmond.

Respectfully yours, Lieutenant Colonel Clayton Parmelee

Brady looked up from the letter. Allison struggled. Finally, she took his hand in hers, fighting back the tears and trying to face the inevitable.

"Please don't let anything happen to you," she said.

It was early winter by the time McCall joined Jackson's Virginia brigade. He had crossed the battle-torn countryside to see the devastation of war that laid waste to his boyhood homeland. It was another shattering reminder of how quickly everything taken for granted can be lost.

He stood angered and shaken at the desecration of the tranquil beauty of the Shenandoah Valley, now reeking of death and destruction, a madness engaged in by both sides.

Parmelee died in battle only days before McCall arrived. He had taken a direct hit from a ten-pounder Union Parrott rifle and, according to the young private who had been entrenched next to Parmelee, "They wasn't enuff a him left to bury."

By August of the following year, McCall had been in more skirmishes and pitched battles than he could even recall. The smell of death followed him everywhere and there was no relief from the suffering. More died from malnutrition, infection, and dysentery than from bullets. The surgeon's tent was a hellish image of human limbs stacked outside and hauled away by the wagonload. Squads of men on burial detail, rags across their faces, formed up in convoys to dump the bodies in shallow graves with not enough dirt thrown over them to keep out the feral dogs that followed them to the graveyards.

Nothing about the war made sense to McCall. The short range and inaccuracy of their rifles turned every battle into a face-to-face confrontation that unnerved men to the point that any sign of panic in the ranks could cause entire companies of soldiers to turn tail and retreat.

Every engagement resulted in the loss of thousands of lives. The braver the soldiers, the greater the losses on both sides. Robert E. Lee's Army of Northern Virginia was scattered from Gainesville, on the Manassas Gap Railroad, all the way up to Jackson's camp at Sudley Ford on Bull Run.

Jackson's brilliant victories in the Shenandoah Valley campaigns earned him a promotion to Major General, and his unwavering battle line at First Manassas had earned him the nickname, *Stonewall*.

By late August the battle lines were once again drawn at Bull Run, as Federal forces referred to Manassas. McCall reported back to Jackson with information that General Pope and his Union forces had entered the battlefield on several fronts, heading toward the Confederates from Centerville.

Jackson, always calm and methodical, deployed his troops near Stony Bridge. General Lee was anxious to move the lines forward but refrained under advice from General Longstreet, who was waiting for a report from General Jeb Stuart.

Jackson took his men and departed. McCall fell in with the movement and watched as Lee grew impatient and wheeled his big, grey horse to the right to go investigate for himself.

Later, McCall would write in a letter to his wife:

Virginia Dec.19, '62

My Dearest Allison,
I trust this letter finds you and Elizabeth and John William all fine and in good health. I myself have no complaints. Compared to most I have been fortunate. The reports you must hear on this war cannot adequately describe the awfulness of it all.
I have never seen men so poorly outfitted for battle as most of the Johnny Rebs on our side. They wear every manner of gear, and some have no shoes.
Lee and Jackson are great leaders and the Blackfoot would say they have powerful medicine, but I fear the Confederacy cannot win out over the Union any more than the Indian can overcome the white man.
I now know for certain Franklin T. Stilwell is somewhere in Virginia, and I believe I see him every time we face the enemy. It grieves me that any day I may face him in battle.
Mostly the weather has been fair. The wind blows more than I remembered.
You all are always in my thoughts and every day I think about the day this war is over and I return to you.
Your loving husband, Brady C. McCall

After their decisive victory at Second Manassas, Lee's Army was buoyed with confidence and, when Jefferson Davis predicted an early end to the war, there was a renewed energy among the rebel soldiers. Their anticipation of walking off the battlefield with their heads held high soon gave way to the realization that defeat grew nearer with each new battle.

McCall was masterful in his ability to move undetected in and out of enemy lines. He quickly learned the back trails and woodcutter roads that provided Jackson with mobility and cover in the heavily guarded area of Northern Virginia where the Confederates imposed a threat on the capitol in Washington.

On April 30, 1863, McCall reported to Jackson after spending six days behind enemy lines scouting Union positions and strength. They sat together on wooden boxes outside Jackson's tent as the bearded general laid out a stained and tattered map. The general hung his hat on the corner pole of the tent and wiped the grey sleeve of his jacket across his forehead. His receding hairline and hawkish nose drew McCall's attention to his intense gaze, as the general studied the map.

"McCall," he said in his commanding voice. "Look at this map and tell me where the Federals have moved to."

McCall sensed that, once again, Jackson had already calculated where the main enemy forces would be and was only looking for confirmation before committing his own strategy. As the general's head scout, he had reviewed hundreds of battle plans with Jackson and each time he was awed by the general's clear ability to assess the enemy's movement and plans.

"They established an offensive line from the Rappahannock down Mineral Spring Road and into Chancellorsville," McCall said.

Jackson nodded. McCall continued.

"The Eleventh Corps is here," he said pointing to the map. "They're on the Old Orange Turnpike. The Third is right here. Here between Old School and Fairview, is the Twelfth Corps."

Jackson thought a moment. "Is there a way around through the wilderness here to allow us to flank them?" Jackson asked.

"Yes sir, there is," said McCall. "I found a woodcutter's road that will bring us in to the west of them on Culpepper Plank Road and up across the Turnpike."

Jackson's eyes traveled back and forth across the map, following his finger as he mentally went through the options and countermoves, trying to determine exactly where the enemy would be, and where they would move in response to any shift in the position of his own forces.

Finally, Jackson looked up.

"Are you sure you can find the way?"

"I can find the way," McCall said.

Jackson finalized the details of the movement with his generals. On May 2nd, while the Union forces were convinced the rebels were in retreat, Jackson's troops fractured the Eleventh Corps in a massive surprise attack that left the Federals in a confused panic. The battle of Chancellorsville raged on, and McCall fought side-by-side with the foot soldiers of the Confederacy.

The rebel armies aggressively pursued the Federals and numerous counter-attacks by Union forces were ineffectual. By nightfall there was a confused clamor in the Confederate ranks as companies and regiments were inextricably mixed. Enlisted men and officers wandered through the chaos attempting to reform with their own units in the dim moonlight.

Jackson sensed his strong advantage and asked McCall to ride forward with him on the Turnpike to assess the situation nearer the Federals' position. Several other aides rode with them in the darkness.

In the path of their retreat, the Union forces had abandoned several important pieces of artillery and the large number of personal items left strewn along the roadway suggested the Federals had incurred great losses.

Muskets, ammo packs, headgear and canteens littered the narrow road.

Eager to get back to camp to organize for tomorrow's forced march, Jackson turned his horse and led the way at a fast trot with McCall riding at his side. Unknown to Jackson's returning party, the Eighteenth North Carolina Regiment had already reformed and was positioned along the Turnpike, braced for a surprise attack from the Union cavalry.

Unaware that Jackson and his aides were on the road, they readied their muskets at the sound of the advancing horses and, when the general was in range, they opened fire. Every man in the North Carolina Regiment, still energized from the earlier fighting, was prepared for another attack.

The first volley was deafening. Before Jackson's party had identified itself, the two aides at the rear of the entourage he had been killed instantly. McCall went to Jackson's defense but was too late. The general had been hit three times.

The first shot of the friendly fire shattered the upper part of the general's left arm, a second shot went through his left forearm, and a third shot broke two fingers on his right hand. Jackson's arms went limp, and he was crippled in the saddle but remained upright.

The smoke and noise panicked Jackson's wild-eyed horse and it bolted. The horse was caught a short distance down the road, with Jackson still mounted but in great pain. As they lowered the general to the ground, artillery fire shook the road, and Jackson was moved to the rear.

On May 3rd, they amputated the general's left arm below the shoulder.

He was convalescing and was moved to Guiney's Station for further recovery. On the tenth of May, his lungs began filling with fluid and, by three in the afternoon, he was dead of pneumonia.

In the meantime, McCall reported to Maj. Gen. A. P. Hill, who took over Jackson's command. They had the Federals on the retreat, but on several fronts resistance was intense. McCall fell in with a company of young Georgia recruits of the remnants of the Twenty-third most of whom had been captured earlier by the northern armies.

On the third night of non-stop battle, a lull in the fighting gave both sides a moment of relief. McCall lay back in exhaustion. His rest was disturbed by the sobbing of a boy who didn't look to be more than sixteen or seventeen years old.

McCall sat back up. The boy sat cross-legged, rocking back and forth. He cried, but there were no tears. McCall put his hand on the boy's arm.

"Son, are you hit anywhere?" he asked.

The boy shook his head from side to side.

"Can you tell me what's wrong, then?"

The boy nodded.

"Go ahead, son. What is it?"

Something in McCall's quiet calmness soothed the boy and he looked up.

"Sir," he said. "I don't think I can do this no more. I'm so tired I can hardly move. I'm scared all the time, and I don't want to keep on killing people."

He sobbed and pointed to the bodies of grey uniformed soldiers lined out for burial.

"My big brother is layin' over yonder with his belly shot out, and I just can't tell my ma and pa I let him die."

McCall put his arm around the boy's shoulder.

"What's your name, son?"

"Jubal. Jubal Sayler. My brother was Robert."

"Well, listen, Jubal. This is a bad war. Every man here is tired and scared."

The boy did not respond.

"We're just all doing what we can—there's no blame."

"My momma told me to trust in the Lord," Jubal said.

McCall tipped his head in the direction of a brushy swale.

"Let's you and me slip on over there where we got some cover and a good line on that clearing."

The boy followed McCall. They found a spot in the shadows that looked out upon the moonlit clearing. They talked for a long time until the boy stopped trembling and his voice settled. He leaned back against a thin sapling to sleep when they saw moon shadows and a tidal wave of blue uniforms advancing toward them. The light reflected off the buttons of their coats and their fixed bayonets.

Jubal sat upright staring wide-eyed at the cadenced movement of advancing soldiers.

Before they were within rifle range, the green company of young rebels opened fire.

"Hold your fire," McCall screamed.

But it was too late. By the time the union soldiers were upon them, more than half of the confederates were caught attempting to reload while the other half fired wildly into the massive blue surge. When the union soldiers opened fire, the rebel soldiers dropped in groups one after the other.

It was a nightmare. In the darkness and the fog the air smelled of sulfur and hung over the dead and dying like some horrific rendition of hell.

Jubal stood by McCall's side, fighting bravely.

"On your left, sir," Jubal yelled, as he stood to defend against a union infantryman with his outstretched bayonet intended for McCall.

McCall sidestepped him. Off balance and with too much forward momentum to correct himself, the bluecoat slipped past McCall. Jubal met him in full stride with a powerful upward stroke of the butt of his rifle, Jubal shattered the jaw of the attacker. McCall nodded to Jubal in appreciation. Jubal smiled and nodded in return. Then Jubal lurched forward and the smile was replaced with a look of surprise. He dropped face-down at McCall's feet, a widening circle of blood spreading across his back.

McCall bent down and gently turned him over. He was still alive, but losing blood at an alarming rate. McCall held the boy's head in his arms.

"Jubal, can you hear me?" McCall asked.

"Yes, sir." The boy sounded clear-minded and McCall prayed he would survive.

Then the boy's eyes closed and a peaceful look came over his face. He began to speak softly of his childhood, his home, and his family. He spoke to each of them as though they were there with him. He rambled on, and then whispered to McCall.

"Sir, please tell my ma and pa their boys died proud."

His chest rattled and his last breath escaped in a slow, relaxed hiss. McCall held him closely, ignoring the battle raging around him. He put his hand gently to the boy's face and closed his eyelids.

"Go on home to God now, Jubal Sayler. You got nothing to be ashamed of," McCall said.

FORTY-THREE

Massaponox Creek, Virginia: July 1863

The battle continued into the night, but by dawn the fractured Federal armies had withdrawn. There was no pursuit. There was no victory. There was no rejoicing.

In the dim light the landscape had taken on definition once again. An acrid layer of smoke hung in the morning air. Only the wounded and delirious made any sounds. Hundreds of survivors sat gazing as in a stupor while others stumbled aimlessly about.

McCall gagged when the darkness lifted and he saw the staggering numbers of dead around him. Bodies in grey and blue uniforms, bloody and torn, lay twisted and deformed. He thought he had grown accustomed to the death and suffering, but this morning it was completely incomprehensible to him.

The dead lay about in massive numbers. Young boys, some no more than children, gave up their lives right alongside the veterans. McCall was struck by the absurdity of it all. In a few days, the ground they fought to win would be abandoned as the battle front moved to other locations, and this place would once again become an insignificant mark on a military map somewhere. The wooded battleground was strewn with so many bodies it was impossible to walk through it without stepping over one dead soldier after another.

For as far as he could see, every tree was pockmarked by the direct hits of thousands of minié balls that had been discharged throughout the night. In the early morning haze McCall pushed his way past the shattered battalions and through the fragmented companies of soldiers who were lost and detached from the real world. Like all good soldiers, they simply waited for someone to give them their next orders.

McCall located Jubal Sayler's body and made sure the young boy from Georgia had a fitting burial with a marked cross, such as it was. He put the boy's name on a scrap of paper and stuffed the paper into his pocket. McCall would be sure to let Jubal's parents know their sons died bravely. He said a short prayer for the young Georgia soldier, and then set out for Chancellorsville to regroup with his company if it still existed.

He forded Massaponox Creek and swung to the northwest to pick up a woodcutter's trail that would take him back to the Turnpike. He made his way through a thickly wooded area and followed a ridge that paralleled a narrow creek, twenty-yards below. McCall calculated that he was still in Confederate territory, but he wasn't sure, so he proceeded cautiously and kept himself concealed as he traveled the backwoods toward Chancellorsville.

The horses that weren't killed when the fighting broke out had run off in the night, leaving McCall and others afoot. He slunk through the thick stands of the trees and stopped when he heard voices coming up from the direction of the creek. He waited. The voices continued toward him, coming closer but still unintelligible when they spoke.

McCall hunkered down and drew back the hammer on his rifle as he waited and tried to determine how many they were and if the voices were Yankee or not. Judging from the direction of the voices, they would cross the clearing directly in McCall's path.

Through the underbrush he barely made out three men. Their uniforms were tattered and filthy, and he couldn't determine if they were grey or blue. They crossed into the clearing thirty yards away, their backs to him—bluecoats—one held up by the other two as they shuffled along. The wounded one favored a bloody leg and a limb that hung loose at his side. In the sunlit clearing there was no mistaking the union uniforms and McCall debated shooting or capturing the hapless trio.

He fell in undetected behind them. One wore trousers too large for him, held up with a section of tent rope tied about his waist. With his pistol leveled at their backs, he spoke up with great authority.

"Hold it right there and don't turn around. You are prisoners of General Lee's Army of Northern Virginia. Welcome to Chancellorsville, you unlucky sons a bitches."

The bluecoats stopped without turning. McCall noticed the hand of the one with the oversized trousers slowly reaching for his sidearm.

"You there. Saggy Britches. You're fixin' to make your last move—you might want to decide if that's the one it's gonna be."

The officer paused. He steadied his wounded comrade and turned his head slowly to look back at the voice. He looked across at his two companions who stood with ashen faces and all hope drained from their eyes.

"It's okay," he said to his men. "It's just some dumbass reb lost from his company."

Franklin T. Stilwell turned and looked at McCall. McCall's eyes widened and a big grin shone on his face. He shook his head and holstered his weapon.

"Damn," he said, holding his thumb and index finger a quarter of an inch apart. "I come this close to shooting your sorry asses."

Then he approached Stilwell and wrapped his arms around him. They laughed and slapped each other on the shoulders. The two union soldiers stood speechless and watched, not knowing whether to run or stay.

It was an improbable reunion by all counts. Brady and Franklin couldn't get over the unlikely odds of meeting, particularly under such remote circumstances. They discovered that they had both been in the same area for the past four months and, while they had never faced one another in battle, their paths had crossed closely several times.

Brady's first concern was for Franklin's condition. Franklin explained that he and his men hadn't eaten in a day and a half, and they had no medical supplies or ammunition except for two unspent rounds in Franklin's revolver. Their company had been trapped in a cross-fire and, as far as they knew, they were the only survivors.

McCall treated the wounded soldier and fed all three men from his own ration pack, then he and Franklin sat down to talk.

"I never thought I'd be happy to see another Johnny Reb again if I lived to be a hundred, but that face of yours is one of the prettiest sights I seen since I been down here," Franklin said.

"All the same, Franklin, you are my prisoners."
Franklin looked up at Brady. Brady wasn't smiling.
"No we ain't."
"You damn sure are."
"No we ain't."
"Are too."
Franklin shook his head.
"Look, I seen you sneaking around up in them bushes like you was getting away with something. Why do you think I let you get the drop on us the way you done?"

"Because you never knew I was there. You three were talking and carrying on like school girls going to a picnic. Hell, you were walking right into the middle of half the damn Confederate army and didn't even know where you were going."

"Well, just so you know, look here on this map and I'll show you where we was going, if you can keep from telling it all to that barefoot, farm-boy army of yours," Franklin said.

He folded out his map and showed McCall where he was trying to rejoin his forces. McCall pointed to the spot on the map just ahead of their present position.

"Franklin, your armies have retreated all the way back to here. The last I heard, they were moving their artillery across the Rappahannock."

He stared across at Franklin who appeared a bit confused.

"You do know you're behind Confederate lines don't you?" McCall asked with grave concern.

"No, we didn't know that," Franklin said. "But I do know we ain't your damn prisoners."

McCall pointed through the brush into a clearing up ahead where a company of rebel soldiers was bivouacked.

"You'll be mine or you'll be theirs," he said, and as he said it the other two soldiers began to move as if to make a break, but Stilwell stopped them.

"What are you thinking, B.C.?"

"Well, you can't travel at night and this place is thick with Confederate soldiers. You give me your weapons and I'll march you through our lines at gunpoint. We get to federal territory and you and your boys can slip on in on your own. Anybody stops us, I'll just tell them I'm delivering my prisoners, and nobody will be the wiser."

Franklin nodded in agreement. "It's the only chance we got," he said. "But, so you know—you didn't capture us—we was baiting you."

Brady pulled out the Gros Ventre knife and drew the flat-edged slowly across his trouser leg without looking up.

"I been following you since last night. I could have taken you in your sleep anytime," he lied.

Franklin shook his head and they laughed. They talked and rested until early afternoon. After they got caught up on all the news, McCall looked over at Franklin.

"I been thinking," McCall said, then he paused.

"I don't need any more of your ideas. Do you remember the last time we had this conversation? You said, *'Wouldn't it be a good idea if we just joined the army?'* Well, I did but you lit out for parts unknown, and that was the last I heard from you."

He settled back and looked off across into the trees. He turned back towards Brady.

"Why is it every time you get an idea I end up getting shot at?"

"It's your nature to get shot at, Franklin. People like shooting at you."

"Not that I'm interested," Franklin said. "But what's your idea this time?"

"Well, I think you and me should get out of this war as quick as we can and get back in the cattle business," Brady said.

Franklin laughed a sarcastic laugh. "Now who doesn't want to get out of this war? I still got eight months to go on my commission—and besides, where are we going to get enough money to get back in the cattle business?"

"We still have a share in the Triple Dot—not that we have any claim to that, but we got the land. We can go down into Texas and Mexico and gather up a couple thousand head of those free-running, longhorn range cows. They'd make us a good start," Brady said.

"Are them cows easy-picking or do we have to hunt them down one at a time?" Franklin asked.

"They're easy picking."

"You sure about that?"

"I'm sure."

Franklin thought about it a minute. "Alright, let's do it," he said, then he smiled as though they could pack up that evening and go get it done.

Brady grinned. "I got another big surprise for you, but I'll save it for later."

Neither man had any way to know the war would drag on, but it did, and they fought through the hot stifling summer and the unmerciful cold of winter. Every time a rebel soldier fell, Franklin prayed it wasn't Brady. Confederate victories came less frequently and soon the Union forces dominated battle after battle. The price of victory was dear, and when the final count would someday be tallied, they would find more than six-hundred thousand soldiers had died.

With their supplies of food, ammunition and clothing depleted, the Confederate armies fought on sheer determination, but it wasn't enough. In the spring of 1865, General Robert E. Lee brought an end to the suffering and relief to both the North and the South when he surrendered with honor and dignity at Appomattox.

Two men, one wearing grey, the other blue, threw down their packs, saddled their horses and rode west.

FORTY-FOUR

Shenandoah Valley, Virginia: April 14, 1865

McCall paused at the summit as he crossed the Appalachian Mountains on his way back to Montana. He turned his horse and looked down into the Shenandoah Valley. He would never again be able to think of Virginia as home.

He followed the sun west and rode straight through the first two days, stopping only to feed and water his horse. At night his mind spun with thoughts of Allison. He wondered how much Elizabeth and John William had grown. Then, hours before sun-up he was back on the trail.

Col. Franklin T. Stilwell resigned his commission in Washington, D.C. the day the war ended. Throngs of people crowded the streets and it seemed that all of humanity was on the move. It was a glorious time of rebirth for a nation whose heart had been cut out by the very men who fought for her well-being. There was hope and excitement in the air. Young and old alike celebrated, not the end of a war, but the beginning of a new country.

Franklin ached to breath the sharp, cool, mountain air and to wake up to the quiet stillness that he always remembered in the unending loudness of war. Somewhere east of Kansas City, he thought about the deal he had made with McCall.

He chuckled to himself. *"I don't know how he thinks me and him are going to run four-thousand head of cows out of Mexico, but I'm damn sure ready to give it a try."*

Well, they did it. Not once, but three different times. Kincaid was happy to have his boys back home. The three of them helped pioneer big cattle drives, they set new trails, and joined the ranks of better known cattlemen like Goodnight, Loving, Chisholm, and a handful of others.

They operated on the fine line that separates the questionable from the illegal, but they never made a dishonest deal and never put an iron on a cow they knew belonged to someone else. That was not a quality shared by many cattlemen, but Kincaid was immovable on the subject. He swore he would hang any man caught altering a brand and would shoot any man he found marking calves with a running iron.

The beef industry went through hard times, and the Triple Dot Ranches swung dangerously close to failure, but each time Kincaid, Stilwell, and McCall were able to readjust and survive.

Over the years, McCall resettled his family on the northernmost ranch of the Triple Dot on the Sweet Grass River. Franklin stayed on and built up the original place in the Gallatin Valley, while Kincaid and Laura ran the big ranch at Ennis Lake.

In 1876, Kincaid made the last drive. He was sixty-nine years old, and they had just delivered over three-thousand troublesome longhorn cattle to the railhead in Abilene,

Kansas. Water had been scarce, the cattle disagreeable, and the weather unpredictable. They watched a quicksand bog swallow a young wrangler and his horse, lost two good cowboys to a stampede that happened for no apparent reason, and were plagued by a lightning storm that struck a horse right out from under one of the night riders.

The drive of '76 would be talked about and remembered by the Triple Dot crew and the drovers who rode with them as the toughest drive any of them had ever experienced. Those who survived it would collect their pay and turn themselves loose on the eagerly waiting town of Abilene. They would drink heartily in honor of those they buried on the trail.

Kincaid sat high on the back of his big dun-colored mare and spoke to the cowboys bunched around the horse corral at the feed lot in Abilene.

"Boys, I just want to tell you two things. Number one, I don't believe I ever rode with better. Number two, you'll draw your pay at the hotel at three o'clock. Well, I said two, but the truth is, I do have a few more things to add."

Kincaid shifted in the saddle and looked over the collection of drovers before him. Most were young. Age showed through on a few. They were tired, dirty, and just plain worn out, but Kincaid knew he could tell them they were going to cover the same trail back the next day, and every one of them would be saddled up at daybreak. Kincaid was proud of his men, and it showed when he spoke.

"There's a permanent job waiting for every one of you that wants to ride for the Triple Dot. The food's good. The winters are long—the pay will just barely cover it—be here tomorrow morning if you're interested. To those of you with better sense—I wish you my best and hope our trails cross again someday."

The air exploded with whoops and hollers, hats flew into the air and, when the dust settled, it was a cowboy foot-race to the nearest bath house and barber shop. Kincaid laughed as he watched his good trail hands disappear around the corner.

He turned the mare out in the corral with fresh hay, hung his saddle over his shoulder and picked up his rifle with his free hand. His fingers ran over the hand-carved in the stock—a special touch added by Brady when he and Allison gave him the rifle as a Christmas gift years ago. He liked the heft of the long, twenty-eight inch octagon barrel and, in spite of its weight, he kept the '73 with him where ever he went.

Kincaid had an unsettling premonition as he headed to the hotel. He had sent John William to meet the buyer and deliver the money to the bank for the sale of the herd. Close to $15,000, a lot of cash for a young man in a town like Abilene where thieves and outlaws followed the herds to the money.

His first inclination was to supervise the deal, but he decided that the boy had done a man's work on the trail and needed to be trusted to do a man's work in town. He had raised Brady and Franklin that way and saw no reason to do otherwise with John William.

The First National Bank of Kansas was a short walk from the buyer's office. John William would have the deposit made and they would be drinking a cool beer in less than fifteen minutes.

Kincaid waited out of the way, near the hotel on the opposite side of the street from the buyer's office.

He watched, inconspicuously, as John William exited the buyer's office followed by the deputy who was to provide security until they got to the bank. John William and the deputy stepped into the street, casually talking as they walked in the direction of the First National.

Kincaid positioned himself on the sidewalk where he had a clear view of both sides of the street. His nerves were on end. He unconsciously turned the latch screw to free the lever on the Winchester, then methodically chambered a cartridge as he watched the two men near the center of the street.

Then, without warning, two men rushed out from the alley alongside the Empire Saloon. They fired two shots. The deputy dropped to his knees.

John William drew his sidearm and fired two shots. The first went astray. The second caught one of the attackers in the cheek. It killed him instantly.

Kincaid stepped into the street and fired a round. It was deflected off the wheel of a wagon drawn between him and the action by a panicked team reacting to the gunfire.

By the time the wagon cleared his line of sight, Kincaid saw the second gunman had disarmed John William and held him hostage at gunpoint.

"Back off, or I'll kill him," the outlaw screamed.

Kincaid held his rifle trained on the desperate man. John William stood without moving.

For an eternity they stood like that, and then the outlaw cocked his pistol and Kincaid pulled the trigger at the same time the outlaw fired at Kincaid.

The outlaw's blood splattered across the face of John William. The weight of the desperado drug the boy to the ground with him.

John William freed himself from the outlaw who lay dead at his feet. John William looked up to see the silhouette of Kincaid standing with the sun at his back, his rifle hanging down at his side.

Kincaid appeared unsteady on his feet. He braced himself with the butt of the rifle. When his big shadow collapsed to the ground, John William ran to him.

"Someone get a doctor," he screamed.

He sat in the dirt of the street holding Kincaid to him.

"Are you okay, Travis?" His voice shook and his hands trembled as he held the old cowboy and tried to stop the blood pumping from Kincaid's chest.

Kincaid shook his head slowly. "I don't think so."

Kincaid put his hand over the wet hand of the boy. He looked up at John William and tried to smile as his whisper of a voice was barely audible. "You tell Brady and Franklin I . . . "

He never finished the sentence.

At the first sound of the shooting, Brady and Franklin knew instinctively that something had gone wrong. Fearing the worst, they spurred their horses from the feedlot at a gallop. When they turned the corner at the end of Commerce Street, a crowd had already gathered in front of the bank. Brady leaped from his horse.

He pushed his way through the spectators and shouted. "Where's my son?"

To his relief, he heard John William call out from the other side of the crowd.

"Over here, Pa. I'm okay, but they shot Travis."

Franklin was at Brady's side, roughly pushing the crowd aside as they hurried to the spot where John William knelt beside the fallen cowboy. Brady dropped to his knees and looked at John William questioningly.

Brady lifted Kincaid up in his arms and held him there, rocking him back and forth. Franklin reached down and closed Kincaid's eyes.

Brady took Travis's gnarled hand in his own, and held it as he looked up at the soft clouds in the sky and imagined grey-haired cowboy in ragged leather chaps and run-down boots, standing at heaven's gate with his thumbs hooked in his front pockets and his battered old hat pushed back, politely waiting his turn to enter.

Brady tried not to weep. He, tried to hold back the tears, but couldn't.

Franklin knelt with them and held his arms around both Kincaid and Brady.

After a long time, Franklin dried his eyes on his sleeve, bent forward, and kissed Travis on the cheek.

∾

In 1881, John William McCall married Anna Martin, the daughter of a miner from Butte, Montana. The following year their son was born. In honor of Travis Kincaid, they named the baby Miles Travis McCall.

Franklin never married. As much as the ladies liked being around him, none of the women he knew was willing to take on the task of trying to rehabilitate his tumble-weed nature. The thought of domesticating Franklin T. Stilwell humbled even the most determined of them.

He had pretty much given up on the idea of marriage by the time he met Jenny Kendrick, a preacher's daughter from Bozeman. She was dark-haired, strong-willed, and fell completely in love with Franklin the first day she met him.

Franklin met his match in Jenny and the two of them talked of marriage, but when he was ready, she had reservations, and when she was ready, he procrastinated, and so it went year after year and, in spite of their indecisiveness, no two people could have been happier together.

Elizabeth McCall grew up loving the Montana wilderness. She was Brady's girl, and he taught her everything he knew about horses. She was as good with a colt as any man on the ranch and, despite her mother's disapproval, she bucked out a few, which made Allison nervous and Brady proud.

She put her trademark on every horse she finished. Each one was gentle and responsive. Never a misfit in her string.

Elizabeth eventually established a good reputation among the local cowboys, many of them eventually coming to her for advice when they had a problem horse. Brady would shake his head and laugh every time he saw his little girl show some raw-boned cowboy how to get over a problem he was having with a new horse. There she would be, barely over five feet tall, hanging on to a rope with a snorting bronc at the other end, while some big cowboy stood by listening to every word she said.

Elizabeth left the Triple Dot when she married a cattleman from the Billings area where she lived and raised a family of her own.

Travis Kincaid and his wife Laura never had children. After Kincaid's death, Franklin and Brady managed Laura's ranch for her along with theirs. Laura was family and, when she grew too old to get by on her own, Brady and Allison moved her in with them.

Laura was Allison's best friend. She was grandmother to the children, mentor to Allison and Anna, and Aunt Laura to Franklin and Brady.

It was a time of change in the West. The speed with which the land and the people gave in to development was incomprehensible to Brady and Franklin. They dug their heels in and resisted. When other cattlemen began switching to the stockier Hereford and Shorthorn breeds, they stayed with the Texas Longhorns. Some of their decisions were good ones, and others proved to be costly, but they held onto their land while others sold theirs off in parcels. The land was their strength.

FORTY-FIVE

Full-Circle: June 1891

Brady McCall's crumpled body lay amidst the blood-stained rocks and dirt at the base of the steep embankment. The struggle had ended quietly. If and when they found the body, they would shake their heads and wonder why he had given up so easily

Flies gathered on McCall's bloody hand and buzzed about the fleshy wound. Buzzards, which had circled above for the past hour, now eyed the carcass and waddled closer. First one, and then another, hissing and flapping as they closed in on the body.

The boldest among them pecked at a boot, then at the trousers, and then stood cocking its head at the bloody hand.

The bird hopped up onto McCall's outstretched legs and positioned itself at the hand. It cocked its head, and then tore a beak full of flesh from the socket.

McCall screamed and sat upright. He made a fist with his good hand, and then punched the bird as he shot to his feet.

He turned, got a handhold on the roots of a small tree, and hauled himself up the bank on the first try. He stumbled to the fire and kicked a glowing branding iron free.

When McCall knelt and thrust the wounded hand against the orange-hot metal, the smell of burning flesh gagged him and the pain sent him to the ground, unconscious.

He awoke with the afternoon sun on his face. The pain from his now cauterized wound seemed to extend to every part of his body. He looked at the hand. It was black and swollen, but the bleeding had stopped. He sat up. His head ached, but he was thankful to be alive.

McCall rose slowly to his feet, staggered, then stopped and listed from side to side until he regained his balance. He stumbled to the edge of a nearby creek where he dropped and drank and rested. When he made his way to the dry creekbed, he retrieved his hat and followed the tracks of the horse and bull where they exited the rocks and entered the brush.

He found the horse with the rope still held fast onto the saddlehorn and wrapped around a tree with the strangled bull lying dead at the end of it. He talked softly to the horse as he approached it, caught up the reins, and cut the rope loose. McCall led the horse to a downhill slope and mounted from the high side. He slumped in the saddle and nudged the horse forward with his heels.

He rode for a long time and, as the last light of day hung on the horizon, he arrived at the brush corrals where the branding crew were heading out for the day.

Deacon Rounder, the ranch foreman, saw him first.

"Long day, Captain?" Deacon asked.

McCall tilted forward and nodded. His hand dropped from inside his shirt.

"What the hell happened?" Deacon asked, as he swung down from the saddle and caught McCall just before he fell out of the saddle.

All McCall could do is nod toward the bloody hand.

"My horse jerked down."

Deacon sat McCall up on the ground and offered him water. McCall drank and seemed to revive some.

"You better get me home, Deke."

When McCall awoke, his eyes opened to the familiar wooden cross-beamed ceiling of his own bedroom. He tried to sit up, but the pain in his chest sent him reeling back. He tried again, only more slowly this time. Finally he succeeded in getting upright. As he adjusted himself, he noticed his ten-year old grandson, Miles, standing at the side of the bed.

"Here Grandpa, you can have this," Miles said, picking up the pillow from the small bed he had made up for himself on the floor next to his grandfather.

Miles stuffed the pillow behind McCall.

"Are you okay, Grandpa?"

McCall nodded. "I'm okay Miles Travis. "How's my boy doing?"

"I'm doing good."

The boy folded back the covers of the makeshift bed on the floor and brought out McCall's Gros Ventre knife.

"I was taking care of this for you," he said.

McCall smiled. "You been sleeping down there?"

"Yeah, I have. You been asleep a long time."

"What time is it?"

"Almost time to eat."

It was mid-day McCall judged by the slant of the sun where it crossed the room. He watched Miles as the dark-haired boy padded barefoot about the room, putting his bed in order, and busying himself with McCall's things.

"Miles, can you bring me my pants and boots?" McCall asked, as he swung his legs tentatively over the edge of the tall bed.

McCall sat there letting his head clear. Miles stood next to him.

"How come you had a finger in your pocket when you came home?"

"What do you mean?"

"When Uncle Franklin took off your vest to put you in bed, he found a finger in it."

McCall laughed. "Oh, I remember now," he said. "I guess I couldn't figure out what else to do with it, and it didn't seem right to just throw it away, so I stuck it in my pocket."

"It was pretty ugly."

"Pretty or ugly?"

"Ugly!"

"Where is it now?"

"Uncle Franklin buried it by the barn."

Miles grimaced.

"But, one of the dogs dug it up and run off with it."

With the help of the boy, McCall managed to get dressed. He was a bit unsteady, but determined. With his good hand on the boy's shoulder, the two rounded the corner into the kitchen when Allison intercepted them.

"Good Lord, Brady! What are you doing out of bed? Sweetheart, are you all right?"

McCall cribbed over to a chair at the table and sat down.

"I'm fine Ally. Except for these ribs—and this."

He held up the bandaged hand.

Miles pulled up a chair next to his grandfather.

"Brady, I've been worried about you. You've been sleeping for two days. You were so groggy when you got here you couldn't even tell us what happened."

She walked over closer and kissed him on the cheek. McCall put his arm around her small waist and pulled her nearer.

"Thinking back on it, there wasn't much to it."

McCall tugged at the bandage and readjusted himself in the chair.

"I got my line on a stray yearling bullock. He jerked my horse down—dumped me into the rocks. Got my hand fouled in the loose rope. Next thing I know, my thumb's gone and I'm bleeding like a stuck pig."

Allison stood with her arms crossed, shaking her head. "Between you and Stilwell, I feel like I've spent my whole life mending the two of you."

She smiled. "I'm just thankful to have you back safe."

She put her arms around his neck and kissed him. She looked over at Miles who was staring up at her.

"Miles you go out there on the porch and sound the dinner bell."

Almost before the last gong faded, McCall heard boots clomping around on the wooden porch. He could see the crew through the window glass, lining up at the wash basin and crowding the doorway.

Franklin came in first, followed by John William and Deke Rounder.

"Well, look who finally got hisself out of bed now that the branding is about finished," Franklin said, hanging his hat on the hall-tree near the door. "We'd about give up on you this time B.C."

McCall grinned. Franklin continued. "In fact, Deke and J.W. here was just arguing over which one would get your new watch and chain if you didn't make it."

Franklin sat across from McCall. John William and Deke looked at one another, both shaking their heads.

"How's that hand?" John William asked, as he gave his father a pat on the shoulder.

"It don't look too good, but I think it will be fine once I get used to it."

Deke spoke up as if to clear the record. "Just so you know, I never said anything about your timepiece."

Franklin didn't look up from spooning fried potatoes onto his plate. "That's 'cause you can't tell time, Deke."

"Well, there is that," Deke said.

The door swung open and three more cowboys came in and took their seats at the table. The first was Pete Caldwell. Next to Deke, Pete was as good a man with a horse and a rope as any that had ever ridden for the ranch. He was steady and reliable on the job, but a hell raiser in town. Pete wore a black hat with a wide brim and a high crown creased down the front and pinched on the sides. He was slightly built and barely five-and-a-half-feet tall. People tended to underestimate Pete, and that invariably proved to be a serious mistake for anyone spoiling for a Saturday night fight.

Get Wood Bell entered behind Pete. He was lanky and easy going.

Franklin grinned when Get Wood sat down. "Sebastian, tell us again how you got the name, Get Wood."

"That was all my dad ever said to me. I thought it was my name."

They had heard the story a hundred times before, but Franklin never tired of hearing it. "Get Wood. Thanks a good name for you," he said.

McCall pointed at the plate of potatoes with his good hand.

"Franklin, pass those around before they get cold."

Get Wood ambled to the table and sat down next to Pete. The two made an unlikely pair. Pete was quick-witted and volatile. Get Wood, slow and easy going, was good-humored and easy to get along with.

The last man through the door was Walter Crow Child, a Blackfoot from northern Montana. Walter was about John William's age. His father, a Blackfoot medicine man, had been a longtime friend of Travis Kincaid. Walter has a serious nature and an aloofness about him that made him appear to be much older than he was.

Franklin, with total disregard for Walter's no nonsense demeanor, went out of his way to test his reserve.

When Franklin heard the door close behind his back, he spoke without turning to see who entered the room.

"Nice of you to make it, Watler," Franklin said, intentionally mispronouncing his name.

"How did you know it was me?"

"Indians smell different."

Allison shook her head. "Franklin!"

She looked at Walter, and then looked around the room. "Judging from the evidence at hand, that may be a compliment," she said.

"That's okay, Miss Allison. At his age, his sense of smell may be the only thing that still works," Walter said.

Franklin made room and Walter sat beside him. Walter and Franklin had built up a special relationship over the years. Walter admired and respected the old ranger, and Franklin was the one who stood with Walter when he was wrongly charged with a robbery that occurred off the reservation. When Walter and his family ran out of money and no one would hire him, it was Franklin who hired him to work at the Triple Dot without making it seem like an act of charity.

Walter nodded to Brady. "Good to see you back, Brady."

"It's good to be back, Walter."

Then Walter spoke to McCall in Blackfoot. McCall nodded in agreement and they both looked at Franklin and smiled. They continued the guttural dialogue with no regard for Franklin. Franklin watched back and forth as the two men spoke, and then he lost his patience.

"Are you two heathens gonna have a tribal council here, or are we gonna eat?"

Deke did his best to choke back the laugh stuck in his throat. Get Wood and Pete stared down at their plates, while Walter and Brady just smiled.

Franklin began calling the Indian, *Watler*, two years ago, after he had instructed Get Wood to paint the names of the permanent hands on the footlockers at the end of their beds.

Get Wood transposed the L and the T in Walter's name, and no one but Franklin noticed the error. Rather than point it out and correct it, Franklin let it stand and it became his private joke. The longer it went on, the more Franklin enjoyed it. The others figured it was just another example of Franklin's inability to master the English language.

FORTY-SIX

Sweet Grass River Ranch, Montana: July 1891

On a lazy Sunday afternoon Brady and Franklin sat on the front porch of McCall's cabin enjoying the sunshine engaged in old man talk and reminiscing.

"B.C., you remember when we could ride out from here and go in any direction and never see a fence?"

He turned his chair to catch more sun on his back. "It sure ain't like it used to be."

McCall nodded in agreement, but didn't say anything.

"Watler and me rode up to Butte this past spring. To get them windmill parts. You remember?"

McCall nodded.

"Well, I don't know when you was there last, but they're smelting copper and digging so many tunnels under the town that the whole damn place is going sink away some day."

He looked over at McCall.

"Nothin' grows there. We was in the post office and heard a sound and felt the ground move. The men in there told us it was miners blasting away in a tunnel nineteen-hundred feet right below where we stood."

Franklin spat off the side of the porch, and then continued.

"You know, if you didn't see it with your own eyes, you wouldn't believe it. I asked Watler if he ever seen a man-dug hole nineteen-hundred feet deep. He says he hadn't. So, we goes on up to the mine at Anaconda. When we gets there, we seen some old boys with a big white mule all trussed up with rope and wrapped in a canvas sheet. They had him on pulleys hanging over the shaft where the men go down into the mine. When we asked what the hell they was doing with the mule, they tells us he's going down to pull the ore cars from the side tunnels to the main shaft, so's they can get the ore out of the ground. Well, I seen Watler a eyeing the mule and he asks them boys how does the mule get back out."

Franklin stared at McCall. McCall just listened.

"You know what they told him?"

McCall shook his head.

"They says the mule don't come back out. They work that damn jackass until he dies or until they give up on that tunnel, then they leave him there. If the mule is lucky, some sombitch shoots him in the head when they leave."

McCall leaned back in his chair and crossed his boots on the porch rail.

"They call that progress, Franklin."

He folded his arms across his chest while he scanned the clouds with his eyes, and then took a deep breath.

"Three years ago, when they voted for Montana statehood and it won—it was a sign that nothing would ever be the same again. It's not just the fences and the mines and more people. It's the idea that they're all so ready to give up them things that men like us value. I sit here and look down at them good horses, then I remember what it was like to ride from the northern Rockies down into Old Mexico and never see a cabin or a fence. It wasn't always easy, but we were free."

Franklin shook his head. His expression was clouded with doubt and concern.

"You don't suppose we're like them old mine mules, do you, B.C.?"

Brady shrugged. Franklin continued.

"We just keep on doing what we're doing while the rest of the world is going on without us, making up new rules as they go."

McCall was surprised at the reflective insight coming from Franklin. He looked over at his friend. Franklin's dark eyes still had that devilish sparkle in them, but the black hair had long ago given way to the silver thatch that now showed beneath his hat. His hands were big-knuckled and rough. They showed strength and a lot of hard work, with only the brown spots of age giving any suggestion that they were the hands of a man almost seventy years old.

The thought of the mule dug into McCall's sensibilities. The more he thought about it, the madder he got.

"Well, I'll tell you one damn thing," McCall said. "I don't want to end up like that, do you?"

He stood, walked over to the edge of the porch, and spat. He stood there looking out over the treed meadow. Franklin watched him without speaking. He spat again and turned to look directly at Franklin. A smile creased the edges of his eyes. Franklin stood and raised in hands in protest.

"No sir. Whatever it is you're thinking, the answer is, absolutely no, B.C."

He looked seriously at McCall. "B.C., I want to get old. I want to sit on this damn porch and tell lies and do the things old men do. I want to take Jenny for buggy rides and I want the kids to bring me coffee or a beer when I want one. And you know what else? I'm done getting shot at."

Brady slipped the old Gros Ventre knife from its tattered sheath, stepped up to the table, and then plunged the blade into the wooden table top right in front of where Franklin sat. He looked Franklin in the eye and stared a long time, still gripping the knife.

"This here's the Triple Dot," he said, twisting the knife point in where it stuck.

He withdrew the knife and stabbed another spot half way across the table from the first one.

"This is Nevada."

Franklin laughed. The sarcasm couldn't have been more obvious.

"Nevada?"

He shook his head in disbelief.

"You know what they got in Nevada, B.C.?"

Brady looked at him.

"Nothing—that's what they got in Nevada."

"They got horses in Nevada," Brady said.

"Horses?"

"Yeah, horses—and lots of them."

"B.C., look around. Do we look like we need any more damn horses?"

Brady leaned forward. His expression was solemn. "No, we don't, but Walter's people do."

Then Brady stood up straight. "We'd be doing it for them."

"We'd be doing what for them?"

"Gatherin' up them horses."

Franklin looked away and shook his head again. He muttered under his breath. Brady ignored him and carried on with all the conviction of an evangelical preacher at a Wednesday night revival meeting.

"Them horses was put on this earth with the sole purpose of running free or working cattle. They wasn't meant for the canner and they wasn't meant to be hunted for sport. Every horse ever made will be in heaven—you can't say that for every man."

Franklin looked at him with a softening eye and a skeptical expression. Then Brady hit him with the altar call of all arguments.

"You and me was spared for some unknown purpose I truly doubt either has yet served. This is our chance to give some back for all we have been given."

Franklin was on the verge of tears.

"To redeem ourselves," Brady added.

And then he waited. He let the spirit of conviction work its way into Franklin's soulful side. Franklin sat back. He crossed his arms. He spat.

"You know, B.C., I never liked doing business with you—ever. You just got to make everything sound so important—like someone up there," he nodded heavenward, "is talking to you and ignoring the rest of us."

"So, you'll do it?" Brady asked smiling.

"Why don't you just shoot me now and be done with it?" Franklin asked. "You been trying all our lives to get me killed."

Brady laughed. "Good. I knew I could count on you."

"Well, before it's a definite *yes*, fill me in on the plan," Franklin said.

Brady explained the plan. He knew where seven or eight-hundred mustangs had been run into a canyon and held by mustangers who would cut out what they needed for each sale, and the horses would be there waiting for them. All the boys had to do was to ride in, break out the horses, and drive them north. It was Franklin's kind of plan and, before they got back to the barn to work out the rest of the details, Franklin was all in.

That evening, after supper, Brady and Franklin continued their talk.

McCall studied his deformed hand as he thought his way through the proposition.

"This could get dicey," he said.

Franklin smiled. "Yeah, it could."

"You can still back out if you want."

Franklin shook his head. "I reckon I'm one digit up on you. You got more to lose than I do."

For the next two weeks every activity at the Triple Dot was focused on the mustang rescue. John William and Walter returned from up north with a dozen Blackfoot riders. Deke had returned the day before from Bozeman with Laird Bingham, the new cook.

Laird, a testy Englishman in his late fifties, limped from an old Civil War wound, wore a bowler hat he never took off, and handled the chuck wagon team like he may have been a top hand in his day. Laird had mothered cowboys on the trail for a long time, and every year his disposition got worse. Talking to Laird was an exercise in frustration. Only Franklin seemed oblivious to his sarcasm, impatience and intolerance.

Laird Bingham was the consummate camp cook with a good reputation, a real asset in getting trail hands to sign on to a job that held as little promise as this one did. He double-checked his list as supplies were loaded on the wagon.

The Triple Dot outfit would roll out for the Medicine Lodge at first light. From there, they would cross over into Nevada. The cowboys who gathered there that afternoon checked out the string of horses milling about the corrals. They spoke of the trail and all they expected to encounter along the way. For all the talk and the excitement, this was about more than the horses and more than helping out the Blackfoot tribe—this was quite possibly the West's last great roundup.

Young Blackfoot braves on their half-broke ponies, and the Triple Dot cowboys on their seasoned cowhorses made for a spectacular vision.

Laura Kincaid watched from the window inside the house with sad eyes that remembered a time when Travis would have been right out there with them. She imagined that he looked down approvingly at what she considered to be the work of little boys acting out their play in old men's bodies.

It warmed her heart to watch Brady and Franklin. She still looked upon the two aging friends as she always remembered them—boys full of mischief and unpredictable behavior. She looked past the grey hair and the lined faces. She never saw two old men—she saw only the boys Travis raised in his own image. She saw him in everything they did and said, and she approved.

That evening, Elizabeth and her family came over to spend the night and be there for the early dawn sendoff. Allison tended Elizabeth's two young ones while Elizabeth and her father walked arm in arm toward the barn where the broodmares were brought up for foaling.

The sweet smell of fresh hay greeted them when Brady pulled the big wooden door open. The mares nickered and stuck their heads over the top rail of the loafing shed fence. Brady and Elizabeth leaned against the rail to look in on the mares.

"See that dun mare over there with the dark stripe running down the middle of her back?" McCall said to his daughter, as he pointed out a well-muscled horse with bulging sides.

Elizabeth beamed. She loved to hear her father talk of horses, and she loved the look in his eyes when he did so. She never stopped being in awe of his knowledge, and she loved that she learned something new from him every time they spoke of horses. She looked at the mare then back at her father.

"Perfect top line," she said. "Well sprung ribs, good hips, good slope to the shoulders, thick in the stifle with strong legs and substantial bone."

She smiled up at her father. "And that nice soft eye we like so much," she added.

"Which bloodline you make her out of?" McCall asked his daughter.

He always tested her this way and she loved the challenge. She furrowed her brow in mock concentration the way she always did to tease him when she knew the answer.

"Well," she said slowly. "If I had to say, I'd say she's all Morning Star on the bottom side and strong Buffalo Dancer on the topside."

Her father grinned. "It's in your blood."

She smiled back at him. "Has been for as long as I can remember," she said, then she put her arms around the old man and didn't say anything for a long time.

When she did speak, she looked over at the mare. "I'll bet you a dollar she has that baby tonight."

McCall looked over at the mare himself. "Based on the pure unpredictability of a mare, I'll take that bet."

They shook. Elizabeth held her father's hand and her expression turned serious.

"Is there any way I can talk you and Uncle Franklin out of this trip?" she asked, as her voice shook.

"Why would you want to do that, Lizzie?" McCall asked.

"I just feel better having you and Uncle Franklin close to us," she said, trying to avoid any references to age or danger.

McCall held her at arm's length. "You really don't want us to go?"

She shook her head from side to side.

"Sweetheart," McCall said. "Your Uncle Franklin and I are at a point in our lives where we may never get another chance like this again. The world is closing in on men like us."

Elizabeth seemed unmoved.

"Nothing is more important to me than your momma and you and your brother and them little grandchildren of ours, but this could be our last go-round. Would you want us sit it out and just wait for time to catch up to us?"

Elizabeth looked up at her father. His eyes were full of love and concern. She bit her bottom lip. Then her expression changed to one of understanding.

"You know what?" She said. "You're right. I don't ever want to see anything bad happen to you or Uncle Franklin, but I will be so proud of you both for doing this."

She smiled big with tears running down her cheeks. She hugged her father tight and tears ran down his cheeks.

"When you come back I want to sit up all night on the porch with the two of you and listen to all your stories and try to figure out which of you tells the biggest lies."

Then she laughed and he laughed, and he knew it was all right.

The dinner bell sounded at the same time Miles Travis stuck his head into the barn and yelled, "Come and get it before the flies do," and he was off.

Every seat at the table was filled. McCall said grace over the food and asked for a safe journey. He prayed for good weather, asked for easy river crossings, and then asked the Lord's hand in helping them with the horses. He asked the Lord's blessing on those present and those who were away. *Amen.*

Franklin looked over at Brady with a serious expression, and said, "B.C., I ain't at all sure it was appropriate for you to ask the Lord to help us steal horses."

"Are we stealing them horses?" Get Wood asked Pete quietly.

"No, not exactly, Sebastian," Pete said mockingly. "We're just going to try to do the right thing by them."

"Is that true, Captain Stilwell?" Get Wood asked, looking confused.

"Well, do you think a sawed-off little shit like Pete would lie to a big sombitch like you, Get Wood?"

Get Wood shook his head, now more confused than ever. "No, I don't reckon he would," Get Wood said, grinning.

Pete glared at Get Wood. "Who you calling a sawed-off little shit?"

"Pete, I never said you was. . ."

Pete cut him off. "Well, best you don't."

Allison carried a huge platter of beef to the table.

"Unless you boys want to eat out in the barn, you best keep your profanities to yourselves in front of these children," she said, scolding the men collectively.

Franklin started to speak. Allison shook her finger at him.

"That goes double for you, Stilwell."

"Yes, ma'am," he said obediently.

Miles sat at the head of the table next to his grandfather. His mother, Anna, sat at the other end of the table with Allison and Elizabeth. Between bites, talk slowed down. The women held their private conversation at one end of the table. The men talked with their mouths full, knowing it would be a while before they ate this good again.

McCall and Get Wood speculated on how far they would travel the first day, while Pete and Franklin talked about the new singer at the Prairie Dog Saloon in Bozeman.

Sitting up straight and as tall as he could, Miles pointed his fork at McCall and spoke out loud and clear. "I'm going with you tomorrow, grandpa."

The room fell silent. All eyes turned Brady's direction. Anna's face went ashen as she reached over and grabbed Allison's arm for moral support. McCall smiled and spoke softly.

"Son, I figured you to stay here and take charge of the ranch while we're gone."

Miles shook his head. "They don't need me here. I'm going with you and Uncle Franklin."

Elizabeth cringed.

"You simply are not going and that is final," Anna said, hoping to end the discussion right then and there.

"Miles, your momma is right," McCall reaffirmed. "You're a mite too young to be thinking about crossing that much territory on horseback with no one to look after you."

The boy set his jaw and stood up. He looked McCall directly in the eye.

"Well, I damn sure ain't. You did it."

His mother's mouth fell open in astonishment. She started to speak, but Allison calmed her with a firm, gentle touch of her hand. "Better let Brady handle this," she whispered.

Miles fought back the tears.

"Grandpa, I'm ten years old. I can shoot and I can ride. I can take care of my own gear. I ain't too young."

Franklin and Brady exchanged pained expressions.

"I remember them stories you and Uncle Franklin told me about what you did when you were my age. No one said you couldn't do it."

Miles fiddled with something beneath the table.

"I even have the knife Aunt Laura give me that used to belong to Uncle Travis," he said resolutely.

Miles laid the knife and its old worn leather sheath out on the table in front of him. Brady and Franklin recognized the knife Kincaid had used the night he rescued them from the Comanche renegades. A wave of emotion ran over both of the old cowboys, but neither spoke.

McCall looked down the table at Anna and Allison, but saw no approval in the eyes of either of them. Franklin shrugged his shoulders in a, let's-let-him-come, gesture.

"Miles," Brady began in a slow, deliberate manner. "What you say is true. I can't think of a better partner than you. But son, you got to understand this is a different time and a different set of circumstances. It just isn't like it used to be."

"It's progress," Franklin muttered to himself.

To Anna's great relief, Brady finally settled the matter.

"It's best you just put it out of your mind. When we get back we can pack back up into the Absarokies and get us a deer for the winter," he said, patting the dejected boy consolingly on the back.

"Uncle Franklin, please tell him it's okay," Miles pleaded.

Franklin was torn. He looked at McCall. "B.C.?" he said weakly, not wanting to make the matter worse.

"Grandpa, please. This is the only chance I'm ever going to get," the boy said, as he stood with his hand on McCall's shoulder.

"Miles, I'm sorry. . ." He looked over at Anna, but she stood firm.

Miles ran from the room, swinging the front door open violently and slamming it against the wall on his way out.

A terrible silence hung over the place. Brady knew how the boy felt. He knew the boy could handle the trip. He wanted to see some give in Anna, but there was none.

Laura Kincaid, in her soft voice, broke the quiet. At the risk of going counter to Anna's wishes, she spoke directly to Brady.

"Brady, do you remember Travis ever telling you there was anything you couldn't do? And you Franklin, he always treated you like a man. I can't remember how many times Travis told me how young and green you two were then, but it never stopped him from treating you like men. Now you got a chance to return the favor to your own grandson. Are you two so old you can't remember what it was like to be a boy getting ready to be a man?"

"Aunt Laura, that was different," Brady said, in feeble defense.

Laura's mind and memory were sharp and unfailing. Everyone at the table except Anna was thinking what only she had the gumption to say. The problem was, no one else could get themselves up to say anything for fear of upsetting Anna, who still thought of Miles as her little baby.

Brady got up from the table and walked toward the door. He took his hat from the hall tree and pulled it down tight on his head.

"Where are you going?" Allison asked.

"I think I'll take a walk down to the broodmare barn. There's a young cowboy down there feeling a little low right about now," Brady answered.

McCall sidestepped in through the partially opened barn door and saw Miles in the pen with the mares. When he approached and looked over the rail, he saw Miles sitting and helping the dun mare clean off her new baby. McCall watched quietly, and Miles looked up at him and smiled.

Finally, the new colt stretched his long, spindly legs out in front of him and pushed his front end up off the ground. Then he made one quick lunge, and he was up on all four feet.

McCall climbed over the rail and stood beside Miles. He put an arm across the boy's shoulder, and Miles put his arm around his grandfather's waist.

Together they watched as the foal found the mare's udder. The colt's legs were still shaky, but he drank his fill, and then began to explore. At first he stayed close to his mother's side, but soon he ventured out in larger circles. The colt walked confidently up to Miles and sniffed the boy's fingers with his soft muzzle. He nibbled at the buttons on the boy's shirt then whirled to return to his mother.

"Looks like we got us a stud colt there, Miles."

Miles smiled and nodded.

"Judging by the way he looks, I would say he is going to be a buckskin. Nice straight legs, good angle to his shoulder. Look at that front end and that butt on him. He's going to be a mover."

"Do you think he likes me grandpa?"

"I don't know. What do you think?"

"I think he does."

"I expect he does too," McCall said, as he looked the baby over like horsemen do."

McCall paused, and watched the boy's eyes as they followed the colt.

"You ever had a buckskin?"

Miles shook his head. "My daddy's ol' brown horse, Jeff Davis, is the only horse I ever had."

"Well, one thing I know for sure, is that every man ought to have him a buckskin horse at least once in his life."

"I'll get me one someday," Miles said, looking back up at his grandfather.

"It takes a heap of hard work to raise a colt," McCall said.

"I'm as hard a worker as there is," Miles said, catching on to Brady's game

"A man's got to be strong to handle a big colt," McCall added.

"I've got muscles I haven't even used yet," Miles said, grinning.

Then McCall looked up as though he were doing some complex mental calculations. Finally, he looked back down at Miles.

"You know, the way I figure it, you're the next one in line for a buckskin horse around here," McCall said.

"I am?" Miles asked, his eyes lighting up and an uncontrollable grin stretching his face back to his ears.

"Yessir. What do you think about that one?"

"I love him," Miles said.

"You best be thinking of a name for him then."

"He's mine?"

"He's yours."

Miles hugged his grandpa, and then inched his way back to the colt. The colt watched the boy through soft, brown eyes. His short bristle-brush mane gave him a carousel-horse appearance, and he stood quietly as Miles touched his soft nose and talked to him in a low voice. Miles touched the foal on the cheek then returned to sit on the fence with his grandfather.

They sat there for almost two hours watching the colt master his small universe as he grew stronger and more confident. He nuzzled his mother, then nursed until the mare became impatient with his head-butting. He found a spot in the clean hay and stretched out on his side and slept.

McCall stepped down from the rail and Miles jumped to the ground next to him. He put his arms around his grandfather.

"I love my new horse, grandpa.

Late that night, after everyone had gone to bed, McCall got up and quietly made his way through the dark house and out onto the porch. The air was cool, and the moon was full. In the silver light McCall saw Miles sitting on the front step watching the mare and her colt, standing in the corral down at the barn.

McCall put his hand on the boy's shoulder and sat down beside him without speaking. The cowboy couldn't remember how many new foals he watched run by their mother's side, but still there was an excitement about it that made it impossible to sleep the first night. He knew Miles would have the same problem, and he understood just how the boy felt.

"Grandpa," Miles said quietly after a long period of silence.

"What is it, son?"

"I got a name for my colt."

Miles turned to his grandfather. In the moonlight McCall thought he saw a little of the man showing through on the boy. He looked down at Miles and saw his own father looking down at him a thousand years earlier.

"What are you going to call him?"

"Buffalo Dancer."

McCall turned away. The sound of the name brought back so many feelings, so many memories. An image of the battle-scarred, buckskin stallion flashed across his mind. A flood of emotion swelled up in the old cowboy's throat and he was unable to speak.

"That's a good name, isn't it?" Miles asked, after the uncomfortable silence.

McCall put his arm around the boy's shoulder and remembered how it felt to be ten-years old and the new owner of a buckskin stallion. Miles looked up. The moonlight light reflected in McCall's eyes and Miles thought he saw a tear when his grandfather replied.

"It's the best."

FORTY-SEVEN

It was an hour before sun-up. The dogs barked and a fat, red rooster stood on the top rail of the fence, crowing and flapping its wings. The line of saddlehorses at the hitch rail pawed the ground and shifted from foot to foot as they nervously watched the activity going on around them.

Laird Bingham was up on the seat of the chuck wagon, one foot on the brake and both hands on the reins. The team was anxious, four horses prancing and tossing their heads, pent-up energy waiting to explode. Just about the time Laird had the team under control, Pete whooped and hollered as the fresh horse he climbed aboard humped up and bucked all the way from the barn, past the chuck wagon, and on his way around the back of the house.

Laird cursed Pete as he went by. "Keep that jug head the hell away from my team."

Pete was hanging on for his life and looked back just long enough to glare at Laird as they bucked off into the dark where Pete and his horse disappeared behind a cloud of dust then around the side of the house.

Laird turned in time to see Deke with one foot in the stirrup as his bronc went straight up in the air with a twist and a grunt. When the big gelding came back down, Deke was still half in and half out of the saddle. The gelding spun his direction, and Deke managed to get his free leg over, but never found the other stirrup. The horse sunfished back up, and a full-grown man could have walked under the space between its belly and the ground.

When the horse came back down Deke was ready. He shortened up a rein, jerked its head around and buried the rowels of his spurs into its sides. The horse stuck out its nose, pointed himself south, and its feet barely touched the ground as he flew down the road.

Laird managed to hold the team in check but, by that time, they were charged with nervous energy and lathered like they had been run all night. The cook watched suspiciously as Pete rode his horse quietly out from behind the house and to the barn. Pete looked as calm as an undertaker as he gathered up his bedroll and tied it on behind his saddle.

Deke trotted his horse back in from the darkness and, even though it was still high-headed and snorty, he had ridden all the kinks out of it and it was ready to go to work.

The family gathered on the front porch. The children still wrapped in blankets and the women with shawls held tightly about their shoulders. Allison shivered, but didn't know if it was from the chill or the excitement.

Over the ridgeline of the mountains to the east, the sky began to take on the hopeful colors of dawn. Allison watched Franklin riding back and forth, waving his arms and shouting orders at everyone and it reminded her of the first river crossing out of St. Joseph. She shuddered at the thought of it. She could see Brady's beaming expression as he sat tall and proud on the bay gelding he rode, and she thought back at how gallant he looked the first time she saw him on the back of that majestic buckskin stallion.

A chill ran down her back. In all the excitement, it had never before occurred to her that she might never see him again. She forced the thought from her mind. She and Brady never said long goodbyes and this time was no exception. They had taken care of that earlier, and now a final wave would do as they riders pulled out.

Brady rode toward the wagons and then pulled his horse up. He suddenly turned and trotted back to the porch. He felt the same thing Allison did and he wanted to make sure nothing was cut short this time. He leaned down from the saddle, gathered her up in one arm and kissed her.

"We'll be back before the snow flies," he said, as he gave her a reassuring wink. "There ain't nothing on this earth I love more than you."

Tears now rolled freely down her cheeks.

"I love you too," she whispered.

The ground shook and a rumbling sound like thunder preceded the remuda as the bell-mare clanked by, leading the charging horses down the road. Get Wood whooped it up as he galloped by with the thirty, stampeding horses he jingled from the lower pasture. He grinned and waved his hat, then spurred his horse on faster. Laird Bingham shook his fist in a fit of obscenities then he whistled and clucked his team in behind as the entire operation was on the move up the road and lined out for the Medicine Lodge River.

Pete fell in behind the chuck wagon with Deke at his side. It was a magnificent sight. The cowboys on horseback tended to their early-dawn duties. The chuck wagon creaked and clattered behind the remuda of well bred horses. Even the small cootie wagon, heavy with bedrolls and equipment, seemed like part of a bygone time, brought to life for this single glorious occasion.

It was just a handful of cowboys with high hopes and a thinly devised plan to rescue a bunch of feral horses for what seemed like a good cause. And, at this point in time, there was nothing more important in the world than these men and this particular Montana morning.

Allison watched with great pride as Brady and Franklin trotted up on their strong, young ponies and fell in with Pete, Deke, and John William. The two old cowboys sat tall in their saddles and they rode with great authority.

They talked and laughed and their hands made great and wild gestures.

Aren't they a handsome pair, Allison said to herself. *Just like two kids*. She smiled and held her arms wrapped tightly about her. She looked over at Laura who stood beside her. There was an eternity of history in the lines on Laura's face. Laura's eyes were wet. She looked at Allison.

"For as long as I can remember, those boys have always ridden good horses," she said with a hint of pride in her voice. "Wouldn't Travis be so proud?"

Allison nodded and simply watched as the procession rolled out the gate. The two old men would forever remain the two young men who changed her life.

The horses pranced and jigged down the road and the riders stood up in their stirrups waving their hats in a grandiose salute. Brady and Franklin grinned at one another. Franklin leaned over to Brady.

"It's like a Saturday night getting ready to visit the peephole, ain't it?"

Brady laughed.

"Yeah, Franklin. It's exactly like a trip to the peephole."

"We sure had us some good times," Franklin said.

Brady looked over at his old friend.

"We did that."

Brady looked down at the Gros Ventre knife on his belt. Franklin's eyes fell to the old relic. Then their eyes met and they both smiled.

Franklin's expression turned serious.

"We surly did have us some good times."

They had settled in their saddles for the long ride when the rapid clatter of shod hooves upon the dry road behind them caused both old cowboys to turn at the same time. A horseman galloped up out of the dark and reined in between them as he jerked his horse down to a walk. He sat up in the saddle and looked first at Franklin then at Brady.

"I'm coming with you," Miles said.

McCall turned quickly in the saddle and looked back at the house. There stood Anna in the yard with her hand to her mouth and tears streaming down both cheeks. She waved and nodded her approval.

McCall looked across at John William and John William smiled. "Takes after his grandpa," J.W. said.

Miles grinned and waved a hand at his father. McCall smiled broadly then turned back to Miles and stuck out his hand. Miles grabbed it and shook it hard.

"Welcome to the outfit, cowboy," McCall said.

THE END

www.ingramcontent.com/pod-product-compliance
Lightning Source LLC
Chambersburg PA
CBHW030829110726
47900CB00006B/1803